THE GRAND TOURNAMENT

COLLECTING ISSUES 1-4

ARTISTS:
ALESSANDRO PERINA,
MARCO MAZZARELLO,
VITALE MANGIATORDI,
LORENZO PASTROVICCHIO,
ALESSANDRO
PASTROVICCHIO

WRITER:
STEFANO AMBROSIO

TRADE COVER:
CORRADO
MASTANTUONO

ASSISTANT EDITOR:
CHRISTOPHER BURNS

TRANSLATION:
SAIDA TEMOFONTE

EDITOR:
CHRISTOPHER MEYER

LETTERER:
DERON BENNETT

DESIGNER:
ERIKA TERRIQUEZ

SPECIAL THANKS TO:
JESSE POST, LAUREN KRESSEL
& ELENA GARBO

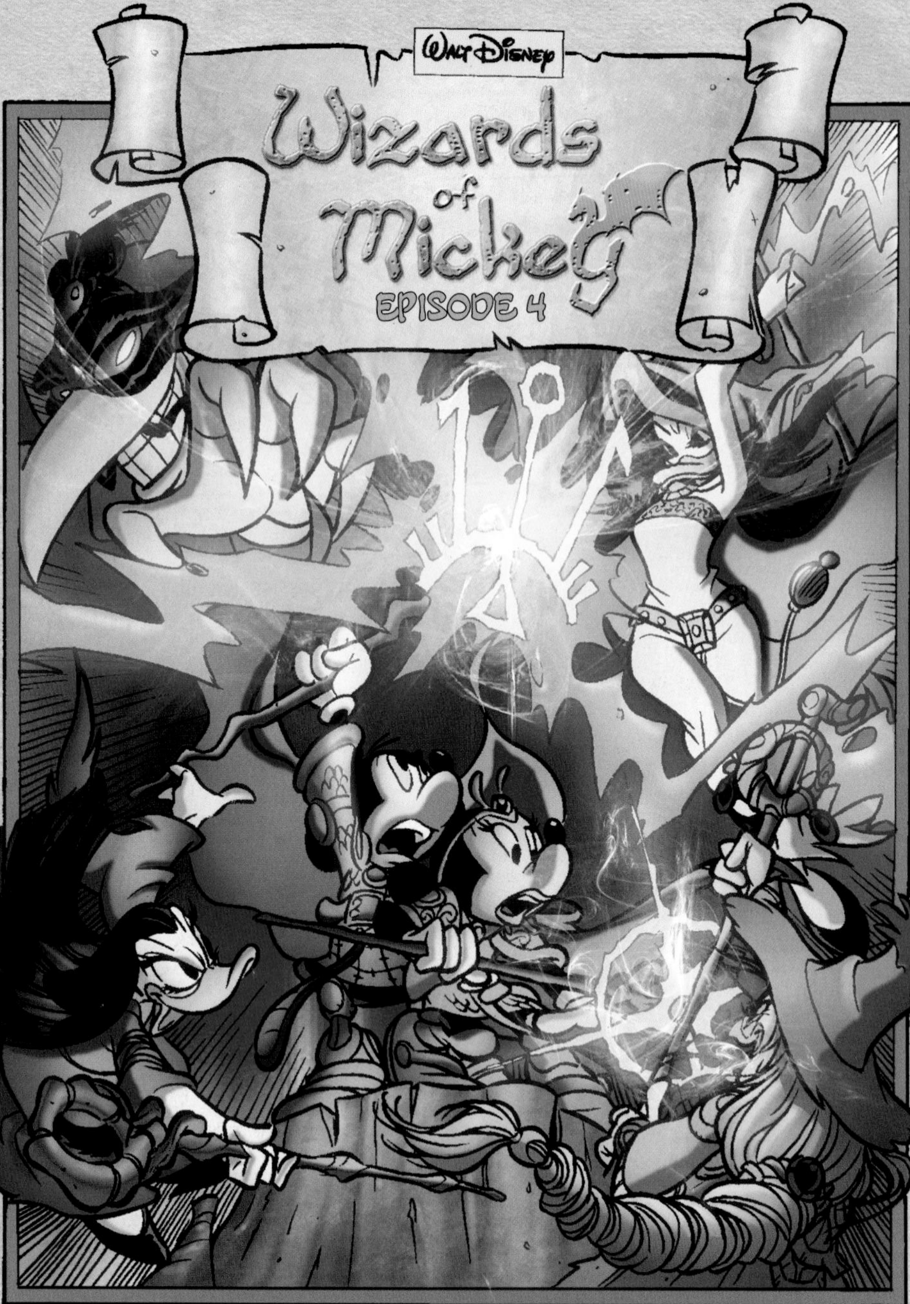
Walt Disney
Wizards of Mickey
Episode 4

O**ur story so far...* ***Mickey has formed the ***Wizards of Mickey*** with ***Donald*** and ***Goofy*** to enter the Great Sorcery Tournament. Here he hopes to win back the Miceland village's Diamagic stolen by ***Peg-Leg Pete,*** under orders from the ***Phantom Blot***. Mickey successfully wins back the Diamagic from Pete's team, however, Mickey learns that the Phantom Blot has taken his master, ***Nereus***, captive. Events take another unexpected turn when the Wizards of Mickey join with ***Team Magma Fire*** after Donald's pet dragon, ***Fafnir***, is kidnapped by Pete's team in their quest to find a way into the dragon kingdom. Together, they foil Phantom Blot's plot and Mickey receives a Techno-charm which lets him communicate with Nereus. Following these events, Mickey's gang befriends ***Team Diamond Moon***, consisting of ***Daisy***, ***Minnie*** and ***Clarabelle.*** Shortly thereafter they defeat ***Team Tapestry*** and recover the Stone Diamagic, hoping to use it to free Nereus from his prison...

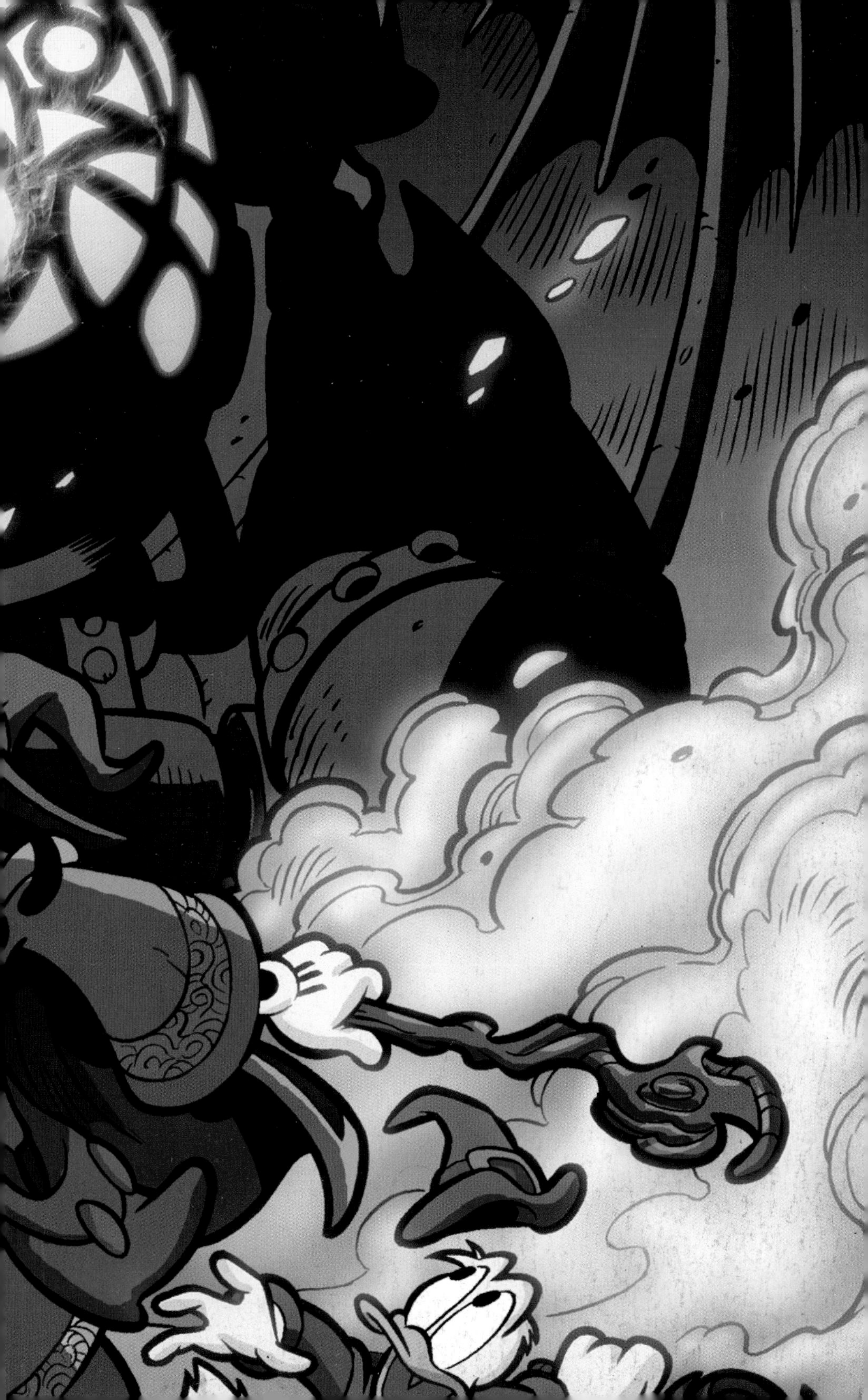

Walt Disney's

Wizards of Mickey

THE GRAND TOURNAMENT

BOOM! STUDIOS

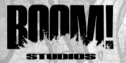

ROSS RICHIE
chief executive officer

MARK WAID
editor-in-chief

ADAM FORTIER
vice president,
new business

WES HARRIS
vice president,
publishing

LANCE KREITER
vice president,
licensing & merchandising

CHIP MOSHER
marketing director

MATT GAGNON
managing editor

FIRST EDITION: MAY 2010

10 9 8 7 6 5 4 3 2 1
FOR INFORMATION REGARDING THE CPSIA ON THIS PRINTED MATERIAL
CALL: 203-595-3636 AND PROVIDE REFERENCE # EAST – 66492

Office of publication: 6310 San Vicente Blvd Ste 404, Los Angeles, CA 90048-5457.

A catalog record for this book is available from OCLC and on our website www.boom-kids.com on the Librarians page.

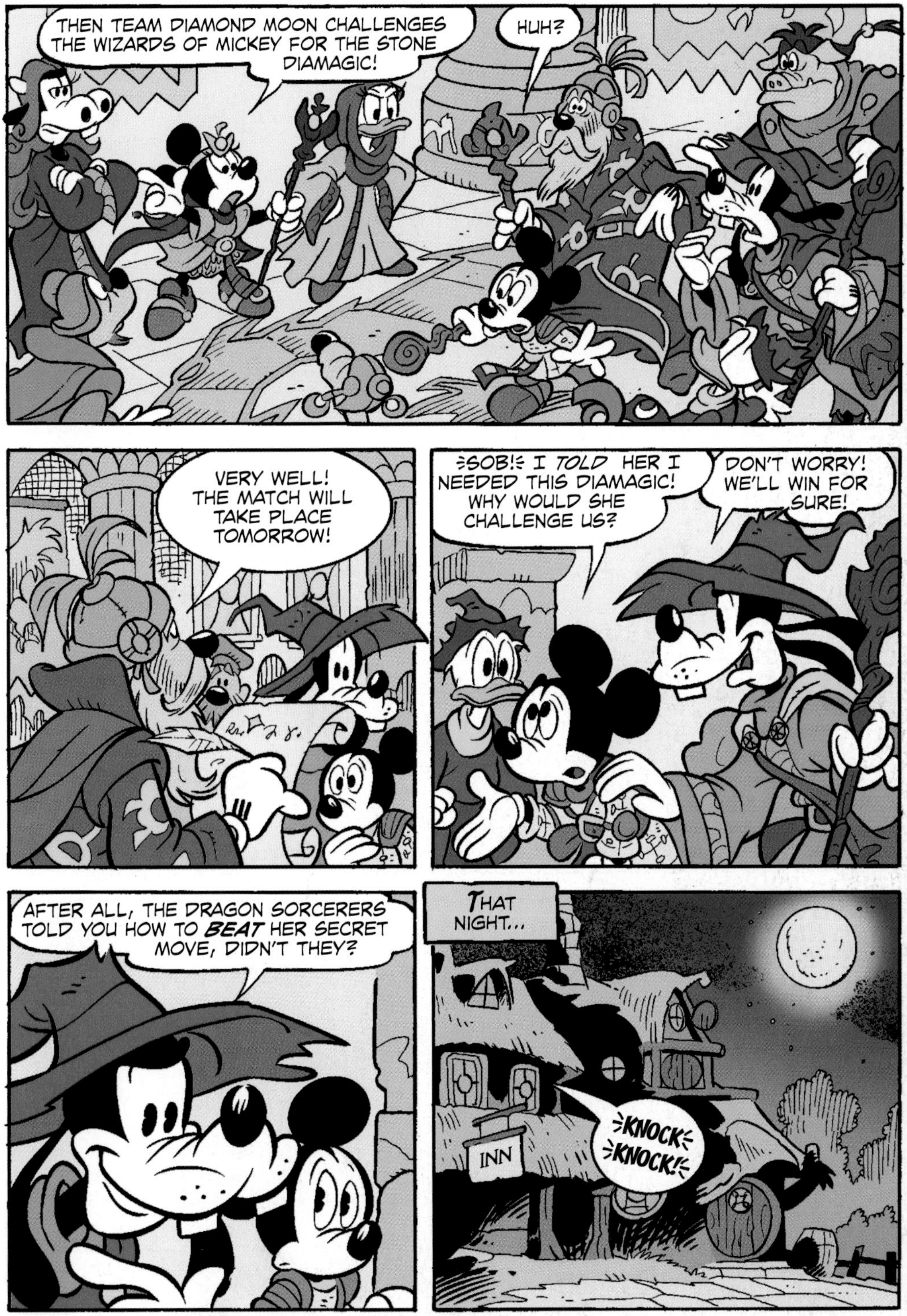
THEN TEAM DIAMOND MOON CHALLENGES THE WIZARDS OF MICKEY FOR THE STONE DIAMAGIC!
HUH?
VERY WELL! THE MATCH WILL TAKE PLACE TOMORROW!
SOB! I TOLD HER I NEEDED THIS DIAMAGIC! WHY WOULD SHE CHALLENGE US?
DON'T WORRY! WE'LL WIN FOR SURE!
AFTER ALL, THE DRAGON SORCERERS TOLD YOU HOW TO BEAT HER SECRET MOVE, DIDN'T THEY?
THAT NIGHT...
INN
KNOCK KNOCK!

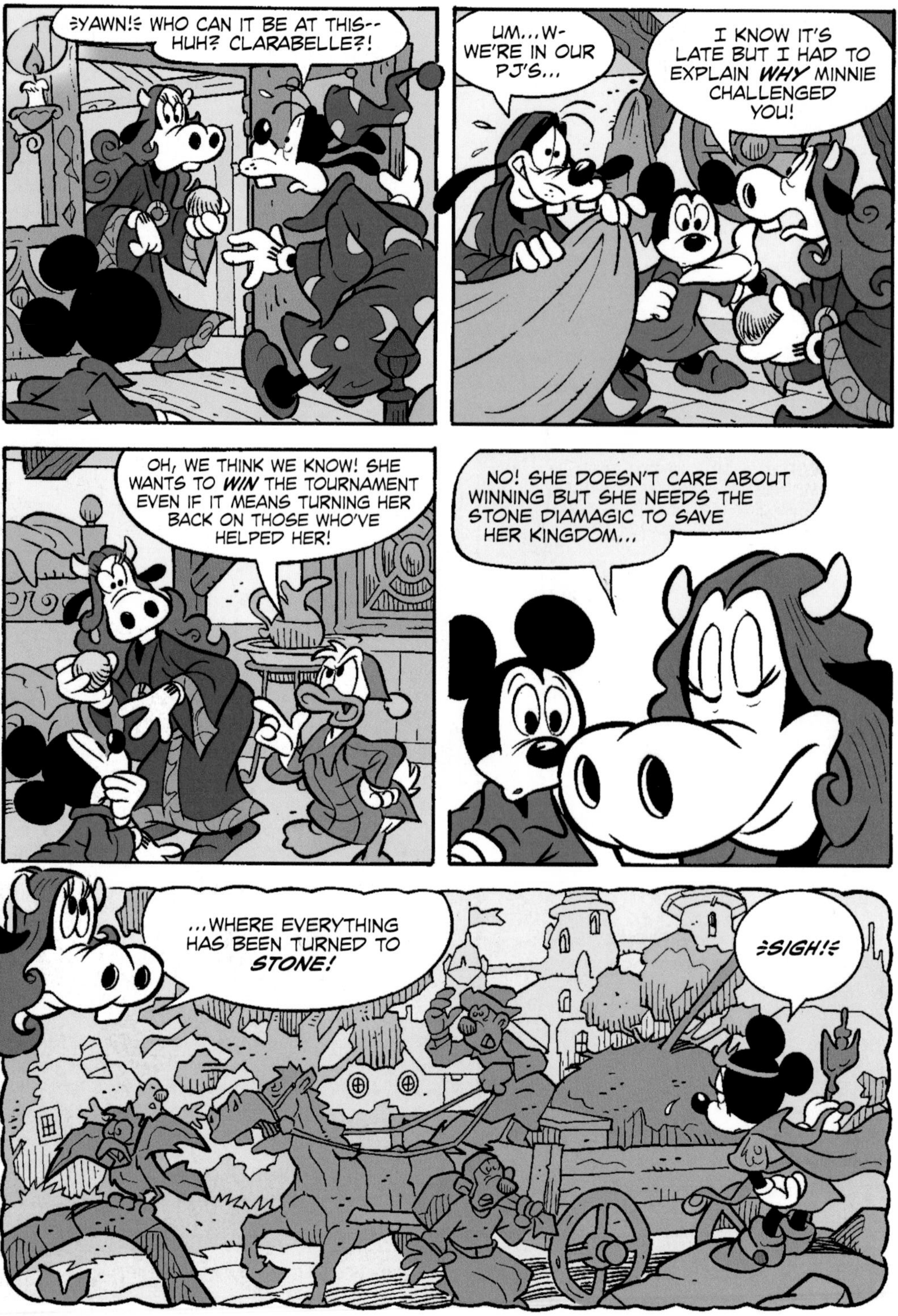

=YAWN!= WHO CAN IT BE AT THIS-- HUH? CLARABELLE?!
UM...W- WE'RE IN OUR PJ'S...
I KNOW IT'S LATE BUT I HAD TO EXPLAIN WHY MINNIE CHALLENGED YOU!
OH, WE THINK WE KNOW! SHE WANTS TO WIN THE TOURNAMENT EVEN IF IT MEANS TURNING HER BACK ON THOSE WHO'VE HELPED HER!
NO! SHE DOESN'T CARE ABOUT WINNING BUT SHE NEEDS THE STONE DIAMAGIC TO SAVE HER KINGDOM...
...WHERE EVERYTHING HAS BEEN TURNED TO STONE!
=SIGH!=

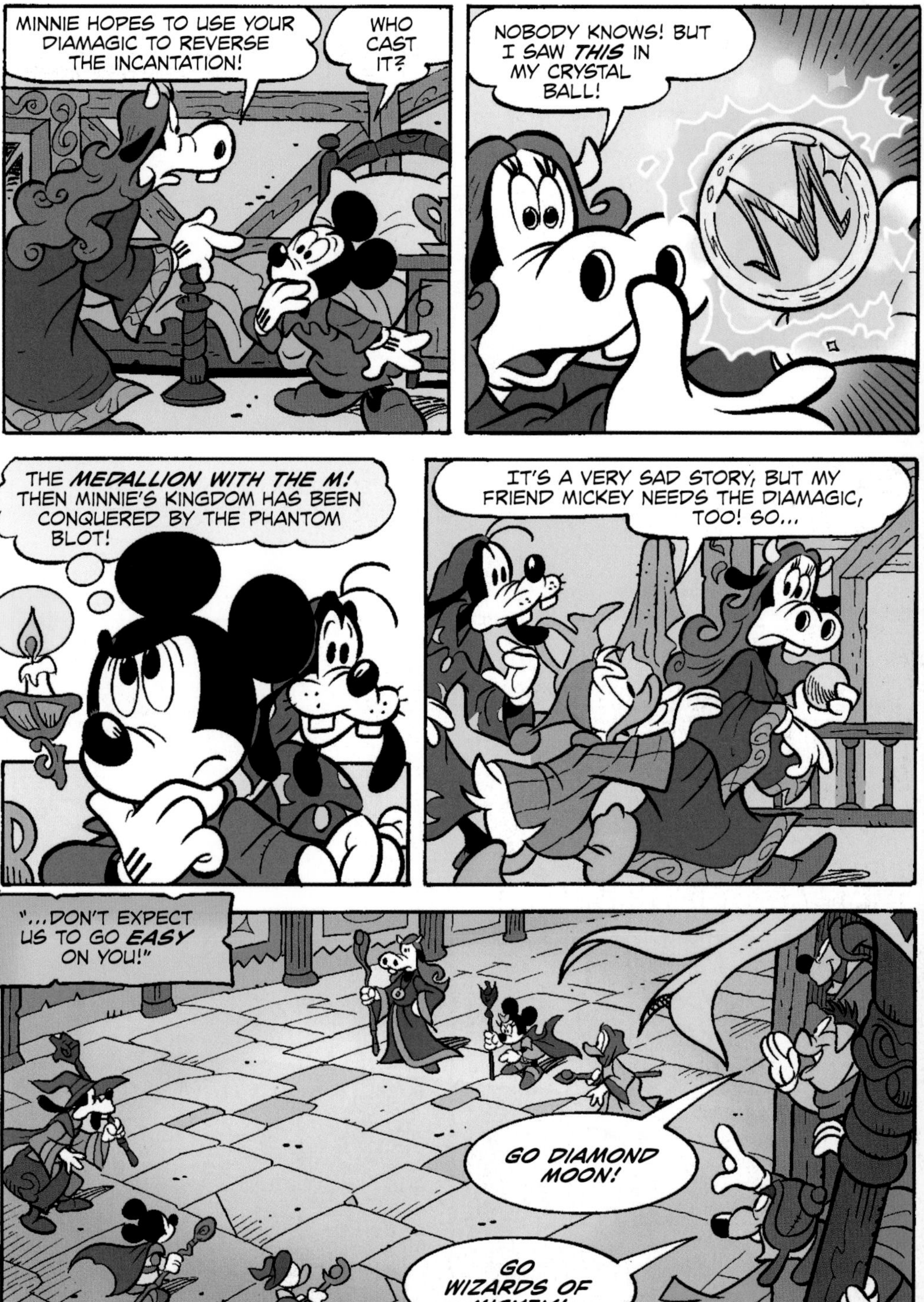
MINNIE HOPES TO USE YOUR DIAMAGIC TO REVERSE THE INCANTATION!
WHO CAST IT?
NOBODY KNOWS! BUT I SAW *THIS* IN MY CRYSTAL BALL!
THE *MEDALLION WITH THE M!* THEN MINNIE'S KINGDOM HAS BEEN CONQUERED BY THE PHANTOM BLOT!
IT'S A VERY SAD STORY, BUT MY FRIEND MICKEY NEEDS THE DIAMAGIC, TOO! SO...
"...DON'T EXPECT US TO GO *EASY* ON YOU!"
GO DIAMOND MOON!
GO WIZARDS OF MICKEY!

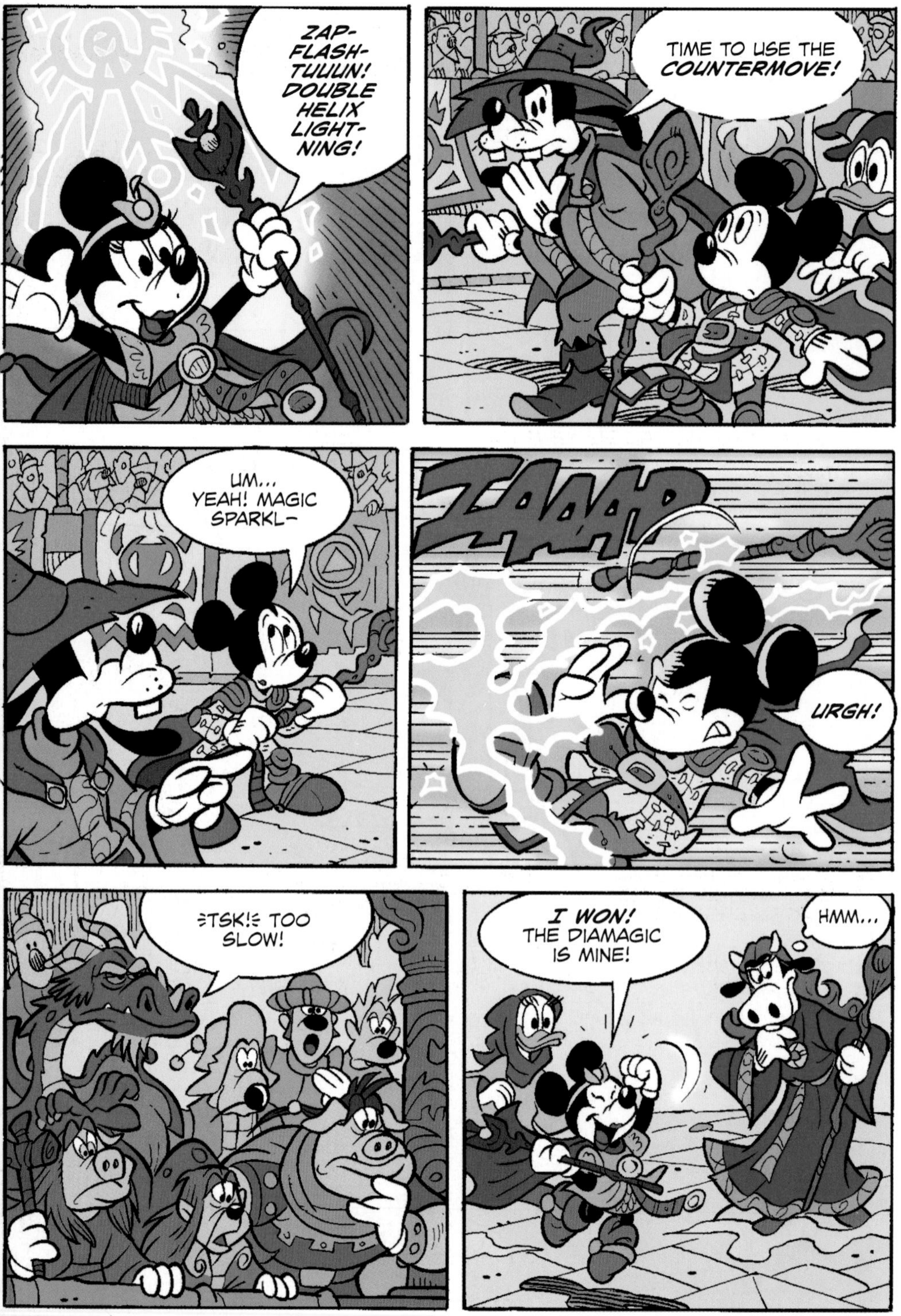
ZAP-FLASH-TUUUN! DOUBLE HELIX LIGHT-NING!
TIME TO USE THE COUNTERMOVE!
UM... YEAH! MAGIC SPARKL–
ZAAAP
URGH!
TSK! TOO SLOW!
I WON! THE DIAMAGIC IS MINE!
HMM...

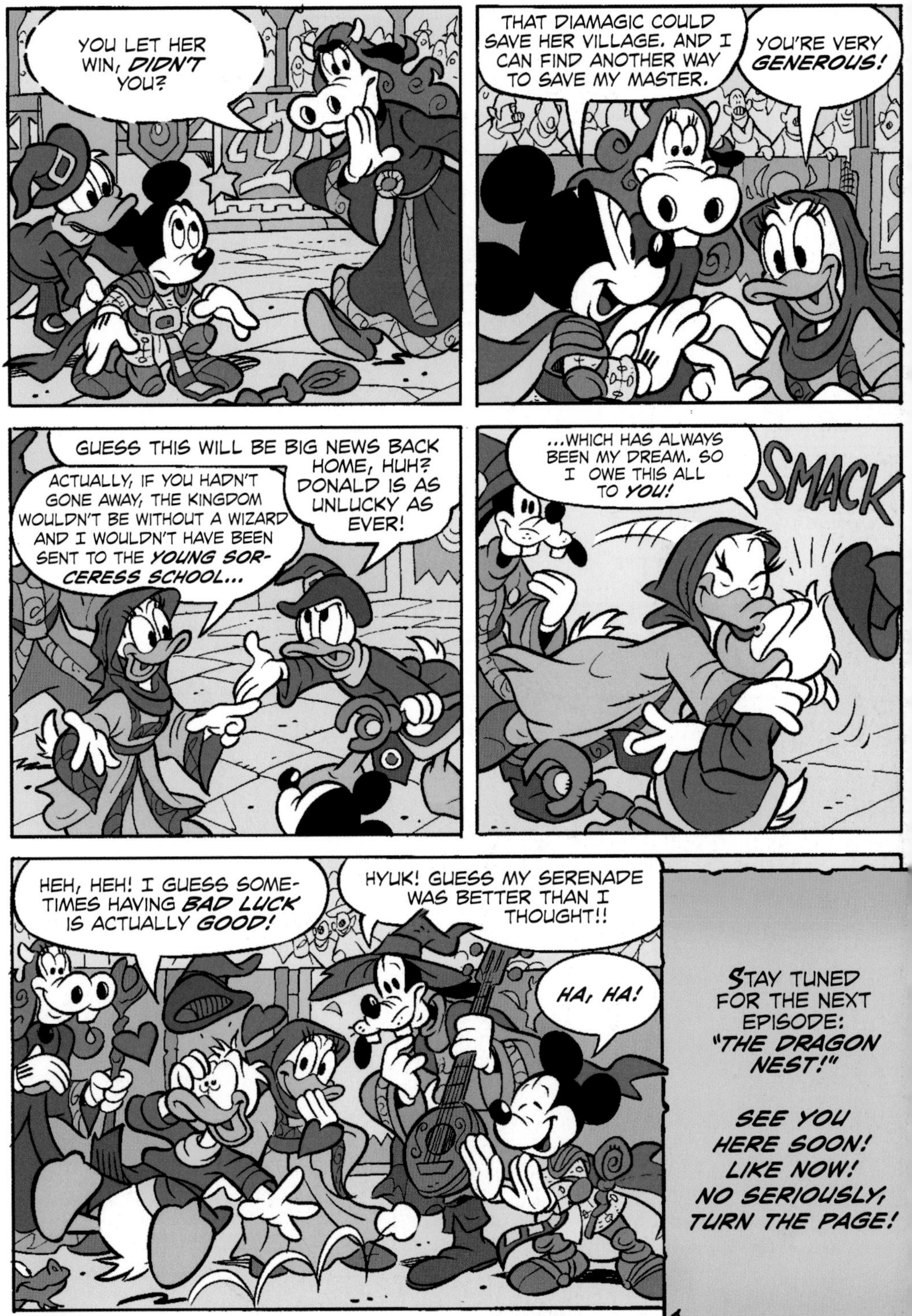
YOU LET HER WIN, *DIDN'T* YOU?
THAT DIAMAGIC COULD SAVE HER VILLAGE. AND I CAN FIND ANOTHER WAY TO SAVE MY MASTER.
YOU'RE VERY *GENEROUS!*
GUESS THIS WILL BE BIG NEWS BACK HOME, HUH? DONALD IS AS UNLUCKY AS EVER!
ACTUALLY, IF YOU HADN'T GONE AWAY, THE KINGDOM WOULDN'T BE WITHOUT A WIZARD AND I WOULDN'T HAVE BEEN SENT TO THE *YOUNG SORCERESS SCHOOL...*
...WHICH HAS ALWAYS BEEN MY DREAM. SO I OWE THIS ALL TO *YOU!*
SMACK
HEH, HEH! I GUESS SOMETIMES HAVING *BAD LUCK* IS ACTUALLY *GOOD!*
HYUK! GUESS MY SERENADE WAS BETTER THAN I THOUGHT!!
HA, HA!
STAY TUNED FOR THE NEXT EPISODE: *"THE DRAGON NEST!"*
SEE YOU HERE SOON! LIKE NOW! NO SERIOUSLY, TURN THE PAGE!

EPISODE 5: THE DRAGON WELL

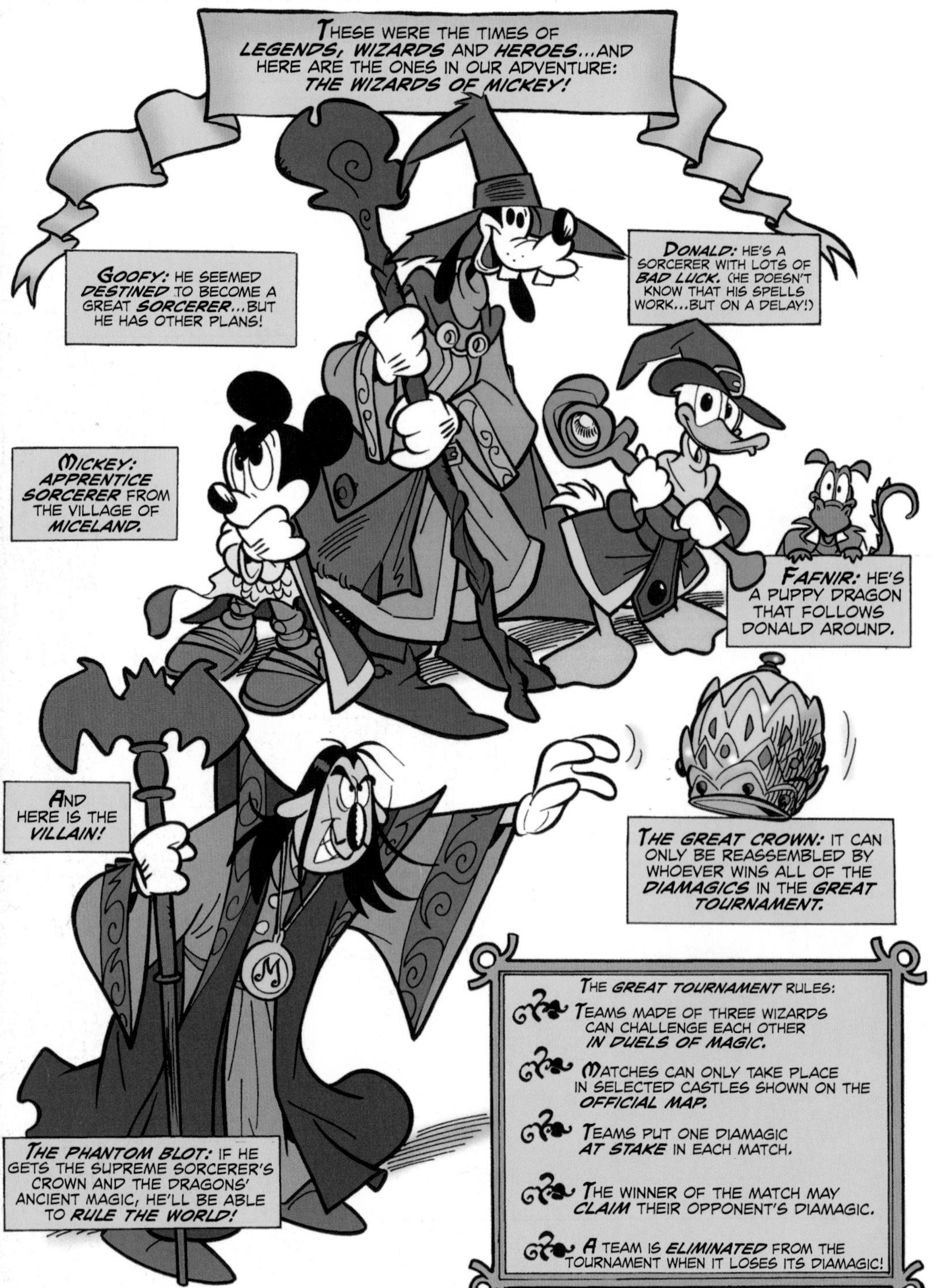
THESE WERE THE TIMES OF LEGENDS, WIZARDS AND HEROES...AND HERE ARE THE ONES IN OUR ADVENTURE: THE WIZARDS OF MICKEY!
GOOFY: HE SEEMED DESTINED TO BECOME A GREAT SORCERER...BUT HE HAS OTHER PLANS!
DONALD: HE'S A SORCERER WITH LOTS OF BAD LUCK. (HE DOESN'T KNOW THAT HIS SPELLS WORK...BUT ON A DELAY!)
MICKEY: APPRENTICE SORCERER FROM THE VILLAGE OF MICELAND.
FAFNIR: HE'S A PUPPY DRAGON THAT FOLLOWS DONALD AROUND.
AND HERE IS THE VILLAIN!
THE GREAT CROWN: IT CAN ONLY BE REASSEMBLED BY WHOEVER WINS ALL OF THE DIAMAGICS IN THE GREAT TOURNAMENT.
THE PHANTOM BLOT: IF HE GETS THE SUPREME SORCERER'S CROWN AND THE DRAGONS' ANCIENT MAGIC, HE'LL BE ABLE TO RULE THE WORLD!
THE GREAT TOURNAMENT RULES:
TEAMS MADE OF THREE WIZARDS CAN CHALLENGE EACH OTHER IN DUELS OF MAGIC.
MATCHES CAN ONLY TAKE PLACE IN SELECTED CASTLES SHOWN ON THE OFFICIAL MAP.
TEAMS PUT ONE DIAMAGIC AT STAKE IN EACH MATCH.
THE WINNER OF THE MATCH MAY CLAIM THEIR OPPONENT'S DIAMAGIC.
A TEAM IS ELIMINATED FROM THE TOURNAMENT WHEN IT LOSES ITS DIAMAGIC!

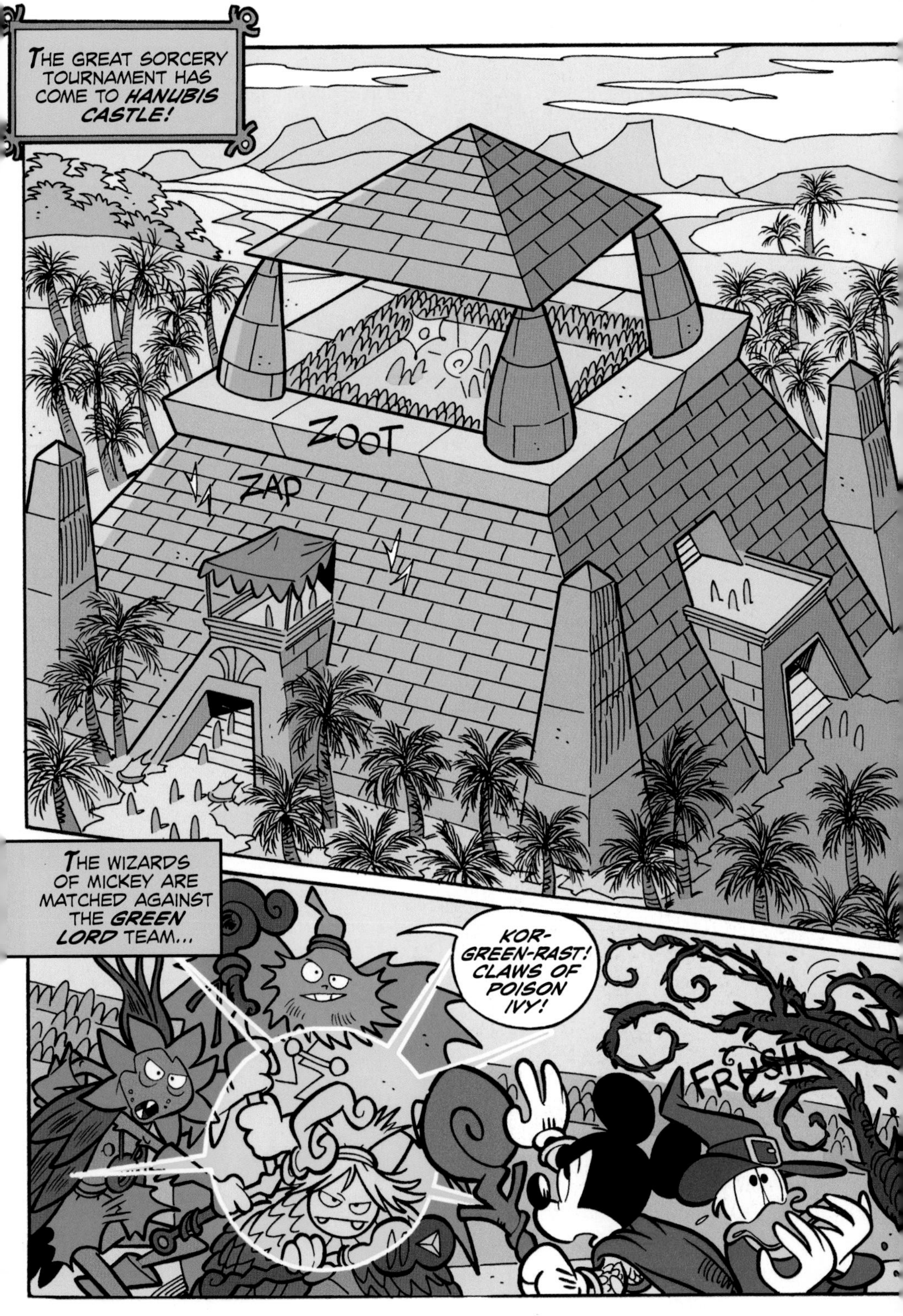
THE GREAT SORCERY TOURNAMENT HAS COME TO HANUBIS CASTLE!
ZOOT
ZAP
THE WIZARDS OF MICKEY ARE MATCHED AGAINST THE GREEN LORD TEAM...
KOR-GREEN-RAST! CLAWS OF POISON IVY!
FRUSH

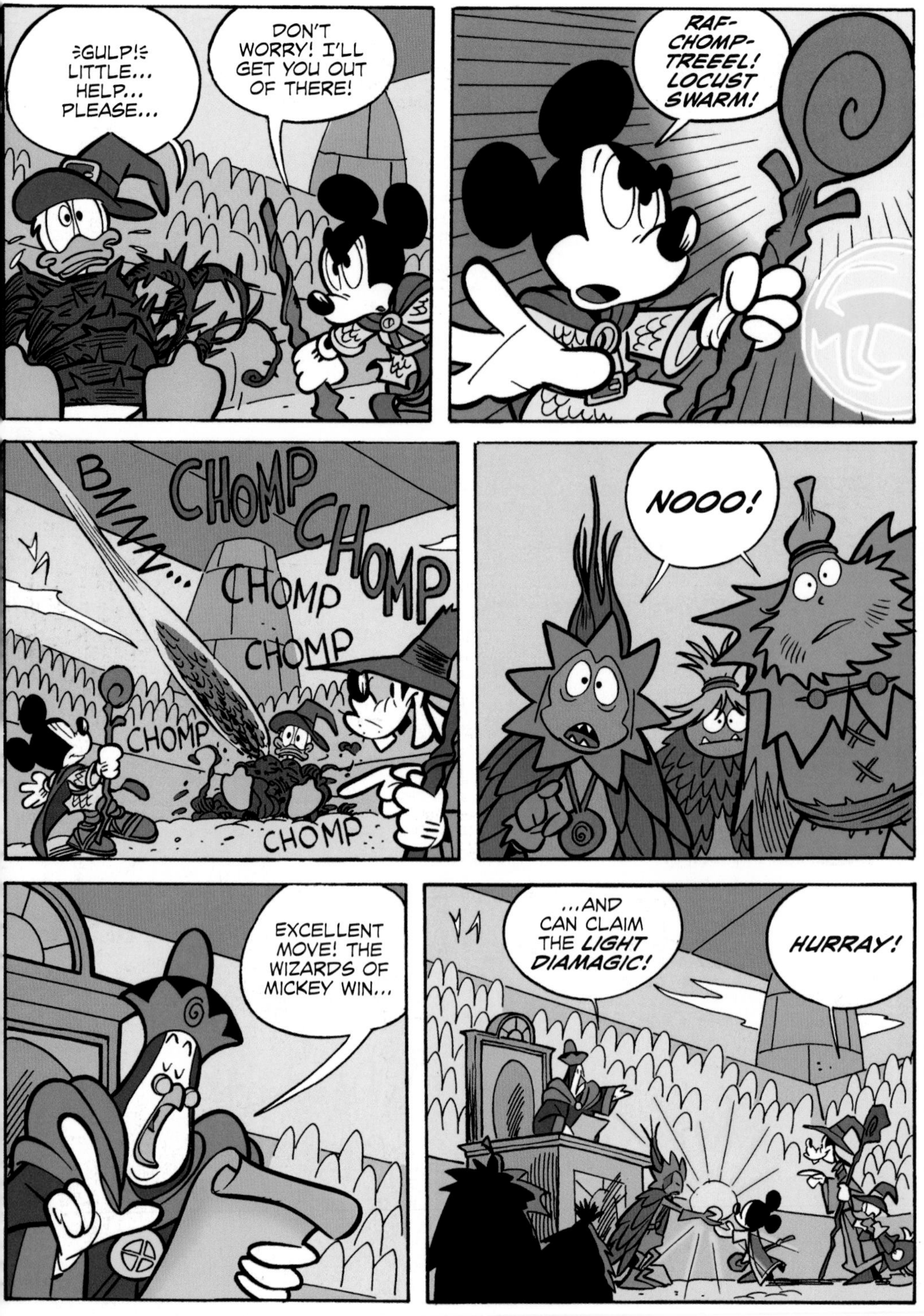

≶GULP!≶ LITTLE... HELP... PLEASE...
DON'T WORRY! I'LL GET YOU OUT OF THERE!
RAF-CHOMP-TREEEL! LOCUST SWARM!
BZZZZ...
CHOMP
CHOMP
CHOMP
CHOMP
CHOMP
CHOMP
NOOO!
EXCELLENT MOVE! THE WIZARDS OF MICKEY WIN...
...AND CAN CLAIM THE *LIGHT DIAMAGIC!*
HURRAY!

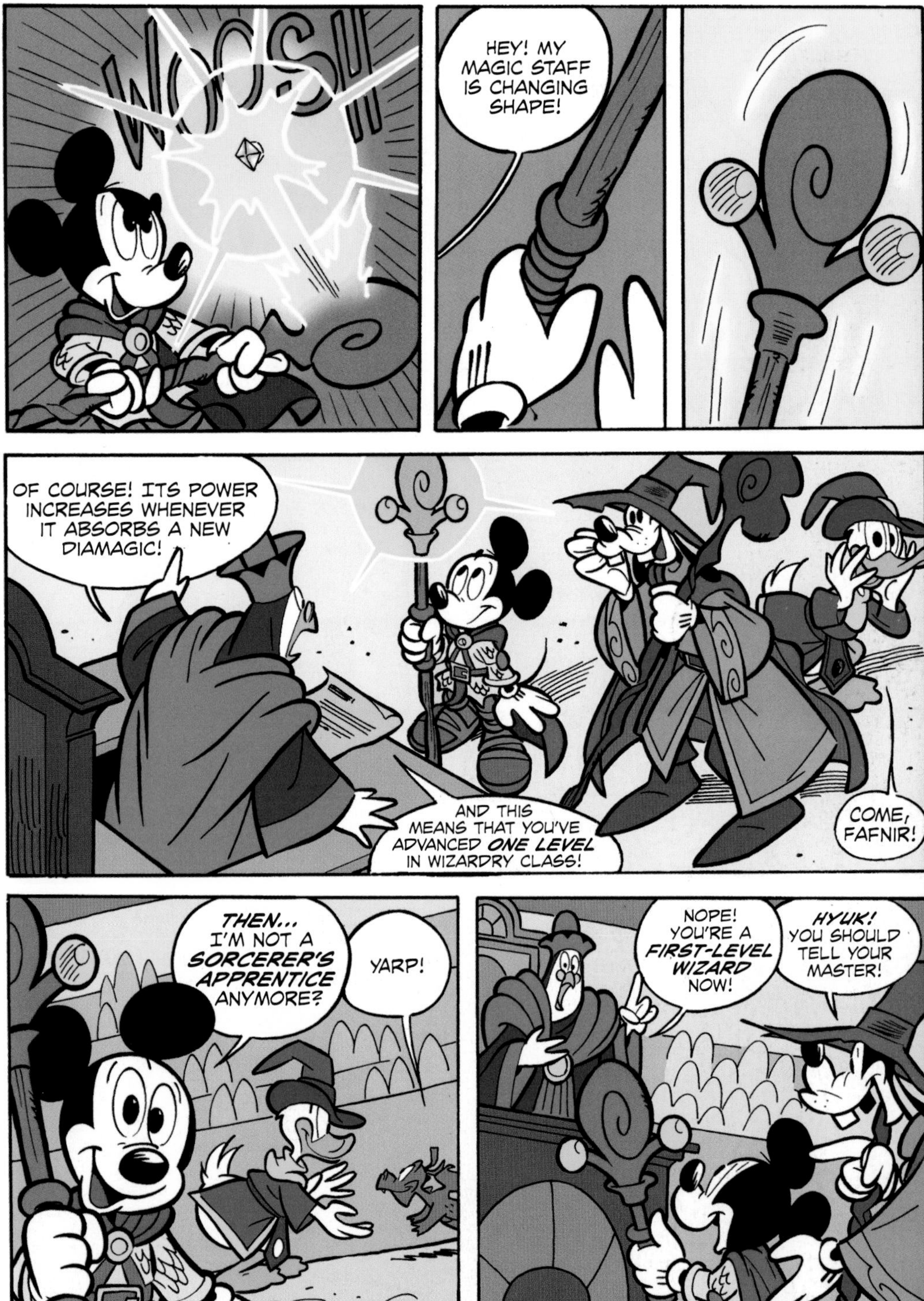
WOOSH!
HEY! MY MAGIC STAFF IS CHANGING SHAPE!
OF COURSE! ITS POWER INCREASES WHENEVER IT ABSORBS A NEW DIAMAGIC!
AND THIS MEANS THAT YOU'VE ADVANCED ONE LEVEL IN WIZARDRY CLASS!
COME, FAFNIR!
THEN... I'M NOT A SORCERER'S APPRENTICE ANYMORE?
YARP!
NOPE! YOU'RE A FIRST-LEVEL WIZARD NOW!
HYUK! YOU SHOULD TELL YOUR MASTER!

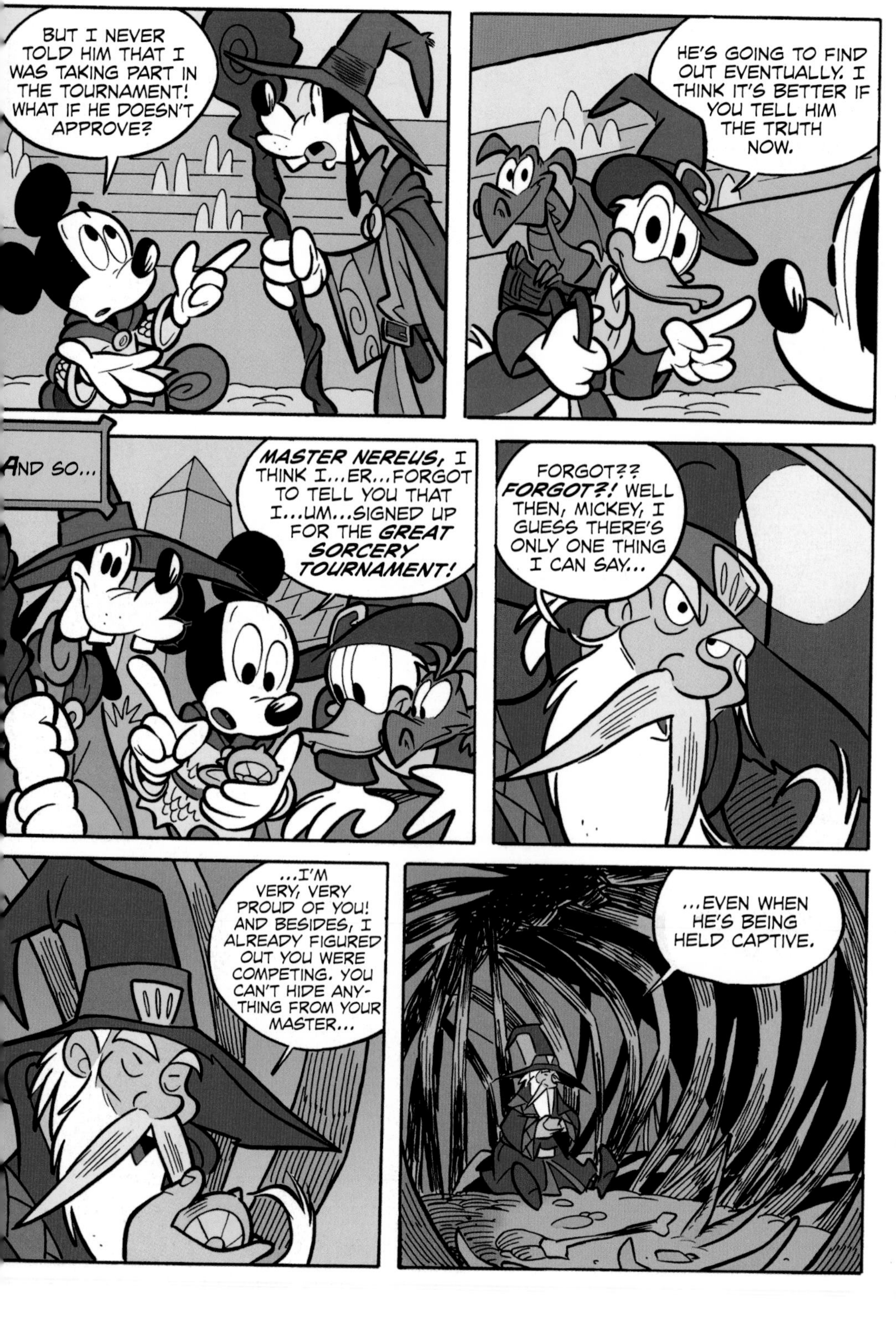
BUT I NEVER TOLD HIM THAT I WAS TAKING PART IN THE TOURNAMENT! WHAT IF HE DOESN'T APPROVE?
HE'S GOING TO FIND OUT EVENTUALLY. I THINK IT'S BETTER IF YOU TELL HIM THE TRUTH NOW.
AND SO...
MASTER NEREUS, I THINK I...ER...FORGOT TO TELL YOU THAT I...UM...SIGNED UP FOR THE GREAT SORCERY TOURNAMENT!
FORGOT?? FORGOT?! WELL THEN, MICKEY, I GUESS THERE'S ONLY ONE THING I CAN SAY...
...I'M VERY, VERY PROUD OF YOU! AND BESIDES, I ALREADY FIGURED OUT YOU WERE COMPETING. YOU CAN'T HIDE ANY-THING FROM YOUR MASTER...
...EVEN WHEN HE'S BEING HELD CAPTIVE.

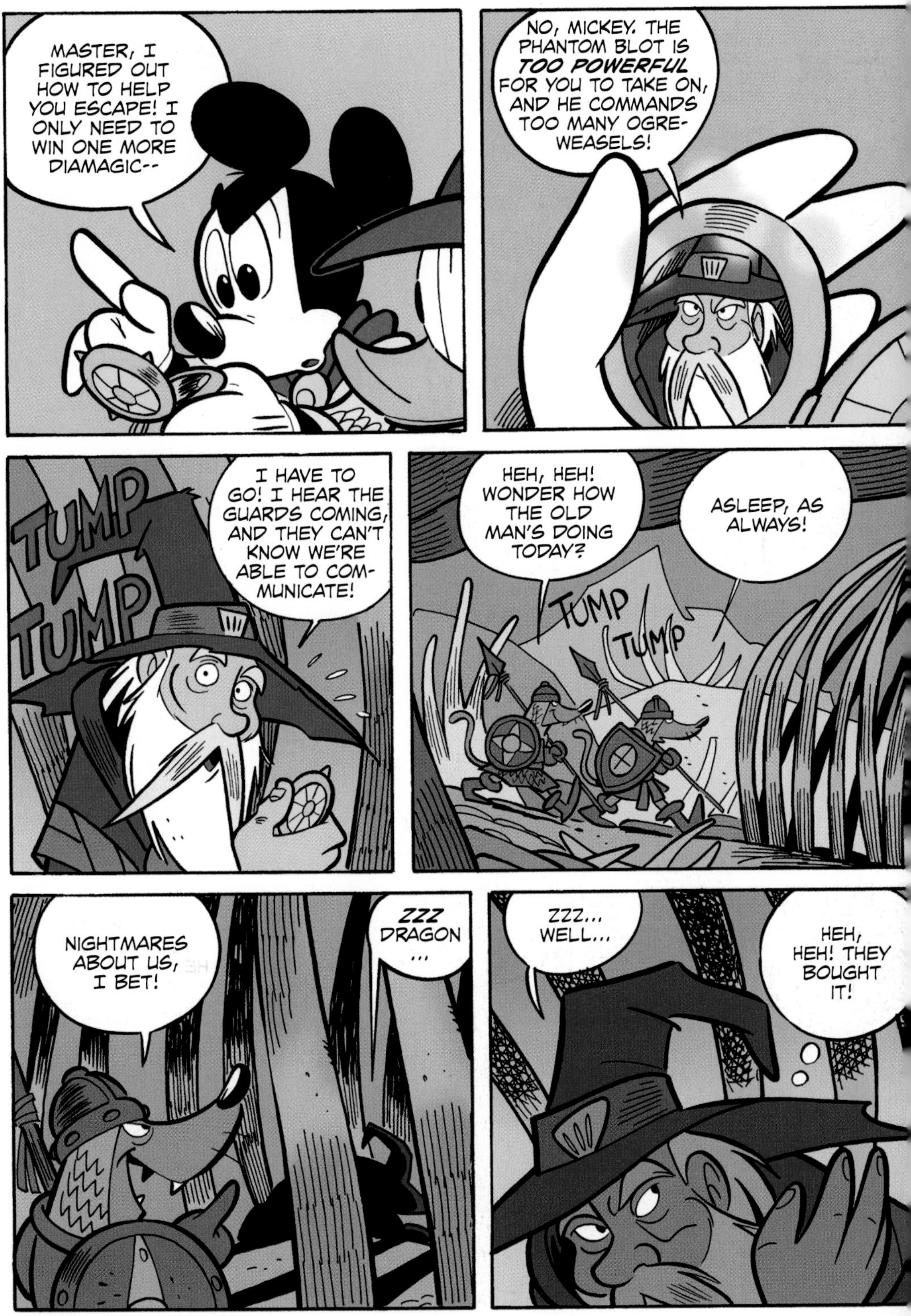
MASTER, I FIGURED OUT HOW TO HELP YOU ESCAPE! I ONLY NEED TO WIN ONE MORE DIAMAGIC--
NO, MICKEY. THE PHANTOM BLOT IS TOO POWERFUL FOR YOU TO TAKE ON, AND HE COMMANDS TOO MANY OGRE-WEASELS!
TUMP TUMP
I HAVE TO GO! I HEAR THE GUARDS COMING, AND THEY CAN'T KNOW WE'RE ABLE TO COMMUNICATE!
HEH, HEH! WONDER HOW THE OLD MAN'S DOING TODAY?
ASLEEP, AS ALWAYS!
TUMP TUMP
NIGHTMARES ABOUT US, I BET!
ZZZ DRAGON ...
ZZZ... WELL...
HEH, HEH! THEY BOUGHT IT!

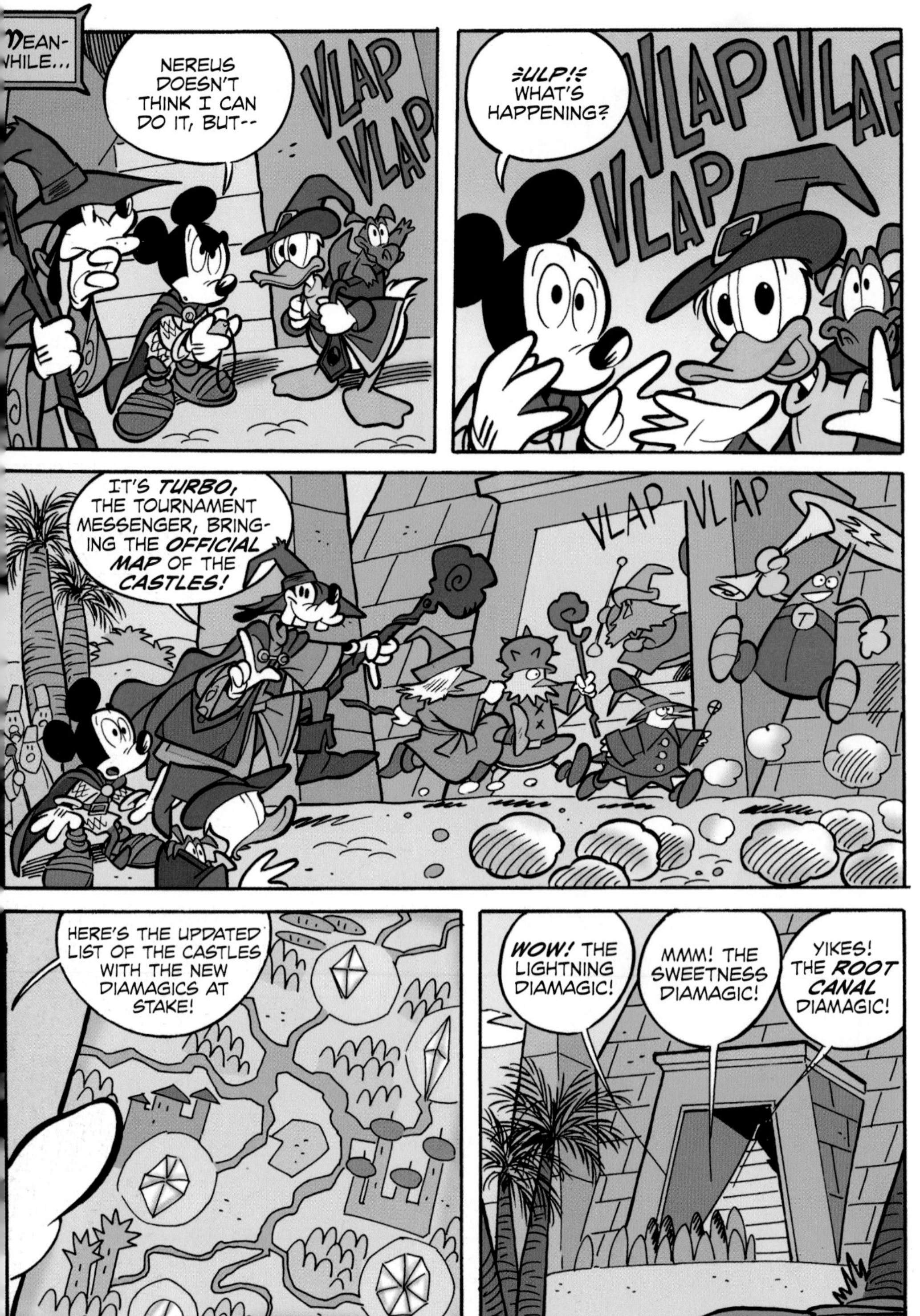
MEANWHILE...
NEREUS DOESN'T THINK I CAN DO IT, BUT--
VLAP VLAP
ULP!! WHAT'S HAPPENING?
VLAP VLAP VLAP VLAP
IT'S TURBO, THE TOURNAMENT MESSENGER, BRINGING THE OFFICIAL MAP OF THE CASTLES!
VLAP VLAP
HERE'S THE UPDATED LIST OF THE CASTLES WITH THE NEW DIAMAGICS AT STAKE!
WOW! THE LIGHTNING DIAMAGIC!
MMM! THE SWEETNESS DIAMAGIC!
YIKES! THE ROOT CANAL DIAMAGIC!

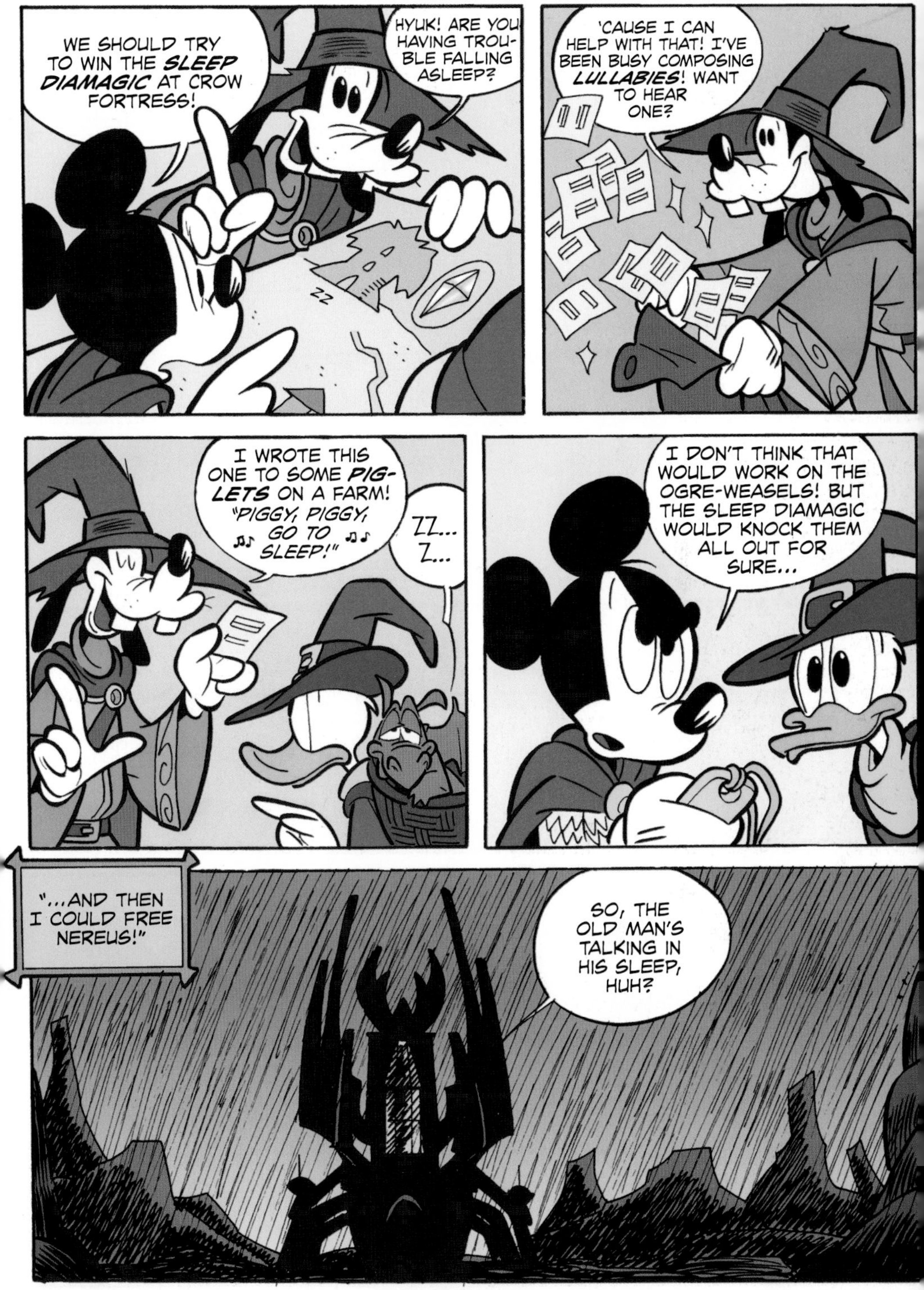
WE SHOULD TRY TO WIN THE SLEEP DIAMAGIC AT CROW FORTRESS!
HYUK! ARE YOU HAVING TROUBLE FALLING ASLEEP?
'CAUSE I CAN HELP WITH THAT! I'VE BEEN BUSY COMPOSING LULLABIES! WANT TO HEAR ONE?
I WROTE THIS ONE TO SOME PIGLETS ON A FARM! "PIGGY, PIGGY, GO TO SLEEP!"
ZZ... Z...
I DON'T THINK THAT WOULD WORK ON THE OGRE-WEASELS! BUT THE SLEEP DIAMAGIC WOULD KNOCK THEM ALL OUT FOR SURE...
"...AND THEN I COULD FREE NEREUS!"
SO, THE OLD MAN'S TALKING IN HIS SLEEP, HUH?

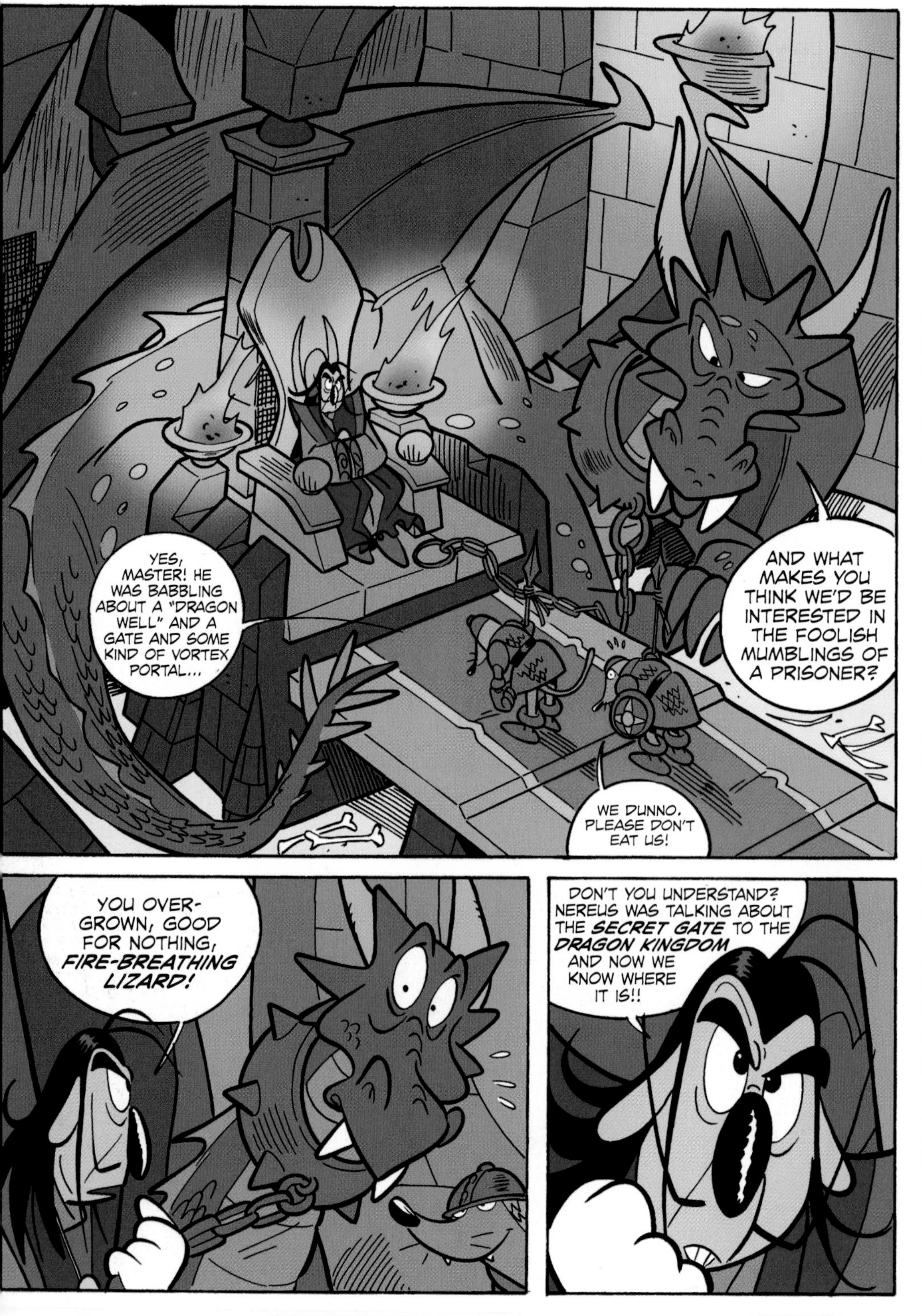
YES, MASTER! HE WAS BABBLING ABOUT A "DRAGON WELL" AND A GATE AND SOME KIND OF VORTEX PORTAL...
AND WHAT MAKES YOU THINK WE'D BE INTERESTED IN THE FOOLISH MUMBLINGS OF A PRISONER?
WE DUNNO. PLEASE DON'T EAT US!
YOU OVER-GROWN, GOOD FOR NOTHING, *FIRE-BREATHING LIZARD!*
DON'T YOU UNDERSTAND? NEREUS WAS TALKING ABOUT THE *SECRET GATE* TO THE *DRAGON KINGDOM* AND NOW WE KNOW WHERE IT IS!!

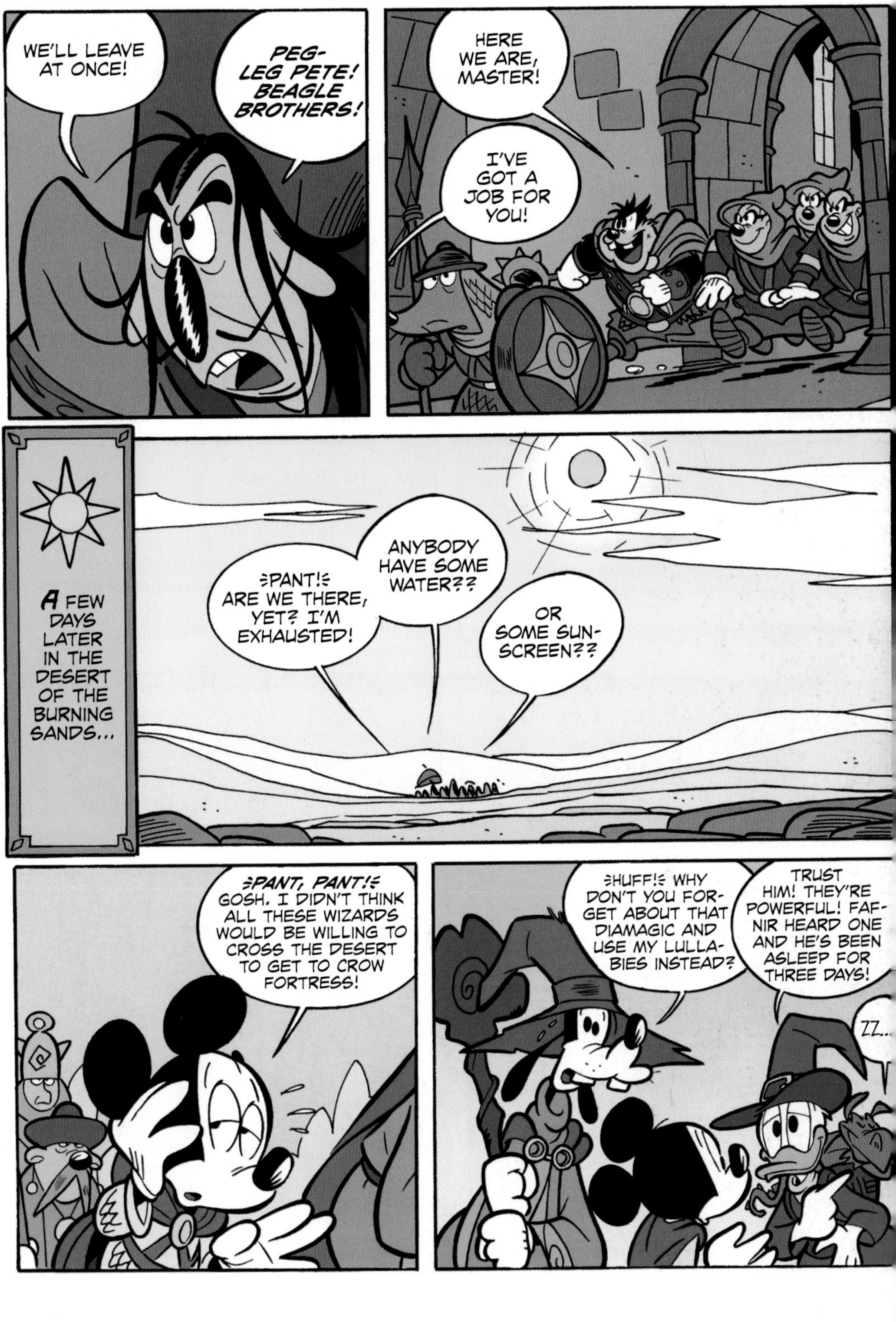

WE'LL LEAVE AT ONCE!
PEG-LEG PETE! BEAGLE BROTHERS!
HERE WE ARE, MASTER!
I'VE GOT A JOB FOR YOU!
A FEW DAYS LATER IN THE DESERT OF THE BURNING SANDS...
=PANT!= ARE WE THERE, YET? I'M EXHAUSTED!
ANYBODY HAVE SOME WATER??
OR SOME SUN-SCREEN??
=PANT, PANT!= GOSH. I DIDN'T THINK ALL THESE WIZARDS WOULD BE WILLING TO CROSS THE DESERT TO GET TO CROW FORTRESS!
=HUFF!= WHY DON'T YOU FOR-GET ABOUT THAT DIAMAGIC AND USE MY LULLA-BIES INSTEAD?
TRUST HIM! THEY'RE POWERFUL! FAF-NIR HEARD ONE AND HE'S BEEN ASLEEP FOR THREE DAYS!
ZZ...

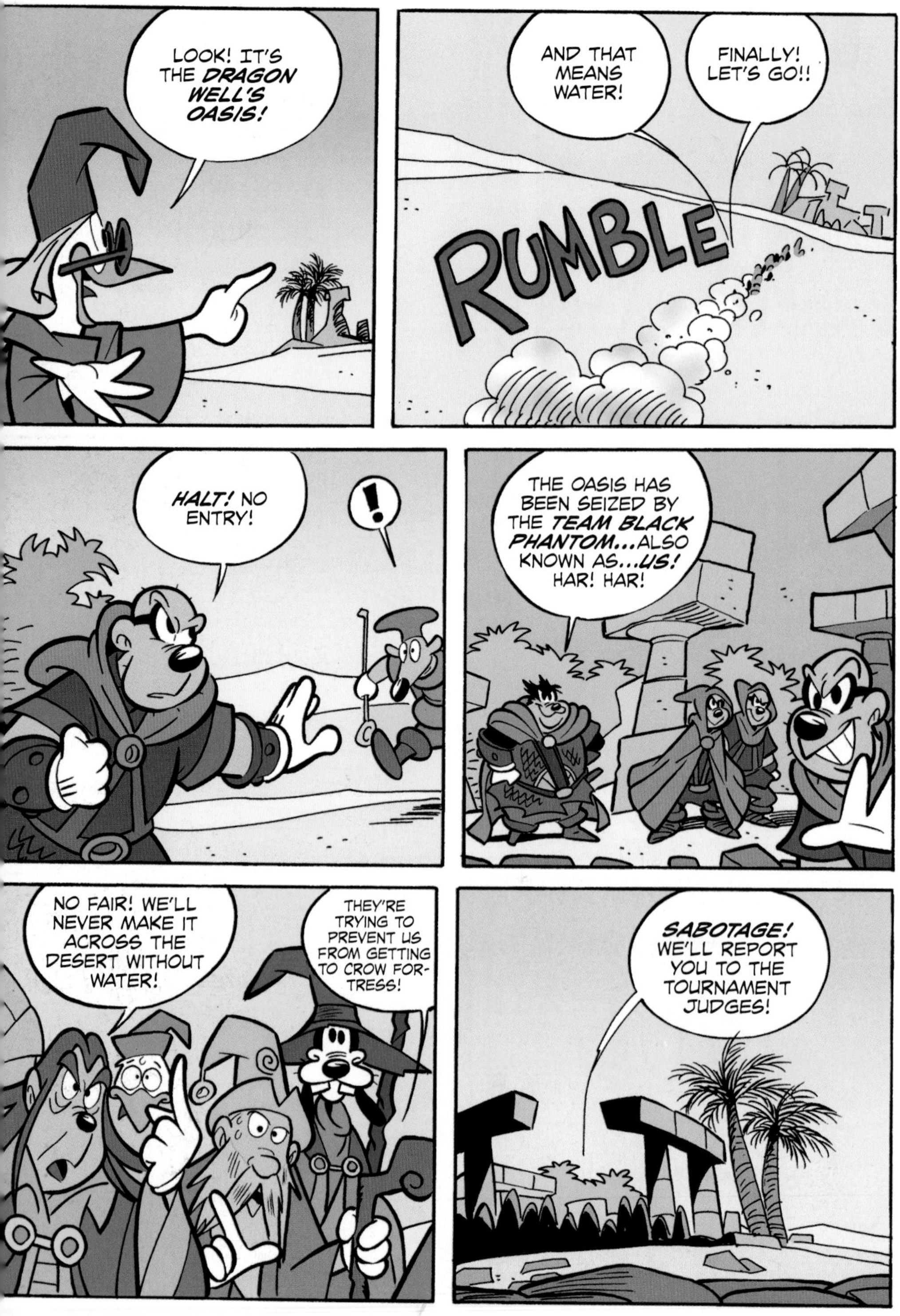
LOOK! IT'S THE *DRAGON WELL'S OASIS!*
AND THAT MEANS WATER!
FINALLY! LET'S GO!!
RUMBLE
HALT! NO ENTRY!
!
THE OASIS HAS BEEN SEIZED BY THE *TEAM BLACK PHANTOM*...ALSO KNOWN AS...*US!* HAR! HAR!
NO FAIR! WE'LL NEVER MAKE IT ACROSS THE DESERT WITHOUT WATER!
THEY'RE TRYING TO PREVENT US FROM GETTING TO CROW FORTRESS!
SABOTAGE! WE'LL REPORT YOU TO THE TOURNAMENT JUDGES!

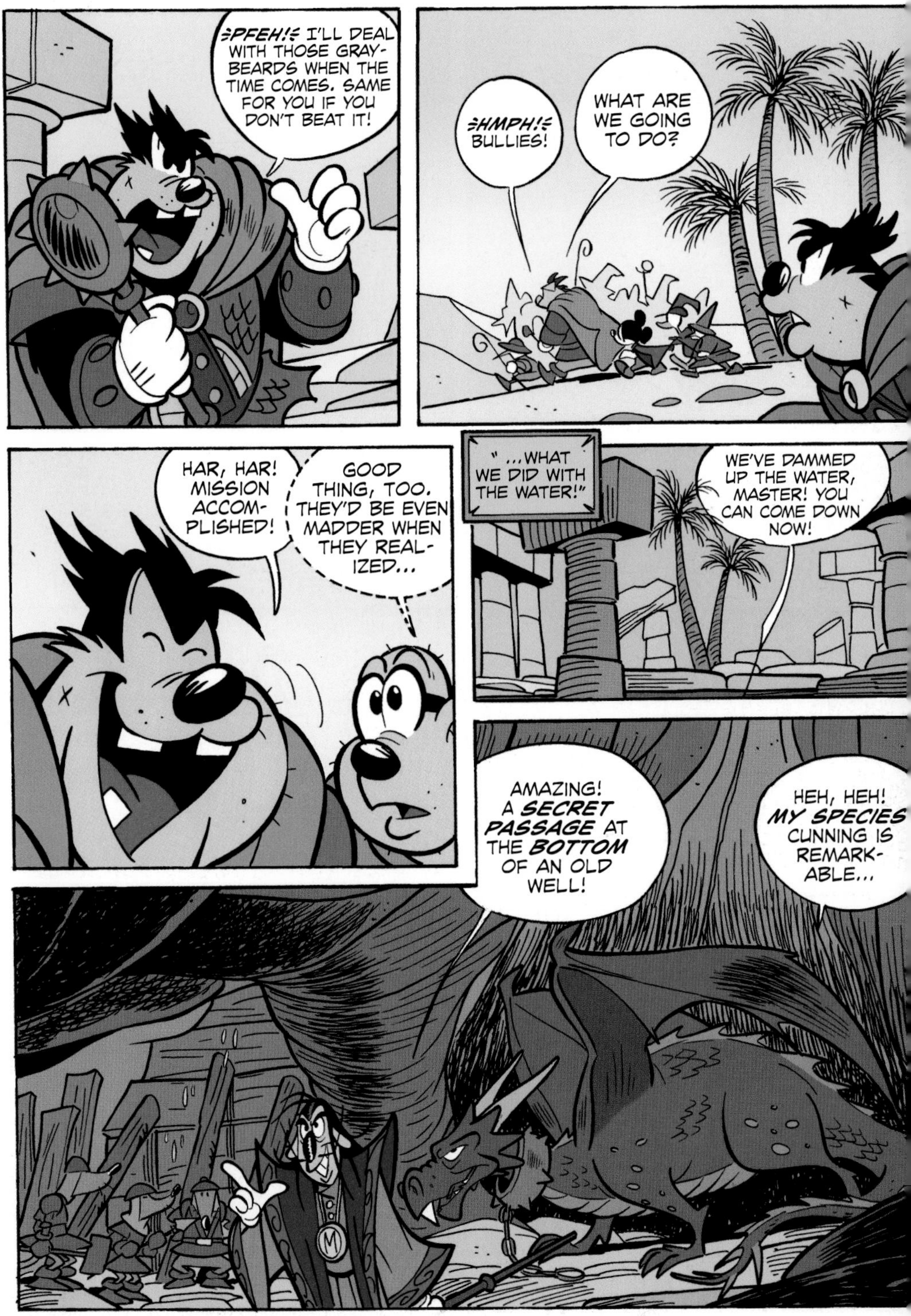

PFEH! I'LL DEAL WITH THOSE GRAY-BEARDS WHEN THE TIME COMES. SAME FOR YOU IF YOU DON'T BEAT IT!
HMPH! BULLIES!
WHAT ARE WE GOING TO DO?
HAR, HAR! MISSION ACCOM-PLISHED!
GOOD THING, TOO. THEY'D BE EVEN MADDER WHEN THEY REAL-IZED...
"...WHAT WE DID WITH THE WATER!"
WE'VE DAMMED UP THE WATER, MASTER! YOU CAN COME DOWN NOW!
AMAZING! A SECRET PASSAGE AT THE BOTTOM OF AN OLD WELL!
HEH, HEH! MY SPECIES CUNNING IS REMARK-ABLE...

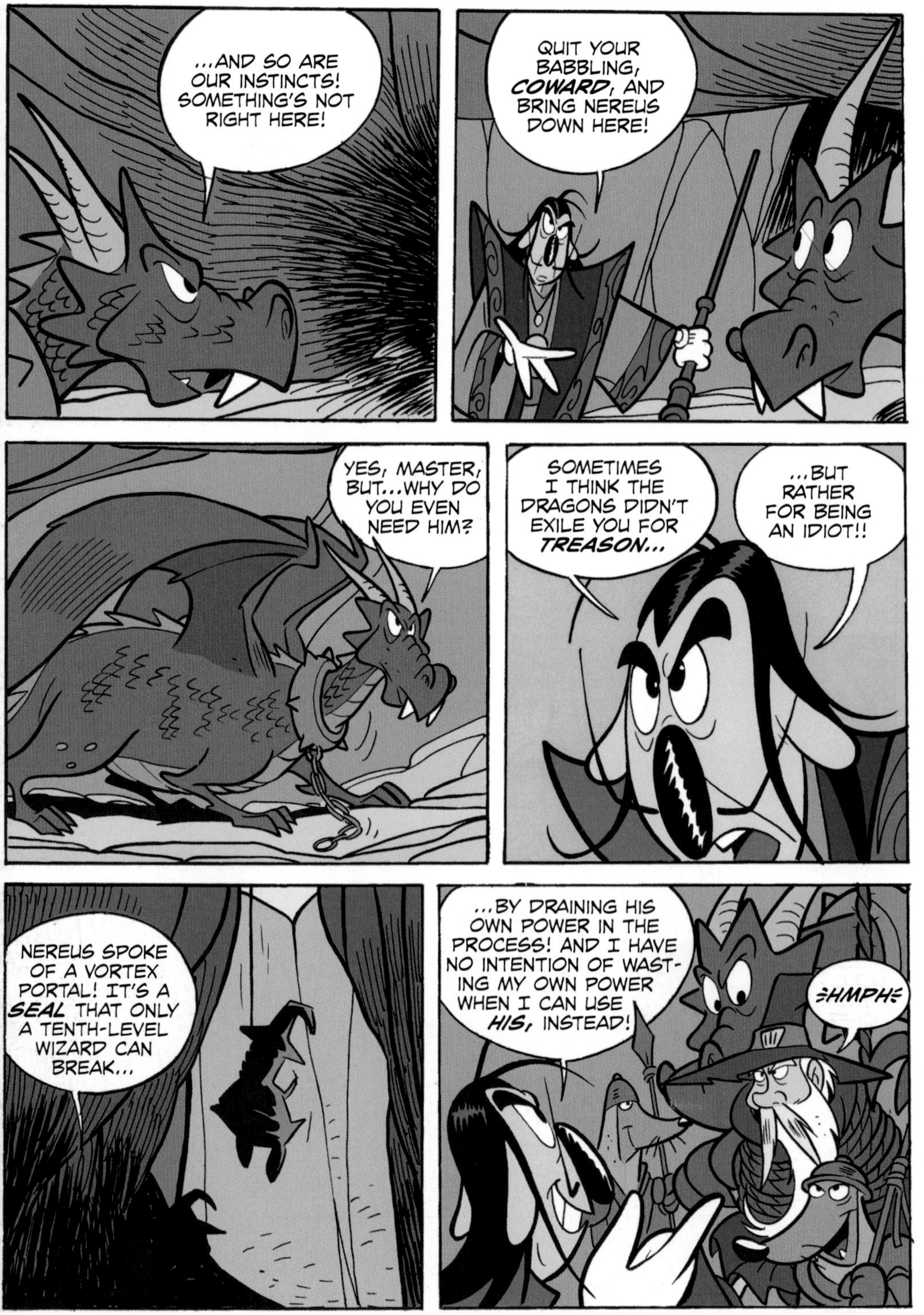
...AND SO ARE OUR INSTINCTS! SOMETHING'S NOT RIGHT HERE!
QUIT YOUR BABBLING, COWARD, AND BRING NEREUS DOWN HERE!
YES, MASTER, BUT...WHY DO YOU EVEN NEED HIM?
SOMETIMES I THINK THE DRAGONS DIDN'T EXILE YOU FOR TREASON...
...BUT RATHER FOR BEING AN IDIOT!!
NEREUS SPOKE OF A VORTEX PORTAL! IT'S A SEAL THAT ONLY A TENTH-LEVEL WIZARD CAN BREAK...
...BY DRAINING HIS OWN POWER IN THE PROCESS! AND I HAVE NO INTENTION OF WASTING MY OWN POWER WHEN I CAN USE HIS, INSTEAD!
HMPH

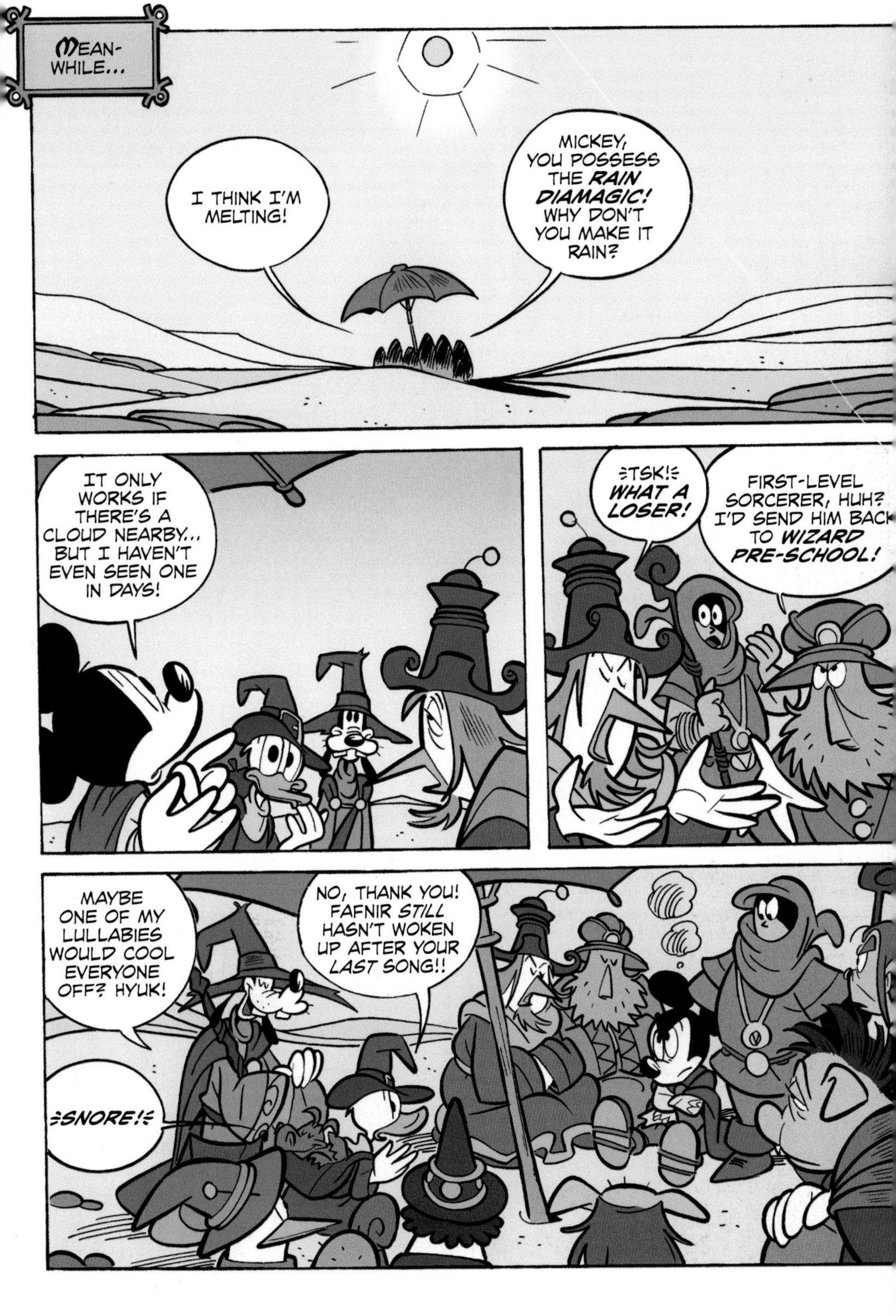
MEAN-WHILE...
I THINK I'M MELTING!
MICKEY, YOU POSSESS THE *RAIN DIAMAGIC!* WHY DON'T YOU MAKE IT RAIN?
IT ONLY WORKS IF THERE'S A CLOUD NEARBY... BUT I HAVEN'T EVEN SEEN ONE IN DAYS!
TSK! *WHAT A LOSER!*
FIRST-LEVEL SORCERER, HUH? I'D SEND HIM BACK TO *WIZARD PRE-SCHOOL!*
MAYBE ONE OF MY LULLABIES WOULD COOL EVERYONE OFF? HYUK!
NO, THANK YOU! FAFNIR *STILL* HASN'T WOKEN UP AFTER YOUR *LAST* SONG!!
SNORE!

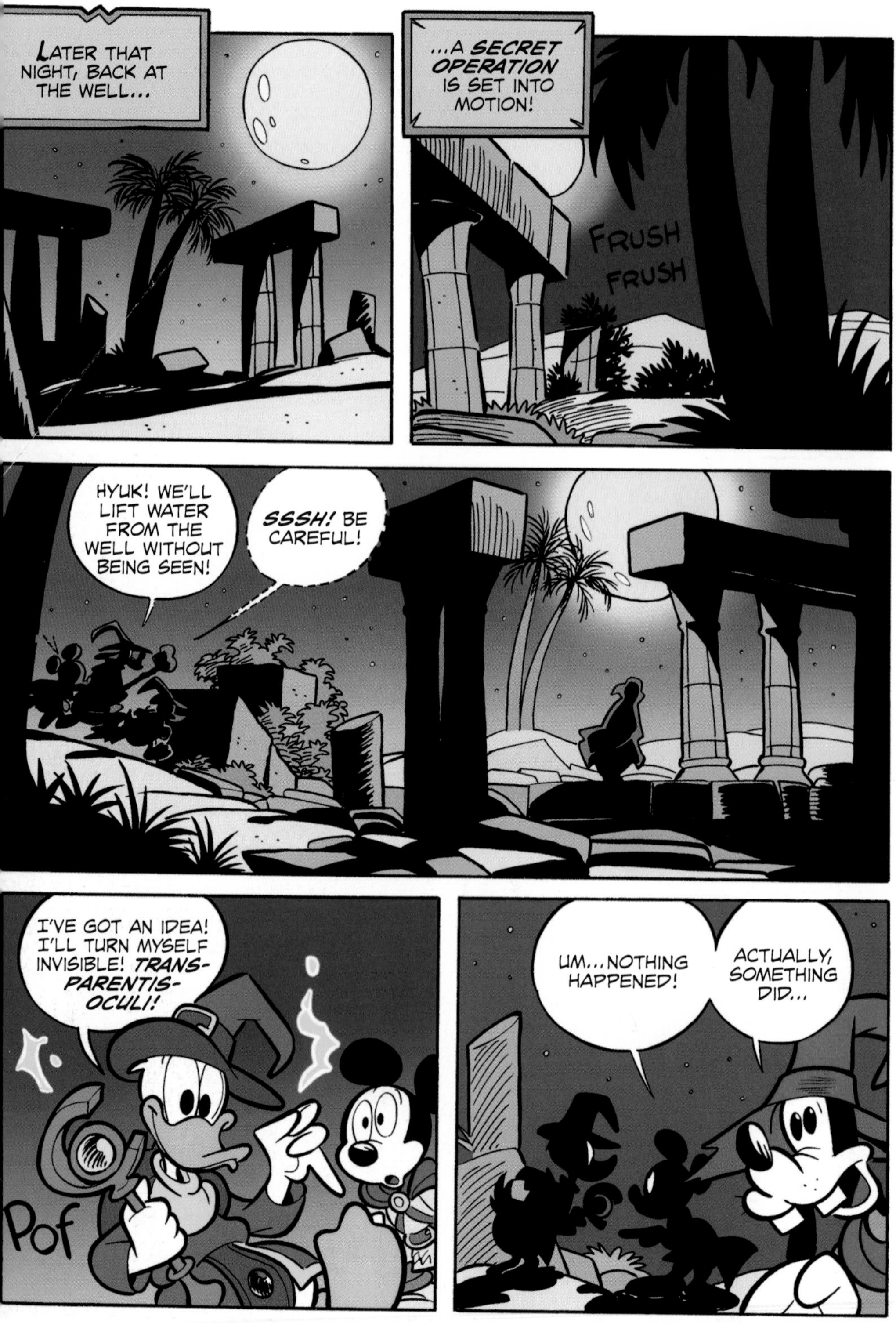
LATER THAT NIGHT, BACK AT THE WELL...
...A SECRET OPERATION IS SET INTO MOTION!
FRUSH FRUSH
HYUK! WE'LL LIFT WATER FROM THE WELL WITHOUT BEING SEEN!
SSSH! BE CAREFUL!
I'VE GOT AN IDEA! I'LL TURN MYSELF INVISIBLE! TRANS-PARENTIS-OCULI!
POF
UM...NOTHING HAPPENED!
ACTUALLY, SOMETHING DID...

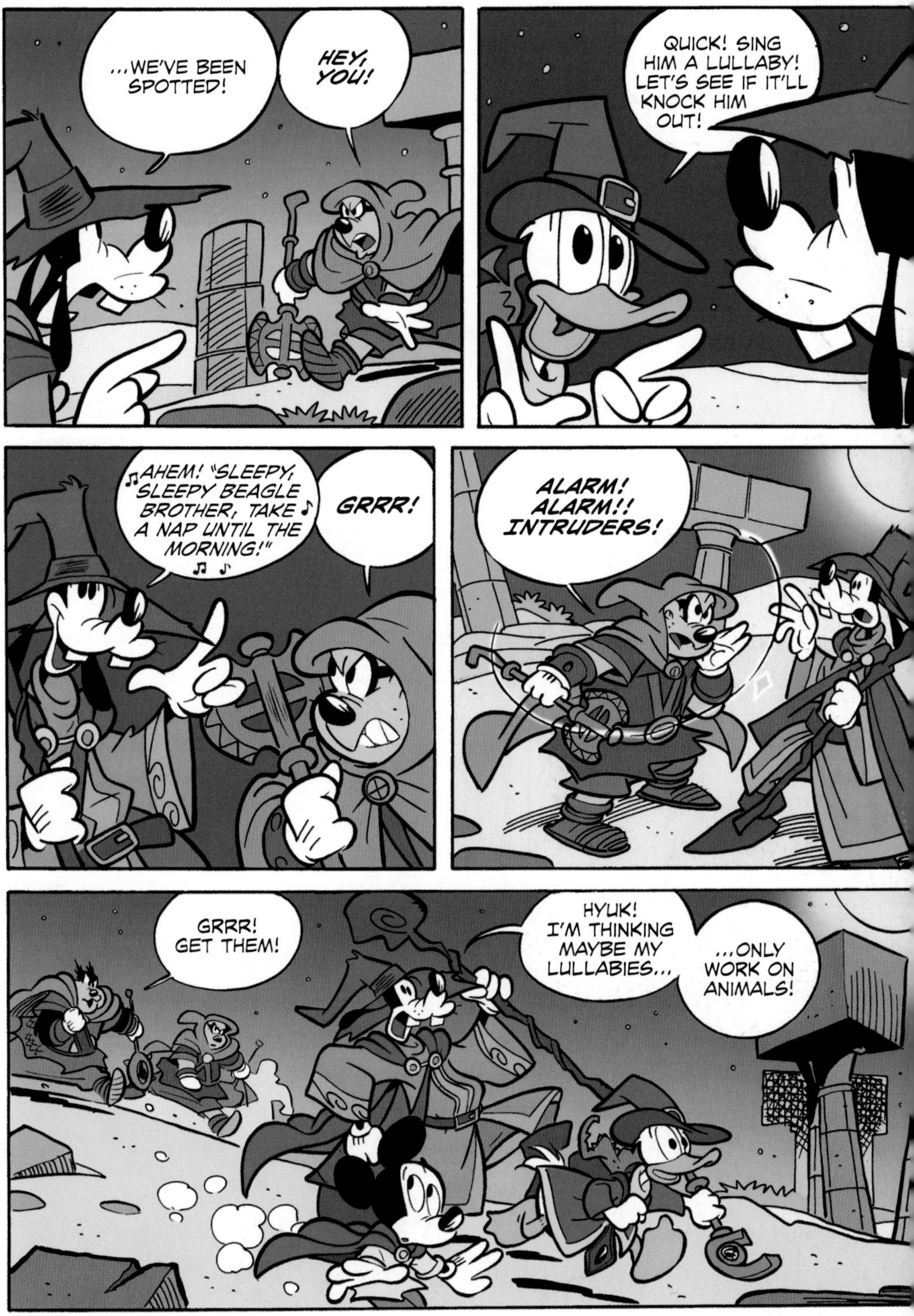
...WE'VE BEEN SPOTTED!
HEY, YOU!
QUICK! SING HIM A LULLABY! LET'S SEE IF IT'LL KNOCK HIM OUT!
AHEM! "SLEEPY, SLEEPY BEAGLE BROTHER, TAKE A NAP UNTIL THE MORNING!"
GRRR!
ALARM! ALARM!! INTRUDERS!
GRRR! GET THEM!
HYUK! I'M THINKING MAYBE MY LULLABIES...
...ONLY WORK ON ANIMALS!

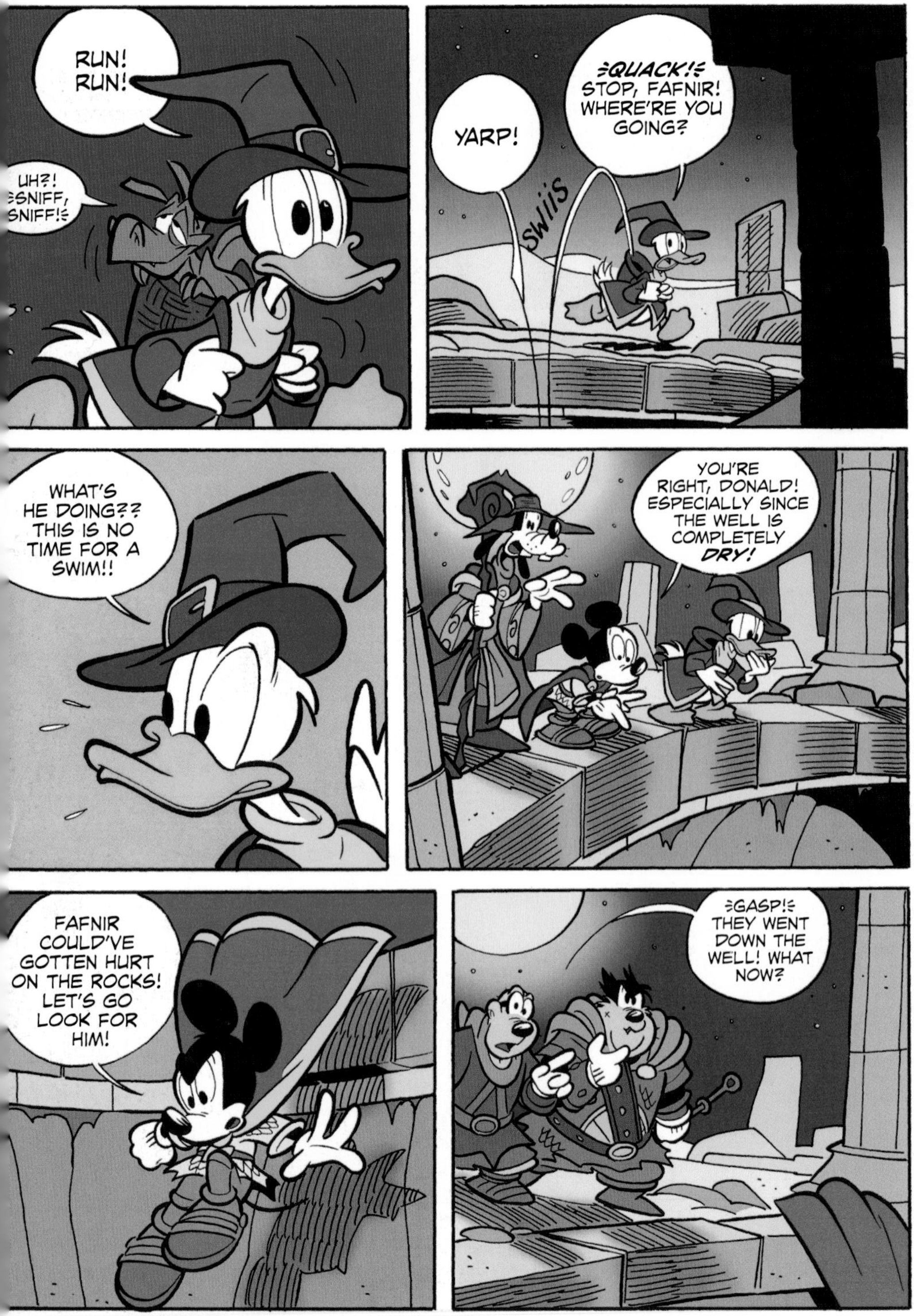
RUN! RUN!
UH?! SNIFF, SNIFF!
YARP!
QUACK! STOP, FAFNIR! WHERE'RE YOU GOING?
SWIIS
WHAT'S HE DOING?? THIS IS NO TIME FOR A SWIM!!
YOU'RE RIGHT, DONALD! ESPECIALLY SINCE THE WELL IS COMPLETELY DRY!
FAFNIR COULD'VE GOTTEN HURT ON THE ROCKS! LET'S GO LOOK FOR HIM!
GASP! THEY WENT DOWN THE WELL! WHAT NOW?

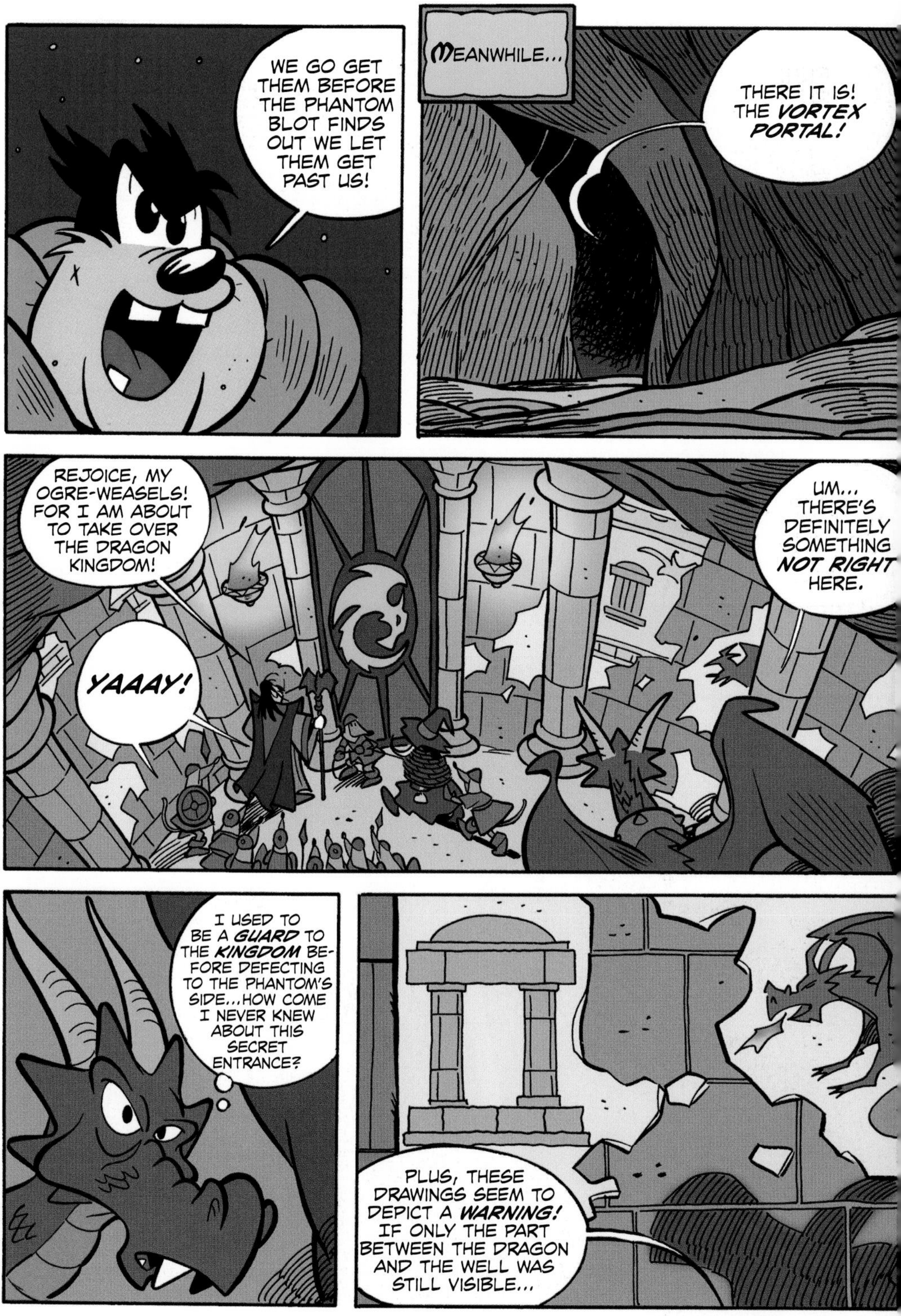
WE GO GET THEM BEFORE THE PHANTOM BLOT FINDS OUT WE LET THEM GET PAST US!
MEANWHILE...
THERE IT IS! THE *VORTEX PORTAL!*
REJOICE, MY OGRE-WEASELS! FOR I AM ABOUT TO TAKE OVER THE DRAGON KINGDOM!
YAAAY!
UM... THERE'S DEFINITELY SOMETHING *NOT RIGHT* HERE.
I USED TO BE A *GUARD* TO THE *KINGDOM* BEFORE DEFECTING TO THE PHANTOM'S SIDE...HOW COME I NEVER KNEW ABOUT THIS SECRET ENTRANCE?
PLUS, THESE DRAWINGS SEEM TO DEPICT A *WARNING!* IF ONLY THE PART BETWEEN THE DRAGON AND THE WELL WAS STILL VISIBLE...

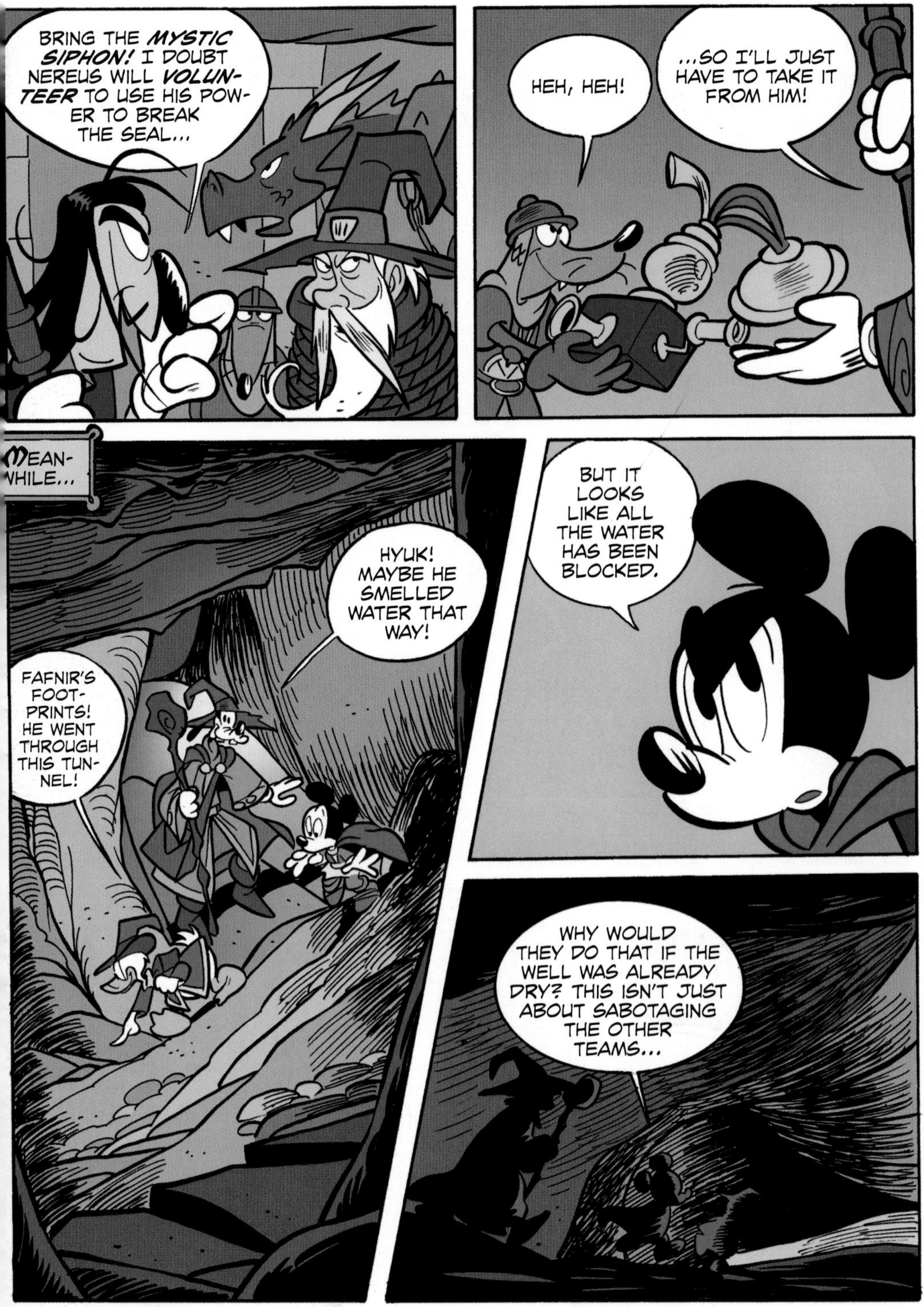
BRING THE MYSTIC SIPHON! I DOUBT NEREUS WILL VOLUNTEER TO USE HIS POWER TO BREAK THE SEAL...
HEH, HEH!
...SO I'LL JUST HAVE TO TAKE IT FROM HIM!
MEANWHILE...
FAFNIR'S FOOTPRINTS! HE WENT THROUGH THIS TUNNEL!
HYUK! MAYBE HE SMELLED WATER THAT WAY!
BUT IT LOOKS LIKE ALL THE WATER HAS BEEN BLOCKED.
WHY WOULD THEY DO THAT IF THE WELL WAS ALREADY DRY? THIS ISN'T JUST ABOUT SABOTAGING THE OTHER TEAMS...

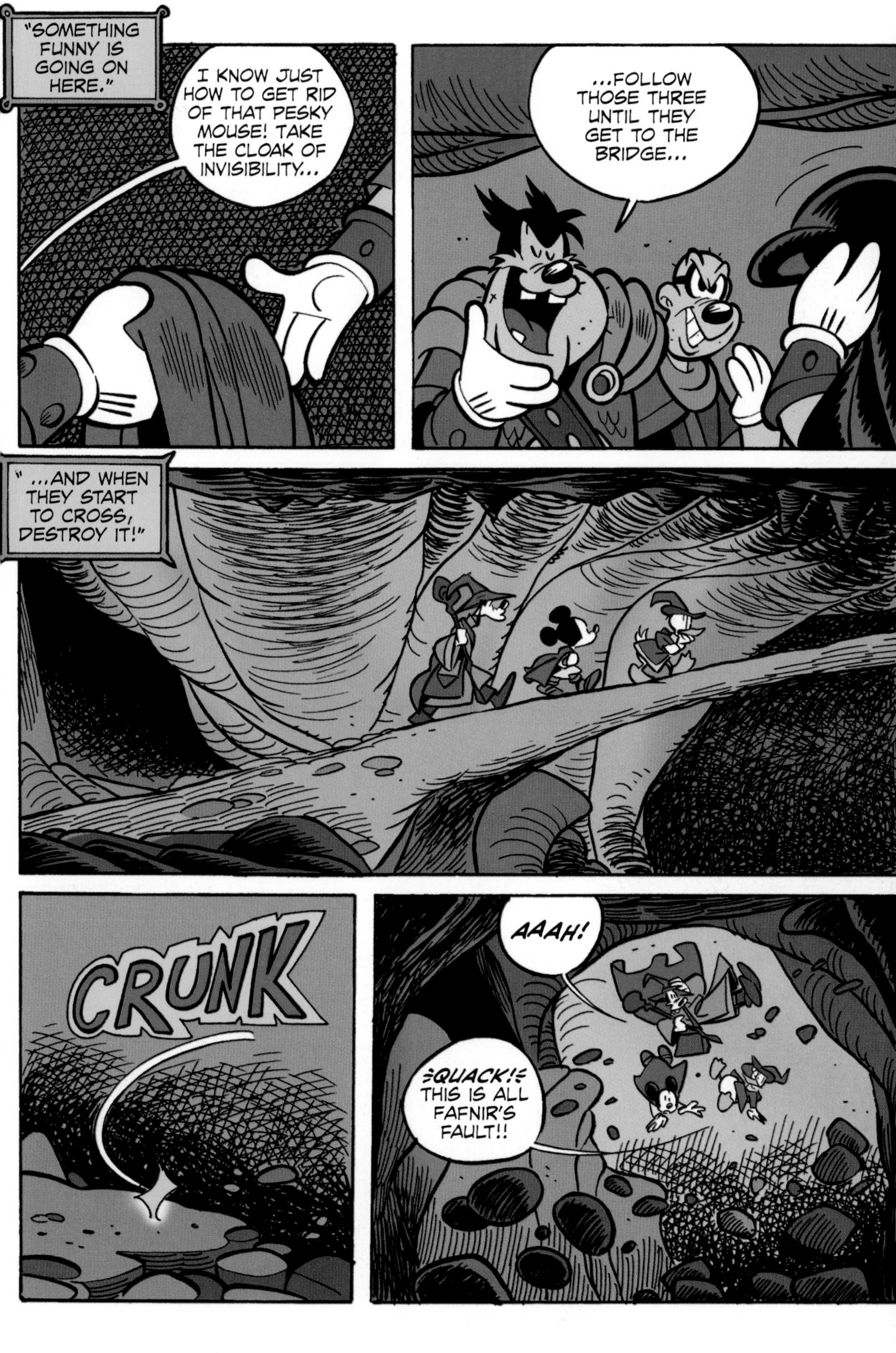
"SOMETHING FUNNY IS GOING ON HERE."
I KNOW JUST HOW TO GET RID OF THAT PESKY MOUSE! TAKE THE CLOAK OF INVISIBILITY...
...FOLLOW THOSE THREE UNTIL THEY GET TO THE BRIDGE...
" ...AND WHEN THEY START TO CROSS, DESTROY IT!"
CRUNK
AAAH!
QUACK! THIS IS ALL FAFNIR'S FAULT!!

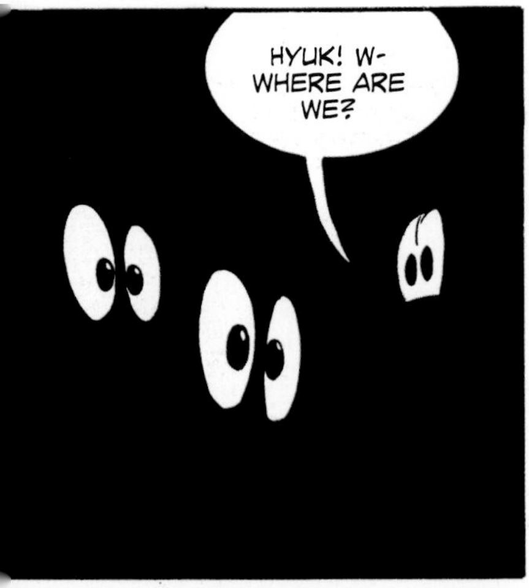
HYUK! W-WHERE ARE WE?

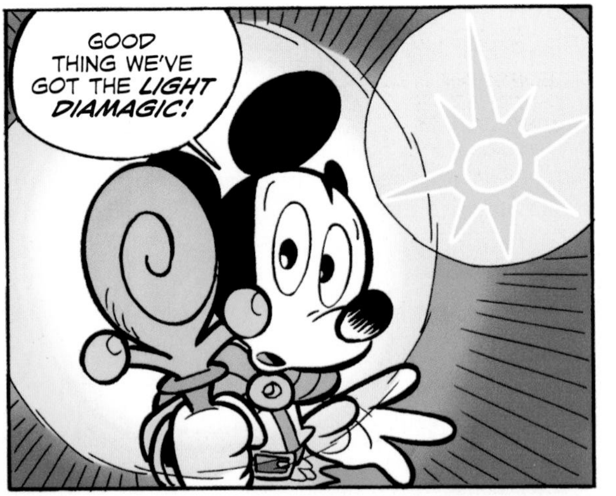
GOOD THING WE'VE GOT THE *LIGHT DIAMAGIC!*

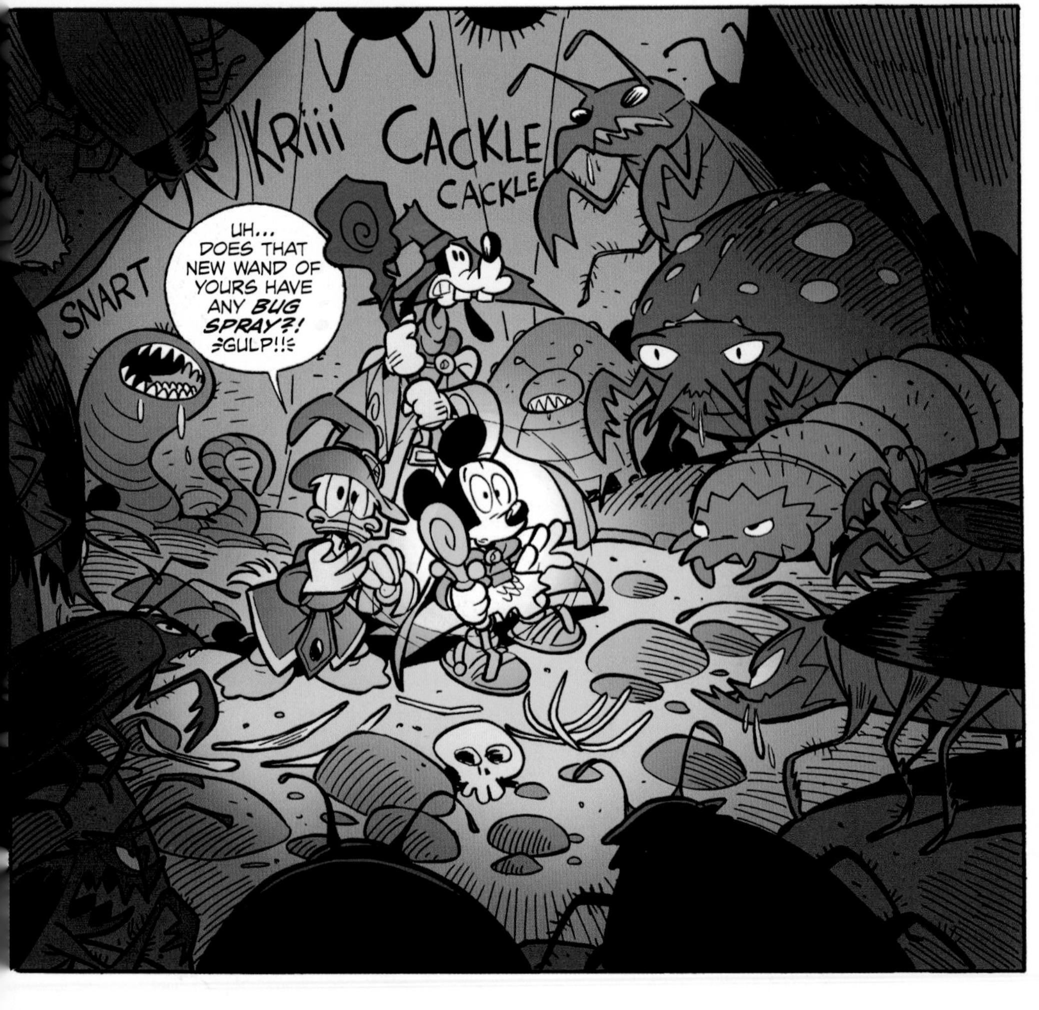
KRIII
CACKLE
CACKLE
SNART
UH... DOES THAT NEW WAND OF YOURS HAVE ANY *BUG SPRAY?!* GULP!!

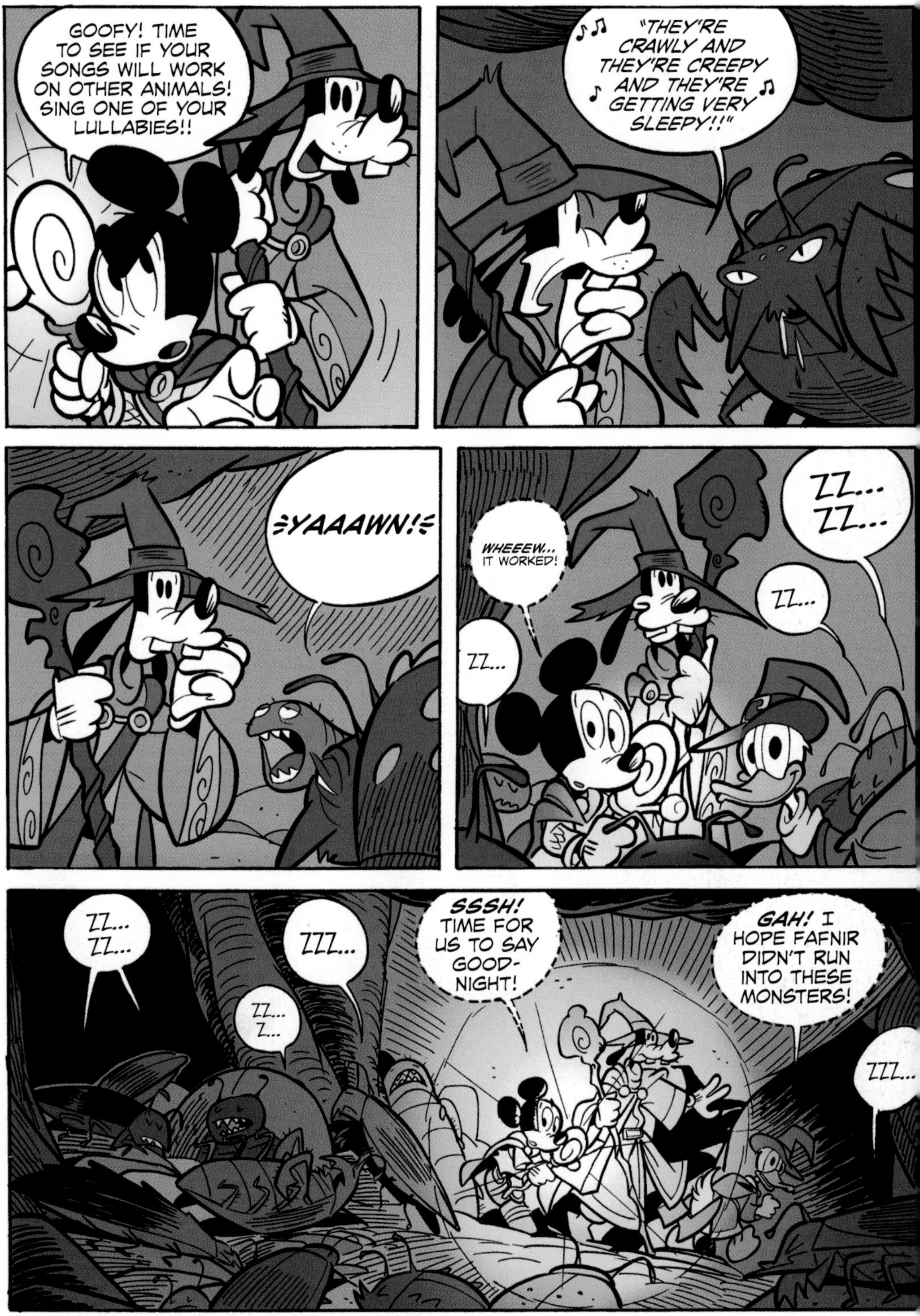
GOOFY! TIME TO SEE IF YOUR SONGS WILL WORK ON OTHER ANIMALS! SING ONE OF YOUR LULLABIES!!
"THEY'RE CRAWLY AND THEY'RE CREEPY AND THEY'RE GETTING VERY SLEEPY!!"
YAAAWN!
WHEEEW... IT WORKED!
ZZ... ZZ...
ZZ...
ZZ...
ZZ... ZZ...
ZZZ...
ZZ... Z...
SSSH! TIME FOR US TO SAY GOOD-NIGHT!
GAH! I HOPE FAFNIR DIDN'T RUN INTO THESE MONSTERS!
ZZZ...

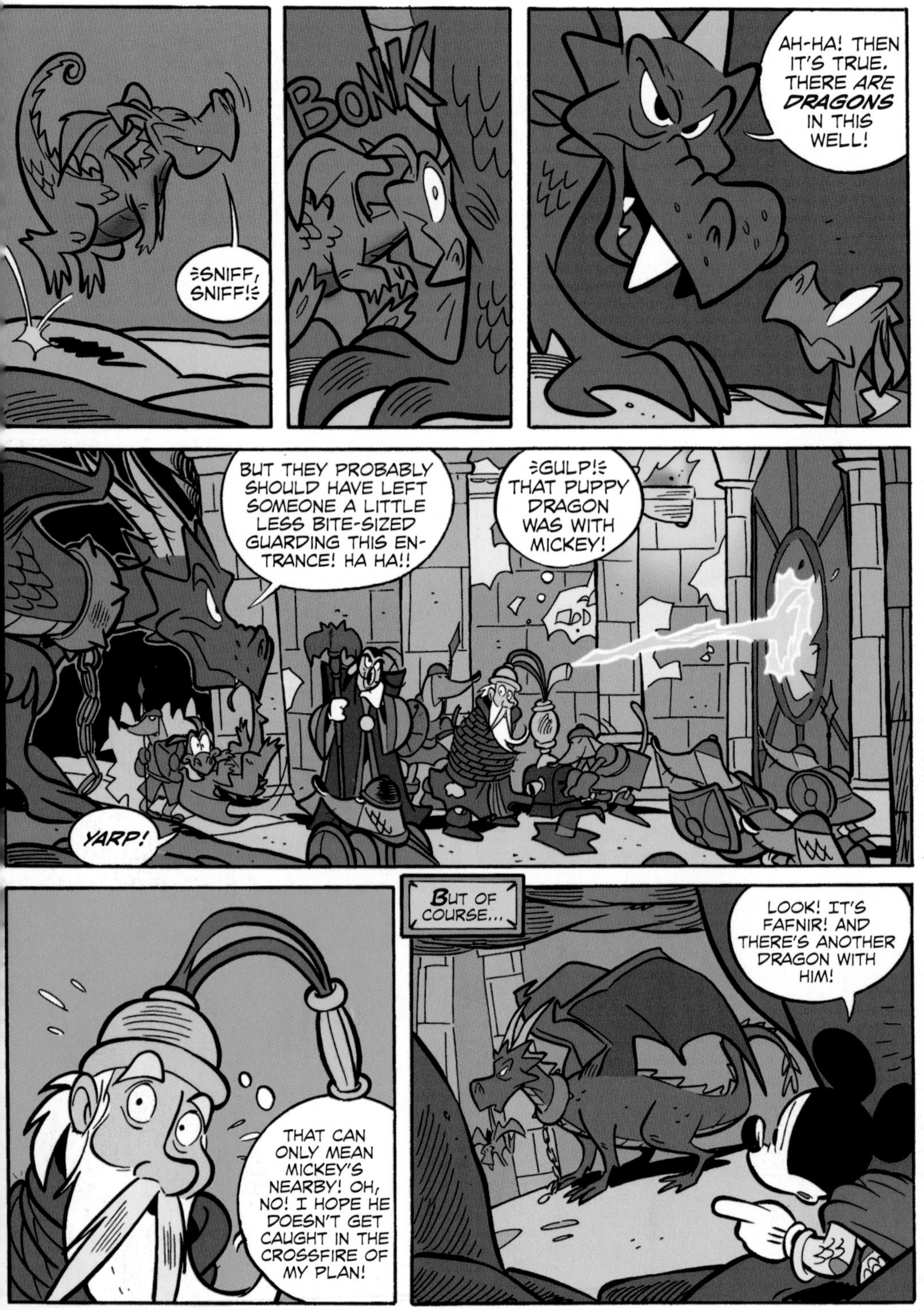
SNIFF, SNIFF!
BONK
AH-HA! THEN IT'S TRUE. THERE *ARE* ***DRAGONS*** IN THIS WELL!
BUT THEY PROBABLY SHOULD HAVE LEFT SOMEONE A LITTLE LESS BITE-SIZED GUARDING THIS ENTRANCE! HA HA!!
GULP! THAT PUPPY DRAGON WAS WITH MICKEY!
YARP!
THAT CAN ONLY MEAN MICKEY'S NEARBY! OH, NO! I HOPE HE DOESN'T GET CAUGHT IN THE CROSSFIRE OF MY PLAN!
BUT OF COURSE...
LOOK! IT'S FAFNIR! AND THERE'S ANOTHER DRAGON WITH HIM!

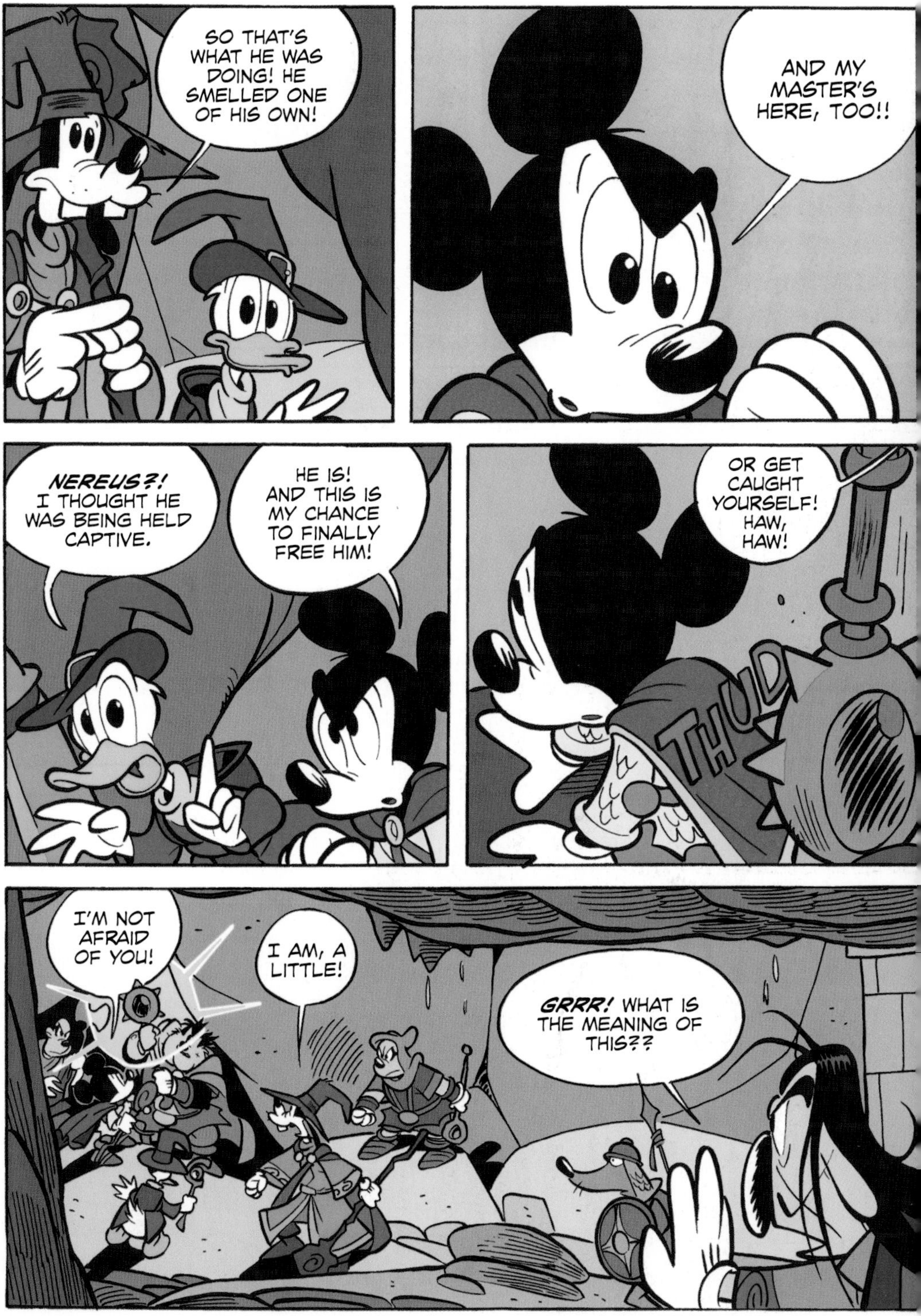

SO THAT'S WHAT HE WAS DOING! HE SMELLED ONE OF HIS OWN!
AND MY MASTER'S HERE, TOO!!
NEREUS?! I THOUGHT HE WAS BEING HELD CAPTIVE.
HE IS! AND THIS IS MY CHANCE TO FINALLY FREE HIM!
OR GET CAUGHT YOURSELF! HAW, HAW!
THUD
I'M NOT AFRAID OF YOU!
I AM, A LITTLE!
GRRR! WHAT IS THE MEANING OF THIS??

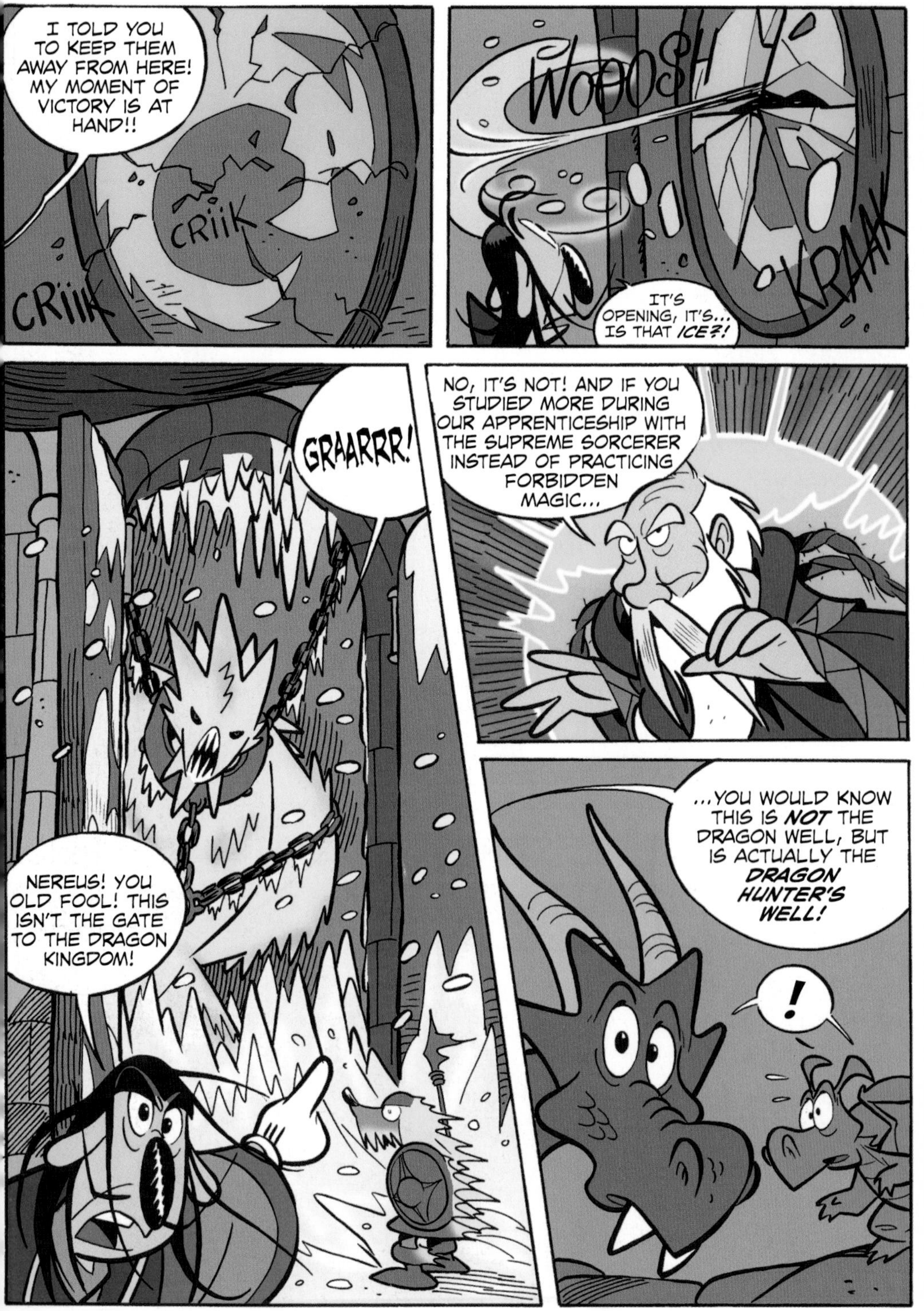
I TOLD YOU TO KEEP THEM AWAY FROM HERE! MY MOMENT OF VICTORY IS AT HAND!!
CRiiK
CRiiK
WOOOSH
KRAAK
IT'S OPENING, IT'S... IS THAT *ICE?!*
GRAARRR!
NEREUS! YOU OLD FOOL! THIS ISN'T THE GATE TO THE DRAGON KINGDOM!
NO, IT'S NOT! AND IF YOU STUDIED MORE DURING OUR APPRENTICESHIP WITH THE SUPREME SORCERER INSTEAD OF PRACTICING FORBIDDEN MAGIC...
...YOU WOULD KNOW THIS IS ***NOT*** THE DRAGON WELL, BUT IS ACTUALLY THE ***DRAGON HUNTER'S WELL!***
!

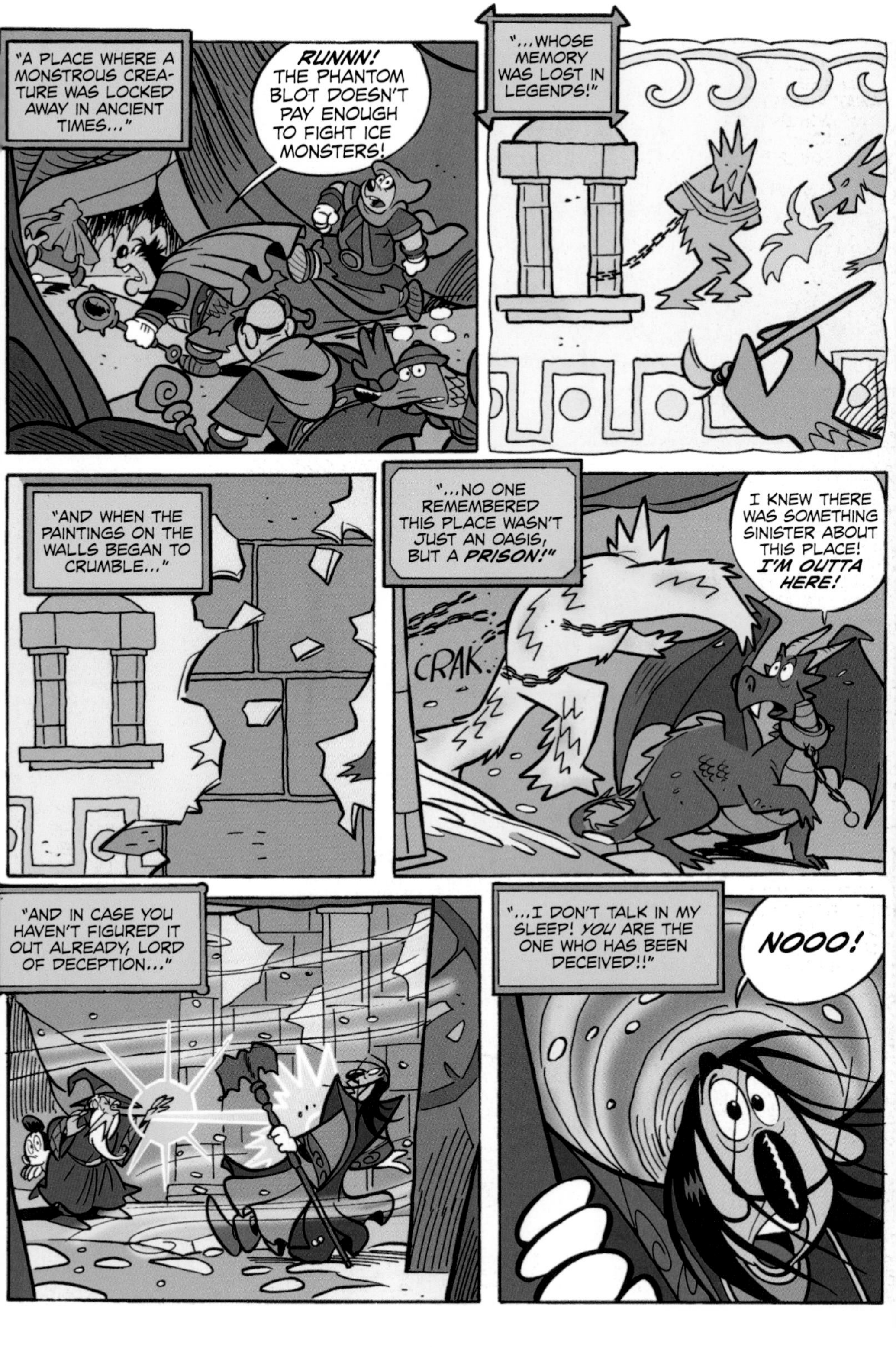
"A PLACE WHERE A MONSTROUS CREATURE WAS LOCKED AWAY IN ANCIENT TIMES..."
RUNNN! THE PHANTOM BLOT DOESN'T PAY ENOUGH TO FIGHT ICE MONSTERS!
"...WHOSE MEMORY WAS LOST IN LEGENDS!"
"AND WHEN THE PAINTINGS ON THE WALLS BEGAN TO CRUMBLE..."
"...NO ONE REMEMBERED THIS PLACE WASN'T JUST AN OASIS, BUT A PRISON!"
I KNEW THERE WAS SOMETHING SINISTER ABOUT THIS PLACE! I'M OUTTA HERE!
CRAK
"AND IN CASE YOU HAVEN'T FIGURED IT OUT ALREADY, LORD OF DECEPTION..."
"...I DON'T TALK IN MY SLEEP! YOU ARE THE ONE WHO HAS BEEN DECEIVED!!"
NOOO!

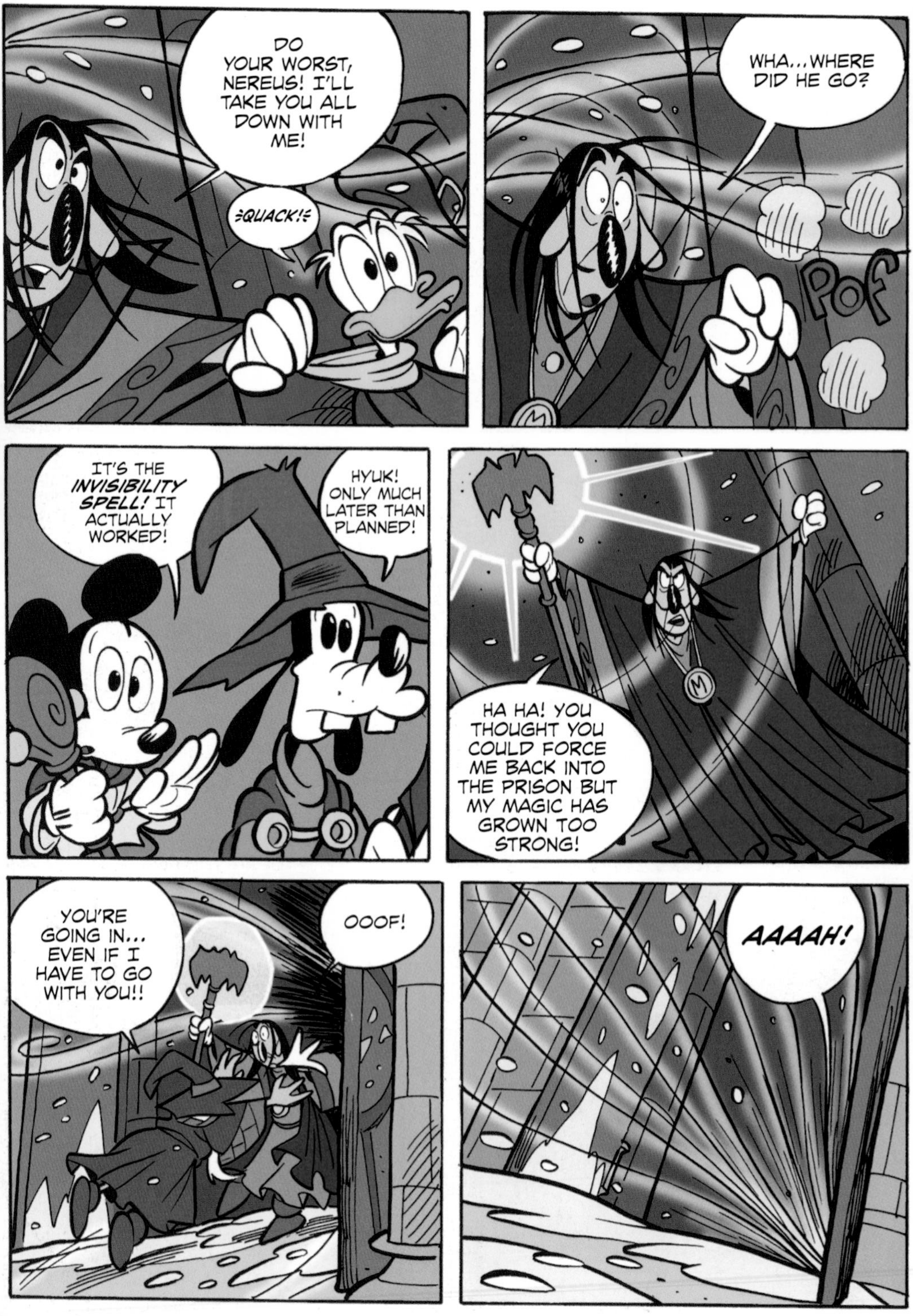
DO YOUR WORST, NEREUS! I'LL TAKE YOU ALL DOWN WITH ME!
QUACK!
WHA...WHERE DID HE GO?
POF
IT'S THE *INVISIBILITY SPELL!* IT ACTUALLY WORKED!
HYUK! ONLY MUCH LATER THAN PLANNED!
HA HA! YOU THOUGHT YOU COULD FORCE ME BACK INTO THE PRISON BUT MY MAGIC HAS GROWN TOO STRONG!
YOU'RE GOING IN... EVEN IF I HAVE TO GO WITH YOU!!
OOOF!
AAAAH!

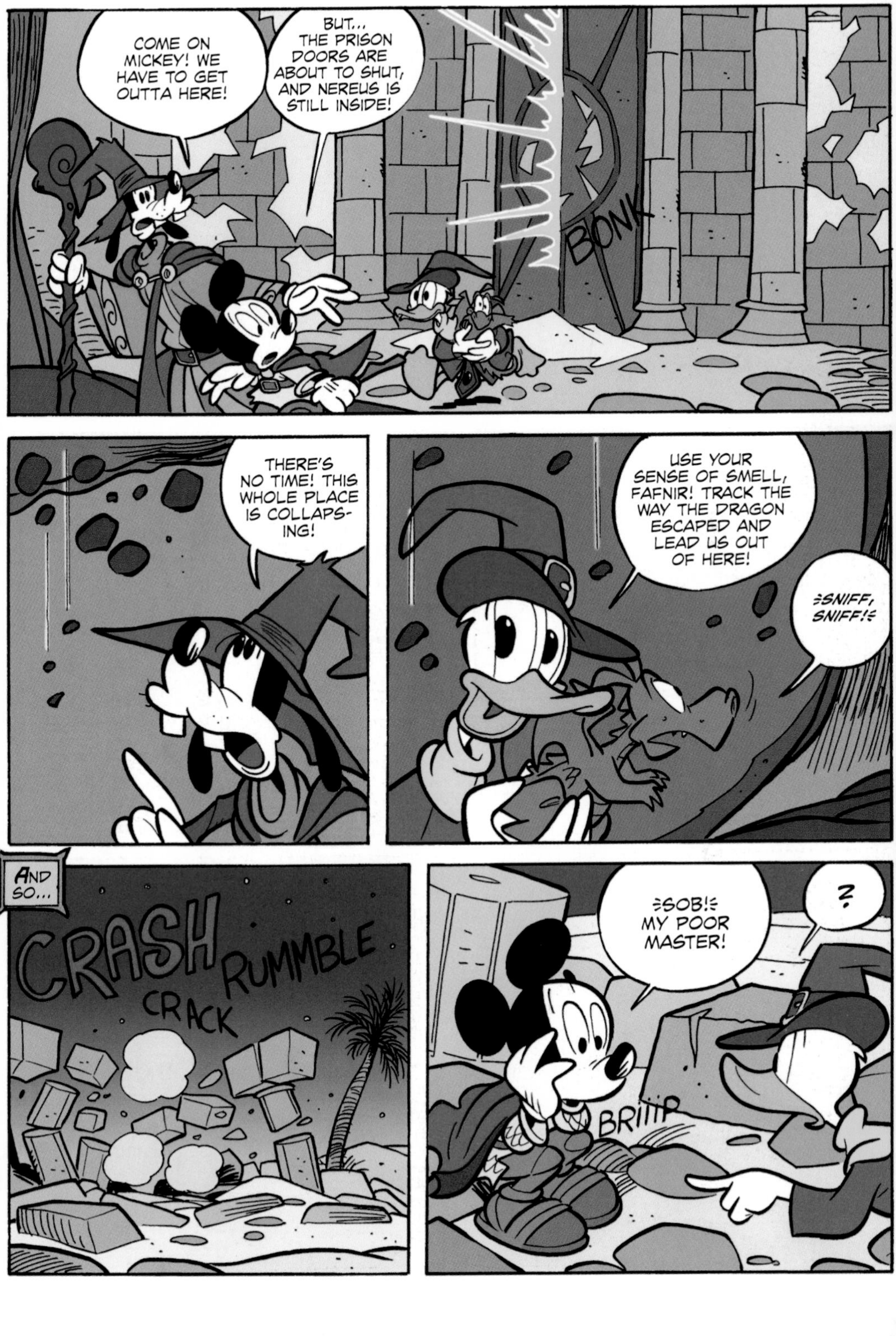
COME ON MICKEY! WE HAVE TO GET OUTTA HERE!
BUT... THE PRISON DOORS ARE ABOUT TO SHUT, AND NEREUS IS STILL INSIDE!
BONK
THERE'S NO TIME! THIS WHOLE PLACE IS COLLAPS-ING!
USE YOUR SENSE OF SMELL, FAFNIR! TRACK THE WAY THE DRAGON ESCAPED AND LEAD US OUT OF HERE!
SNIFF, SNIFF!
AND SO...
CRASH
RUMMBLE
CRACK
SOB! MY POOR MASTER!
?
BRIIIP

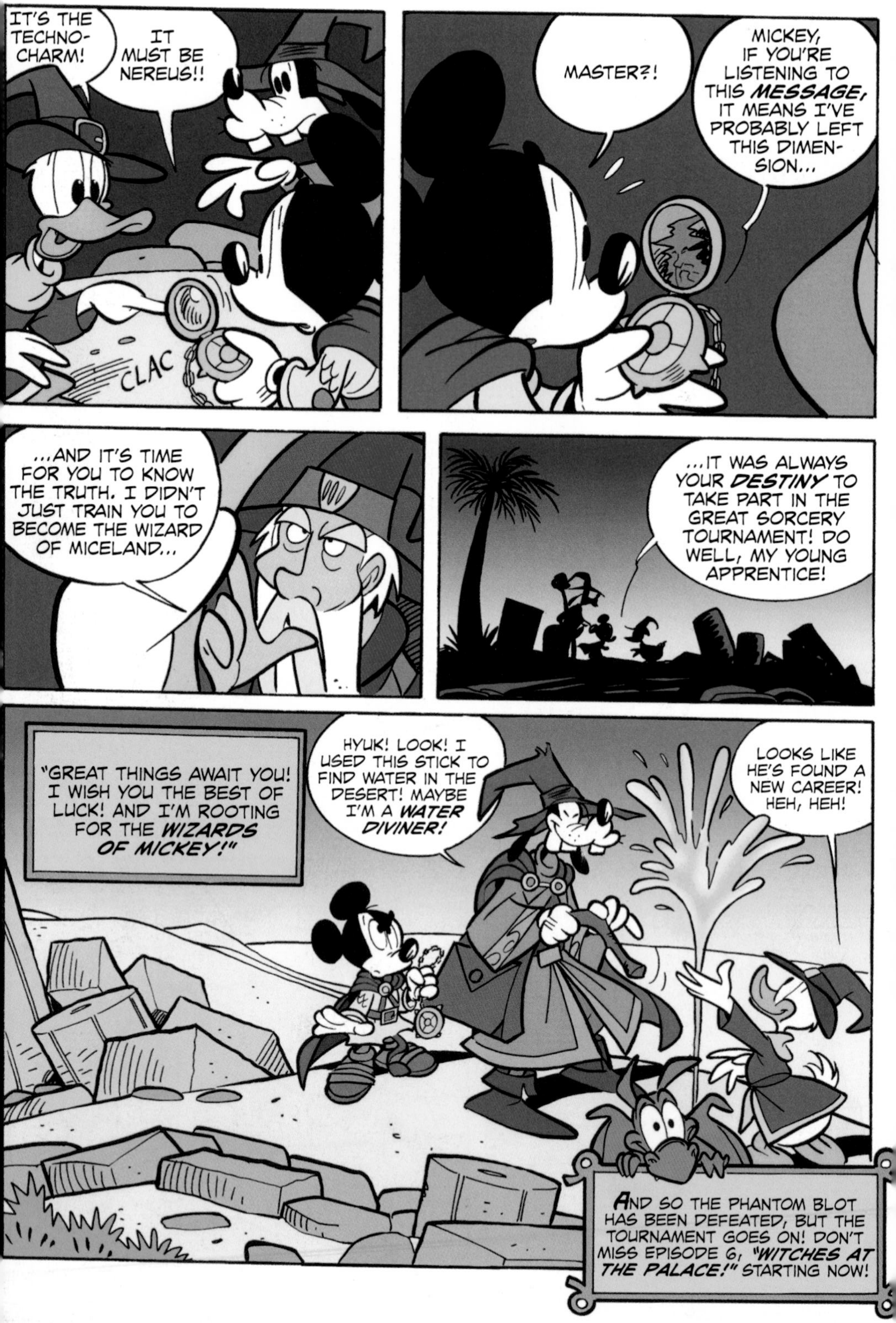
IT'S THE TECHNO-CHARM!
IT MUST BE NEREUS!!
CLAC
MASTER?!
MICKEY, IF YOU'RE LISTENING TO THIS MESSAGE, IT MEANS I'VE PROBABLY LEFT THIS DIMENSION...
...AND IT'S TIME FOR YOU TO KNOW THE TRUTH. I DIDN'T JUST TRAIN YOU TO BECOME THE WIZARD OF MICELAND...
...IT WAS ALWAYS YOUR DESTINY TO TAKE PART IN THE GREAT SORCERY TOURNAMENT! DO WELL, MY YOUNG APPRENTICE!
"GREAT THINGS AWAIT YOU! I WISH YOU THE BEST OF LUCK! AND I'M ROOTING FOR THE WIZARDS OF MICKEY!"
HYUK! LOOK! I USED THIS STICK TO FIND WATER IN THE DESERT! MAYBE I'M A WATER DIVINER!
LOOKS LIKE HE'S FOUND A NEW CAREER! HEH, HEH!
AND SO THE PHANTOM BLOT HAS BEEN DEFEATED, BUT THE TOURNAMENT GOES ON! DON'T MISS EPISODE 6, "WITCHES AT THE PALACE!" STARTING NOW!

Episode 6

WITCHES AT THE PALACE

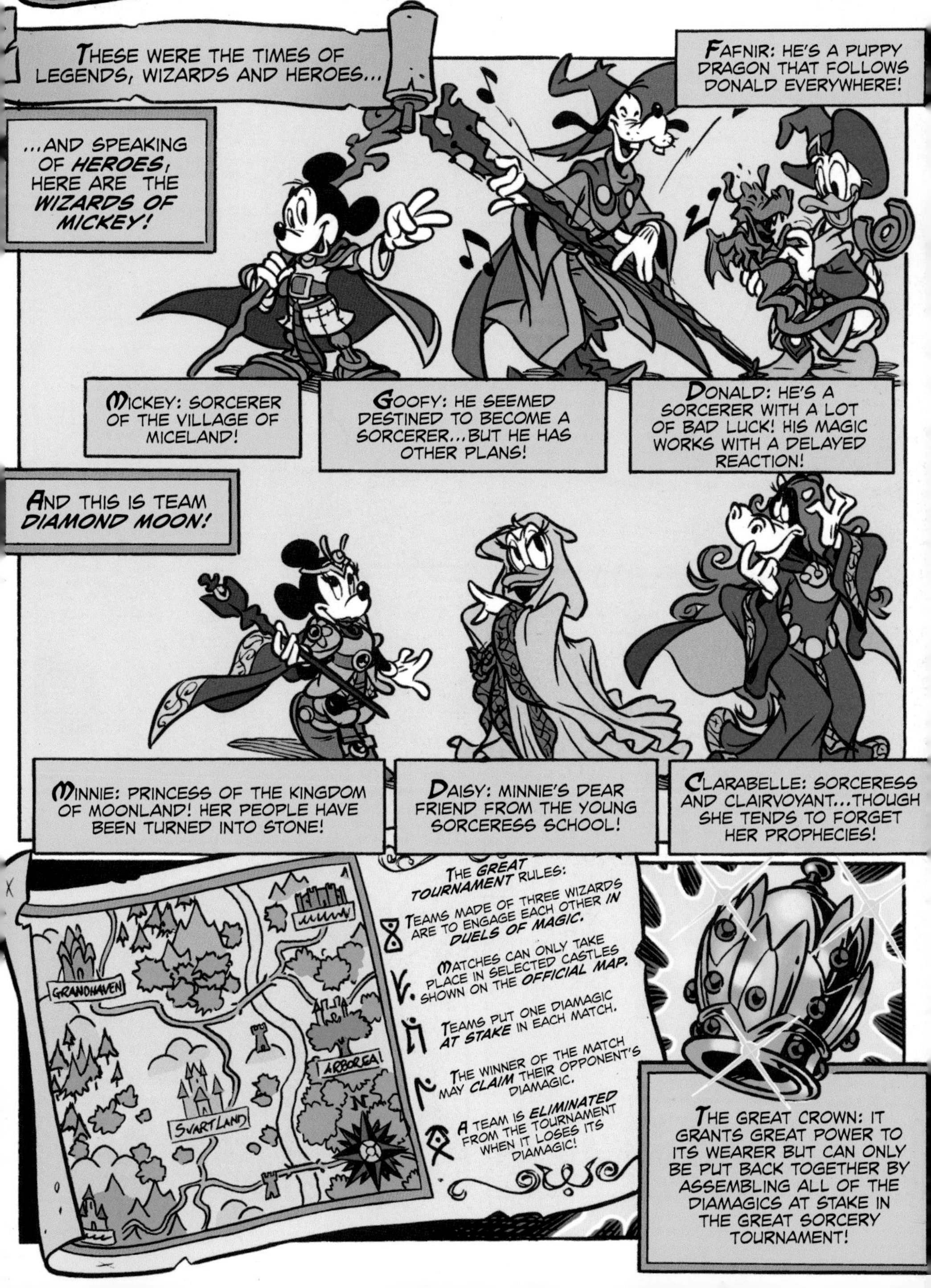
THESE WERE THE TIMES OF LEGENDS, WIZARDS AND HEROES...
FAFNIR: HE'S A PUPPY DRAGON THAT FOLLOWS DONALD EVERYWHERE!
...AND SPEAKING OF HEROES, HERE ARE THE WIZARDS OF MICKEY!
MICKEY: SORCERER OF THE VILLAGE OF MICELAND!
GOOFY: HE SEEMED DESTINED TO BECOME A SORCERER...BUT HE HAS OTHER PLANS!
DONALD: HE'S A SORCERER WITH A LOT OF BAD LUCK! HIS MAGIC WORKS WITH A DELAYED REACTION!
AND THIS IS TEAM DIAMOND MOON!
MINNIE: PRINCESS OF THE KINGDOM OF MOONLAND! HER PEOPLE HAVE BEEN TURNED INTO STONE!
DAISY: MINNIE'S DEAR FRIEND FROM THE YOUNG SORCERESS SCHOOL!
CLARABELLE: SORCERESS AND CLAIRVOYANT...THOUGH SHE TENDS TO FORGET HER PROPHECIES!
GRANDHAVEN
ARBOREA
SVARTLAND
THE GREAT TOURNAMENT RULES:
TEAMS MADE OF THREE WIZARDS ARE TO ENGAGE EACH OTHER IN DUELS OF MAGIC.
MATCHES CAN ONLY TAKE PLACE IN SELECTED CASTLES SHOWN ON THE OFFICIAL MAP.
TEAMS PUT ONE DIAMAGIC AT STAKE IN EACH MATCH.
THE WINNER OF THE MATCH MAY CLAIM THEIR OPPONENT'S DIAMAGIC.
A TEAM IS ELIMINATED FROM THE TOURNAMENT WHEN IT LOSES ITS DIAMAGIC!
THE GREAT CROWN: IT GRANTS GREAT POWER TO ITS WEARER BUT CAN ONLY BE PUT BACK TOGETHER BY ASSEMBLING ALL OF THE DIAMAGICS AT STAKE IN THE GREAT SORCERY TOURNAMENT!

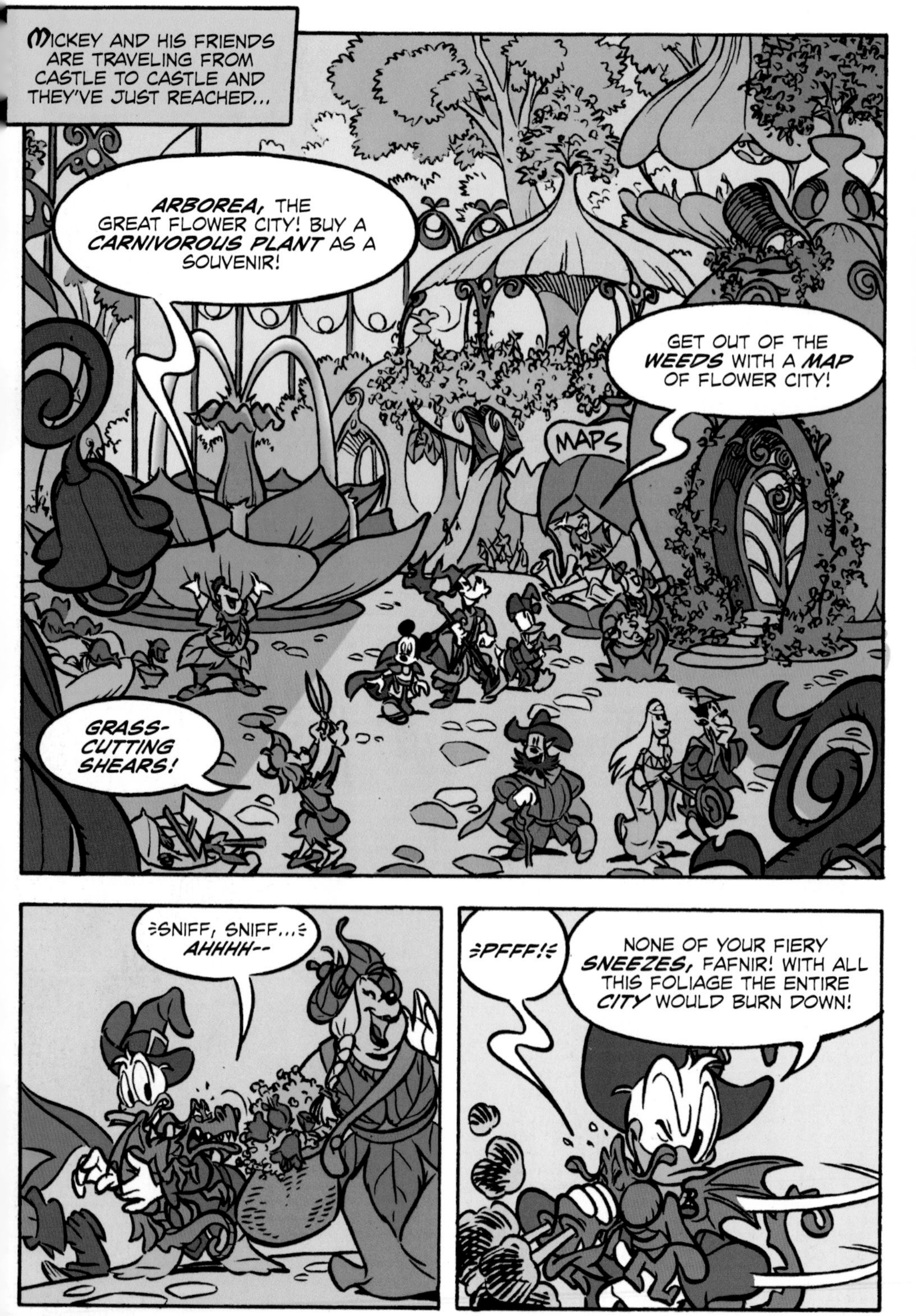
MICKEY AND HIS FRIENDS ARE TRAVELING FROM CASTLE TO CASTLE AND THEY'VE JUST REACHED...
ARBOREA, THE GREAT FLOWER CITY! BUY A CARNIVOROUS PLANT AS A SOUVENIR!
GET OUT OF THE WEEDS WITH A MAP OF FLOWER CITY!
MAPS
GRASS-CUTTING SHEARS!
SNIFF, SNIFF... AHHHH--
PFFF!
NONE OF YOUR FIERY SNEEZES, FAFNIR! WITH ALL THIS FOLIAGE THE ENTIRE CITY WOULD BURN DOWN!

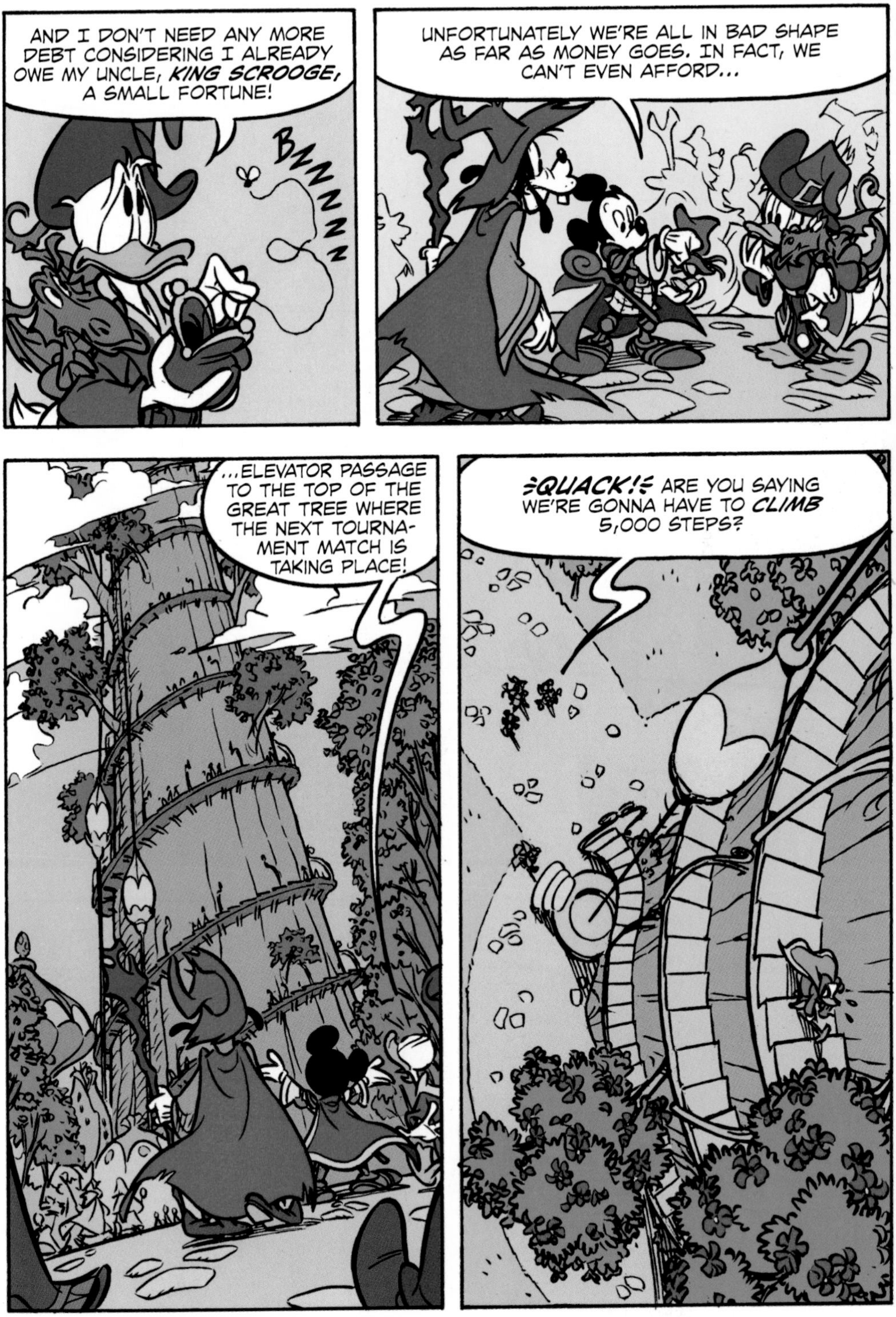
AND I DON'T NEED ANY MORE DEBT CONSIDERING I ALREADY OWE MY UNCLE, KING SCROOGE, A SMALL FORTUNE!
BZZZZZZ
UNFORTUNATELY WE'RE ALL IN BAD SHAPE AS FAR AS MONEY GOES. IN FACT, WE CAN'T EVEN AFFORD...
...ELEVATOR PASSAGE TO THE TOP OF THE GREAT TREE WHERE THE NEXT TOURNAMENT MATCH IS TAKING PLACE!
QUACK! ARE YOU SAYING WE'RE GONNA HAVE TO CLIMB 5,000 STEPS?

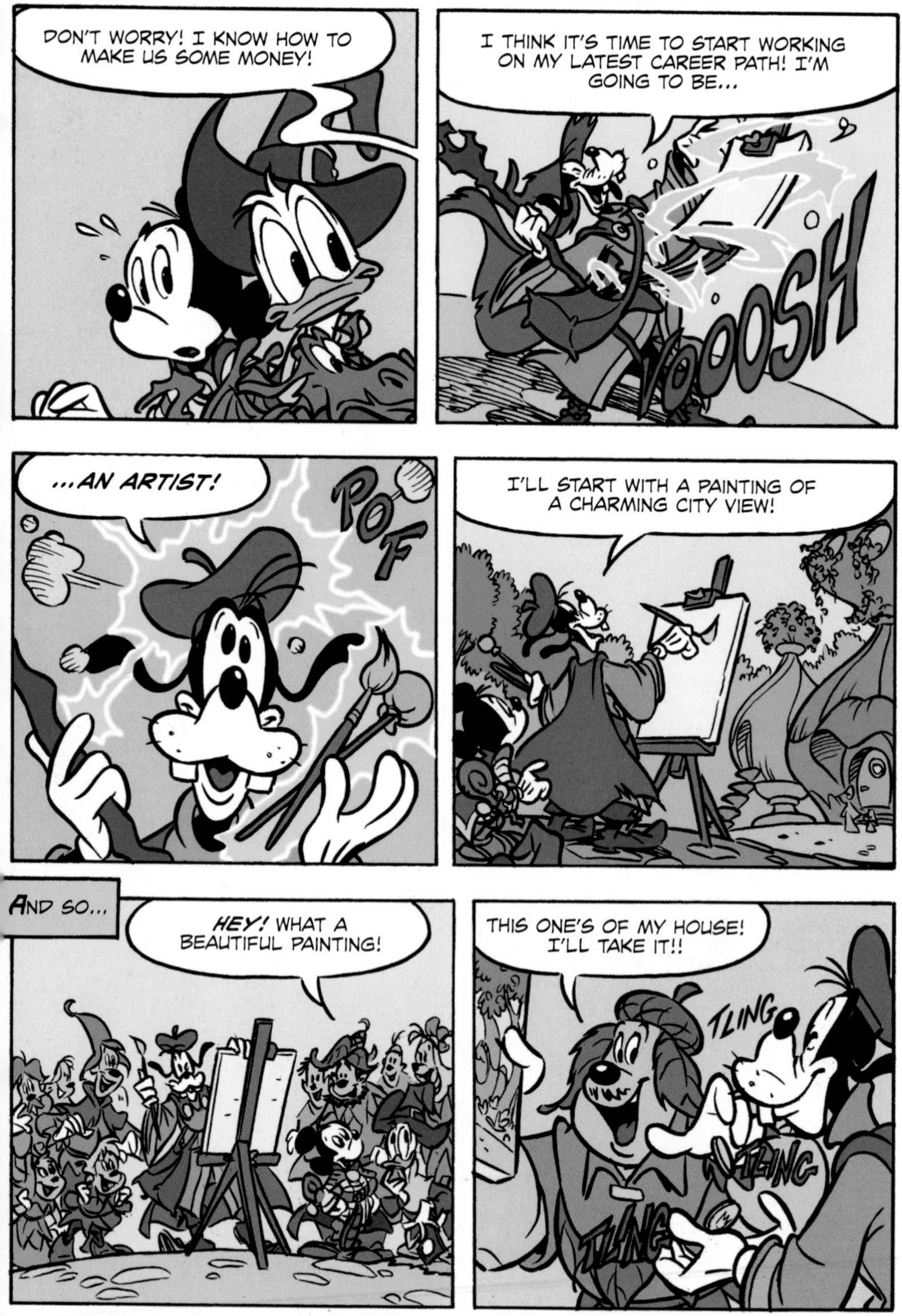
DON'T WORRY! I KNOW HOW TO MAKE US SOME MONEY!
I THINK IT'S TIME TO START WORKING ON MY LATEST CAREER PATH! I'M GOING TO BE...
VOOOOSH
...AN ARTIST!
POF
I'LL START WITH A PAINTING OF A CHARMING CITY VIEW!
AND SO...
HEY! WHAT A BEAUTIFUL PAINTING!
THIS ONE'S OF MY HOUSE! I'LL TAKE IT!!
TLING
TLING
TLING

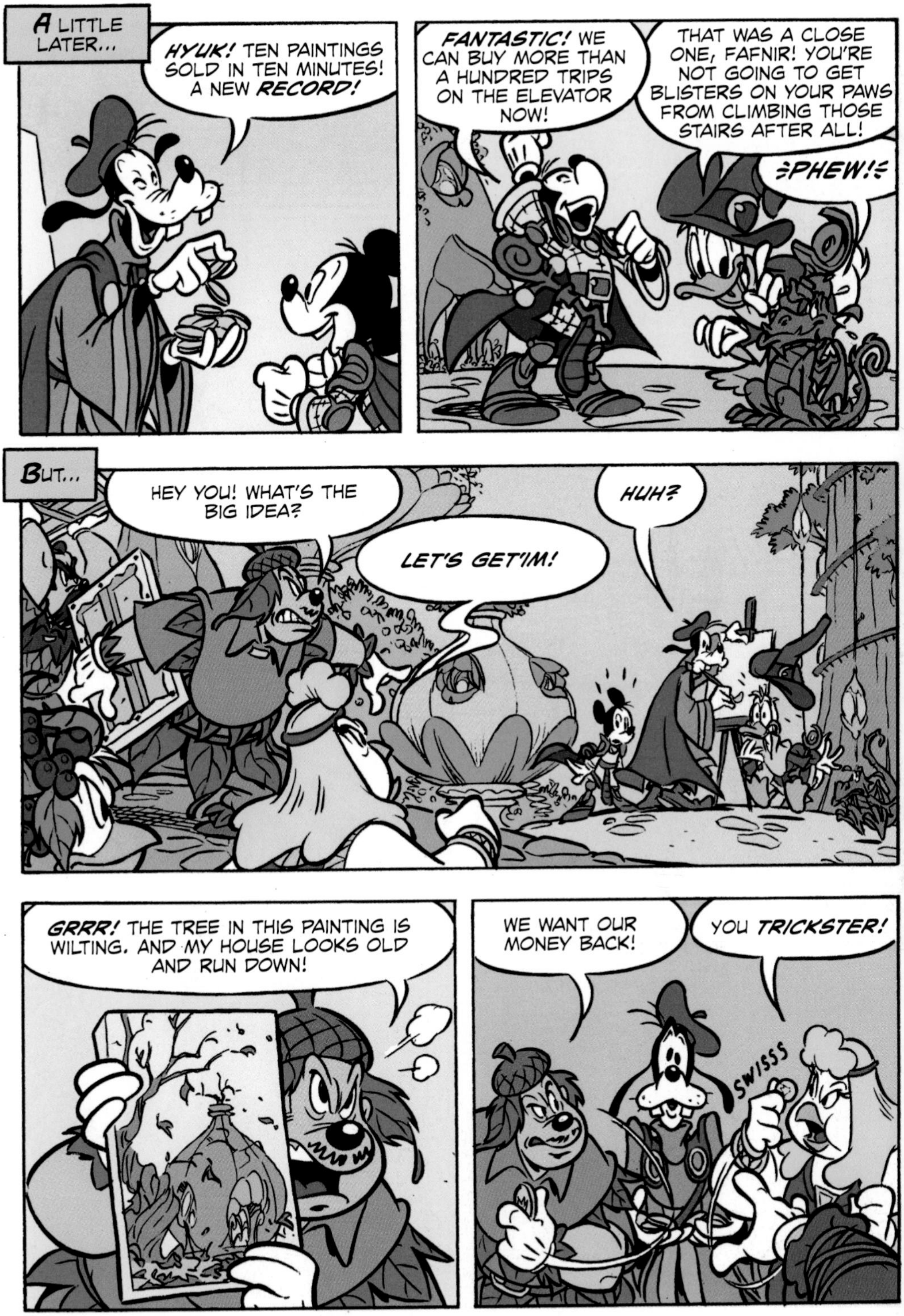
A LITTLE LATER...
HYUK! TEN PAINTINGS SOLD IN TEN MINUTES! A NEW RECORD!
FANTASTIC! WE CAN BUY MORE THAN A HUNDRED TRIPS ON THE ELEVATOR NOW!
THAT WAS A CLOSE ONE, FAFNIR! YOU'RE NOT GOING TO GET BLISTERS ON YOUR PAWS FROM CLIMBING THOSE STAIRS AFTER ALL!
PHEW!
BUT...
HEY YOU! WHAT'S THE BIG IDEA?
LET'S GET'IM!
HUH?
GRRR! THE TREE IN THIS PAINTING IS WILTING. AND MY HOUSE LOOKS OLD AND RUN DOWN!
WE WANT OUR MONEY BACK!
YOU TRICKSTER!
SWISSS

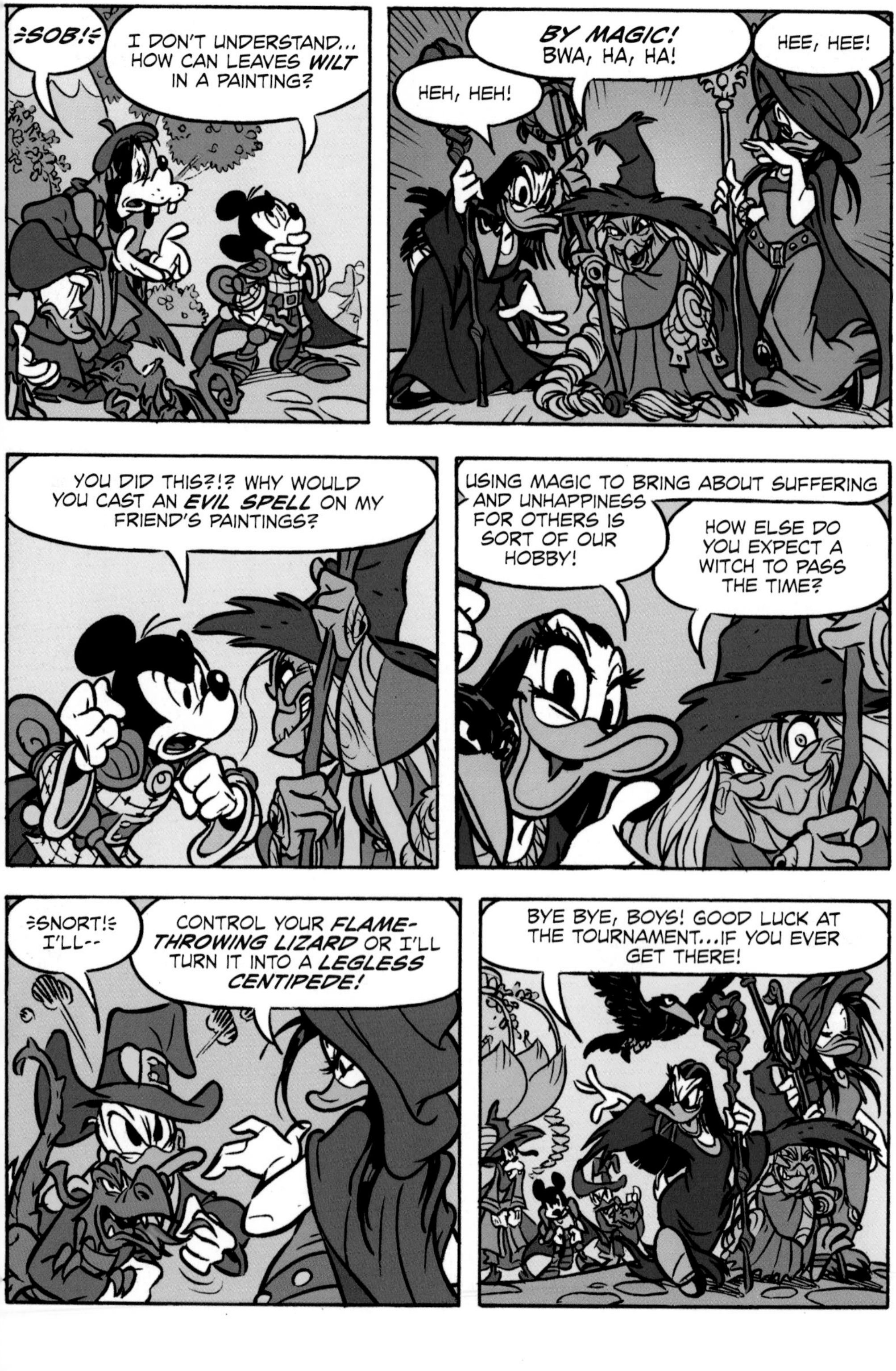

≈SOB!≈
I DON'T UNDERSTAND... HOW CAN LEAVES *WILT* IN A PAINTING?
HEH, HEH!
BY MAGIC! BWA, HA, HA!
HEE, HEE!
YOU DID THIS?!? WHY WOULD YOU CAST AN *EVIL SPELL* ON MY FRIEND'S PAINTINGS?
USING MAGIC TO BRING ABOUT SUFFERING AND UNHAPPINESS FOR OTHERS IS SORT OF OUR HOBBY!
HOW ELSE DO YOU EXPECT A WITCH TO PASS THE TIME?
≈SNORT!≈ I'LL--
CONTROL YOUR *FLAME-THROWING LIZARD* OR I'LL TURN IT INTO A *LEGLESS CENTIPEDE!*
BYE BYE, BOYS! GOOD LUCK AT THE TOURNAMENT...IF YOU EVER GET THERE!

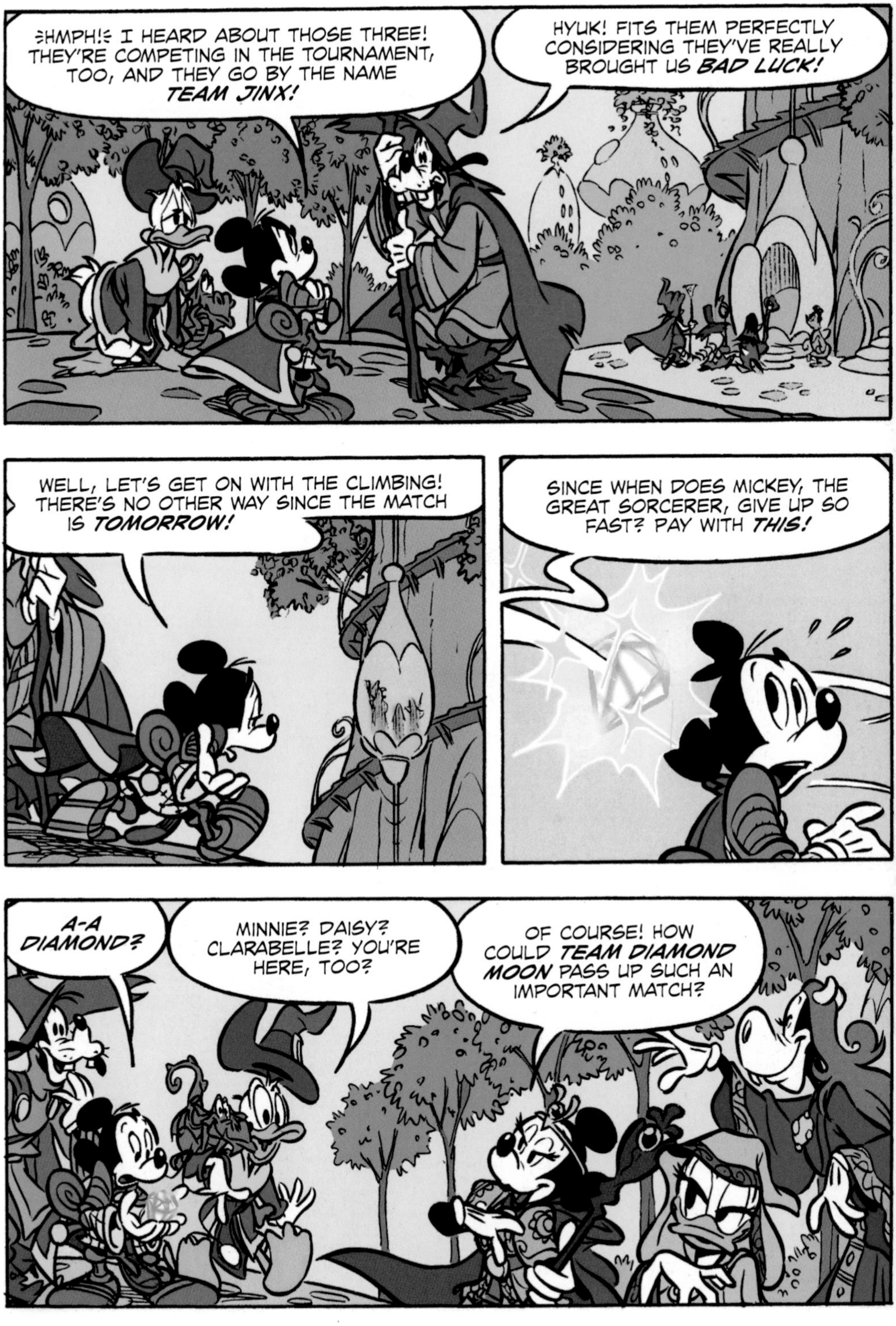

HMPH! I HEARD ABOUT THOSE THREE! THEY'RE COMPETING IN THE TOURNAMENT, TOO, AND THEY GO BY THE NAME TEAM JINX!
HYUK! FITS THEM PERFECTLY CONSIDERING THEY'VE REALLY BROUGHT US BAD LUCK!
WELL, LET'S GET ON WITH THE CLIMBING! THERE'S NO OTHER WAY SINCE THE MATCH IS TOMORROW!
SINCE WHEN DOES MICKEY, THE GREAT SORCERER, GIVE UP SO FAST? PAY WITH THIS!
A-A DIAMOND?
MINNIE? DAISY? CLARABELLE? YOU'RE HERE, TOO?
OF COURSE! HOW COULD TEAM DIAMOND MOON PASS UP SUCH AN IMPORTANT MATCH?

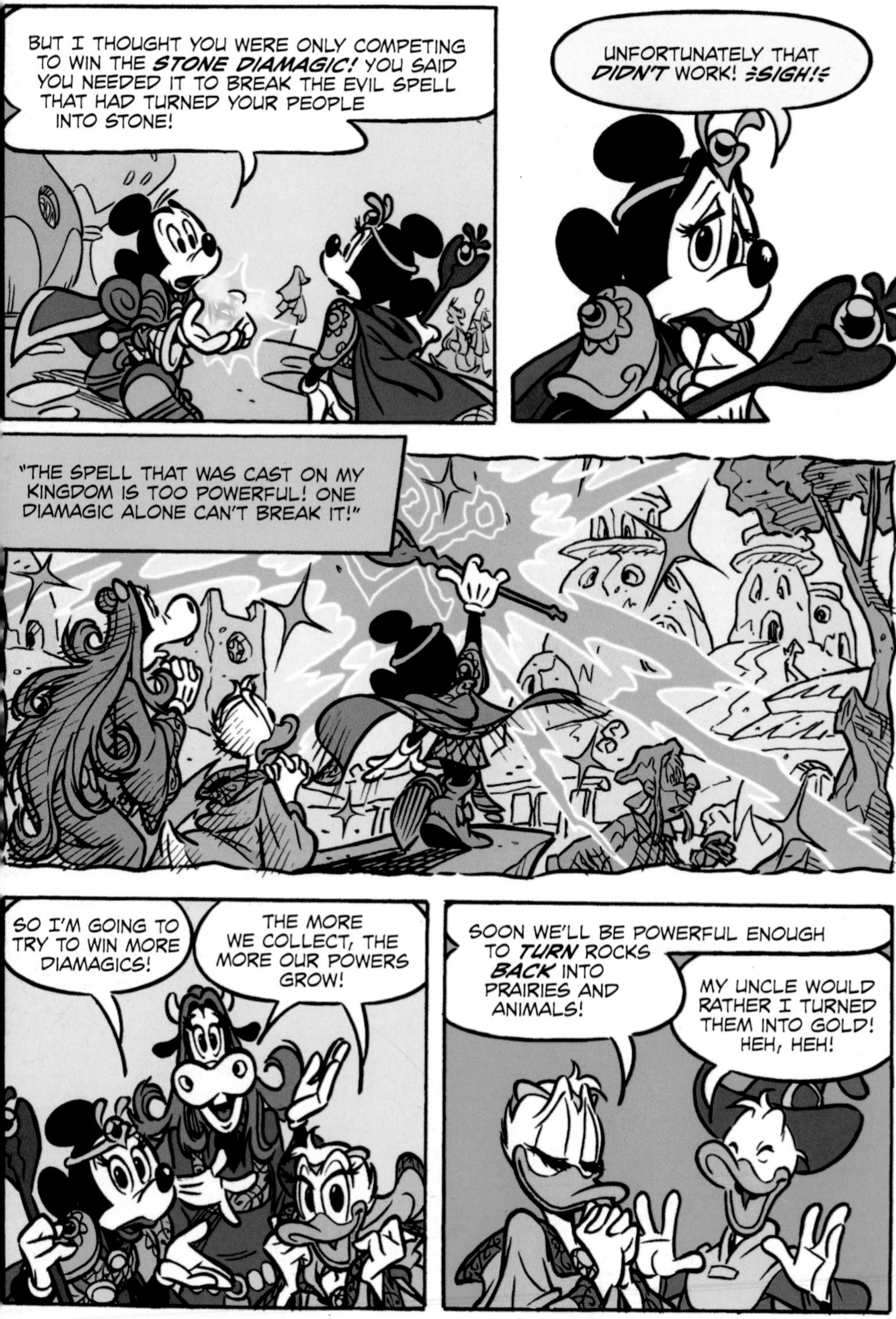

BUT I THOUGHT YOU WERE ONLY COMPETING TO WIN THE STONE DIAMAGIC! YOU SAID YOU NEEDED IT TO BREAK THE EVIL SPELL THAT HAD TURNED YOUR PEOPLE INTO STONE!
UNFORTUNATELY THAT DIDN'T WORK! SIGH!
"THE SPELL THAT WAS CAST ON MY KINGDOM IS TOO POWERFUL! ONE DIAMAGIC ALONE CAN'T BREAK IT!"
SO I'M GOING TO TRY TO WIN MORE DIAMAGICS!
THE MORE WE COLLECT, THE MORE OUR POWERS GROW!
SOON WE'LL BE POWERFUL ENOUGH TO TURN ROCKS BACK INTO PRAIRIES AND ANIMALS!
MY UNCLE WOULD RATHER I TURNED THEM INTO GOLD! HEH, HEH!

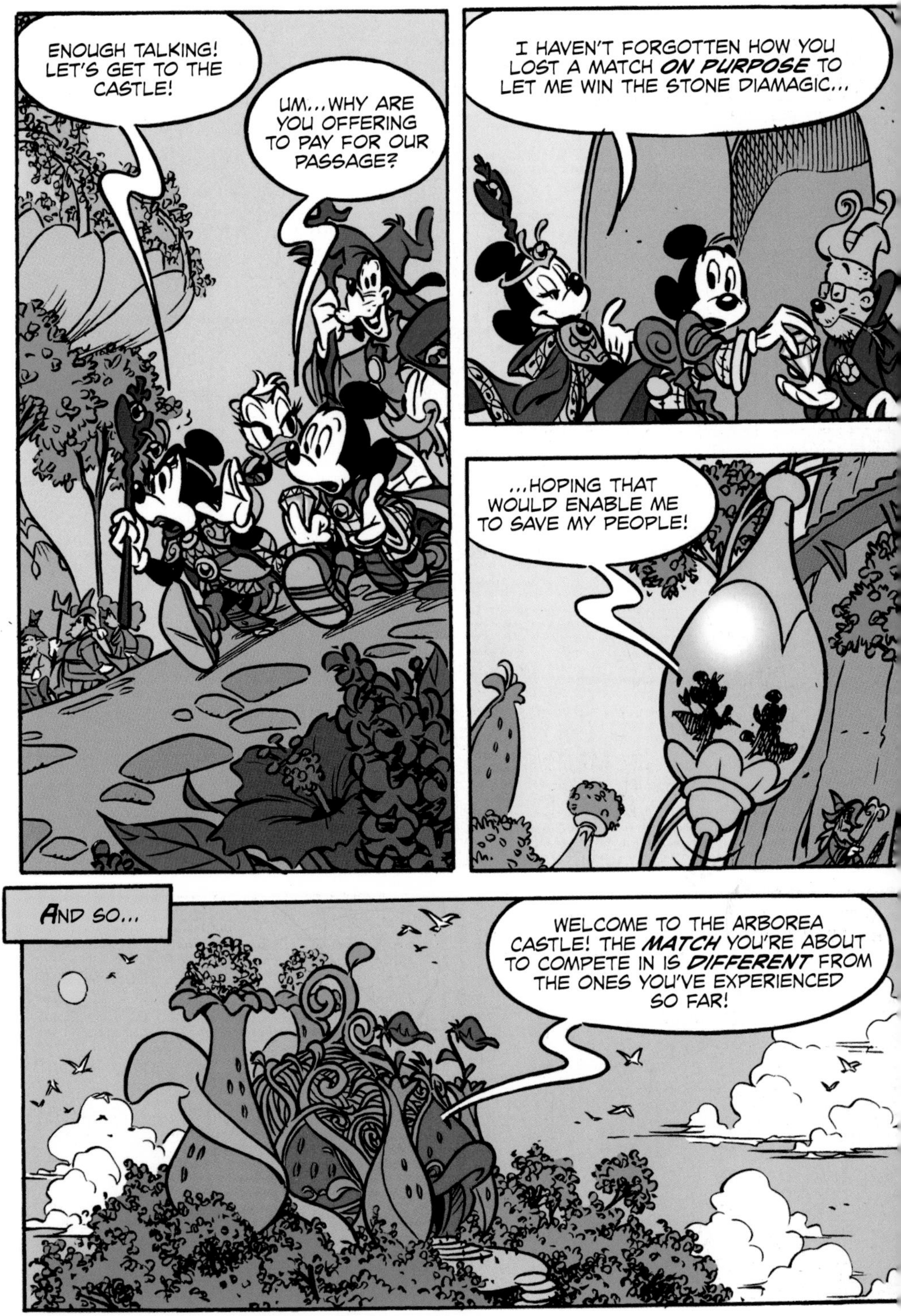
ENOUGH TALKING! LET'S GET TO THE CASTLE!
UM...WHY ARE YOU OFFERING TO PAY FOR OUR PASSAGE?
I HAVEN'T FORGOTTEN HOW YOU LOST A MATCH ON PURPOSE TO LET ME WIN THE STONE DIAMAGIC...
...HOPING THAT WOULD ENABLE ME TO SAVE MY PEOPLE!
AND SO...
WELCOME TO THE ARBOREA CASTLE! THE MATCH YOU'RE ABOUT TO COMPETE IN IS DIFFERENT FROM THE ONES YOU'VE EXPERIENCED SO FAR!

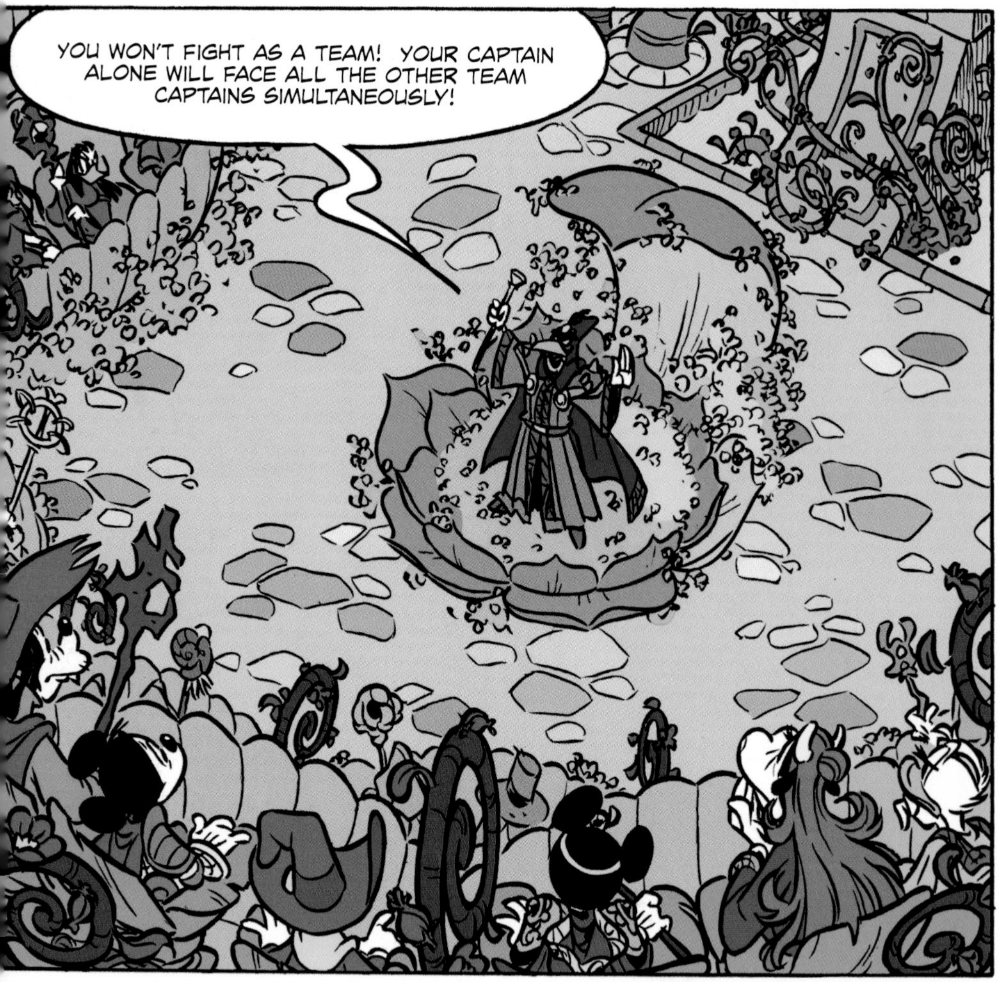
YOU WON'T FIGHT AS A TEAM! YOUR CAPTAIN ALONE WILL FACE ALL THE OTHER TEAM CAPTAINS SIMULTANEOUSLY!

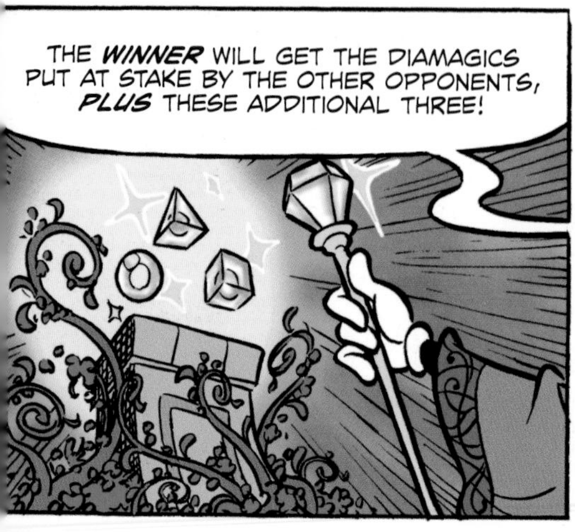
THE *WINNER* WILL GET THE DIAMAGICS PUT AT STAKE BY THE OTHER OPPONENTS, *PLUS* THESE ADDITIONAL THREE!

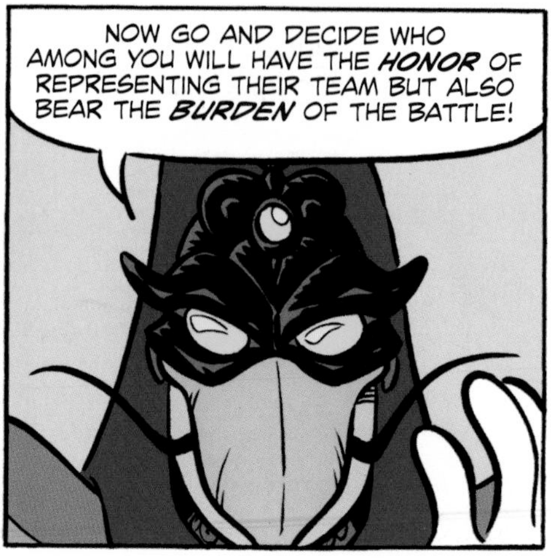
NOW GO AND DECIDE WHO AMONG YOU WILL HAVE THE *HONOR* OF REPRESENTING THEIR TEAM BUT ALSO BEAR THE *BURDEN* OF THE BATTLE!

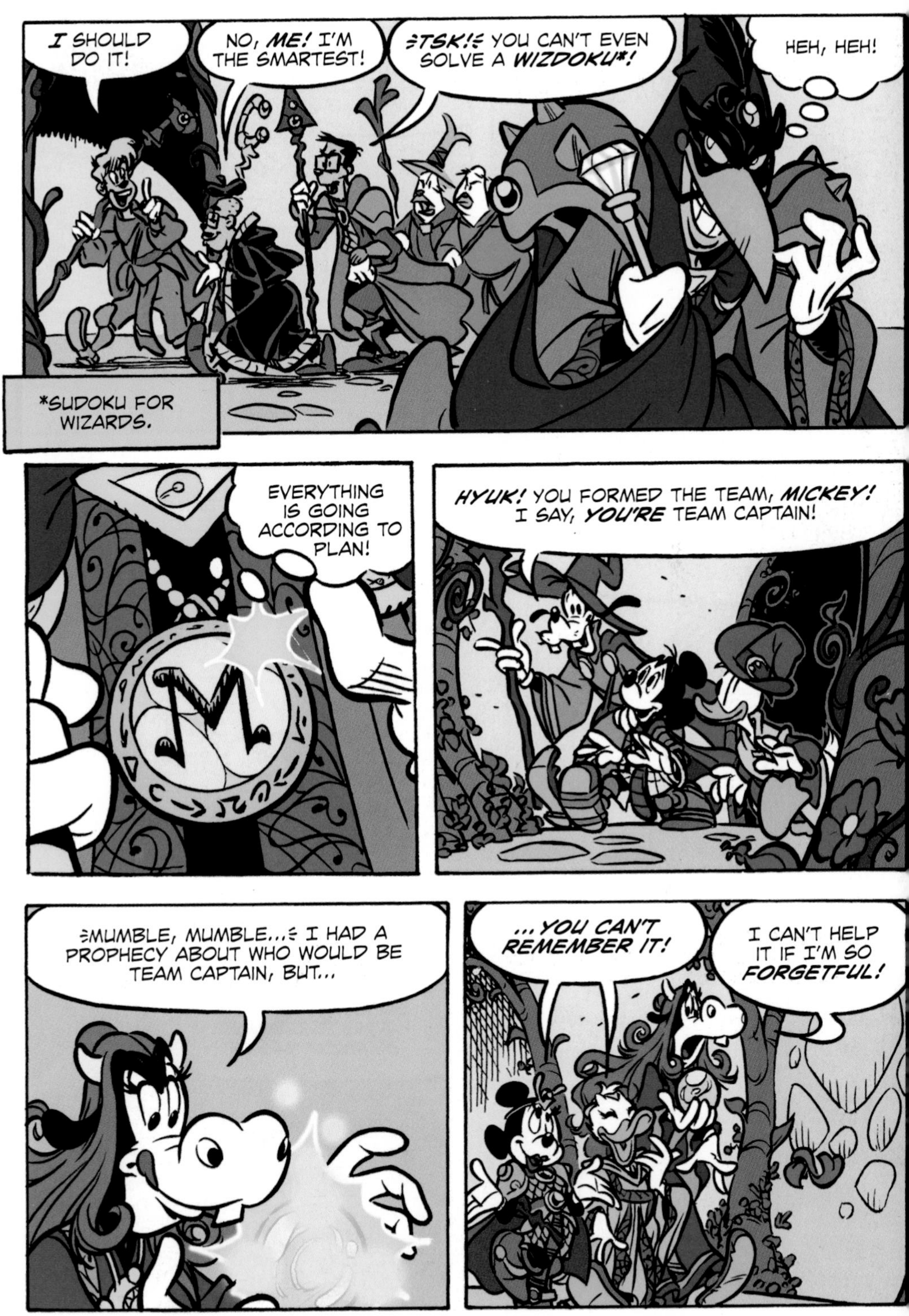

I SHOULD DO IT!
NO, ME! I'M THE SMARTEST!
=TSK!= YOU CAN'T EVEN SOLVE A WIZDOKU*!
HEH, HEH!
*SUDOKU FOR WIZARDS.
EVERYTHING IS GOING ACCORDING TO PLAN!
HYUK! YOU FORMED THE TEAM, MICKEY! I SAY, YOU'RE TEAM CAPTAIN!
=MUMBLE, MUMBLE...= I HAD A PROPHECY ABOUT WHO WOULD BE TEAM CAPTAIN, BUT...
...YOU CAN'T REMEMBER IT!
I CAN'T HELP IT IF I'M SO FORGETFUL!

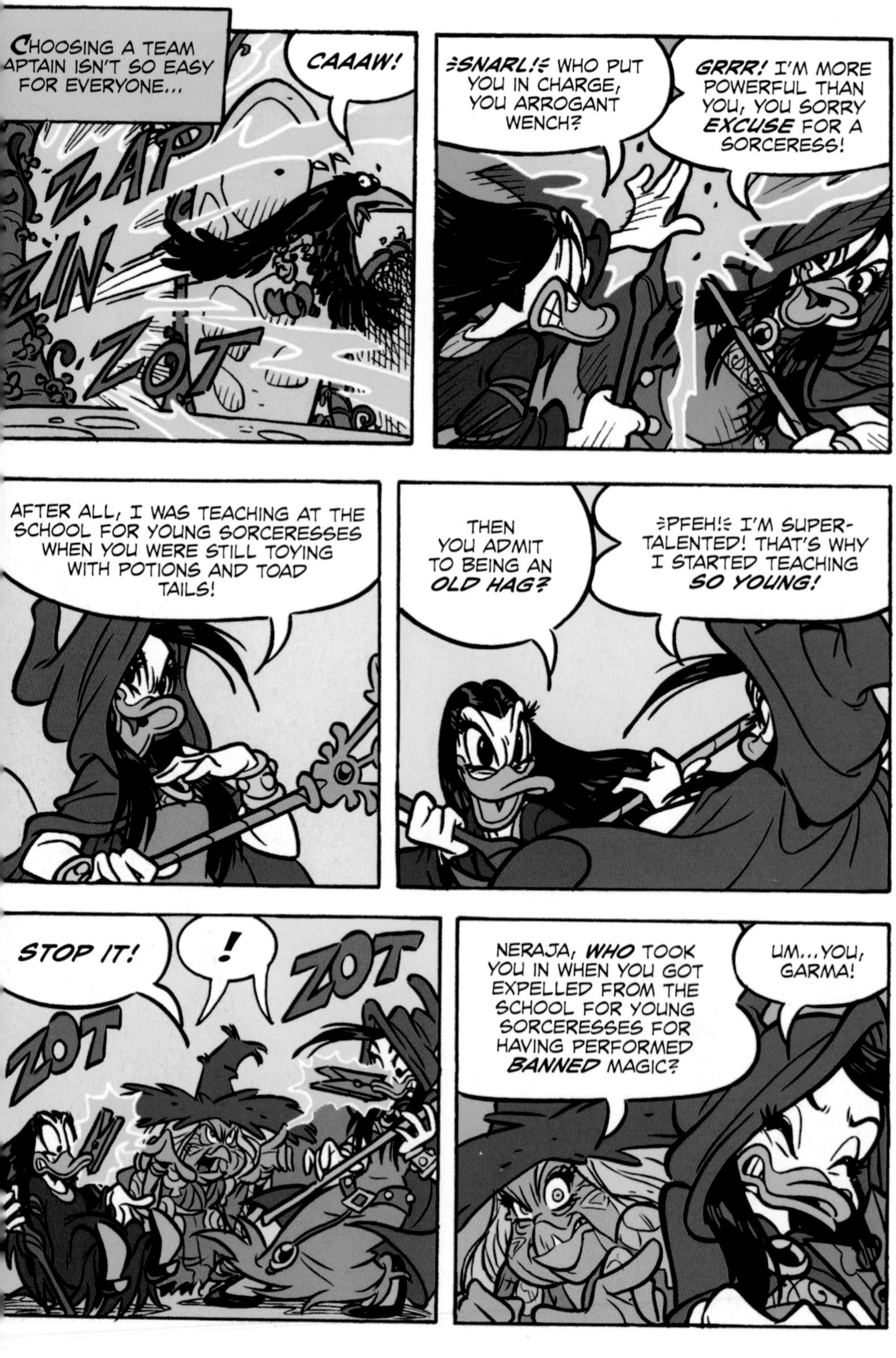
CHOOSING A TEAM APTAIN ISN'T SO EASY FOR EVERYONE...
CAAAW!
ZAP
ZIN
ZOT
SNARL! WHO PUT YOU IN CHARGE, YOU ARROGANT WENCH?
GRRR! I'M MORE POWERFUL THAN YOU, YOU SORRY EXCUSE FOR A SORCERESS!
AFTER ALL, I WAS TEACHING AT THE SCHOOL FOR YOUNG SORCERESSES WHEN YOU WERE STILL TOYING WITH POTIONS AND TOAD TAILS!
THEN YOU ADMIT TO BEING AN OLD HAG?
PFEH! I'M SUPER-TALENTED! THAT'S WHY I STARTED TEACHING SO YOUNG!
STOP IT!
!
ZOT
ZOT
NERAJA, WHO TOOK YOU IN WHEN YOU GOT EXPELLED FROM THE SCHOOL FOR YOUNG SORCERESSES FOR HAVING PERFORMED BANNED MAGIC?
UM...YOU, GARMA!

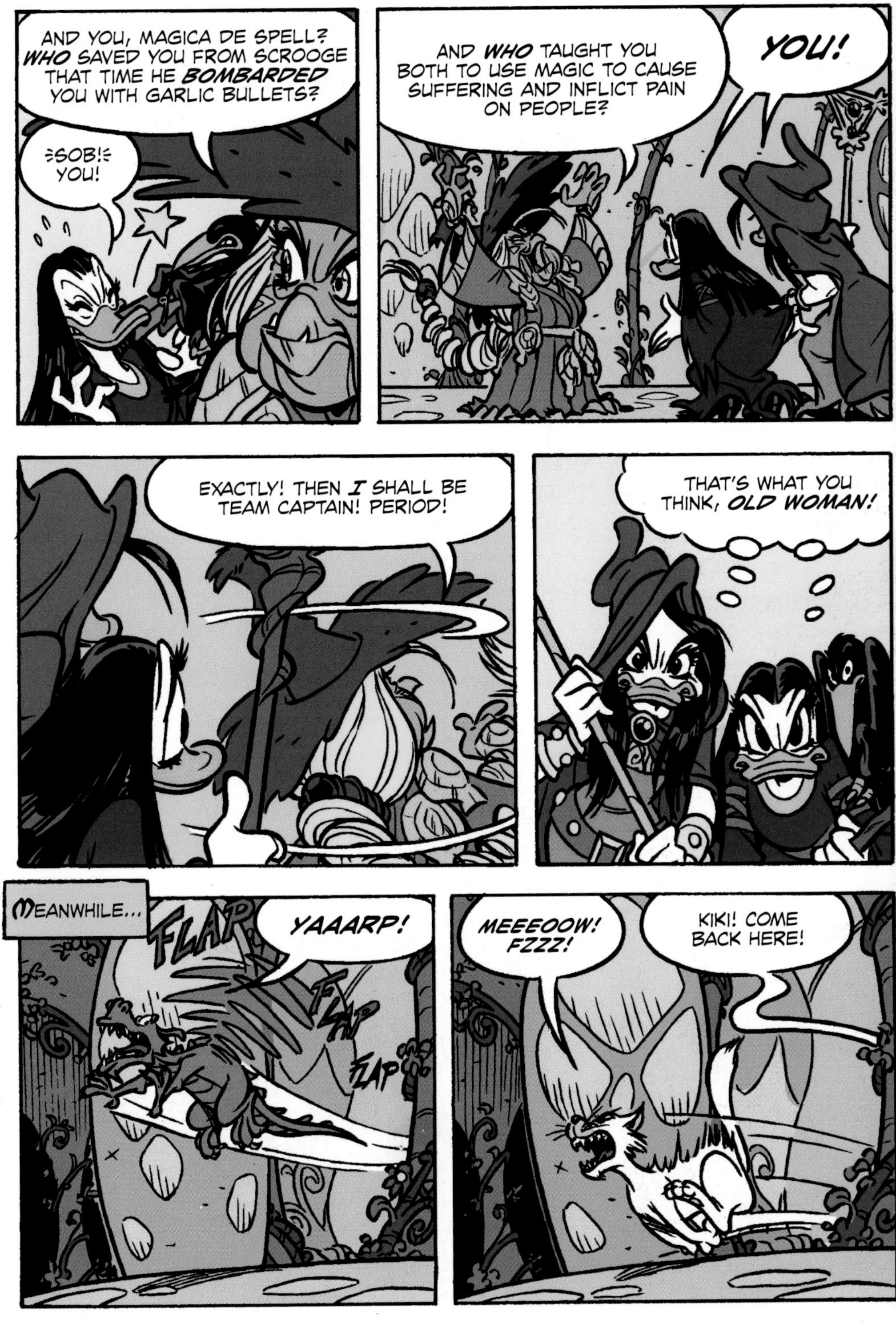
AND YOU, MAGICA DE SPELL? *WHO* SAVED YOU FROM SCROOGE THAT TIME HE *BOMBARDED* YOU WITH GARLIC BULLETS?
≑SOB!≑ YOU!
AND *WHO* TAUGHT YOU BOTH TO USE MAGIC TO CAUSE SUFFERING AND INFLICT PAIN ON PEOPLE?
YOU!
EXACTLY! THEN *I* SHALL BE TEAM CAPTAIN! PERIOD!
THAT'S WHAT YOU THINK, *OLD WOMAN!*
MEANWHILE...
FLAP
YAAARP!
FLAP
FLAP
MEEEOOW! FZZZ!
KIKI! COME BACK HERE!

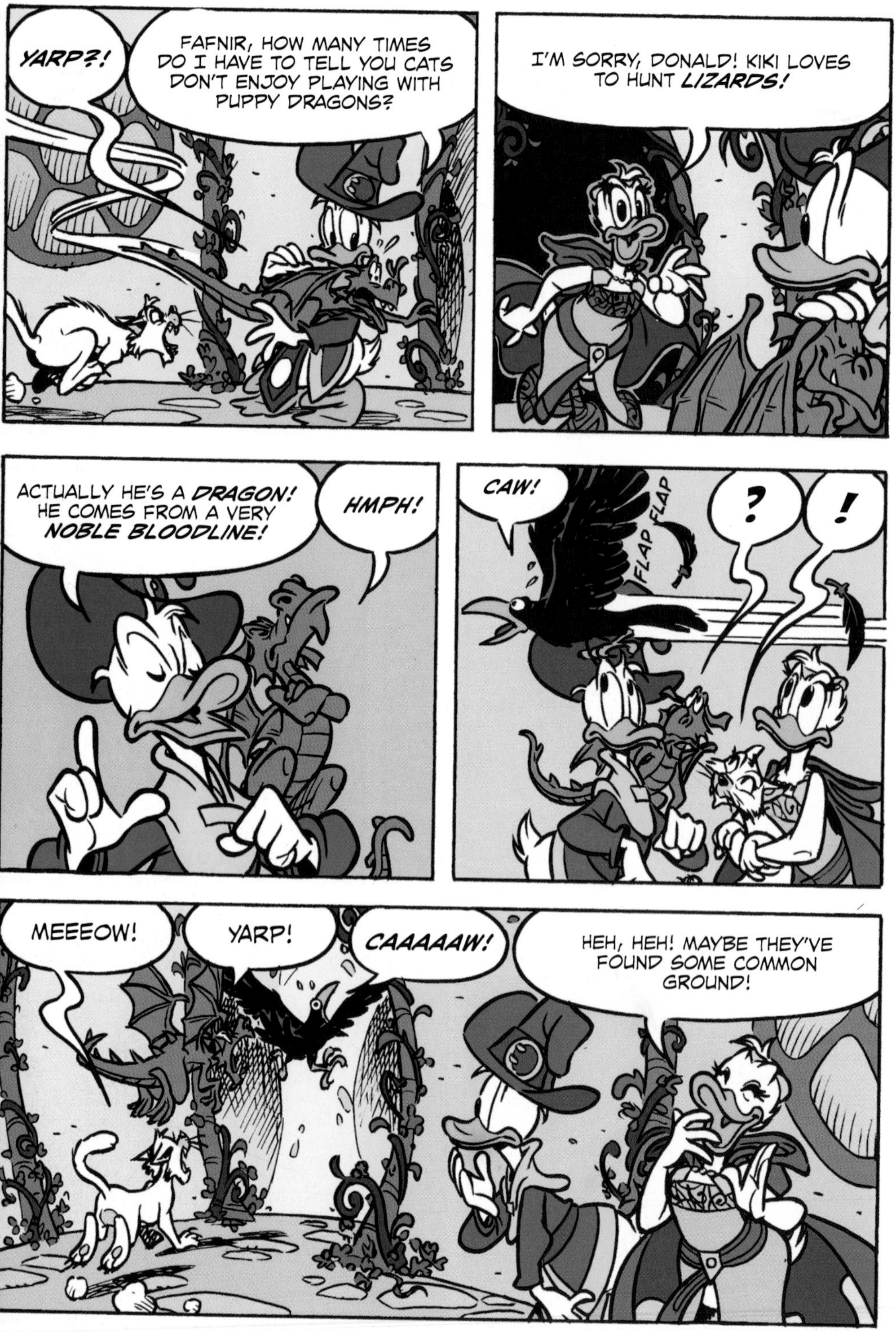
YARP?!
FAFNIR, HOW MANY TIMES DO I HAVE TO TELL YOU CATS DON'T ENJOY PLAYING WITH PUPPY DRAGONS?
I'M SORRY, DONALD! KIKI LOVES TO HUNT LIZARDS!
ACTUALLY HE'S A DRAGON! HE COMES FROM A VERY NOBLE BLOODLINE!
HMPH!
CAW!
FLAP FLAP
?
!
MEEEOW!
YARP!
CAAAAAW!
HEH, HEH! MAYBE THEY'VE FOUND SOME COMMON GROUND!

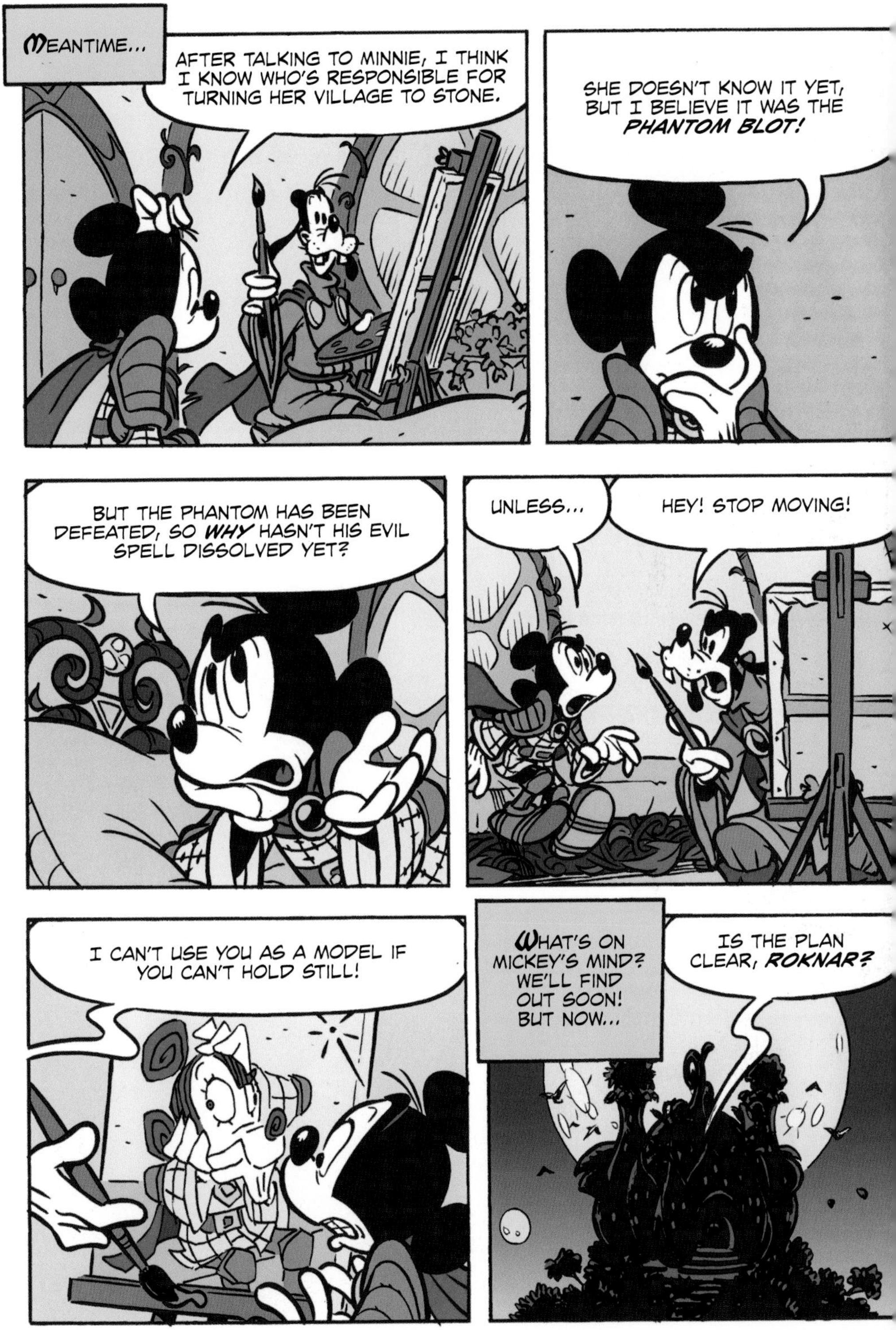
MEANTIME...
AFTER TALKING TO MINNIE, I THINK I KNOW WHO'S RESPONSIBLE FOR TURNING HER VILLAGE TO STONE.
SHE DOESN'T KNOW IT YET, BUT I BELIEVE IT WAS THE PHANTOM BLOT!
BUT THE PHANTOM HAS BEEN DEFEATED, SO WHY HASN'T HIS EVIL SPELL DISSOLVED YET?
UNLESS...
HEY! STOP MOVING!
I CAN'T USE YOU AS A MODEL IF YOU CAN'T HOLD STILL!
WHAT'S ON MICKEY'S MIND? WE'LL FIND OUT SOON! BUT NOW...
IS THE PLAN CLEAR, ROKNAR?

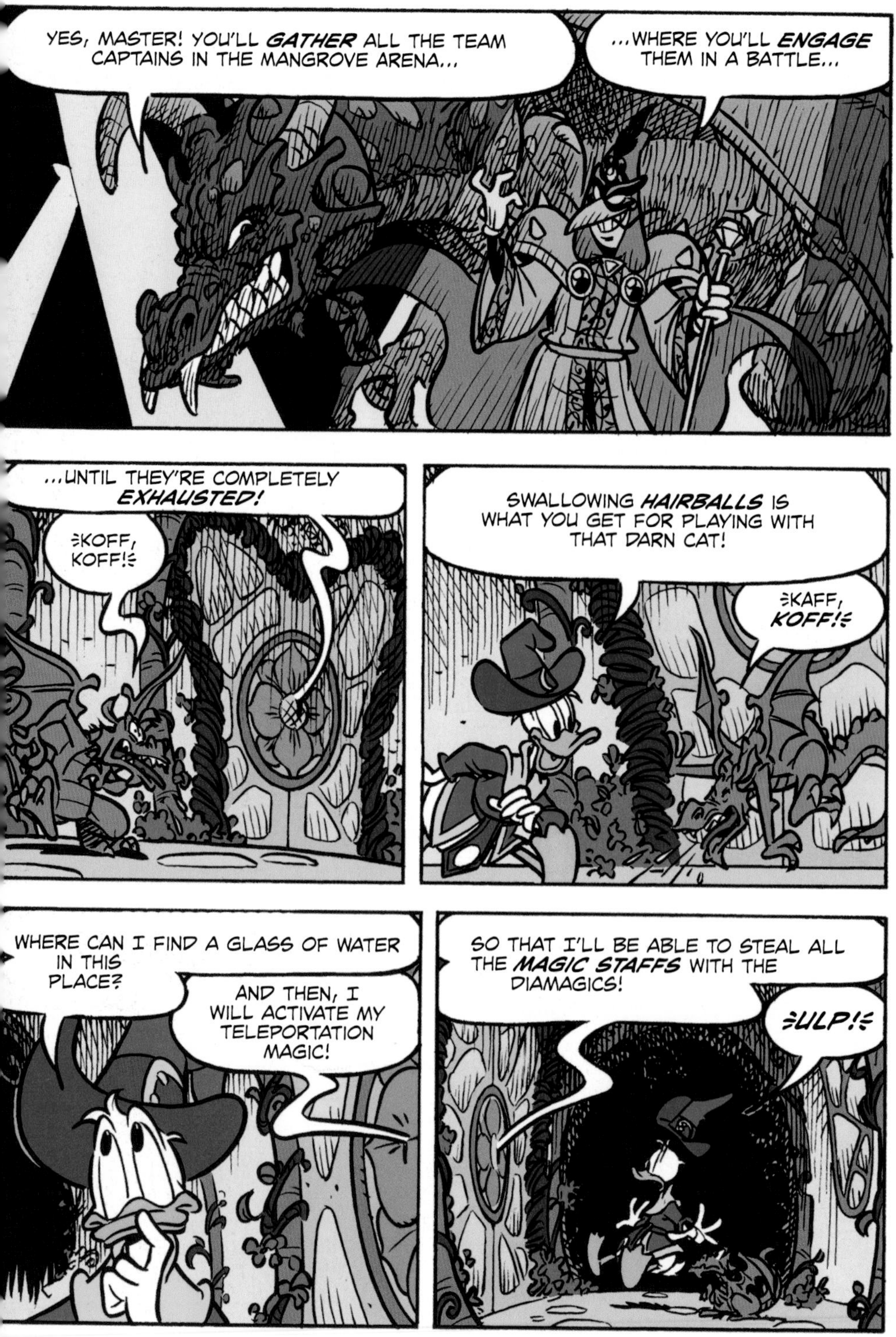
YES, MASTER! YOU'LL GATHER ALL THE TEAM CAPTAINS IN THE MANGROVE ARENA...
...WHERE YOU'LL ENGAGE THEM IN A BATTLE...
...UNTIL THEY'RE COMPLETELY EXHAUSTED!
KOFF, KOFF!
SWALLOWING HAIRBALLS IS WHAT YOU GET FOR PLAYING WITH THAT DARN CAT!
KAFF, KOFF!
WHERE CAN I FIND A GLASS OF WATER IN THIS PLACE?
AND THEN, I WILL ACTIVATE MY TELEPORTATION MAGIC!
SO THAT I'LL BE ABLE TO STEAL ALL THE MAGIC STAFFS WITH THE DIAMAGICS!
ULP!

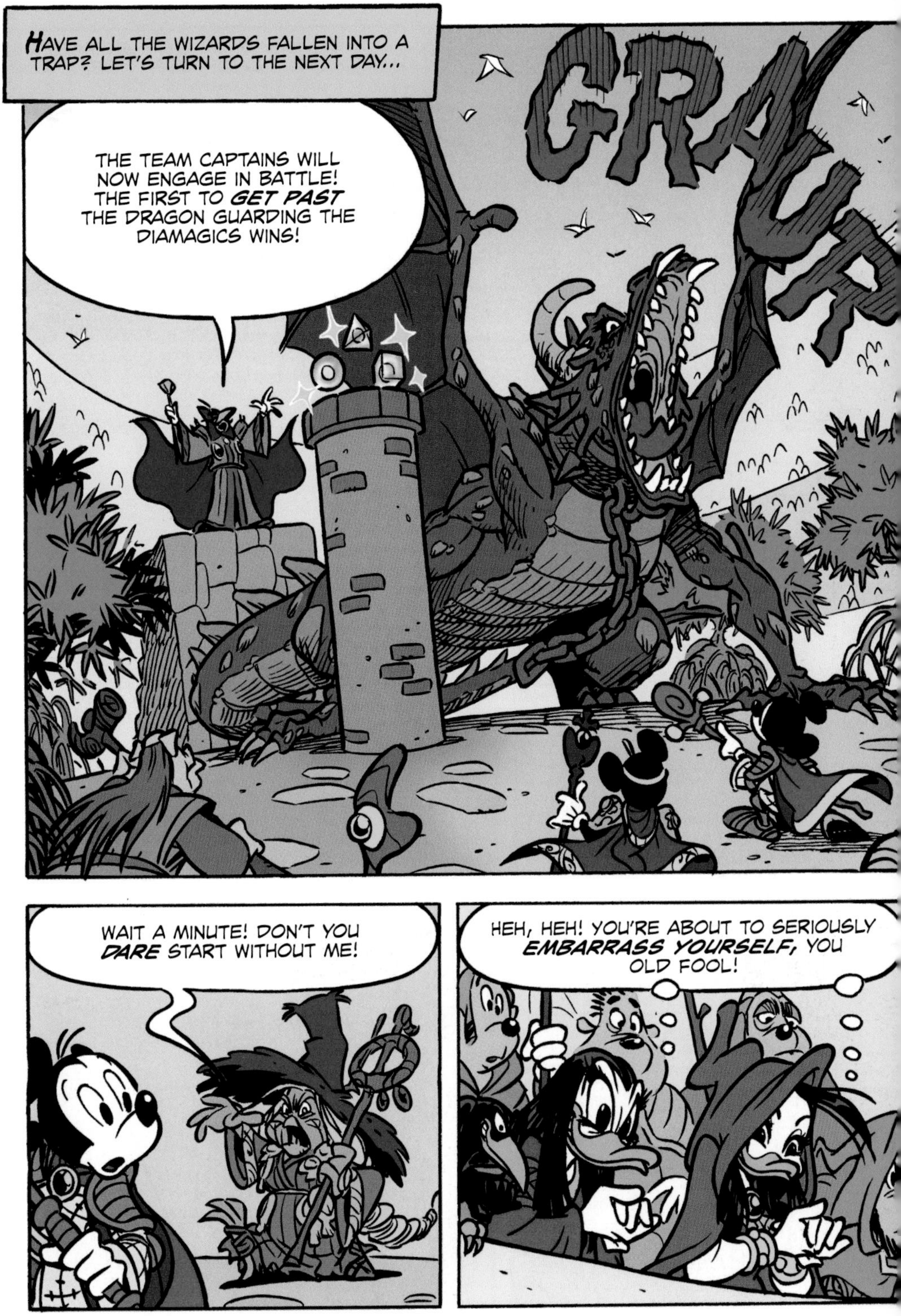
HAVE ALL THE WIZARDS FALLEN INTO A TRAP? LET'S TURN TO THE NEXT DAY...
THE TEAM CAPTAINS WILL NOW ENGAGE IN BATTLE! THE FIRST TO *GET PAST* THE DRAGON GUARDING THE DIAMAGICS WINS!
GRAUR
WAIT A MINUTE! DON'T YOU *DARE* START WITHOUT ME!
HEH, HEH! YOU'RE ABOUT TO SERIOUSLY *EMBARRASS YOURSELF,* YOU OLD FOOL!

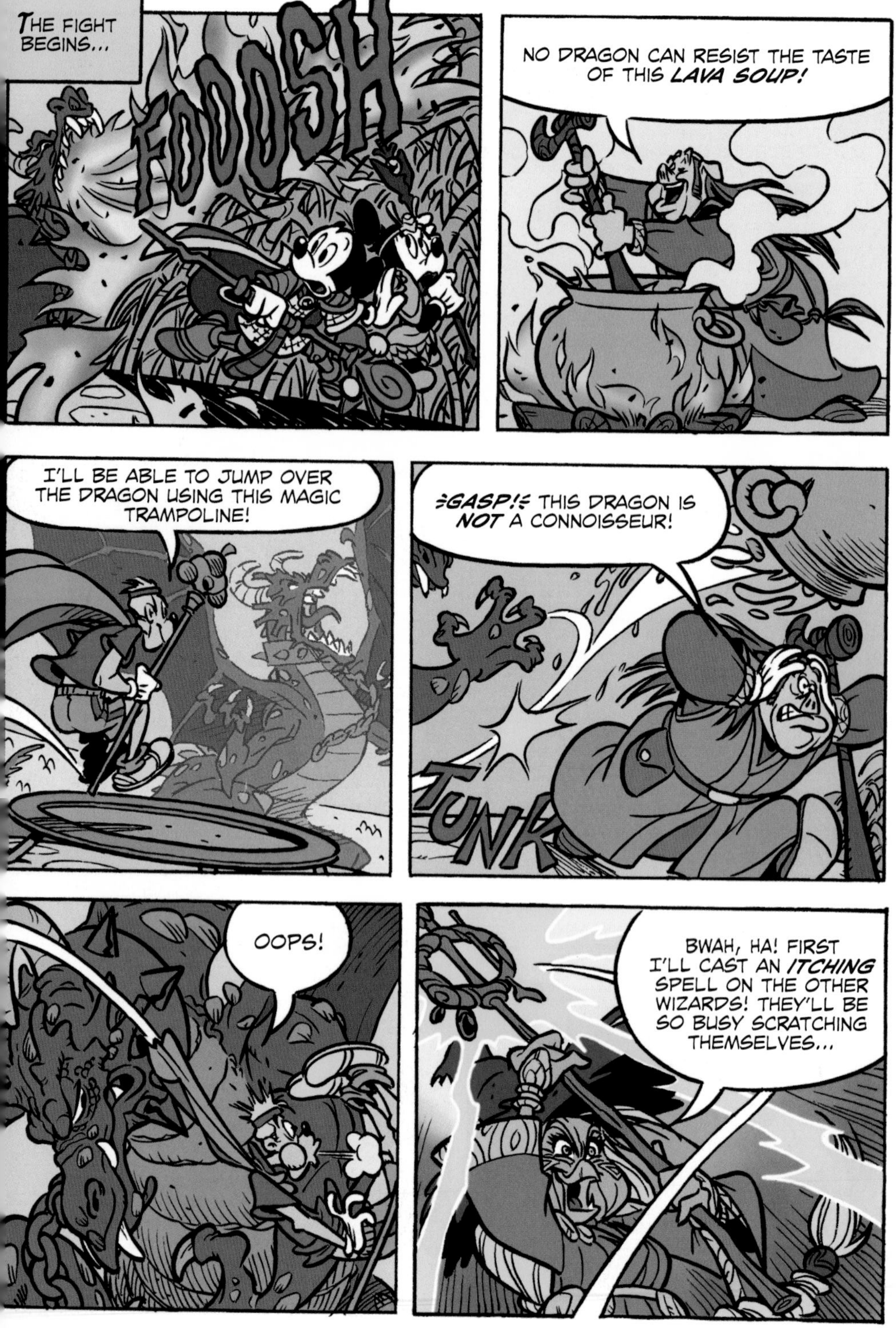
THE FIGHT BEGINS...
FOOOSH
NO DRAGON CAN RESIST THE TASTE OF THIS LAVA SOUP!
I'LL BE ABLE TO JUMP OVER THE DRAGON USING THIS MAGIC TRAMPOLINE!
GASP! THIS DRAGON IS NOT A CONNOISSEUR!
TUNK
OOPS!
BWAH, HA! FIRST I'LL CAST AN ITCHING SPELL ON THE OTHER WIZARDS! THEY'LL BE SO BUSY SCRATCHING THEMSELVES...

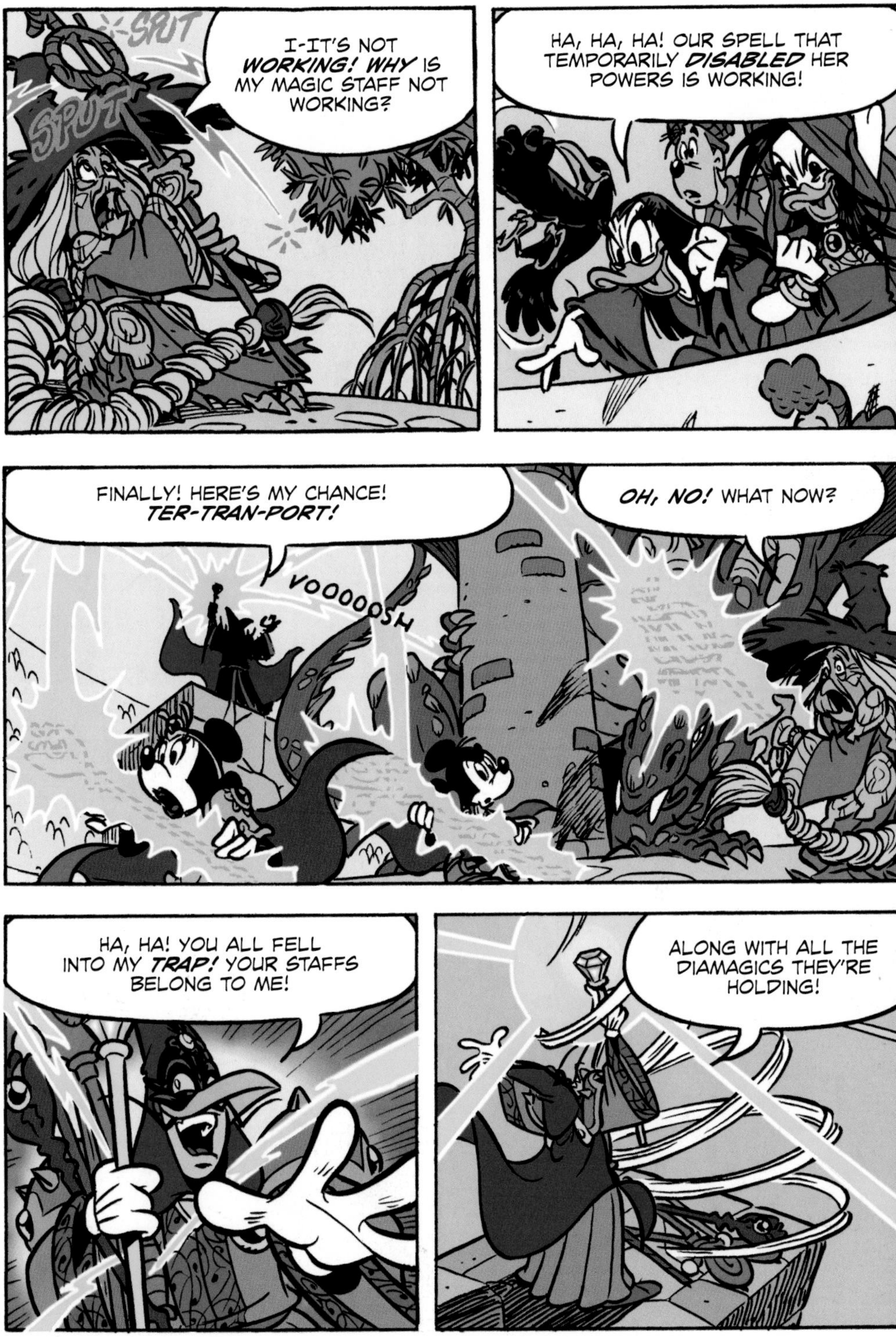
SPUT
SPUT
I-IT'S NOT WORKING! WHY IS MY MAGIC STAFF NOT WORKING?
HA, HA, HA! OUR SPELL THAT TEMPORARILY DISABLED HER POWERS IS WORKING!
FINALLY! HERE'S MY CHANCE! TER-TRAN-PORT!
VOOOOOOSH
OH, NO! WHAT NOW?
HA, HA! YOU ALL FELL INTO MY TRAP! YOUR STAFFS BELONG TO ME!
ALONG WITH ALL THE DIAMAGICS THEY'RE HOLDING!

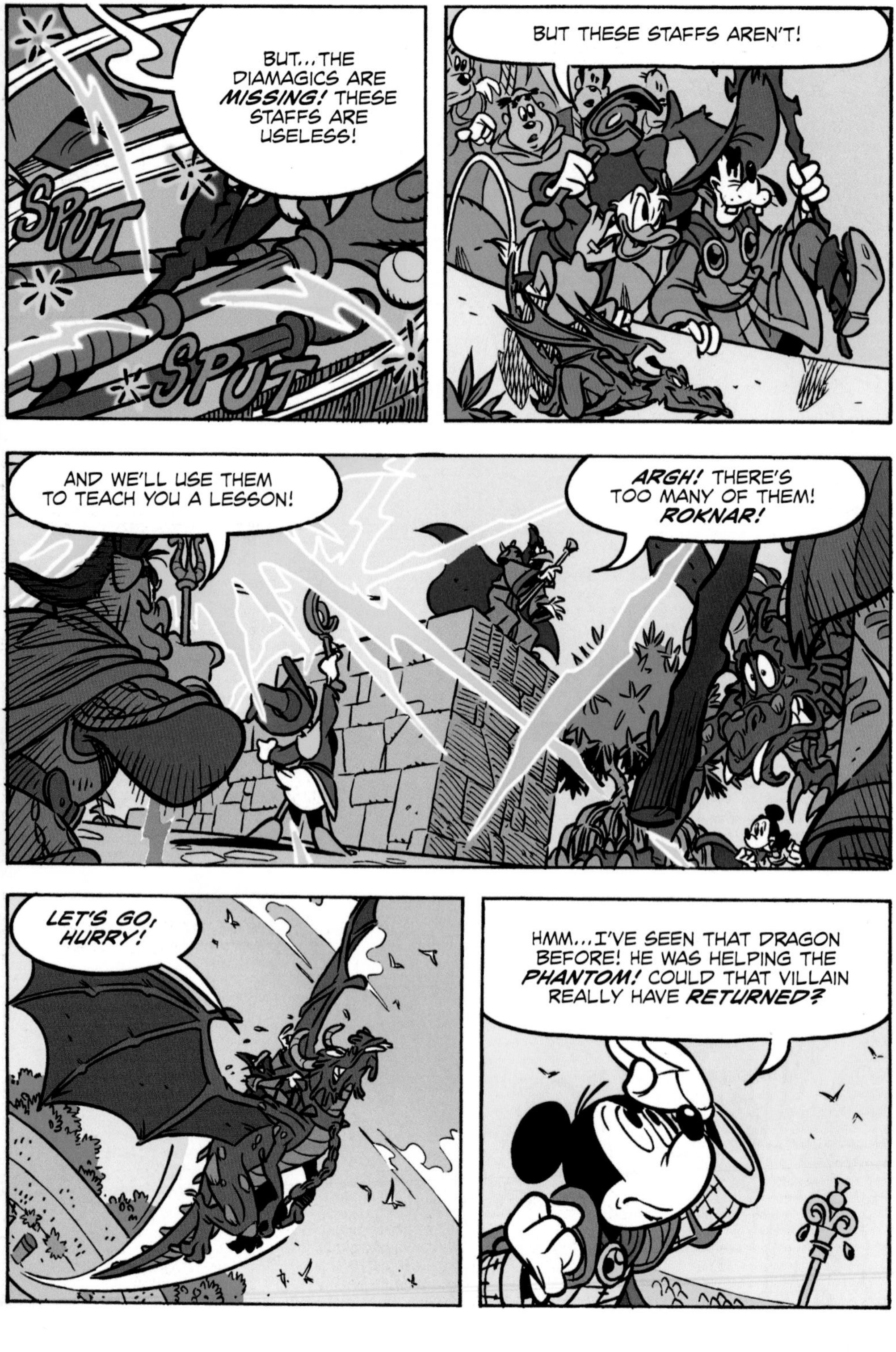

BUT...THE DIAMAGICS ARE MISSING! THESE STAFFS ARE USELESS!
SPUT
SPUT
BUT THESE STAFFS AREN'T!
AND WE'LL USE THEM TO TEACH YOU A LESSON!
ARGH! THERE'S TOO MANY OF THEM! ROKNAR!
LET'S GO, HURRY!
HMM...I'VE SEEN THAT DRAGON BEFORE! HE WAS HELPING THE PHANTOM! COULD THAT VILLAIN REALLY HAVE RETURNED?

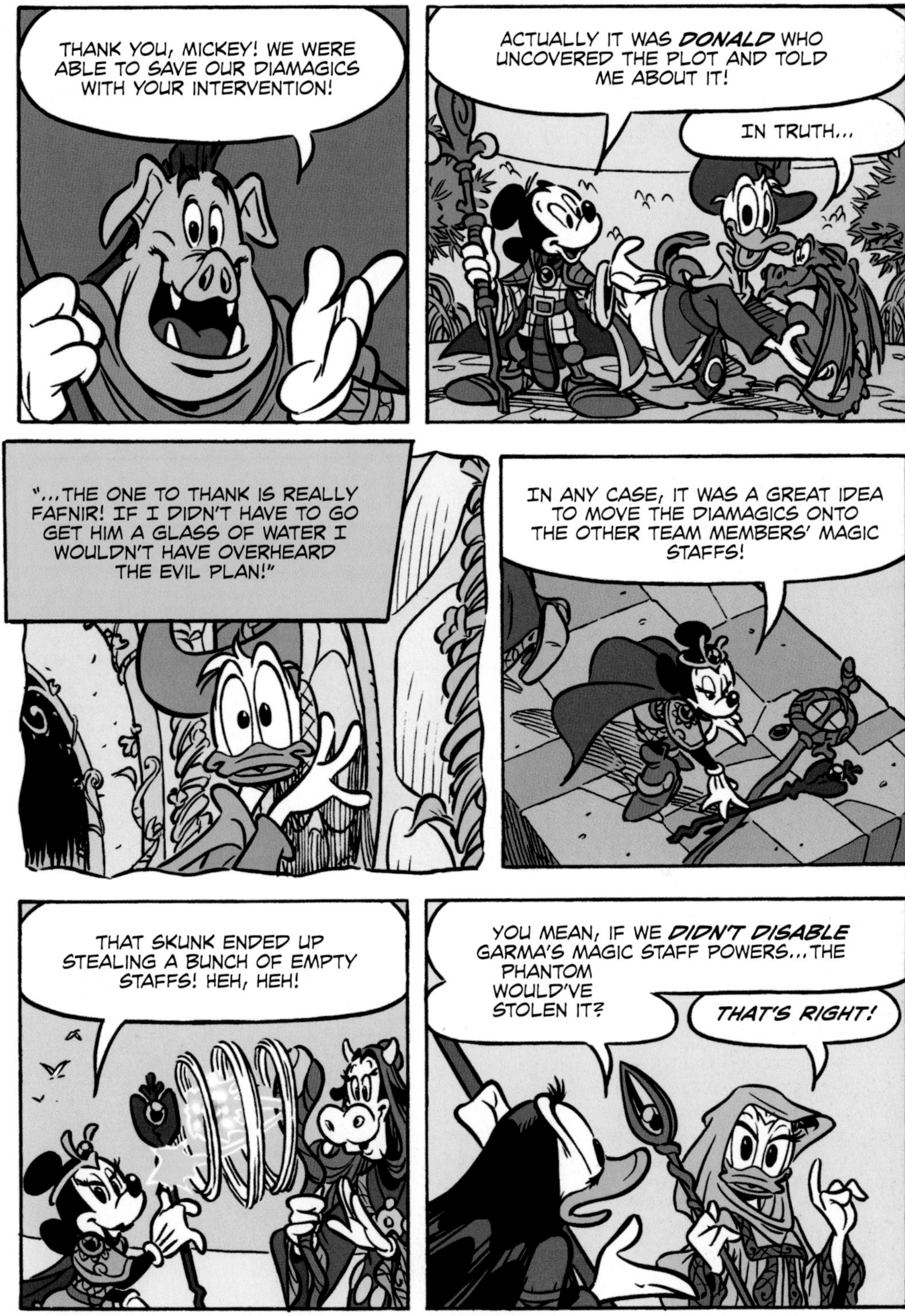
THANK YOU, MICKEY! WE WERE ABLE TO SAVE OUR DIAMAGICS WITH YOUR INTERVENTION!
ACTUALLY IT WAS DONALD WHO UNCOVERED THE PLOT AND TOLD ME ABOUT IT!
IN TRUTH...
"...THE ONE TO THANK IS REALLY FAFNIR! IF I DIDN'T HAVE TO GO GET HIM A GLASS OF WATER I WOULDN'T HAVE OVERHEARD THE EVIL PLAN!"
IN ANY CASE, IT WAS A GREAT IDEA TO MOVE THE DIAMAGICS ONTO THE OTHER TEAM MEMBERS' MAGIC STAFFS!
THAT SKUNK ENDED UP STEALING A BUNCH OF EMPTY STAFFS! HEH, HEH!
YOU MEAN, IF WE DIDN'T DISABLE GARMA'S MAGIC STAFF POWERS...THE PHANTOM WOULD'VE STOLEN IT?
THAT'S RIGHT!

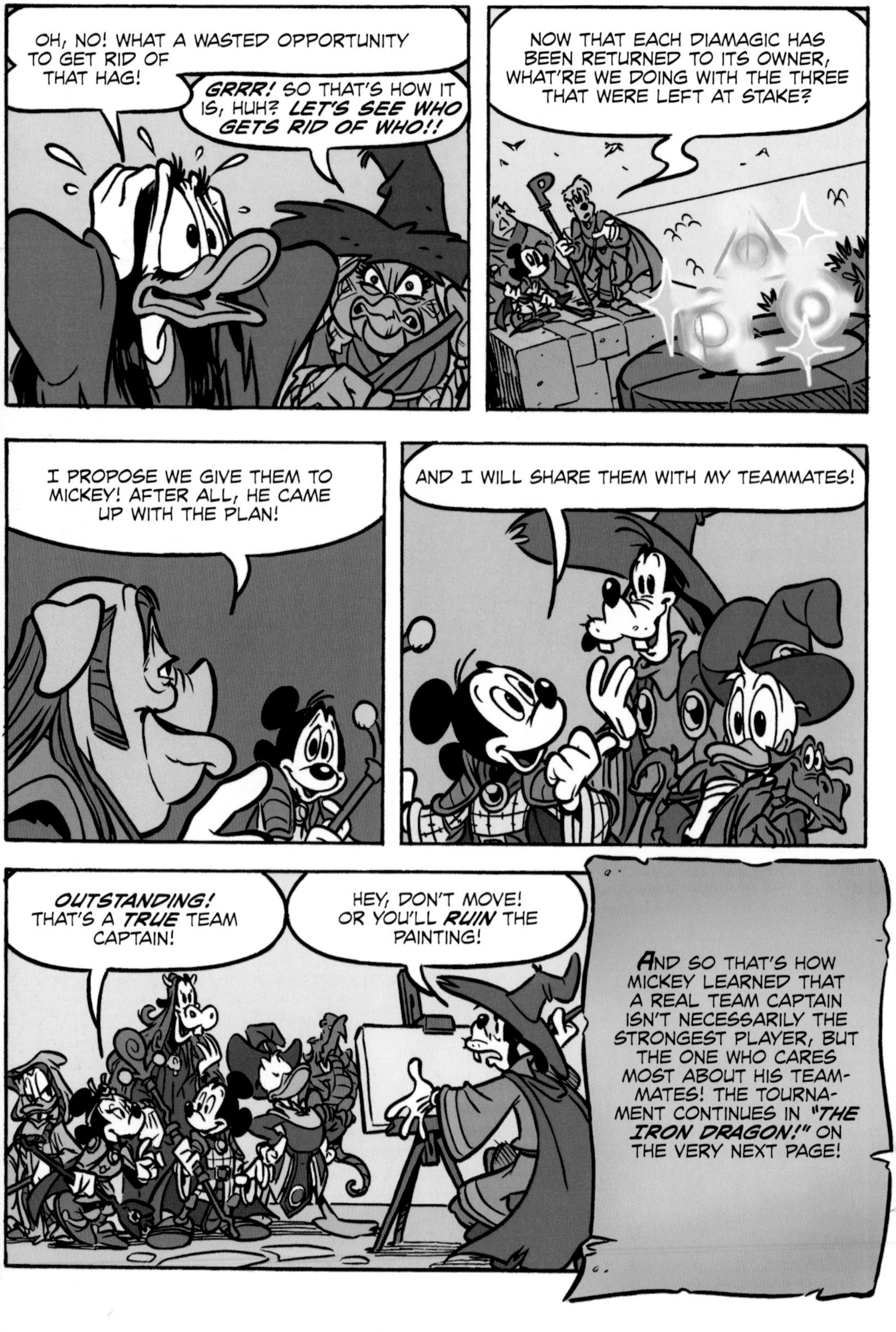
OH, NO! WHAT A WASTED OPPORTUNITY TO GET RID OF THAT HAG!
GRRR! SO THAT'S HOW IT IS, HUH? LET'S SEE WHO GETS RID OF WHO!!
NOW THAT EACH DIAMAGIC HAS BEEN RETURNED TO ITS OWNER, WHAT'RE WE DOING WITH THE THREE THAT WERE LEFT AT STAKE?
I PROPOSE WE GIVE THEM TO MICKEY! AFTER ALL, HE CAME UP WITH THE PLAN!
AND I WILL SHARE THEM WITH MY TEAMMATES!
OUTSTANDING! THAT'S A TRUE TEAM CAPTAIN!
HEY, DON'T MOVE! OR YOU'LL RUIN THE PAINTING!
AND SO THAT'S HOW MICKEY LEARNED THAT A REAL TEAM CAPTAIN ISN'T NECESSARILY THE STRONGEST PLAYER, BUT THE ONE WHO CARES MOST ABOUT HIS TEAM-MATES! THE TOURNA-MENT CONTINUES IN "THE IRON DRAGON!" ON THE VERY NEXT PAGE!

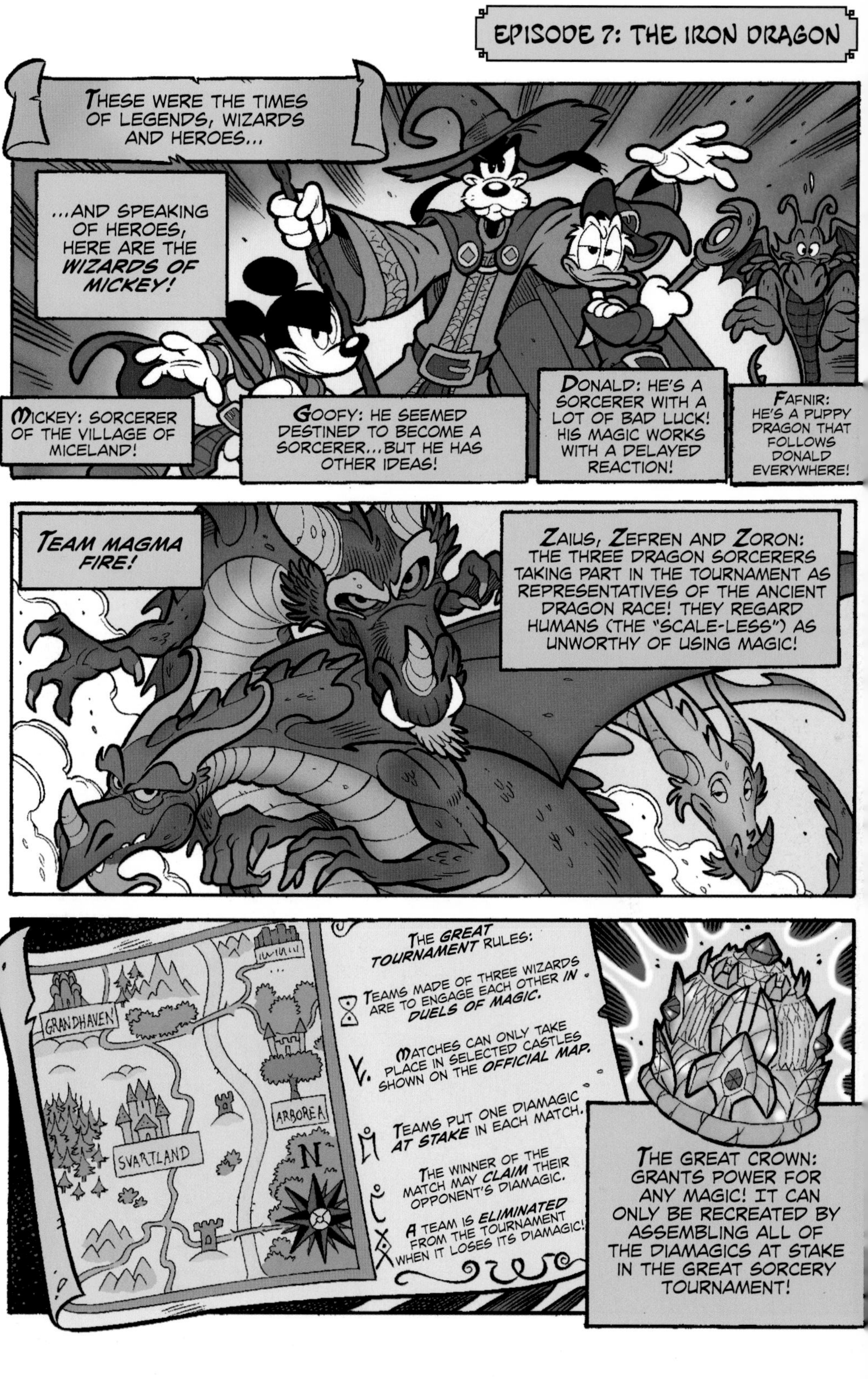
EPISODE 7: THE IRON DRAGON
THESE WERE THE TIMES OF LEGENDS, WIZARDS AND HEROES...
...AND SPEAKING OF HEROES, HERE ARE THE WIZARDS OF MICKEY!
MICKEY: SORCERER OF THE VILLAGE OF MICELAND!
GOOFY: HE SEEMED DESTINED TO BECOME A SORCERER...BUT HE HAS OTHER IDEAS!
DONALD: HE'S A SORCERER WITH A LOT OF BAD LUCK! HIS MAGIC WORKS WITH A DELAYED REACTION!
FAFNIR: HE'S A PUPPY DRAGON THAT FOLLOWS DONALD EVERYWHERE!
TEAM MAGMA FIRE!
ZAIUS, ZEFREN AND ZORON: THE THREE DRAGON SORCERERS TAKING PART IN THE TOURNAMENT AS REPRESENTATIVES OF THE ANCIENT DRAGON RACE! THEY REGARD HUMANS (THE "SCALE-LESS") AS UNWORTHY OF USING MAGIC!
GRANDHAVEN
ARBOREA
SVARTLAND
N
THE GREAT TOURNAMENT RULES:
TEAMS MADE OF THREE WIZARDS ARE TO ENGAGE EACH OTHER IN DUELS OF MAGIC.
MATCHES CAN ONLY TAKE PLACE IN SELECTED CASTLES SHOWN ON THE OFFICIAL MAP.
TEAMS PUT ONE DIAMAGIC AT STAKE IN EACH MATCH.
THE WINNER OF THE MATCH MAY CLAIM THEIR OPPONENT'S DIAMAGIC.
A TEAM IS ELIMINATED FROM THE TOURNAMENT WHEN IT LOSES ITS DIAMAGIC!
THE GREAT CROWN: GRANTS POWER FOR ANY MAGIC! IT CAN ONLY BE RECREATED BY ASSEMBLING ALL OF THE DIAMAGICS AT STAKE IN THE GREAT SORCERY TOURNAMENT!

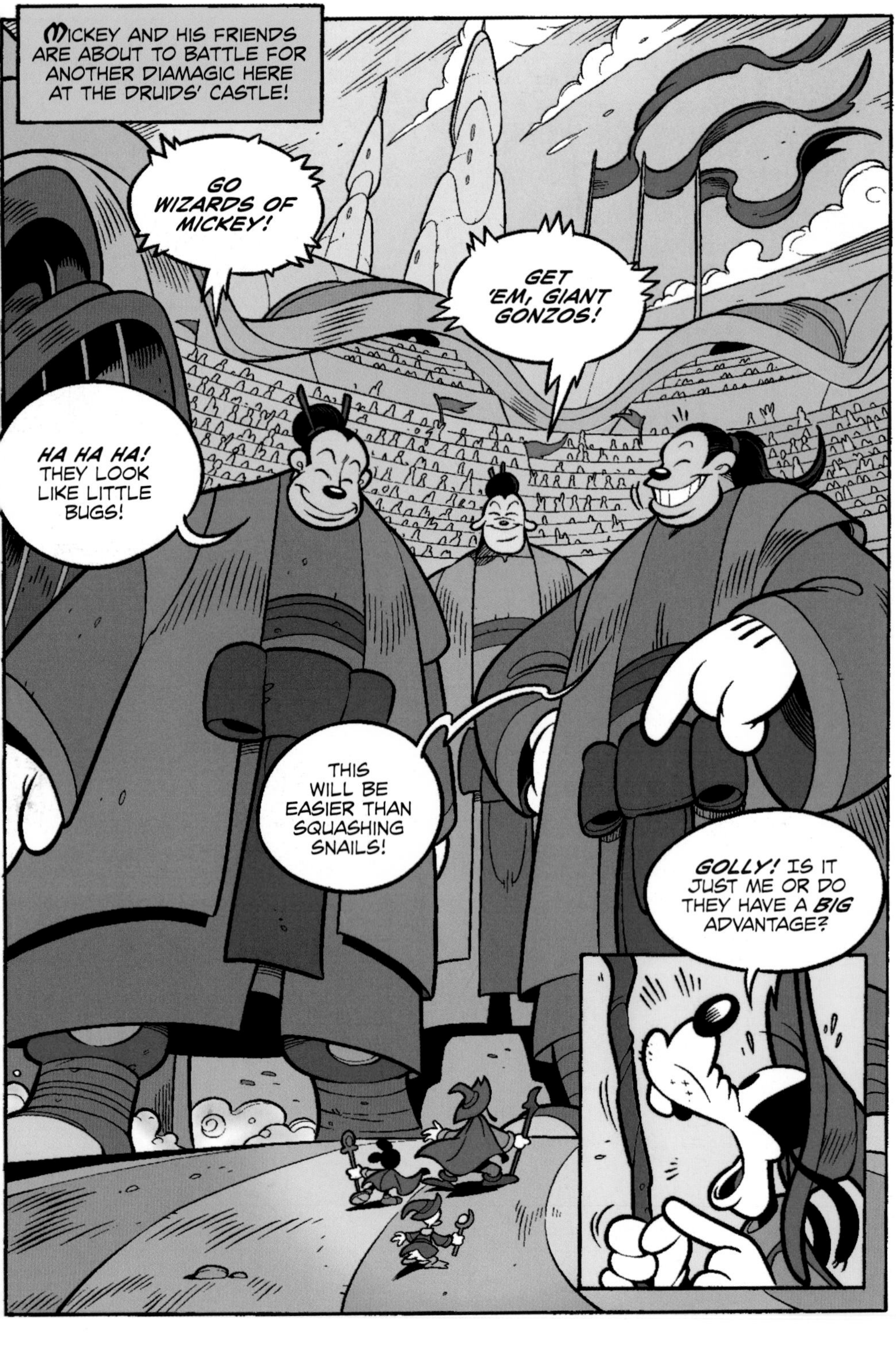
MICKEY AND HIS FRIENDS ARE ABOUT TO BATTLE FOR ANOTHER DIAMAGIC HERE AT THE DRUIDS' CASTLE!
GO WIZARDS OF MICKEY!
GET 'EM, GIANT GONZOS!
HA HA HA! THEY LOOK LIKE LITTLE BUGS!
THIS WILL BE EASIER THAN SQUASHING SNAILS!
GOLLY! IS IT JUST ME OR DO THEY HAVE A BIG ADVANTAGE?

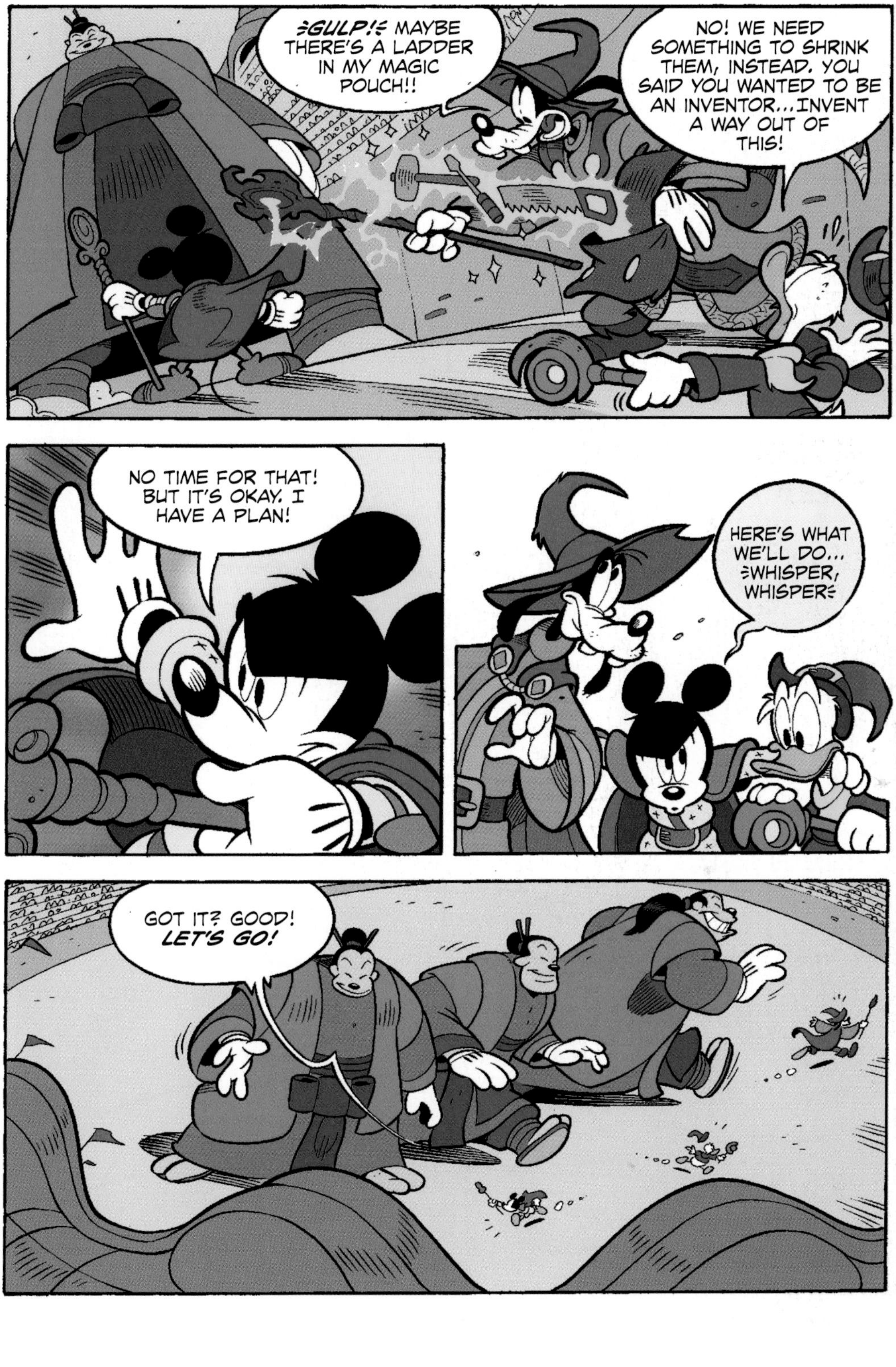

=GULP!= MAYBE THERE'S A LADDER IN MY MAGIC POUCH!!
NO! WE NEED SOMETHING TO SHRINK THEM, INSTEAD. YOU SAID YOU WANTED TO BE AN INVENTOR...INVENT A WAY OUT OF THIS!
NO TIME FOR THAT! BUT IT'S OKAY. I HAVE A PLAN!
HERE'S WHAT WE'LL DO... =WHISPER, WHISPER=
GOT IT? GOOD! LET'S GO!

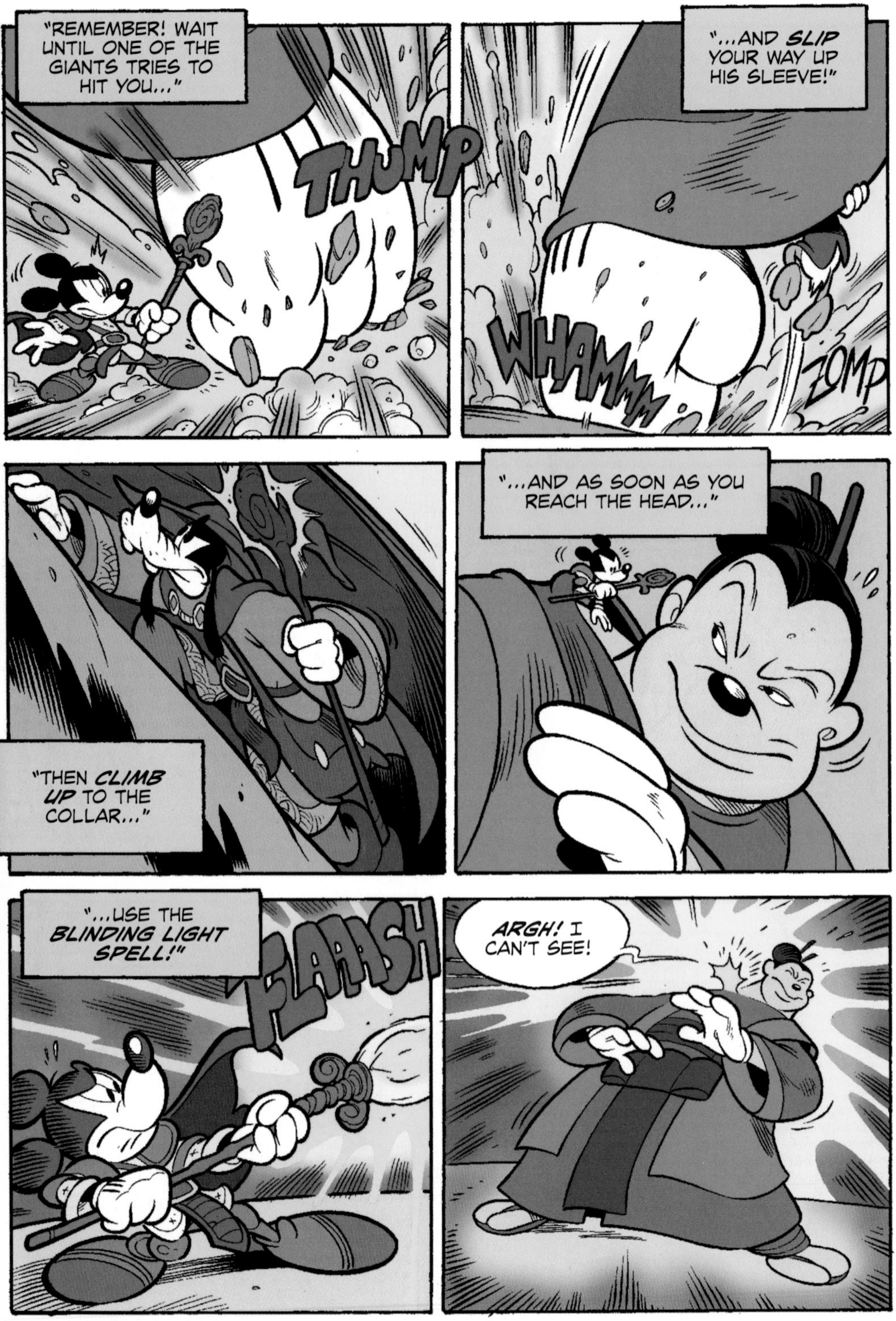
"REMEMBER! WAIT UNTIL ONE OF THE GIANTS TRIES TO HIT YOU..."
THUMP
"...AND *SLIP* YOUR WAY UP HIS SLEEVE!"
WHAMMMM
ZOMP
"THEN *CLIMB UP* TO THE COLLAR..."
"...AND AS SOON AS YOU REACH THE HEAD..."
"...USE THE *BLINDING LIGHT SPELL!*"
FLAAASH
ARGH! I CAN'T SEE!

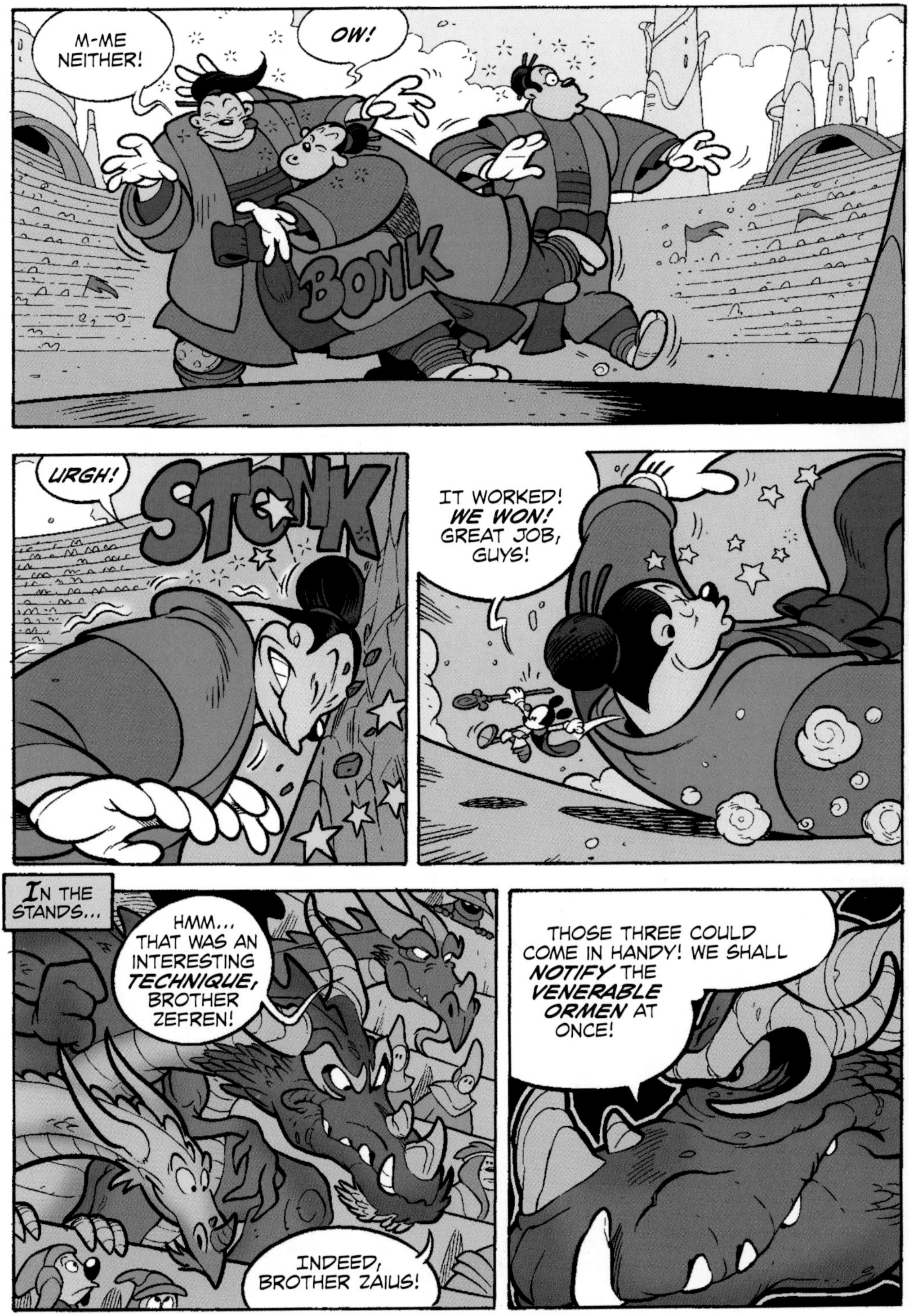
M-ME NEITHER!
OW!
BONK
URGH!
STONK
IT WORKED! WE WON! GREAT JOB, GUYS!
IN THE STANDS...
HMM... THAT WAS AN INTERESTING TECHNIQUE, BROTHER ZEFREN!
INDEED, BROTHER ZAIUS!
THOSE THREE COULD COME IN HANDY! WE SHALL NOTIFY THE VENERABLE ORMEN AT ONCE!

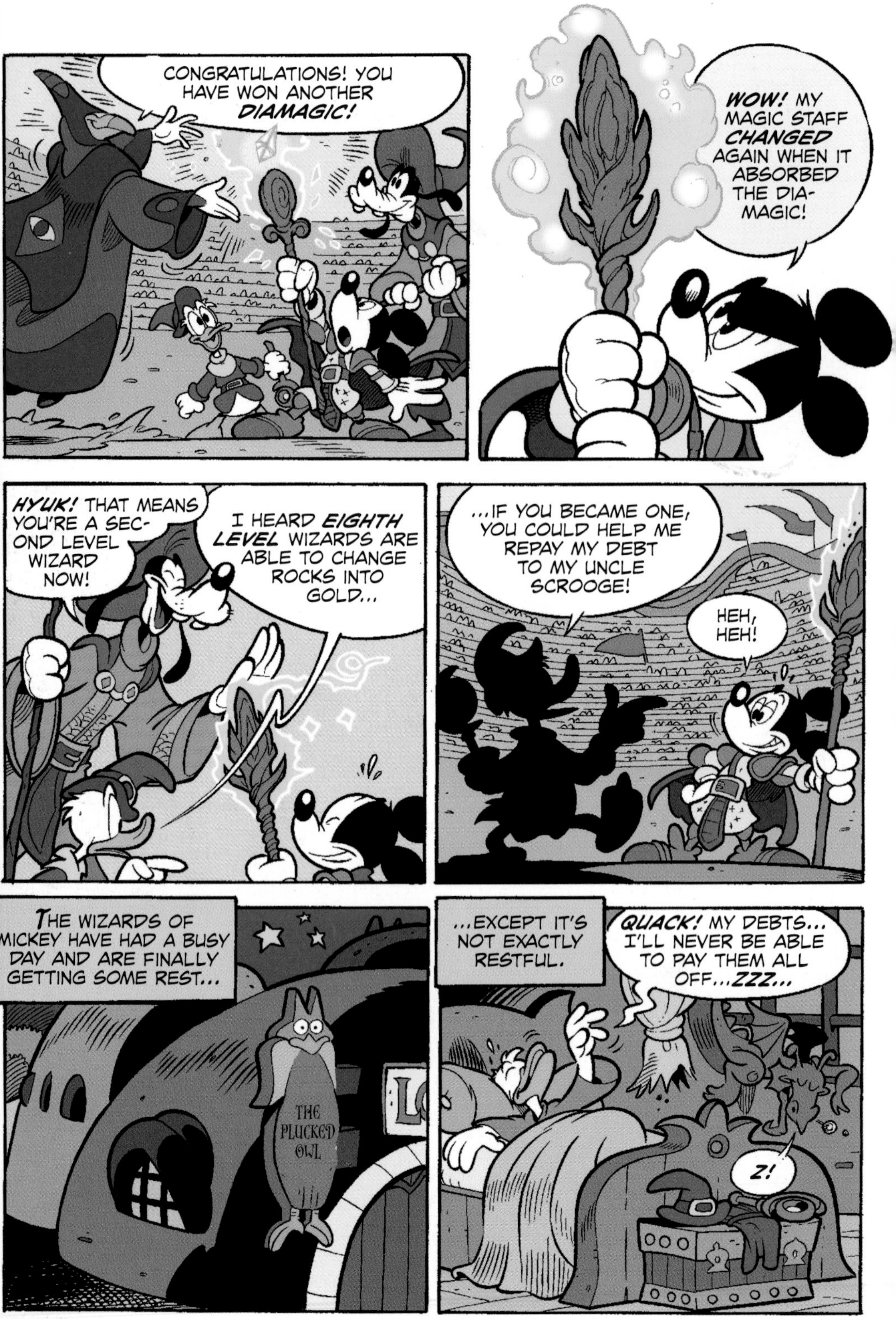
CONGRATULATIONS! YOU HAVE WON ANOTHER DIAMAGIC!
WOW! MY MAGIC STAFF CHANGED AGAIN WHEN IT ABSORBED THE DIA-MAGIC!
HYUK! THAT MEANS YOU'RE A SEC-OND LEVEL WIZARD NOW!
I HEARD EIGHTH LEVEL WIZARDS ARE ABLE TO CHANGE ROCKS INTO GOLD...
...IF YOU BECAME ONE, YOU COULD HELP ME REPAY MY DEBT TO MY UNCLE SCROOGE!
HEH, HEH!
THE WIZARDS OF MICKEY HAVE HAD A BUSY DAY AND ARE FINALLY GETTING SOME REST...
THE PLUCKED OWL
...EXCEPT IT'S NOT EXACTLY RESTFUL.
QUACK! MY DEBTS... I'LL NEVER BE ABLE TO PAY THEM ALL OFF...ZZZ...
Z!

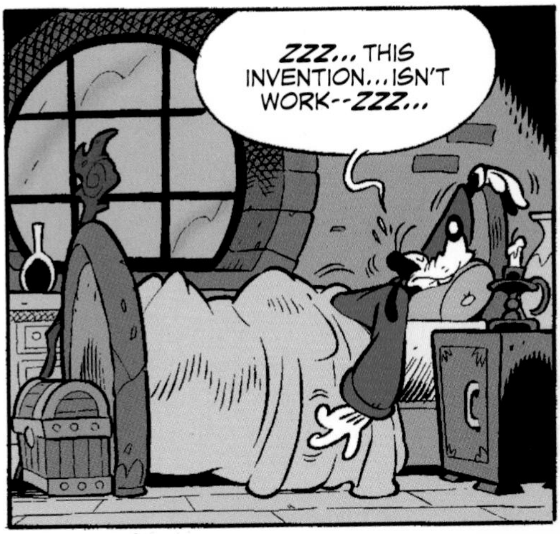
ZZZ... THIS INVENTION... ISN'T WORK--ZZZ...

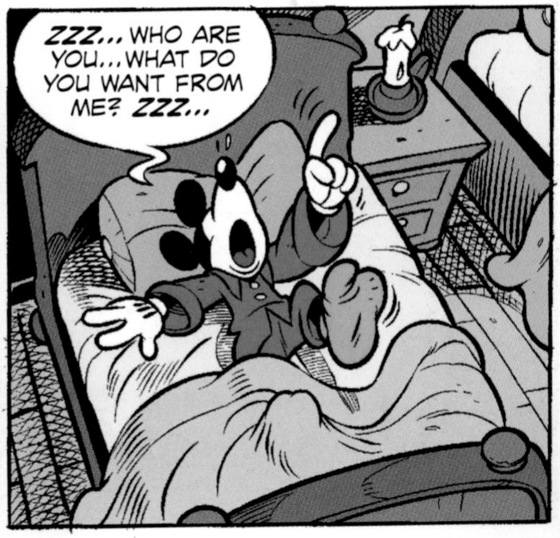
ZZZ... WHO ARE YOU... WHAT DO YOU WANT FROM ME? ZZZ...

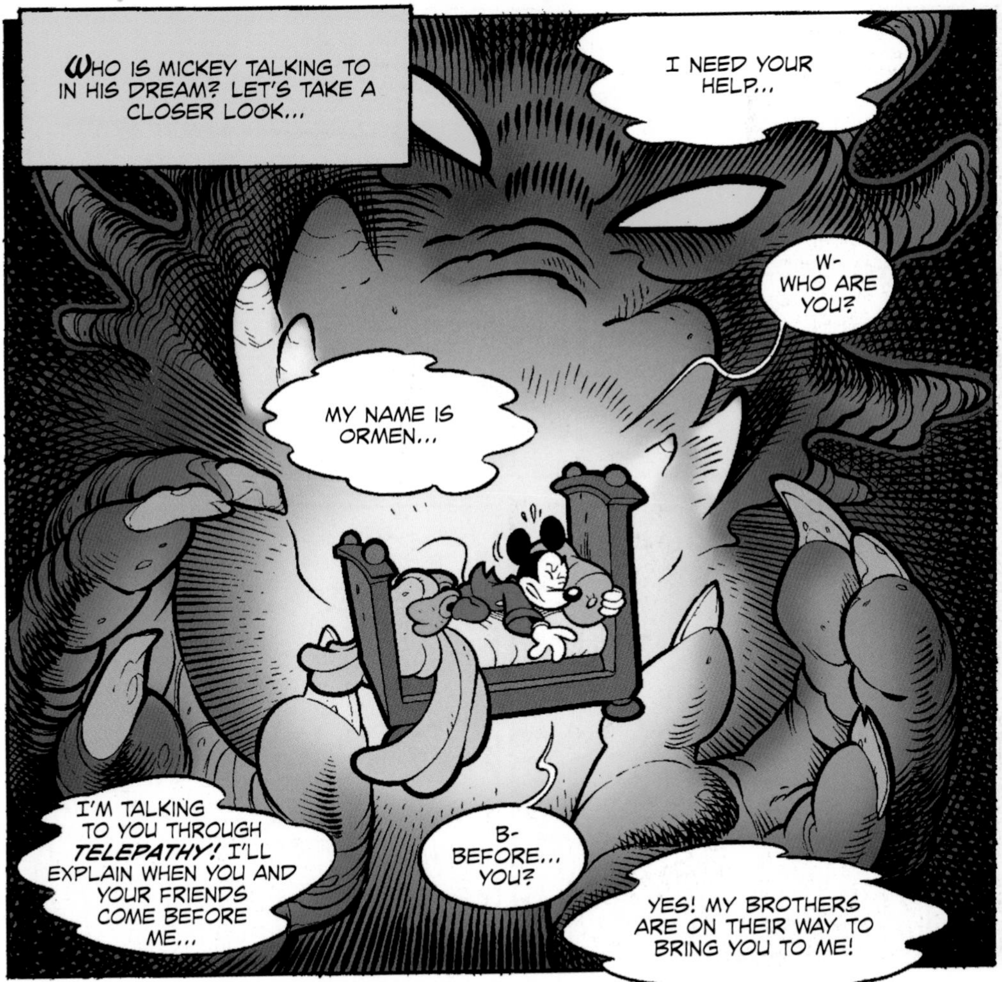
WHO IS MICKEY TALKING TO IN HIS DREAM? LET'S TAKE A CLOSER LOOK...
I NEED YOUR HELP...
W- WHO ARE YOU?
MY NAME IS ORMEN...
I'M TALKING TO YOU THROUGH TELEPATHY! I'LL EXPLAIN WHEN YOU AND YOUR FRIENDS COME BEFORE ME...
B- BEFORE... YOU?
YES! MY BROTHERS ARE ON THEIR WAY TO BRING YOU TO ME!

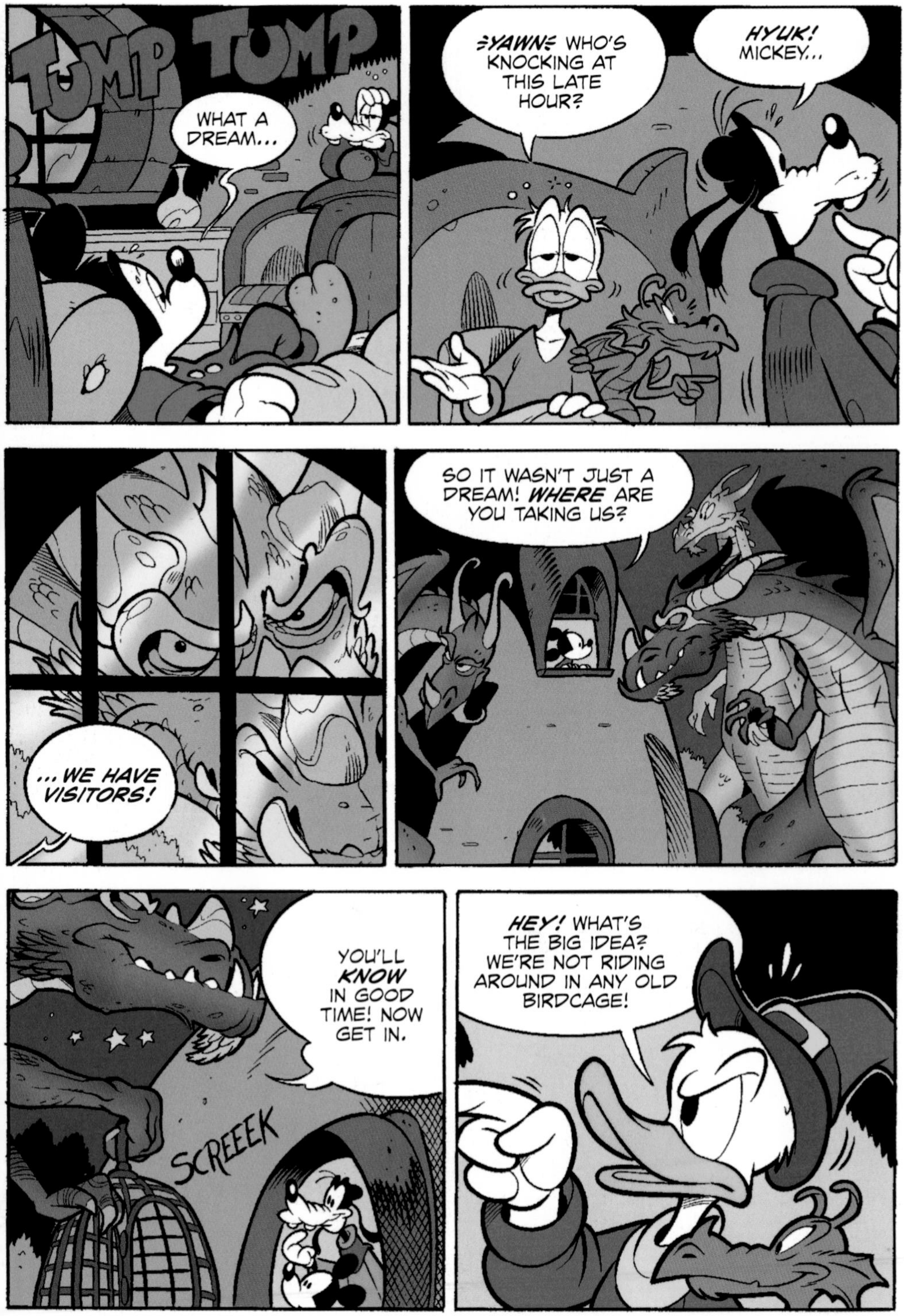
TUMP TUMP
WHAT A DREAM...
=YAWN= WHO'S KNOCKING AT THIS LATE HOUR?
HYUK! MICKEY...
...WE HAVE VISITORS!
SO IT WASN'T JUST A DREAM! WHERE ARE YOU TAKING US?
YOU'LL KNOW IN GOOD TIME! NOW GET IN.
SCREEEK
HEY! WHAT'S THE BIG IDEA? WE'RE NOT RIDING AROUND IN ANY OLD BIRDCAGE!

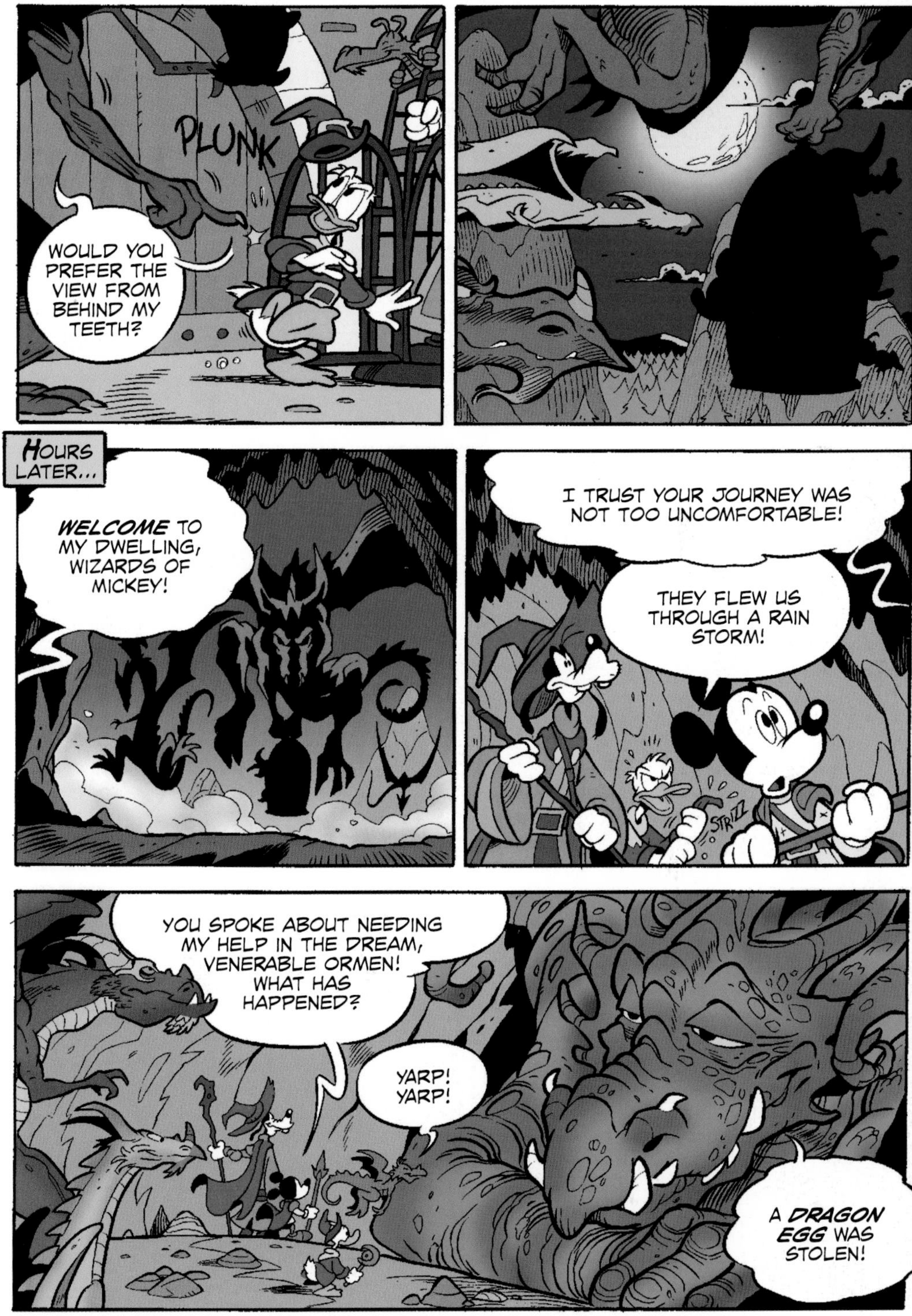
PLUNK
WOULD YOU PREFER THE VIEW FROM BEHIND MY TEETH?
HOURS LATER...
WELCOME TO MY DWELLING, WIZARDS OF MICKEY!
I TRUST YOUR JOURNEY WAS NOT TOO UNCOMFORTABLE!
THEY FLEW US THROUGH A RAIN STORM!
STRIZZ
YOU SPOKE ABOUT NEEDING MY HELP IN THE DREAM, VENERABLE ORMEN! WHAT HAS HAPPENED?
YARP! YARP!
A DRAGON EGG WAS STOLEN!

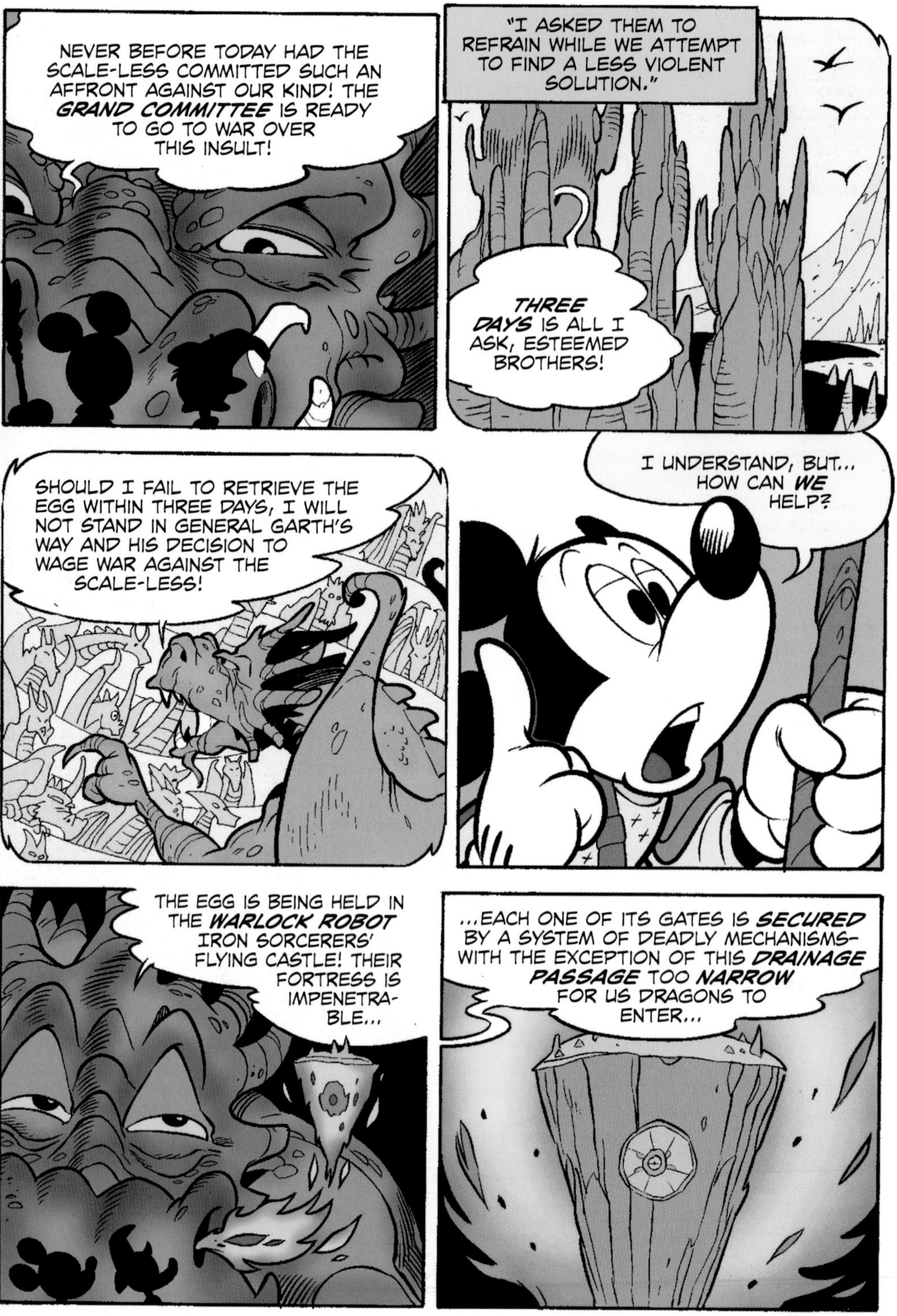
NEVER BEFORE TODAY HAD THE SCALE-LESS COMMITTED SUCH AN AFFRONT AGAINST OUR KIND! THE GRAND COMMITTEE IS READY TO GO TO WAR OVER THIS INSULT!
"I ASKED THEM TO REFRAIN WHILE WE ATTEMPT TO FIND A LESS VIOLENT SOLUTION."
THREE DAYS IS ALL I ASK, ESTEEMED BROTHERS!
SHOULD I FAIL TO RETRIEVE THE EGG WITHIN THREE DAYS, I WILL NOT STAND IN GENERAL GARTH'S WAY AND HIS DECISION TO WAGE WAR AGAINST THE SCALE-LESS!
I UNDERSTAND, BUT... HOW CAN WE HELP?
THE EGG IS BEING HELD IN THE WARLOCK ROBOT IRON SORCERERS' FLYING CASTLE! THEIR FORTRESS IS IMPENETRA-BLE...
...EACH ONE OF ITS GATES IS SECURED BY A SYSTEM OF DEADLY MECHANISMS- WITH THE EXCEPTION OF THIS DRAINAGE PASSAGE TOO NARROW FOR US DRAGONS TO ENTER...

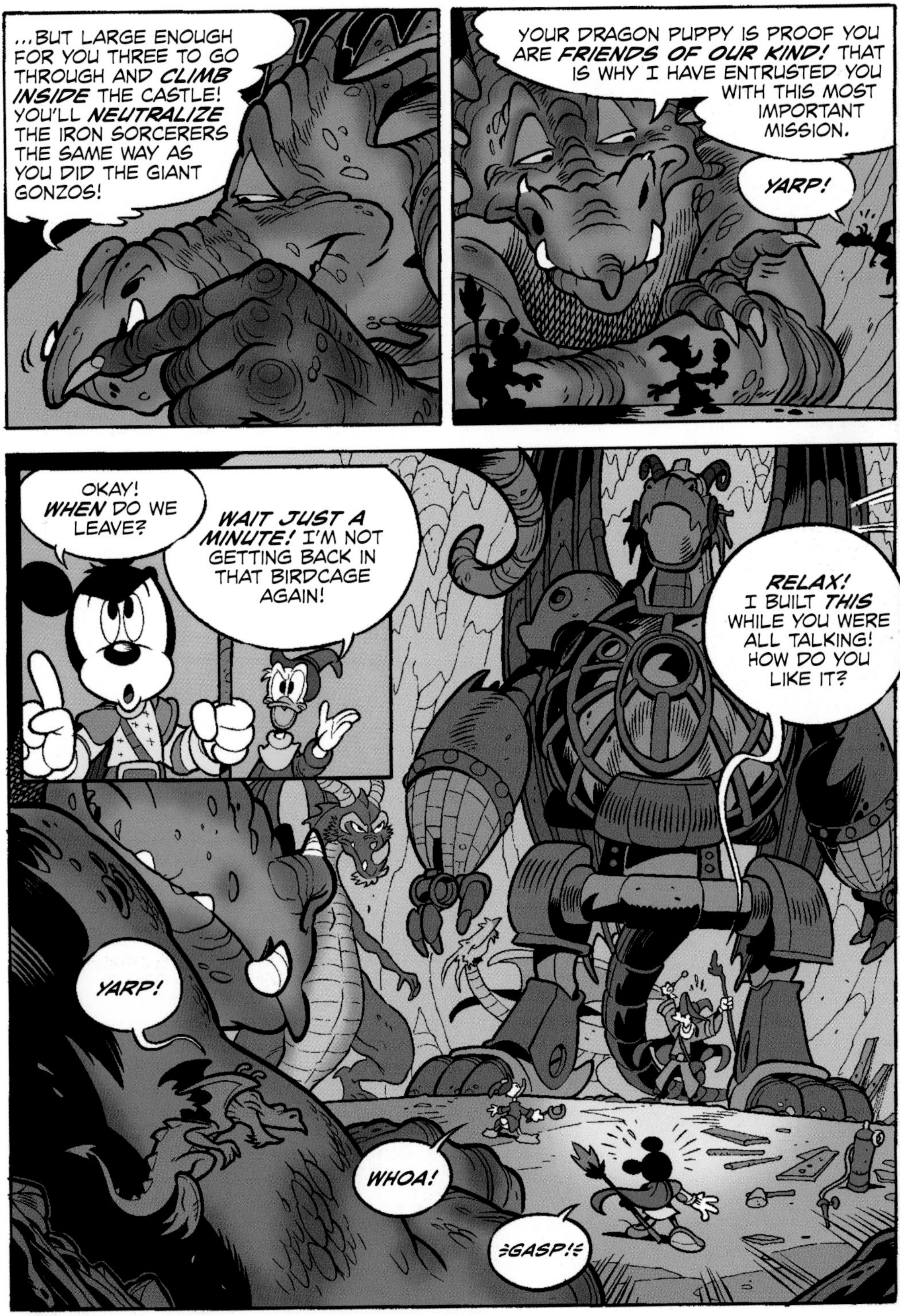
...BUT LARGE ENOUGH FOR YOU THREE TO GO THROUGH AND CLIMB INSIDE THE CASTLE! YOU'LL NEUTRALIZE THE IRON SORCERERS THE SAME WAY AS YOU DID THE GIANT GONZOS!
YOUR DRAGON PUPPY IS PROOF YOU ARE FRIENDS OF OUR KIND! THAT IS WHY I HAVE ENTRUSTED YOU WITH THIS MOST IMPORTANT MISSION.
YARP!
OKAY! WHEN DO WE LEAVE?
WAIT JUST A MINUTE! I'M NOT GETTING BACK IN THAT BIRDCAGE AGAIN!
RELAX! I BUILT THIS WHILE YOU WERE ALL TALKING! HOW DO YOU LIKE IT?
YARP!
WHOA!
GASP!

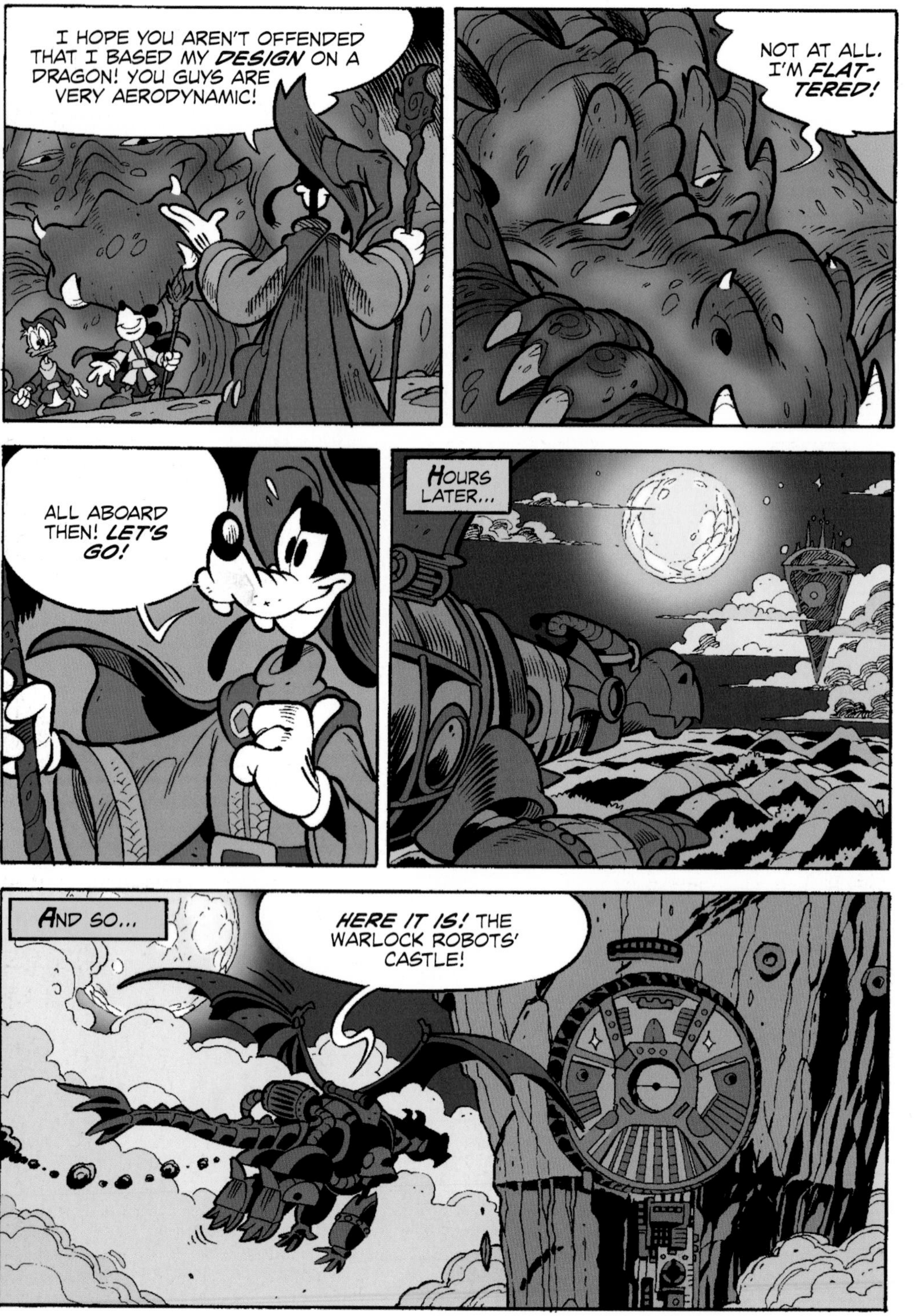
I HOPE YOU AREN'T OFFENDED THAT I BASED MY DESIGN ON A DRAGON! YOU GUYS ARE VERY AERODYNAMIC!
NOT AT ALL. I'M FLAT-TERED!
ALL ABOARD THEN! LET'S GO!
HOURS LATER...
AND SO...
HERE IT IS! THE WARLOCK ROBOTS' CASTLE!

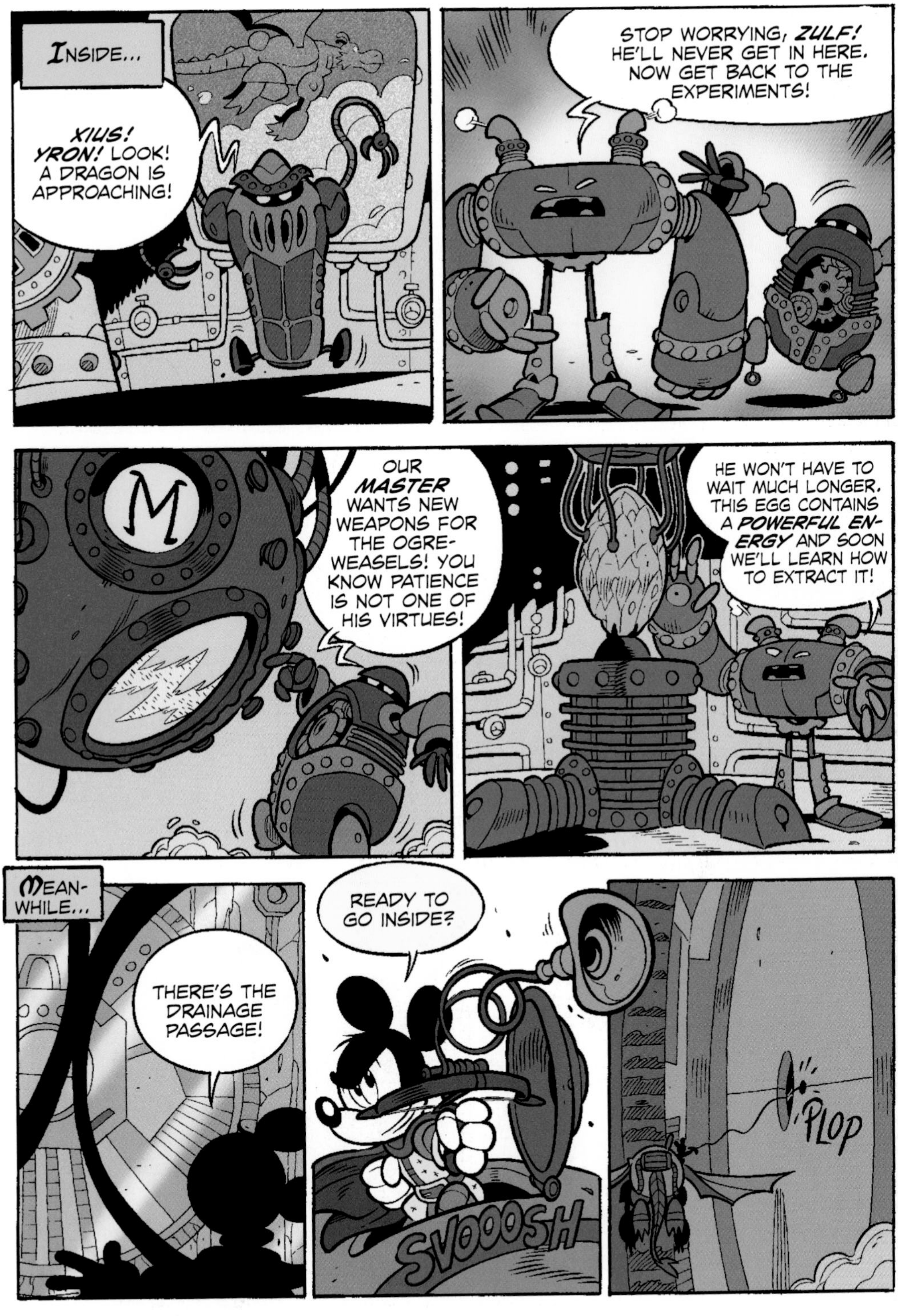
INSIDE...
XIUS! YRON! LOOK! A DRAGON IS APPROACHING!
STOP WORRYING, ZULF! HE'LL NEVER GET IN HERE. NOW GET BACK TO THE EXPERIMENTS!
OUR MASTER WANTS NEW WEAPONS FOR THE OGRE-WEASELS! YOU KNOW PATIENCE IS NOT ONE OF HIS VIRTUES!
HE WON'T HAVE TO WAIT MUCH LONGER. THIS EGG CONTAINS A POWERFUL ENERGY AND SOON WE'LL LEARN HOW TO EXTRACT IT!
MEANWHILE...
THERE'S THE DRAINAGE PASSAGE!
READY TO GO INSIDE?
SVOOOSH
PLOP

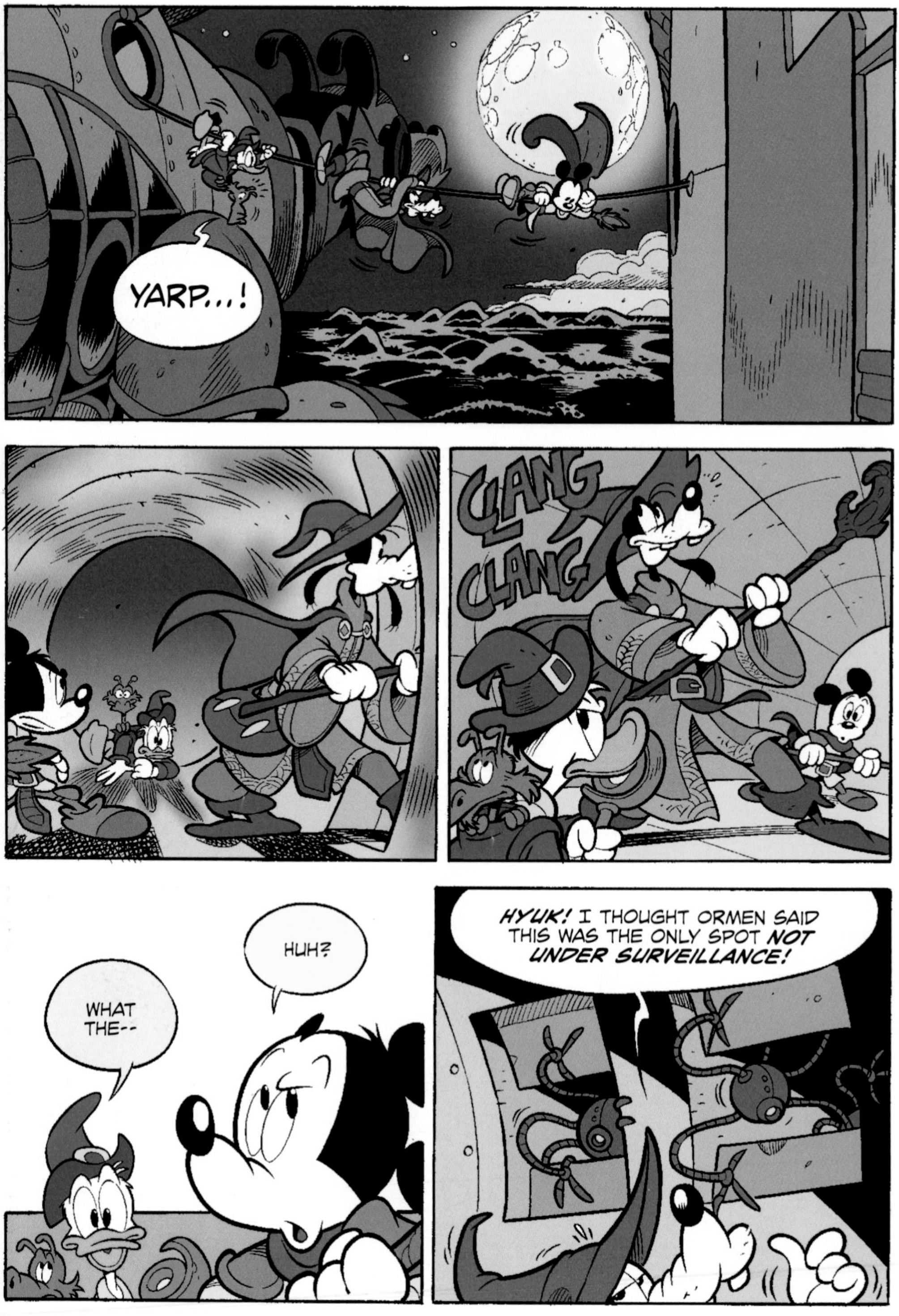
YARP...!
CLANG
CLANG
WHAT THE--
HUH?
HYUK! I THOUGHT ORMEN SAID THIS WAS THE ONLY SPOT NOT UNDER SURVEILLANCE!

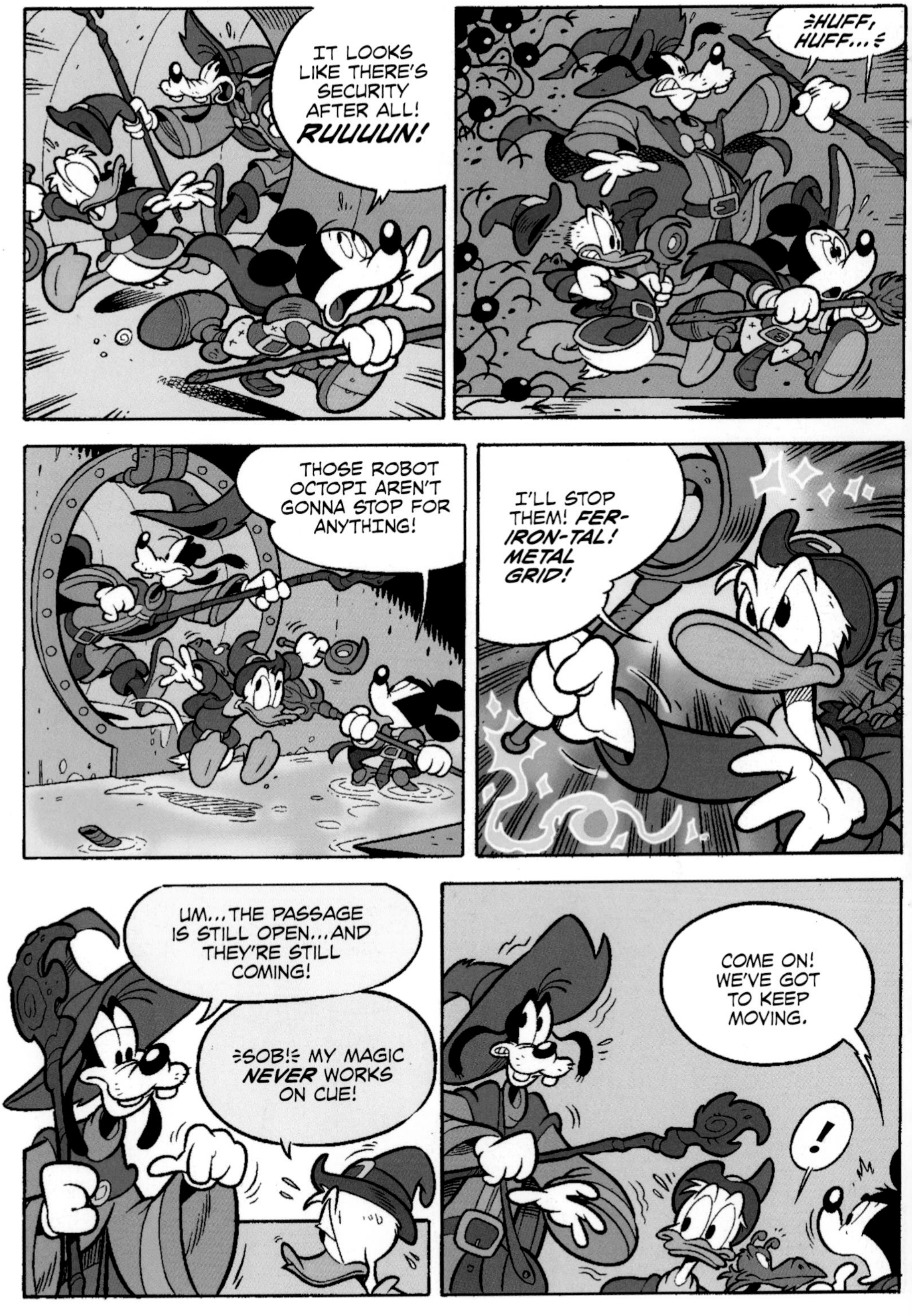
IT LOOKS LIKE THERE'S SECURITY AFTER ALL! *RUUUUN!*
≈HUFF, HUFF...≈
THOSE ROBOT OCTOPI AREN'T GONNA STOP FOR ANYTHING!
I'LL STOP THEM! *FER-IRON-TAL! METAL GRID!*
UM...THE PASSAGE IS STILL OPEN...AND THEY'RE STILL COMING!
≈SOB!≈ MY MAGIC *NEVER* WORKS ON CUE!
COME ON! WE'VE GOT TO KEEP MOVING.
!

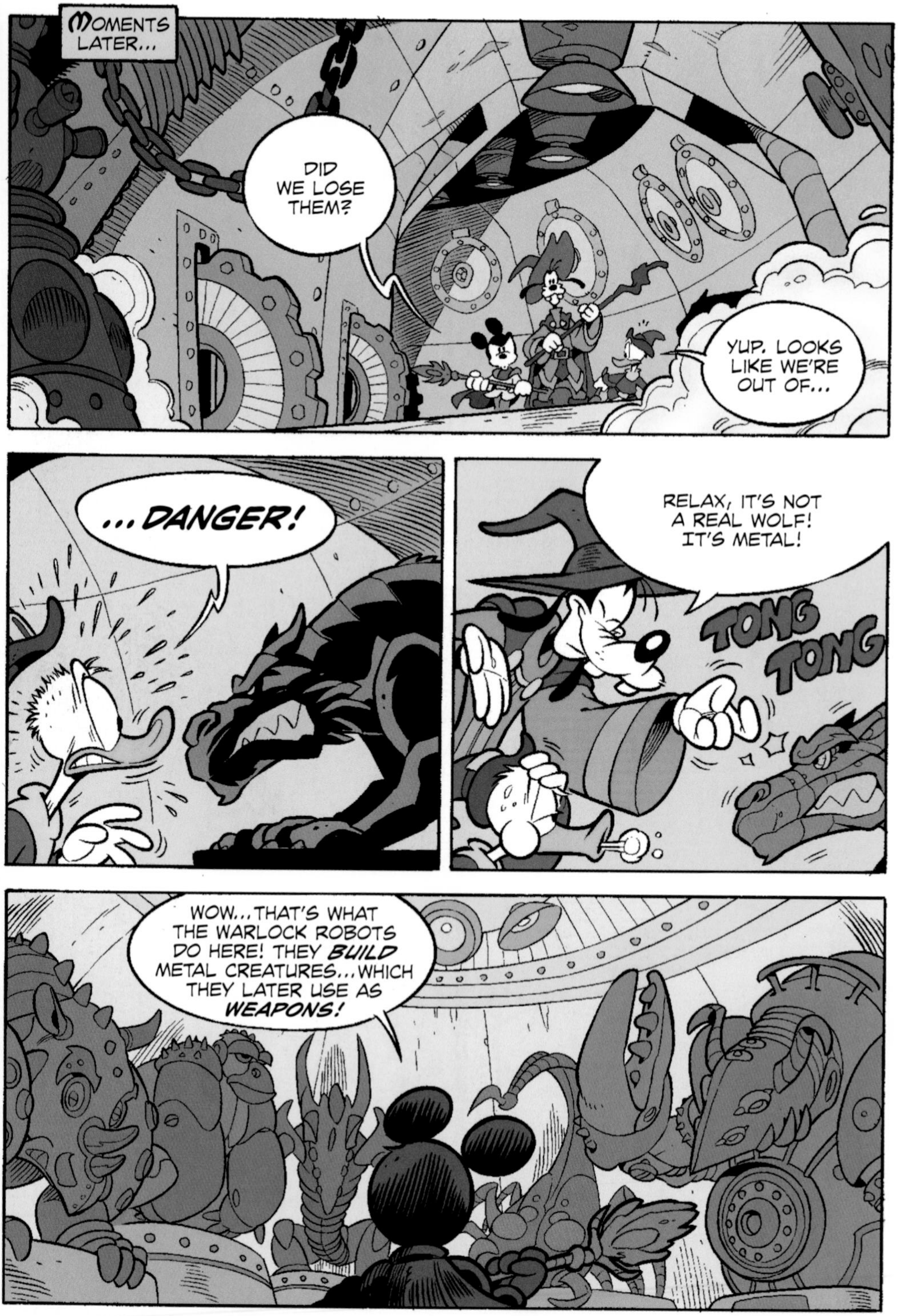
MOMENTS LATER...
DID WE LOSE THEM?
YUP. LOOKS LIKE WE'RE OUT OF...
...DANGER!
RELAX, IT'S NOT A REAL WOLF! IT'S METAL!
TONG TONG
WOW...THAT'S WHAT THE WARLOCK ROBOTS DO HERE! THEY BUILD METAL CREATURES...WHICH THEY LATER USE AS WEAPONS!

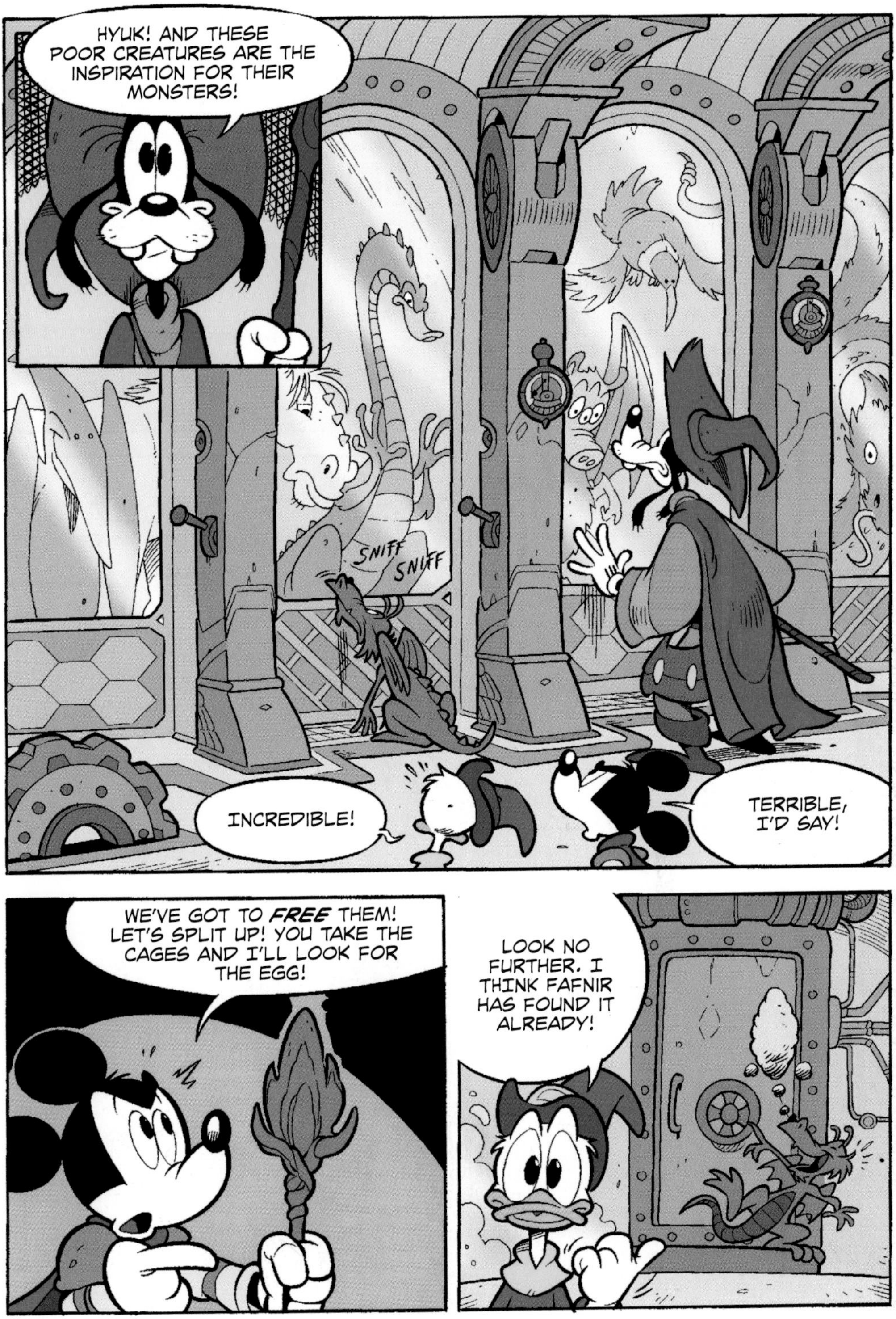
HYUK! AND THESE POOR CREATURES ARE THE INSPIRATION FOR THEIR MONSTERS!
SNIFF SNIFF
INCREDIBLE!
TERRIBLE, I'D SAY!
WE'VE GOT TO FREE THEM! LET'S SPLIT UP! YOU TAKE THE CAGES AND I'LL LOOK FOR THE EGG!
LOOK NO FURTHER. I THINK FAFNIR HAS FOUND IT ALREADY!

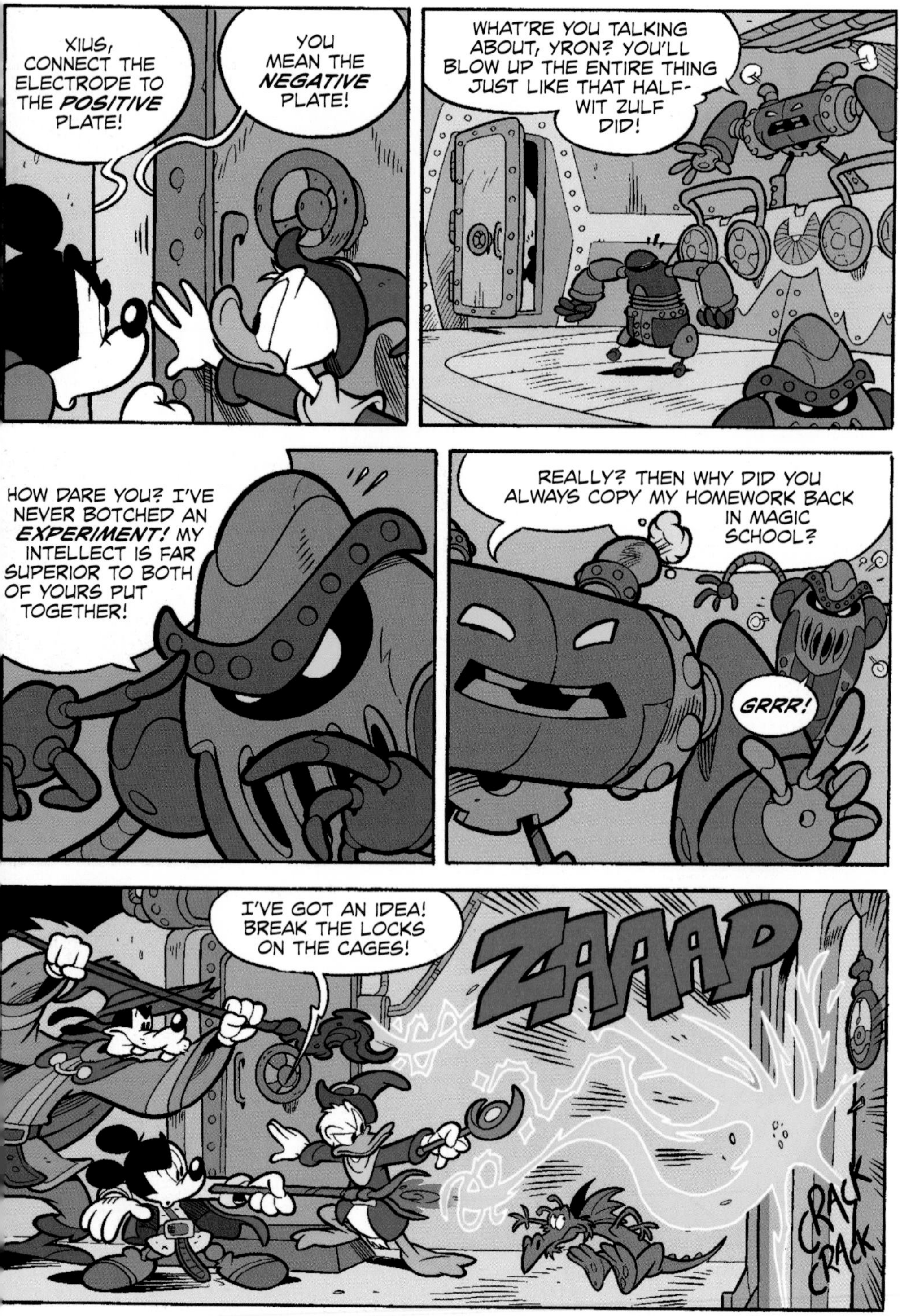
XIUS, CONNECT THE ELECTRODE TO THE *POSITIVE* PLATE!
YOU MEAN THE *NEGATIVE* PLATE!
WHAT'RE YOU TALKING ABOUT, YRON? YOU'LL BLOW UP THE ENTIRE THING JUST LIKE THAT HALF-WIT ZULF DID!
HOW DARE YOU? I'VE NEVER BOTCHED AN *EXPERIMENT!* MY INTELLECT IS FAR SUPERIOR TO BOTH OF YOURS PUT TOGETHER!
REALLY? THEN WHY DID YOU ALWAYS COPY MY HOMEWORK BACK IN MAGIC SCHOOL?
GRRR!
I'VE GOT AN IDEA! BREAK THE LOCKS ON THE CAGES!
ZAAAP
CRACK
CRACK

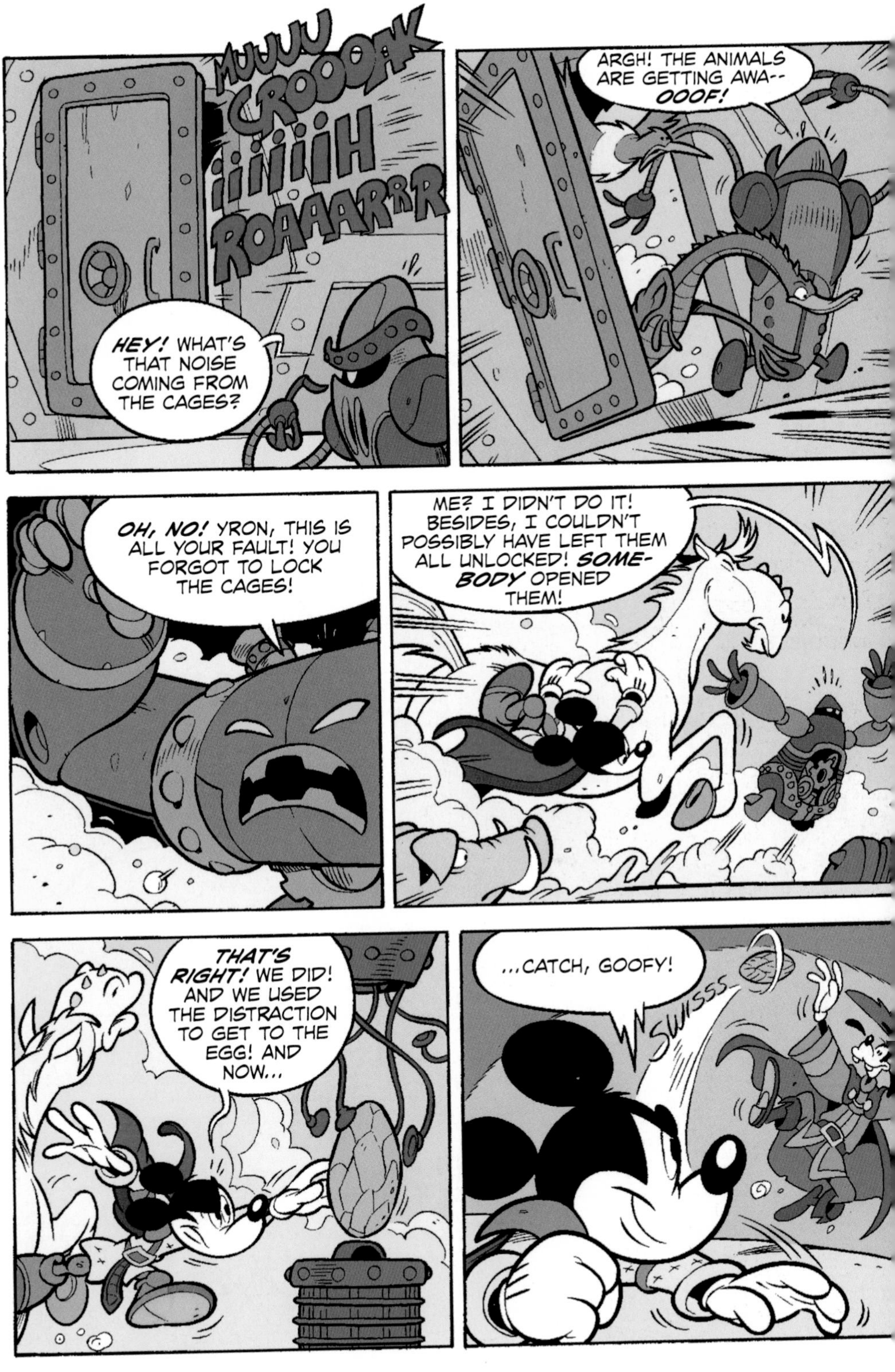
MUUUU
CROOOAK
iiiiiiH
ROAAARRR
HEY! WHAT'S THAT NOISE COMING FROM THE CAGES?
ARGH! THE ANIMALS ARE GETTING AWA-- OOOF!
OH, NO! YRON, THIS IS ALL YOUR FAULT! YOU FORGOT TO LOCK THE CAGES!
ME? I DIDN'T DO IT! BESIDES, I COULDN'T POSSIBLY HAVE LEFT THEM ALL UNLOCKED! SOME-BODY OPENED THEM!
THAT'S RIGHT! WE DID! AND WE USED THE DISTRACTION TO GET TO THE EGG! AND NOW...
...CATCH, GOOFY!
SWISSS

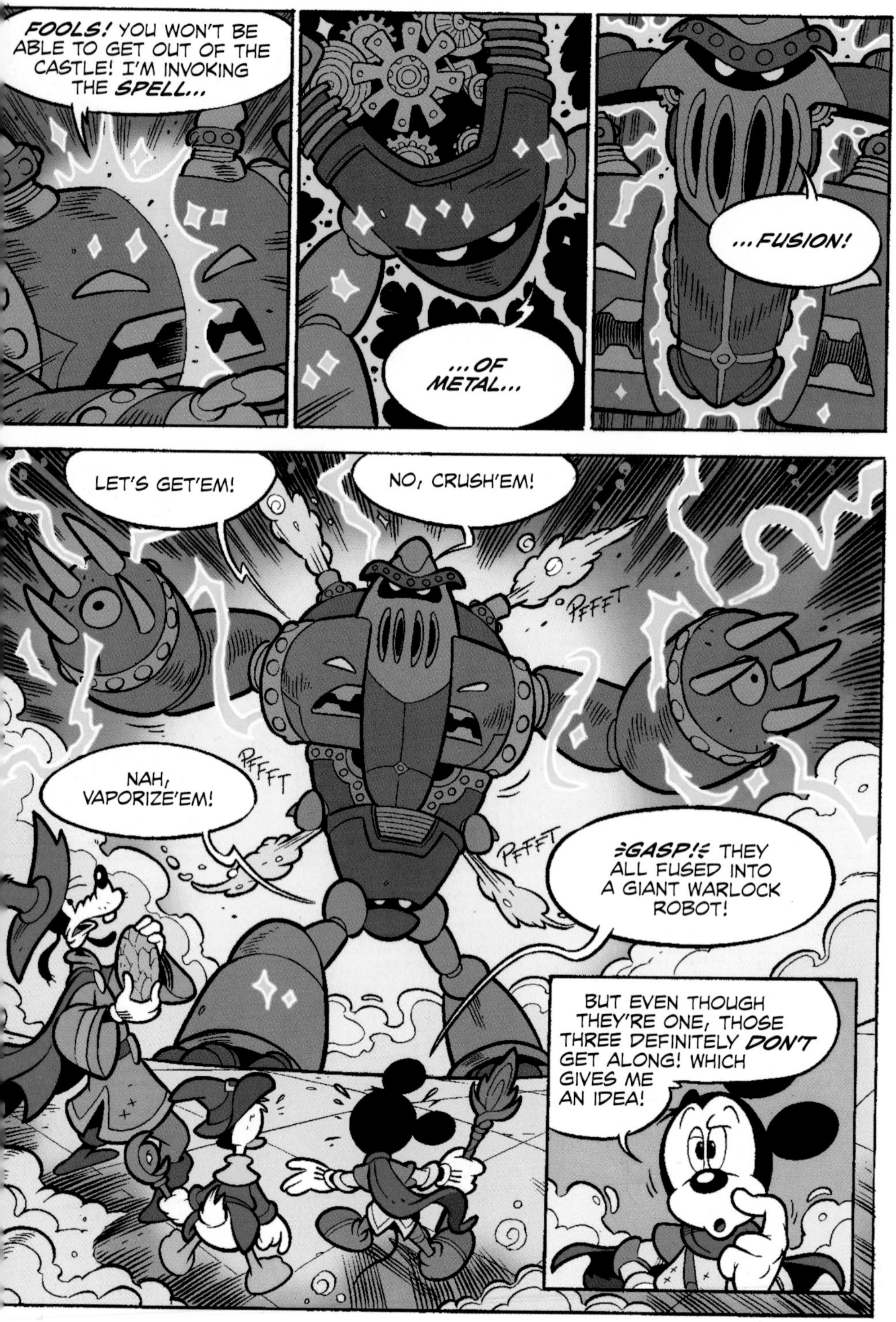
FOOLS! YOU WON'T BE ABLE TO GET OUT OF THE CASTLE! I'M INVOKING THE SPELL...
...OF METAL...
...FUSION!
LET'S GET'EM!
NO, CRUSH'EM!
PFFFT
NAH, VAPORIZE'EM!
PFFFT
PFFFT
GASP! THEY ALL FUSED INTO A GIANT WARLOCK ROBOT!
BUT EVEN THOUGH THEY'RE ONE, THOSE THREE DEFINITELY DON'T GET ALONG! WHICH GIVES ME AN IDEA!

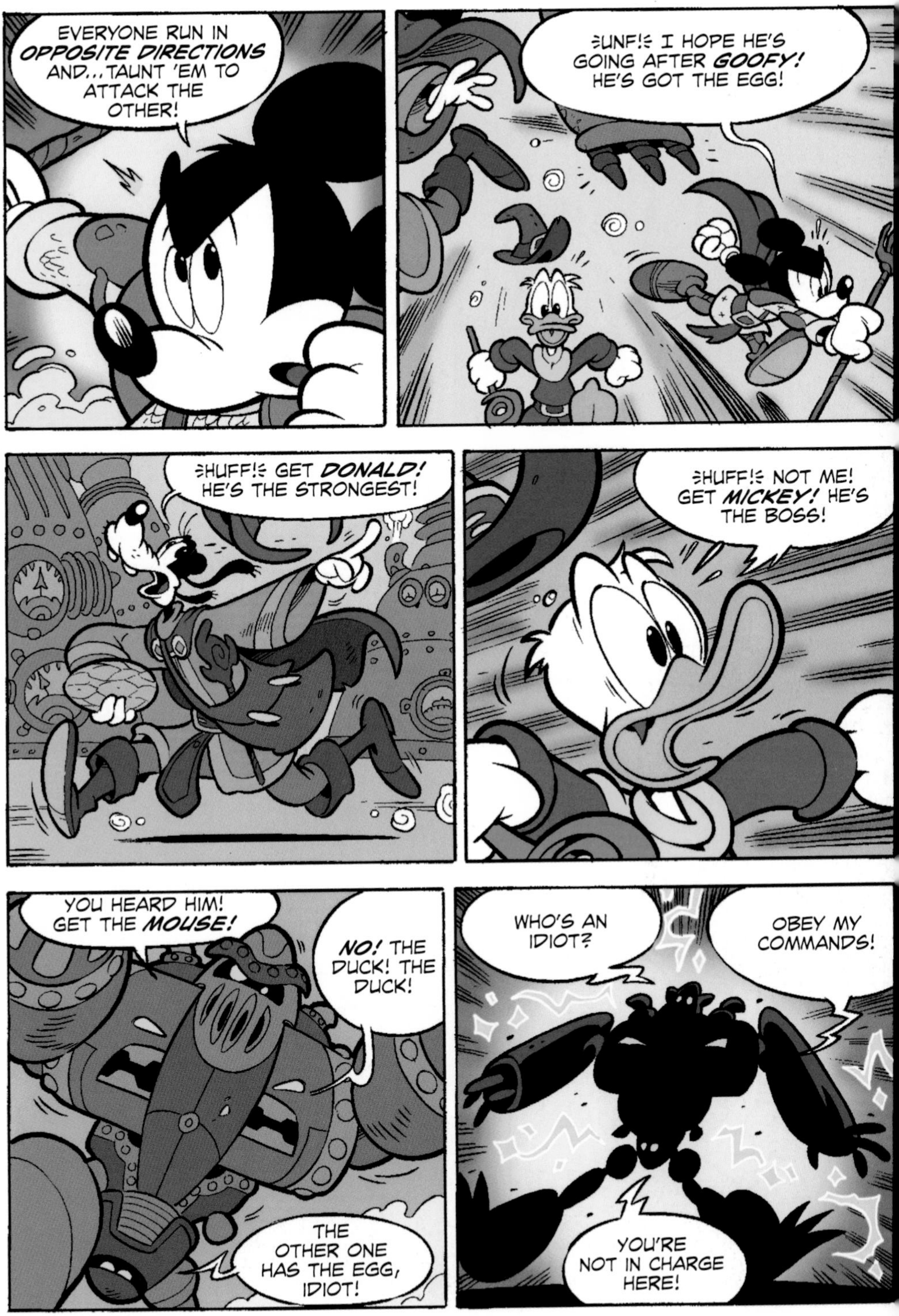
EVERYONE RUN IN OPPOSITE DIRECTIONS AND...TAUNT 'EM TO ATTACK THE OTHER!
UNF! I HOPE HE'S GOING AFTER GOOFY! HE'S GOT THE EGG!
HUFF! GET DONALD! HE'S THE STRONGEST!
HUFF! NOT ME! GET MICKEY! HE'S THE BOSS!
YOU HEARD HIM! GET THE MOUSE!
NO! THE DUCK! THE DUCK!
THE OTHER ONE HAS THE EGG, IDIOT!
WHO'S AN IDIOT?
OBEY MY COMMANDS!
YOU'RE NOT IN CHARGE HERE!

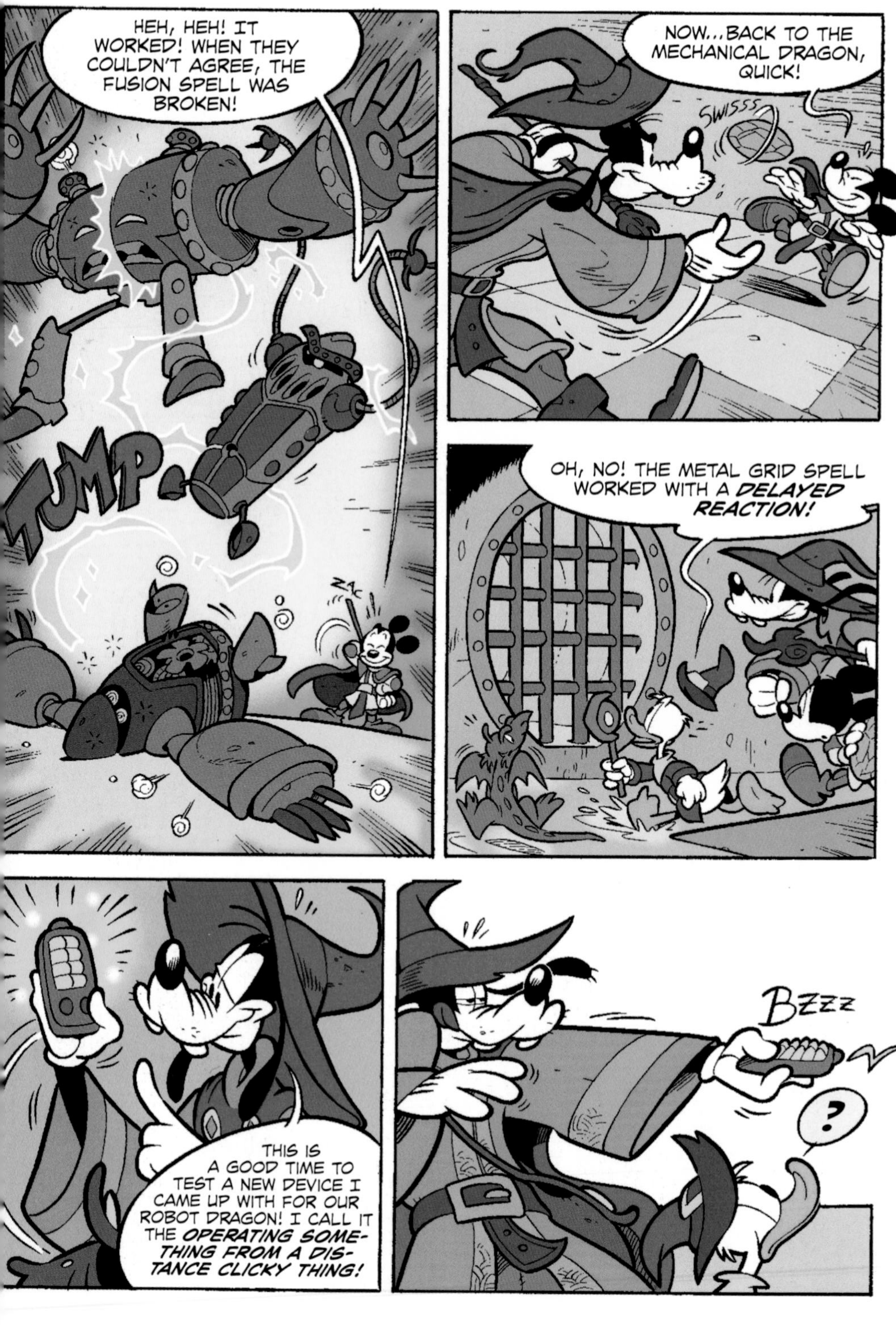
HEH, HEH! IT WORKED! WHEN THEY COULDN'T AGREE, THE FUSION SPELL WAS BROKEN!
TUMP
ZAC
NOW... BACK TO THE MECHANICAL DRAGON, QUICK!
SWISSS
OH, NO! THE METAL GRID SPELL WORKED WITH A DELAYED REACTION!
THIS IS A GOOD TIME TO TEST A NEW DEVICE I CAME UP WITH FOR OUR ROBOT DRAGON! I CALL IT THE OPERATING SOMETHING FROM A DISTANCE CLICKY THING!
BZZZ
?

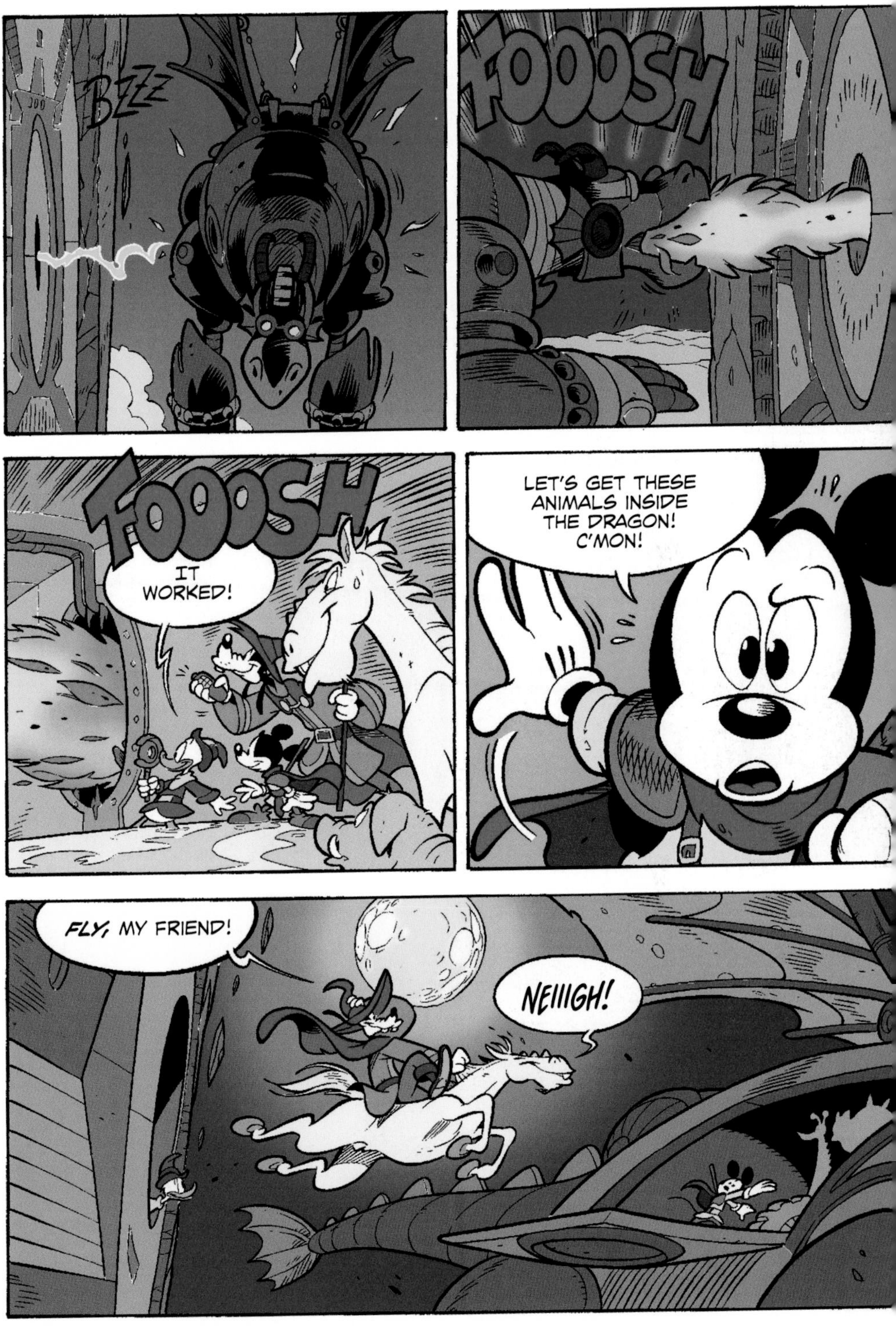
BZZZ
FOOOOSH
FOOOSH
IT WORKED!
LET'S GET THESE ANIMALS INSIDE THE DRAGON! C'MON!
FLY, MY FRIEND!
NEIIIGH!

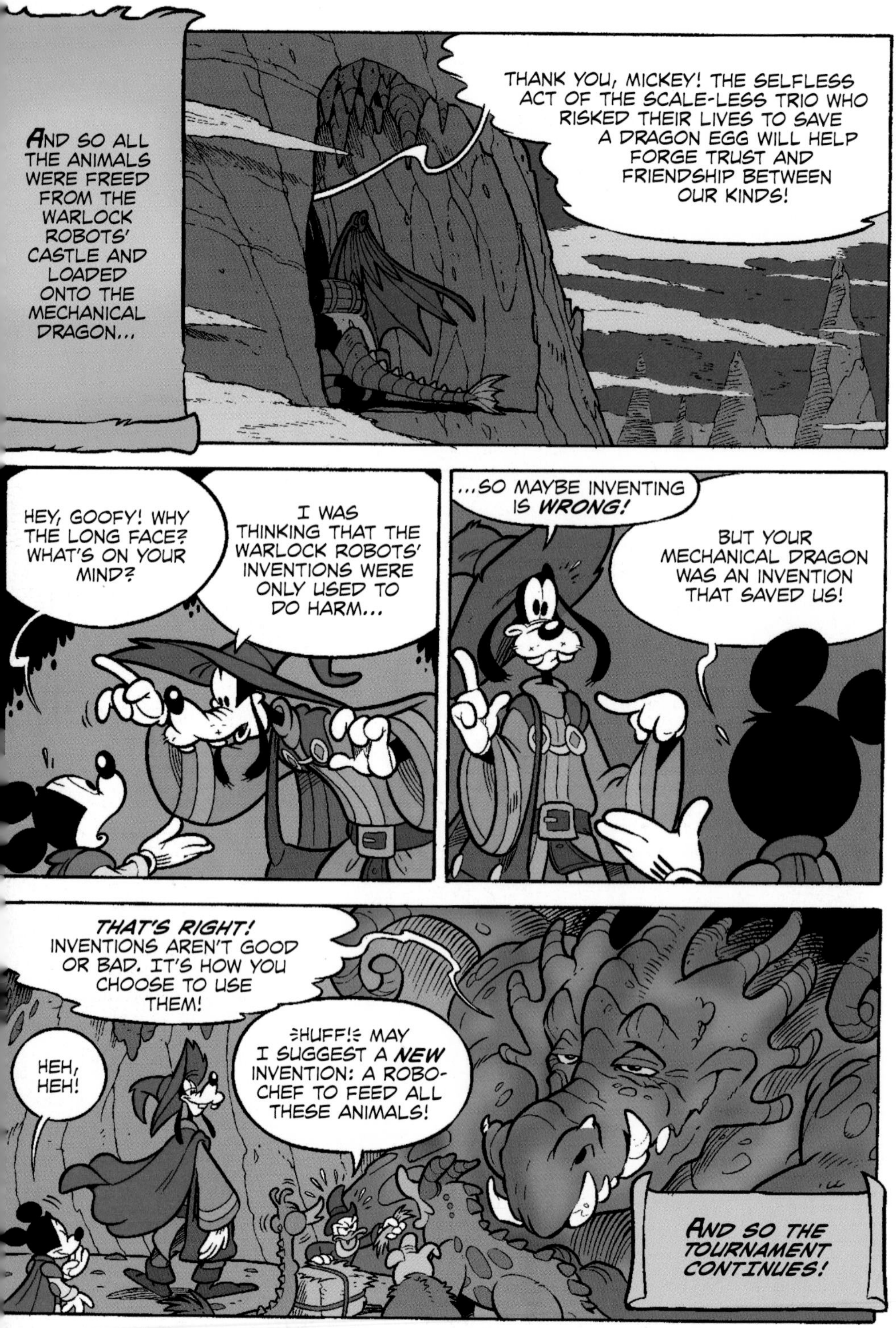
AND SO ALL THE ANIMALS WERE FREED FROM THE WARLOCK ROBOTS' CASTLE AND LOADED ONTO THE MECHANICAL DRAGON...
THANK YOU, MICKEY! THE SELFLESS ACT OF THE SCALE-LESS TRIO WHO RISKED THEIR LIVES TO SAVE A DRAGON EGG WILL HELP FORGE TRUST AND FRIENDSHIP BETWEEN OUR KINDS!
HEY, GOOFY! WHY THE LONG FACE? WHAT'S ON YOUR MIND?
I WAS THINKING THAT THE WARLOCK ROBOTS' INVENTIONS WERE ONLY USED TO DO HARM...
...SO MAYBE INVENTING IS WRONG!
BUT YOUR MECHANICAL DRAGON WAS AN INVENTION THAT SAVED US!
THAT'S RIGHT! INVENTIONS AREN'T GOOD OR BAD. IT'S HOW YOU CHOOSE TO USE THEM!
HEH, HEH!
HUFF! MAY I SUGGEST A NEW INVENTION: A ROBO-CHEF TO FEED ALL THESE ANIMALS!
AND SO THE TOURNAMENT CONTINUES!

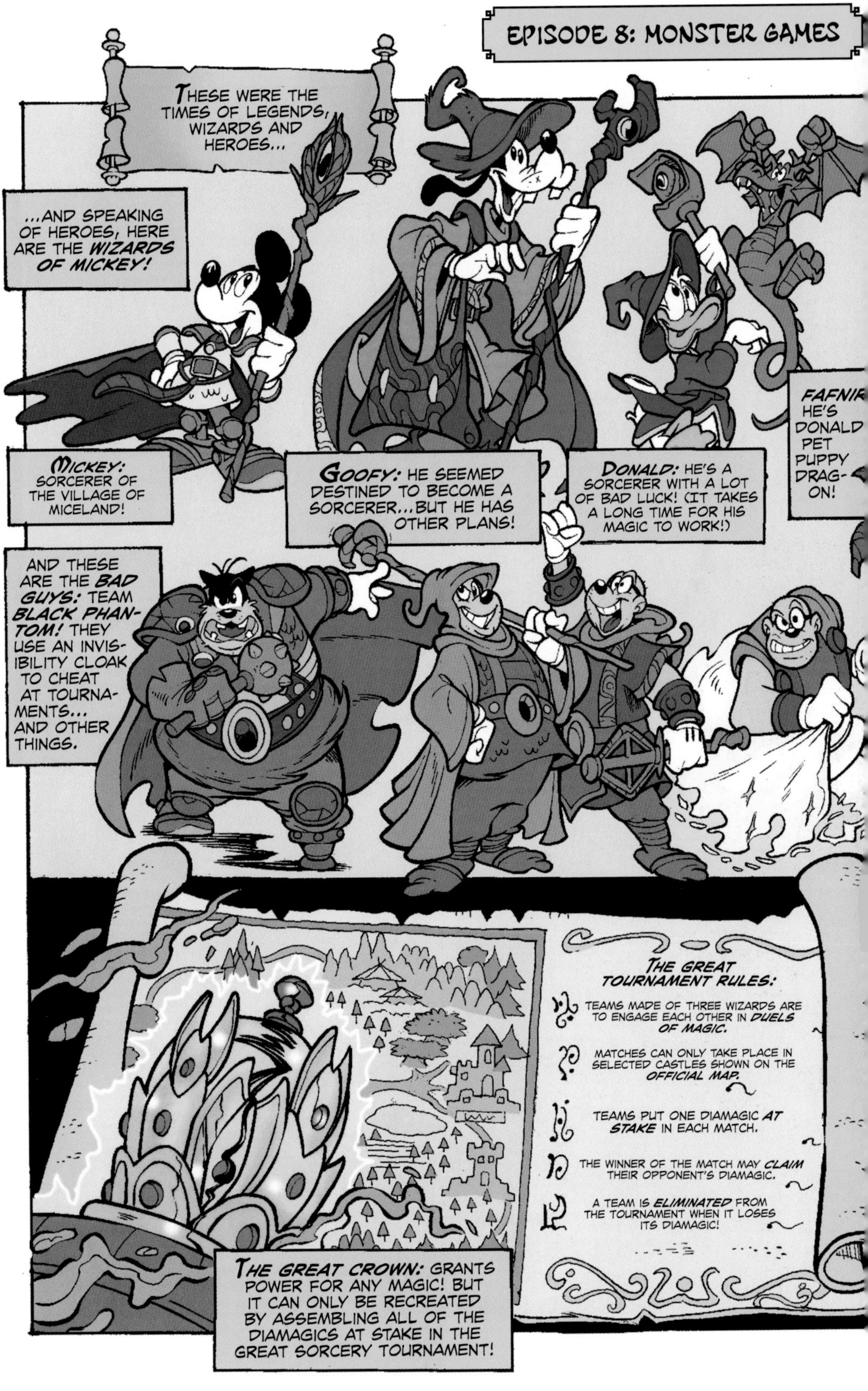
EPISODE 8: MONSTER GAMES
THESE WERE THE TIMES OF LEGENDS, WIZARDS AND HEROES...
...AND SPEAKING OF HEROES, HERE ARE THE WIZARDS OF MICKEY!
MICKEY: SORCERER OF THE VILLAGE OF MICELAND!
GOOFY: HE SEEMED DESTINED TO BECOME A SORCERER...BUT HE HAS OTHER PLANS!
DONALD: HE'S A SORCERER WITH A LOT OF BAD LUCK! (IT TAKES A LONG TIME FOR HIS MAGIC TO WORK!)
FAFNIR HE'S DONALD PET PUPPY DRAG-ON!
AND THESE ARE THE BAD GUYS: TEAM BLACK PHANTOM! THEY USE AN INVISIBILITY CLOAK TO CHEAT AT TOURNAMENTS... AND OTHER THINGS.
THE GREAT TOURNAMENT RULES:
TEAMS MADE OF THREE WIZARDS ARE TO ENGAGE EACH OTHER IN DUELS OF MAGIC.
MATCHES CAN ONLY TAKE PLACE IN SELECTED CASTLES SHOWN ON THE OFFICIAL MAP.
TEAMS PUT ONE DIAMAGIC AT STAKE IN EACH MATCH.
THE WINNER OF THE MATCH MAY CLAIM THEIR OPPONENT'S DIAMAGIC.
A TEAM IS ELIMINATED FROM THE TOURNAMENT WHEN IT LOSES ITS DIAMAGIC!
THE GREAT CROWN: GRANTS POWER FOR ANY MAGIC! BUT IT CAN ONLY BE RECREATED BY ASSEMBLING ALL OF THE DIAMAGICS AT STAKE IN THE GREAT SORCERY TOURNAMENT!

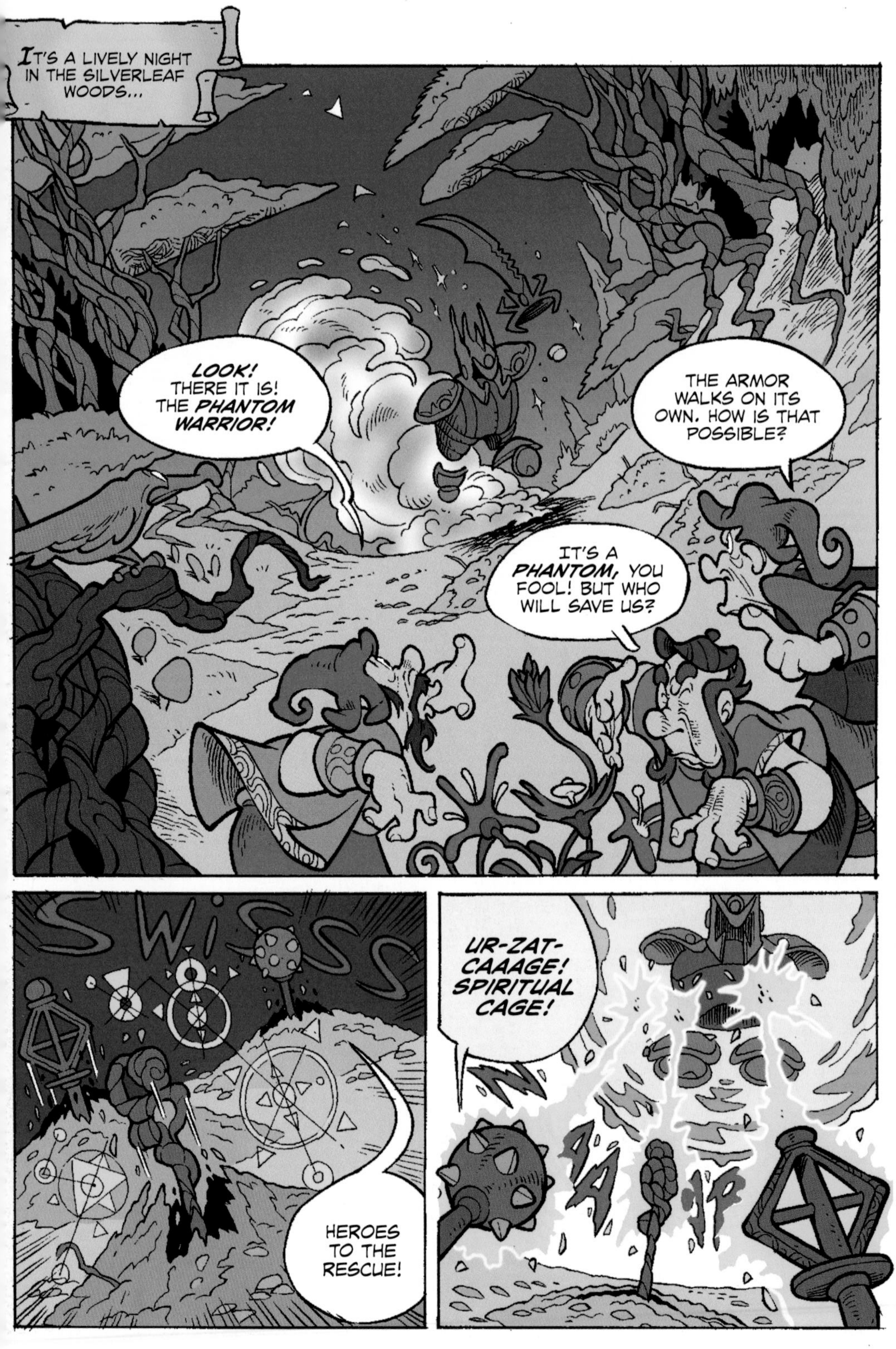
IT'S A LIVELY NIGHT IN THE SILVERLEAF WOODS...
LOOK! THERE IT IS! THE *PHANTOM WARRIOR!*
THE ARMOR WALKS ON ITS OWN. HOW IS THAT POSSIBLE?
IT'S A *PHANTOM,* YOU FOOL! BUT WHO WILL SAVE US?
SWISSS
HEROES TO THE RESCUE!
UR-ZAT-CAAAGE! SPIRITUAL CAGE!

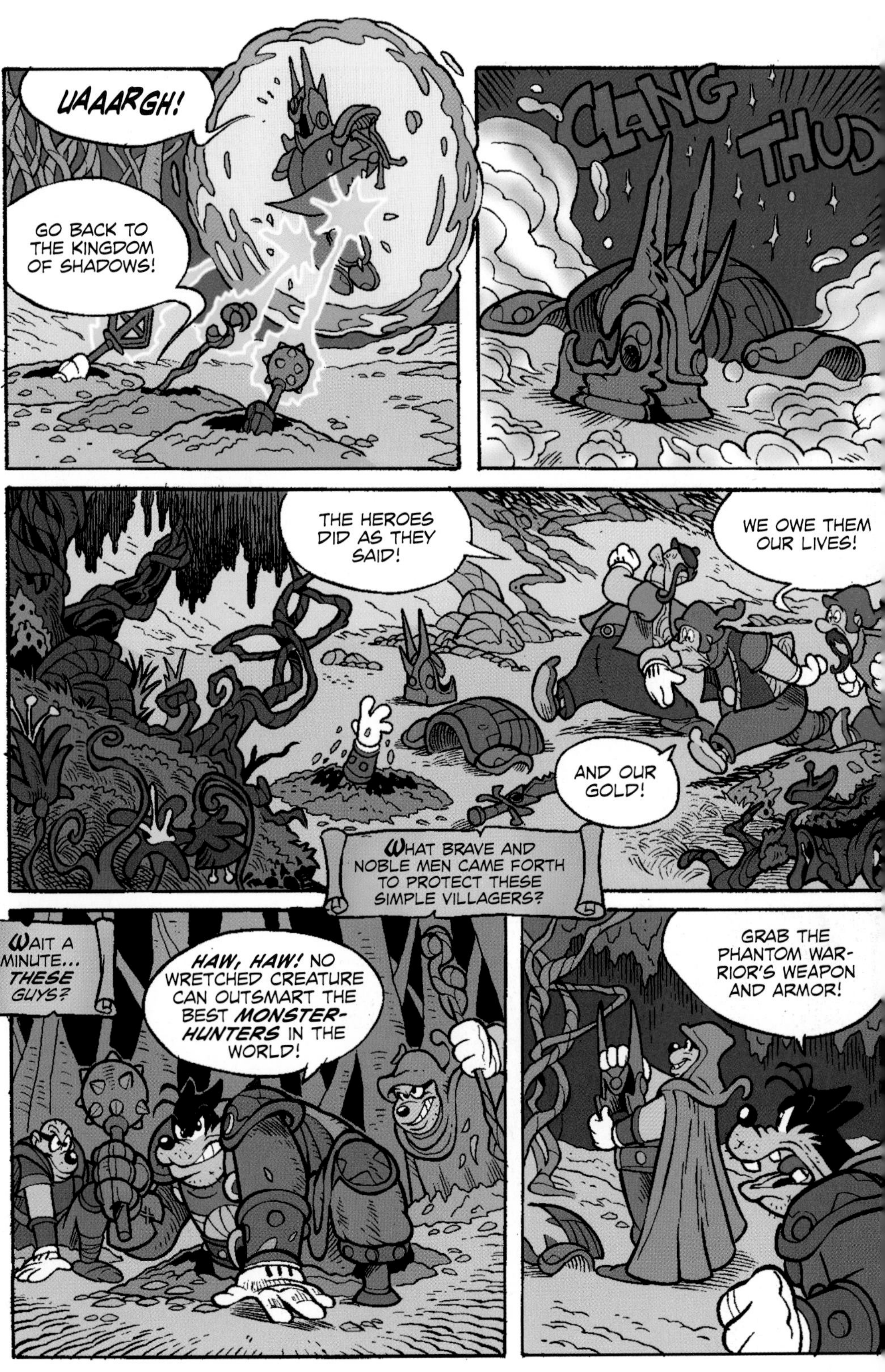
UAAARGH!
GO BACK TO THE KINGDOM OF SHADOWS!
CLANG
THUD
THE HEROES DID AS THEY SAID!
WE OWE THEM OUR LIVES!
AND OUR GOLD!
WHAT BRAVE AND NOBLE MEN CAME FORTH TO PROTECT THESE SIMPLE VILLAGERS?
WAIT A MINUTE... THESE GUYS?
HAW, HAW! NO WRETCHED CREATURE CAN OUTSMART THE BEST MONSTER-HUNTERS IN THE WORLD!
GRAB THE PHANTOM WARRIOR'S WEAPON AND ARMOR!

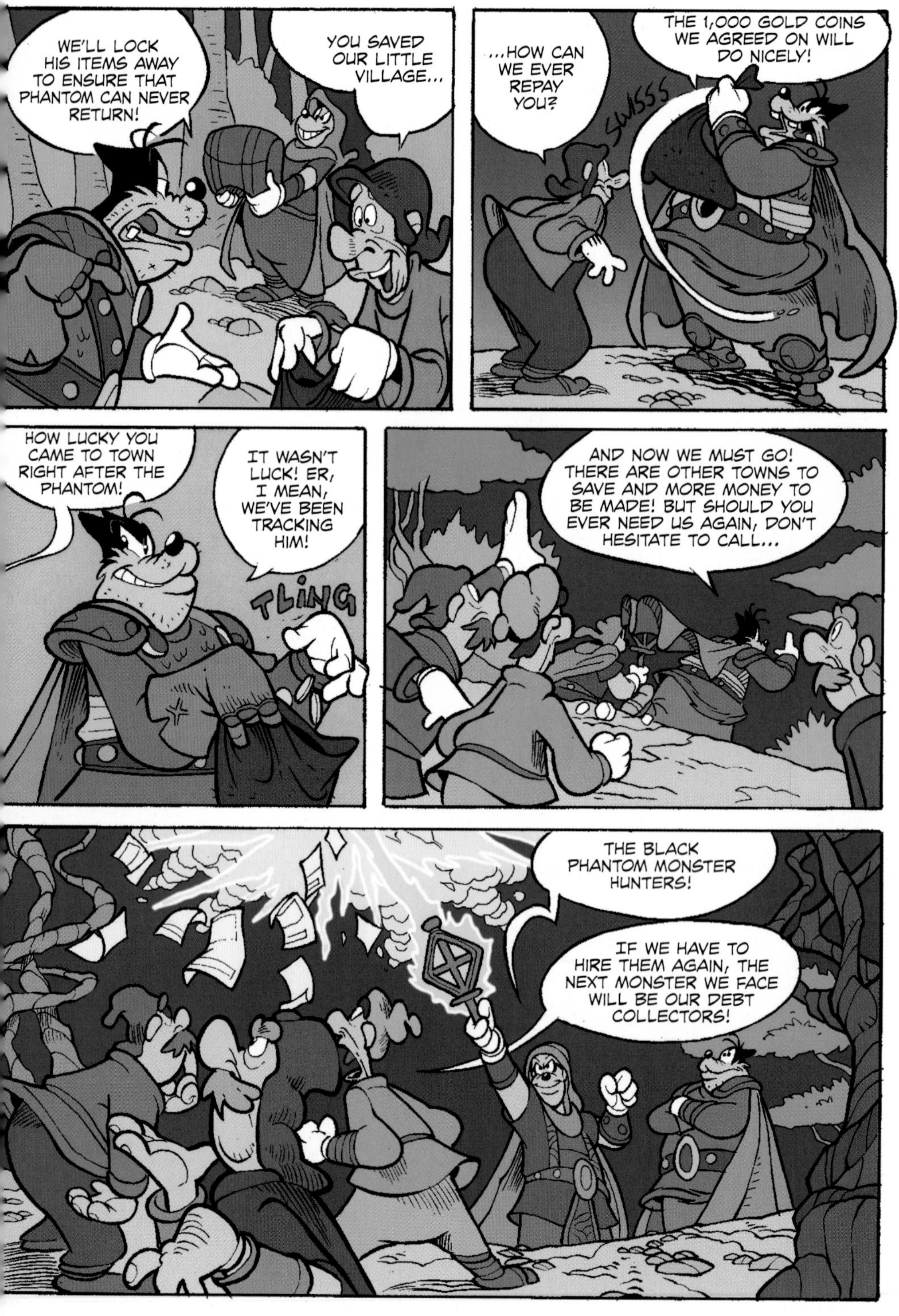
WE'LL LOCK HIS ITEMS AWAY TO ENSURE THAT PHANTOM CAN NEVER RETURN!
YOU SAVED OUR LITTLE VILLAGE...
...HOW CAN WE EVER REPAY YOU?
THE 1,000 GOLD COINS WE AGREED ON WILL DO NICELY!
SWISSS
HOW LUCKY YOU CAME TO TOWN RIGHT AFTER THE PHANTOM!
IT WASN'T LUCK! ER, I MEAN, WE'VE BEEN TRACKING HIM!
TLING
AND NOW WE MUST GO! THERE ARE OTHER TOWNS TO SAVE AND MORE MONEY TO BE MADE! BUT SHOULD YOU EVER NEED US AGAIN, DON'T HESITATE TO CALL...
THE BLACK PHANTOM MONSTER HUNTERS!
IF WE HAVE TO HIRE THEM AGAIN, THE NEXT MONSTER WE FACE WILL BE OUR DEBT COLLECTORS!

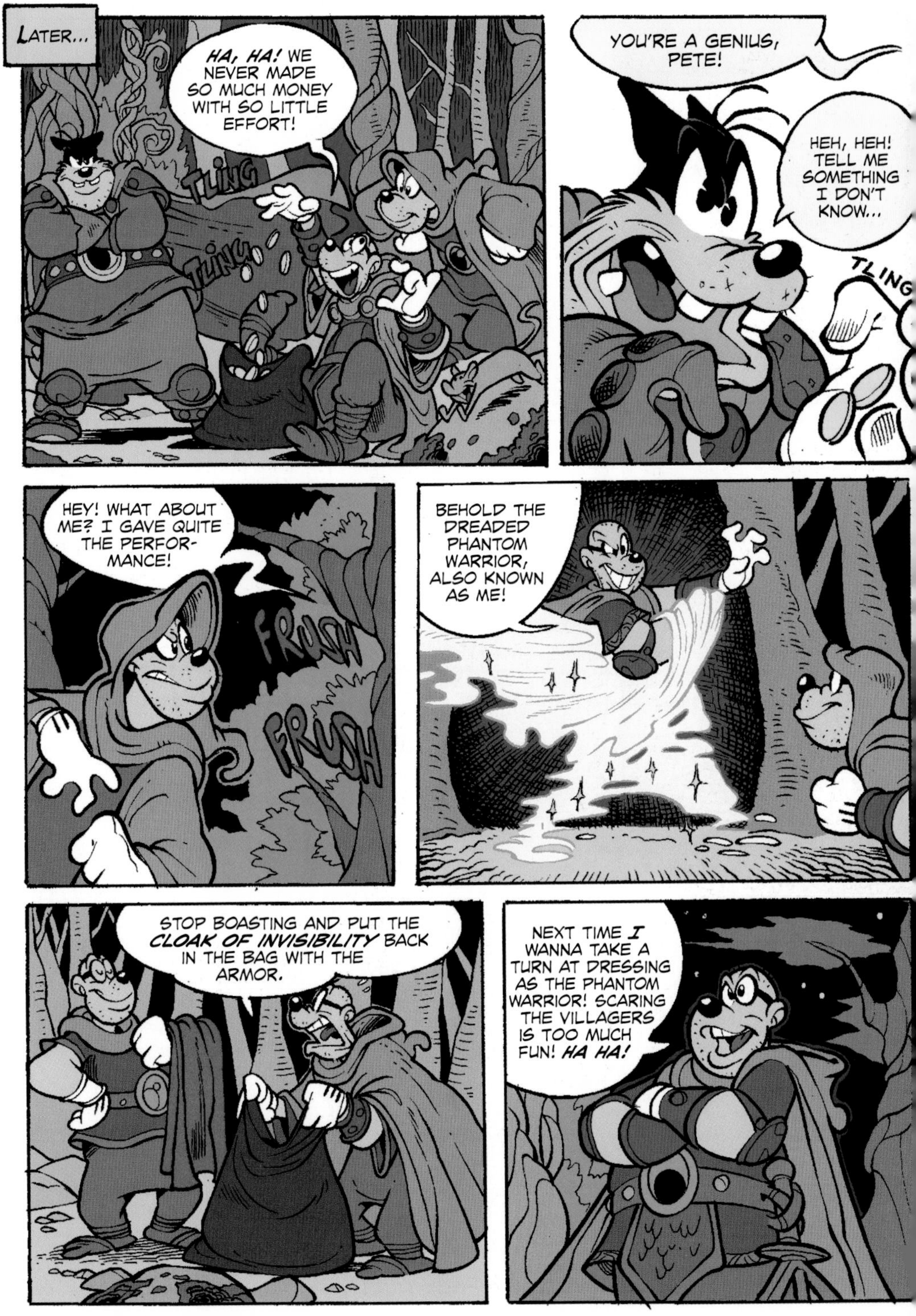
LATER...
HA, HA! WE NEVER MADE SO MUCH MONEY WITH SO LITTLE EFFORT!
TLING
TLING
YOU'RE A GENIUS, PETE!
HEH, HEH! TELL ME SOMETHING I DON'T KNOW...
TLING
HEY! WHAT ABOUT ME? I GAVE QUITE THE PERFOR-MANCE!
FRUSH
FRUSH
BEHOLD THE DREADED PHANTOM WARRIOR, ALSO KNOWN AS ME!
STOP BOASTING AND PUT THE CLOAK OF INVISIBILITY BACK IN THE BAG WITH THE ARMOR.
NEXT TIME I WANNA TAKE A TURN AT DRESSING AS THE PHANTOM WARRIOR! SCARING THE VILLAGERS IS TOO MUCH FUN! HA HA!

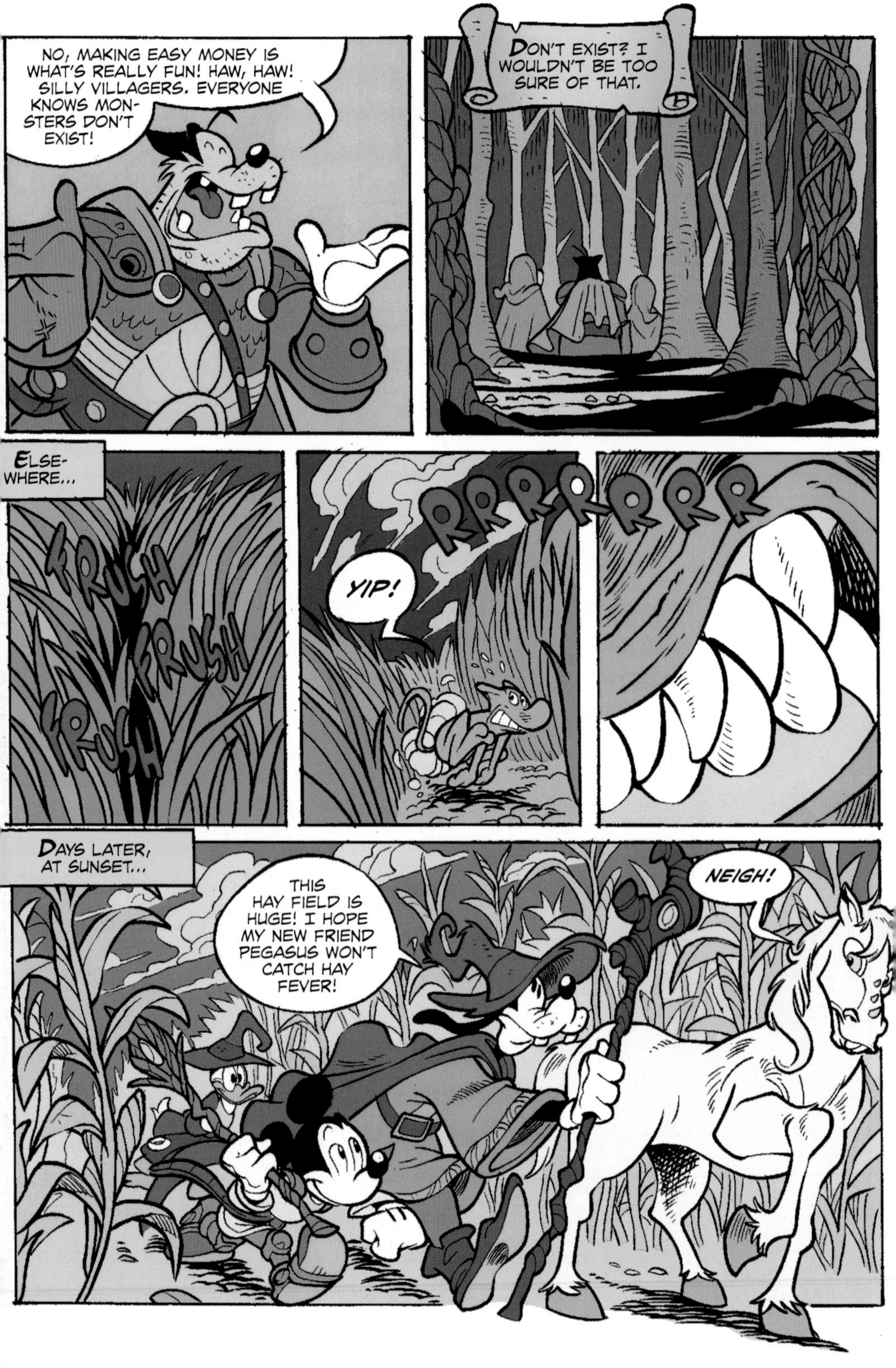
NO, MAKING EASY MONEY IS WHAT'S REALLY FUN! HAW, HAW! SILLY VILLAGERS. EVERYONE KNOWS MONSTERS DON'T EXIST!
DON'T EXIST? I WOULDN'T BE TOO SURE OF THAT.
ELSEWHERE...
FRUSH
FRUSH
FRUSH
RRRRRRRR
YIP!
DAYS LATER, AT SUNSET...
THIS HAY FIELD IS HUGE! I HOPE MY NEW FRIEND PEGASUS WON'T CATCH HAY FEVER!
NEIGH!

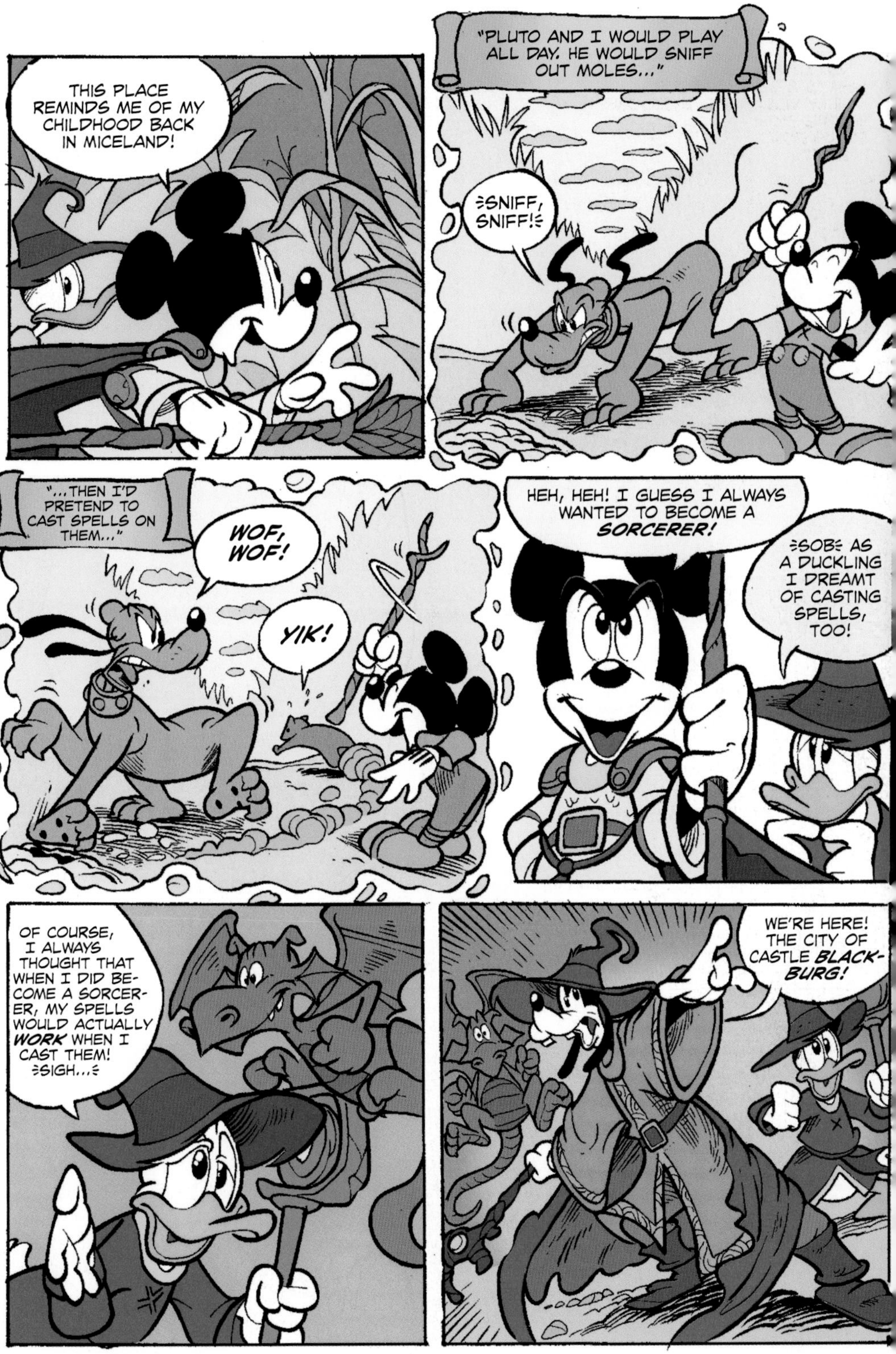
THIS PLACE REMINDS ME OF MY CHILDHOOD BACK IN MICELAND!
"PLUTO AND I WOULD PLAY ALL DAY. HE WOULD SNIFF OUT MOLES..."
SNIFF, SNIFF!
"...THEN I'D PRETEND TO CAST SPELLS ON THEM..."
WOF, WOF!
YIK!
HEH, HEH! I GUESS I ALWAYS WANTED TO BECOME A SORCERER!
SOB AS A DUCKLING I DREAMT OF CASTING SPELLS, TOO!
OF COURSE, I ALWAYS THOUGHT THAT WHEN I DID BECOME A SORCERER, MY SPELLS WOULD ACTUALLY WORK WHEN I CAST THEM! SIGH...
WE'RE HERE! THE CITY OF CASTLE BLACKBURG!

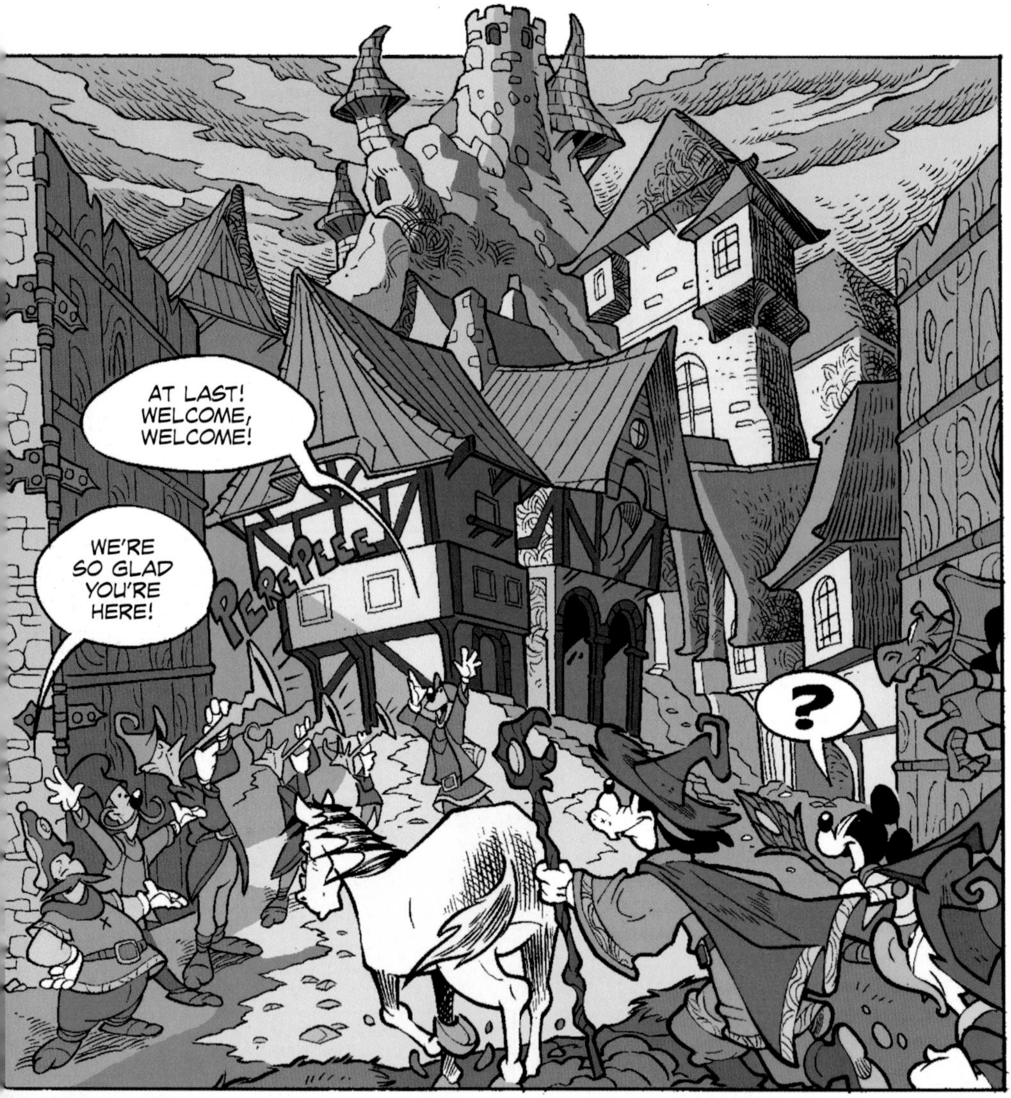
AT LAST! WELCOME, WELCOME!
WE'RE SO GLAD YOU'RE HERE!
PEREPEEE
?

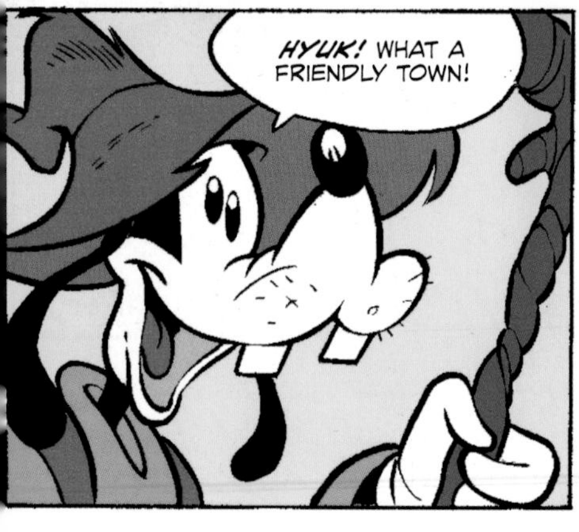
HYUK! WHAT A FRIENDLY TOWN!

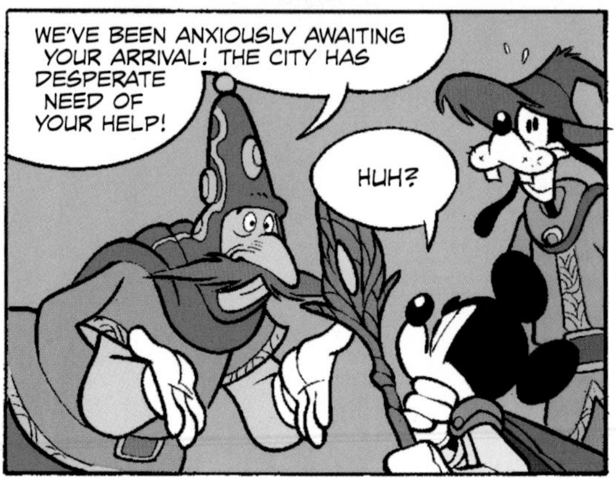
WE'VE BEEN ANXIOUSLY AWAITING YOUR ARRIVAL! THE CITY HAS DESPERATE NEED OF YOUR HELP!
HUH?

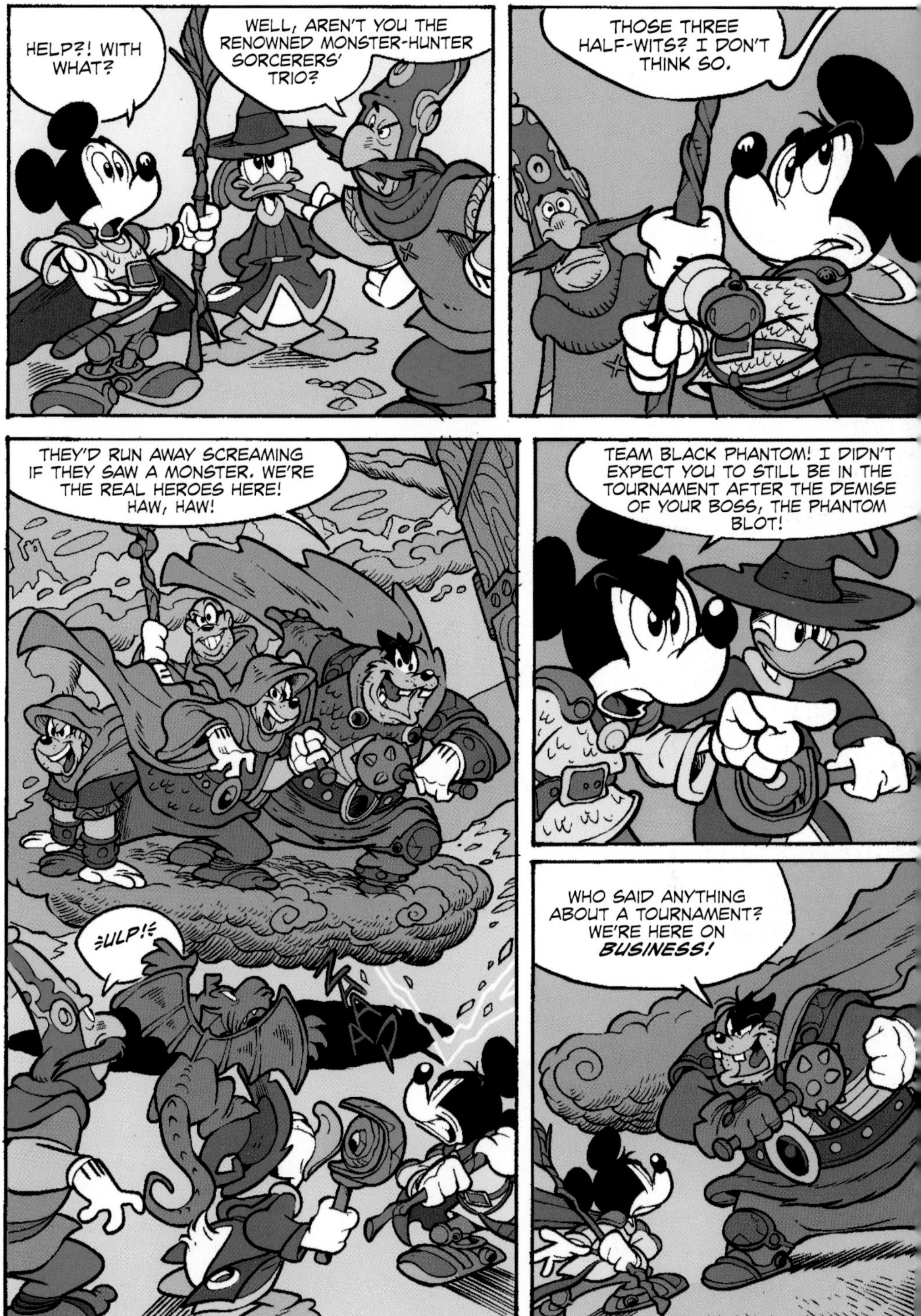
HELP?! WITH WHAT?
WELL, AREN'T YOU THE RENOWNED MONSTER-HUNTER SORCERERS' TRIO?
THOSE THREE HALF-WITS? I DON'T THINK SO.
THEY'D RUN AWAY SCREAMING IF THEY SAW A MONSTER. WE'RE THE REAL HEROES HERE! HAW, HAW!
ULP!
TEAM BLACK PHANTOM! I DIDN'T EXPECT YOU TO STILL BE IN THE TOURNAMENT AFTER THE DEMISE OF YOUR BOSS, THE PHANTOM BLOT!
WHO SAID ANYTHING ABOUT A TOURNAMENT? WE'RE HERE ON BUSINESS!

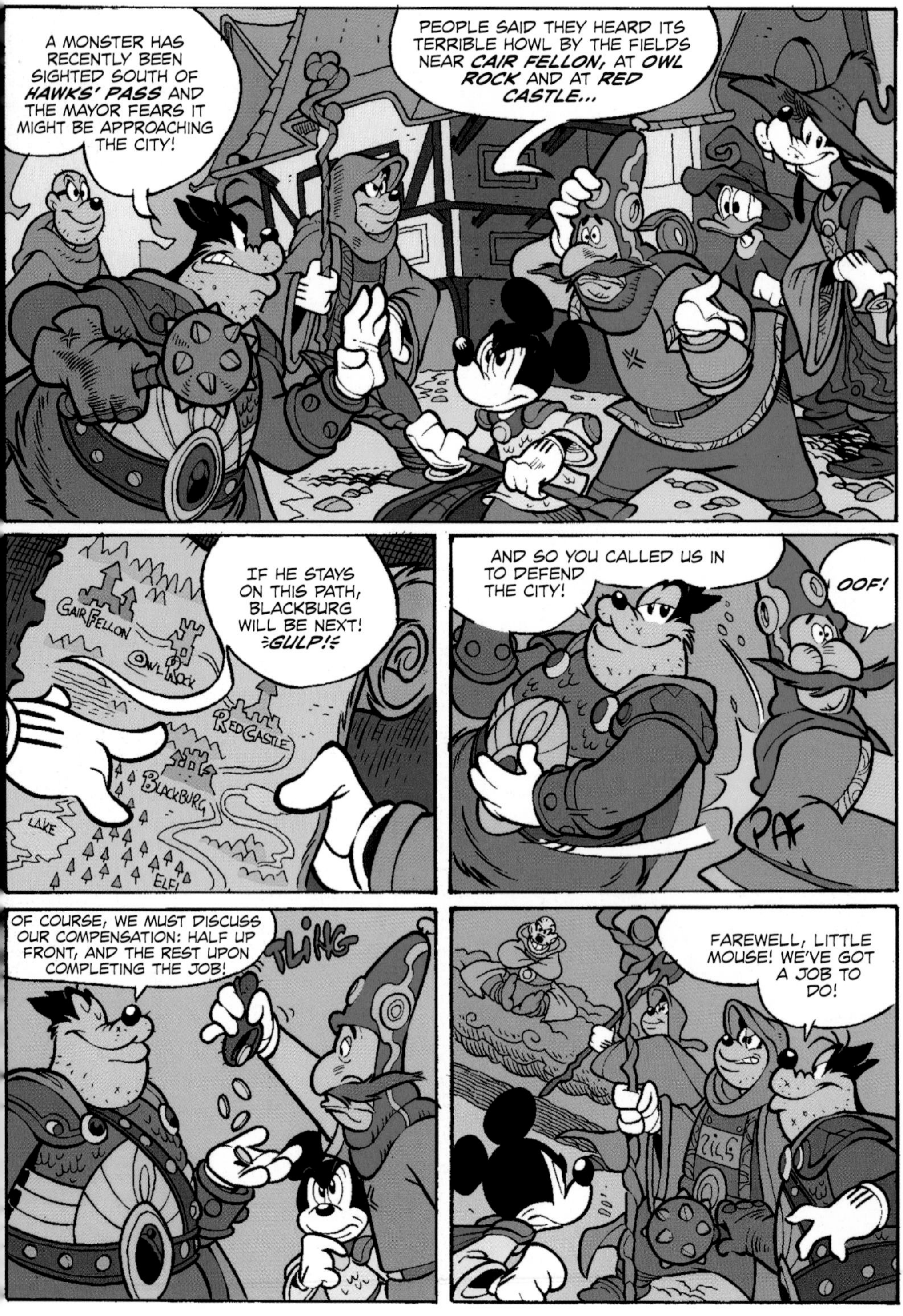
A MONSTER HAS RECENTLY BEEN SIGHTED SOUTH OF HAWKS' PASS AND THE MAYOR FEARS IT MIGHT BE APPROACHING THE CITY!
PEOPLE SAID THEY HEARD ITS TERRIBLE HOWL BY THE FIELDS NEAR CAIR FELLON, AT OWL ROCK AND AT RED CASTLE...
GAIR FELLON
OWL ROCK
RED CASTLE
BLACKBURG
LAKE
ELFI
IF HE STAYS ON THIS PATH, BLACKBURG WILL BE NEXT! GULP!
AND SO YOU CALLED US IN TO DEFEND THE CITY!
OOF!
PAF
OF COURSE, WE MUST DISCUSS OUR COMPENSATION: HALF UP FRONT, AND THE REST UPON COMPLETING THE JOB!
TLING
FAREWELL, LITTLE MOUSE! WE'VE GOT A JOB TO DO!

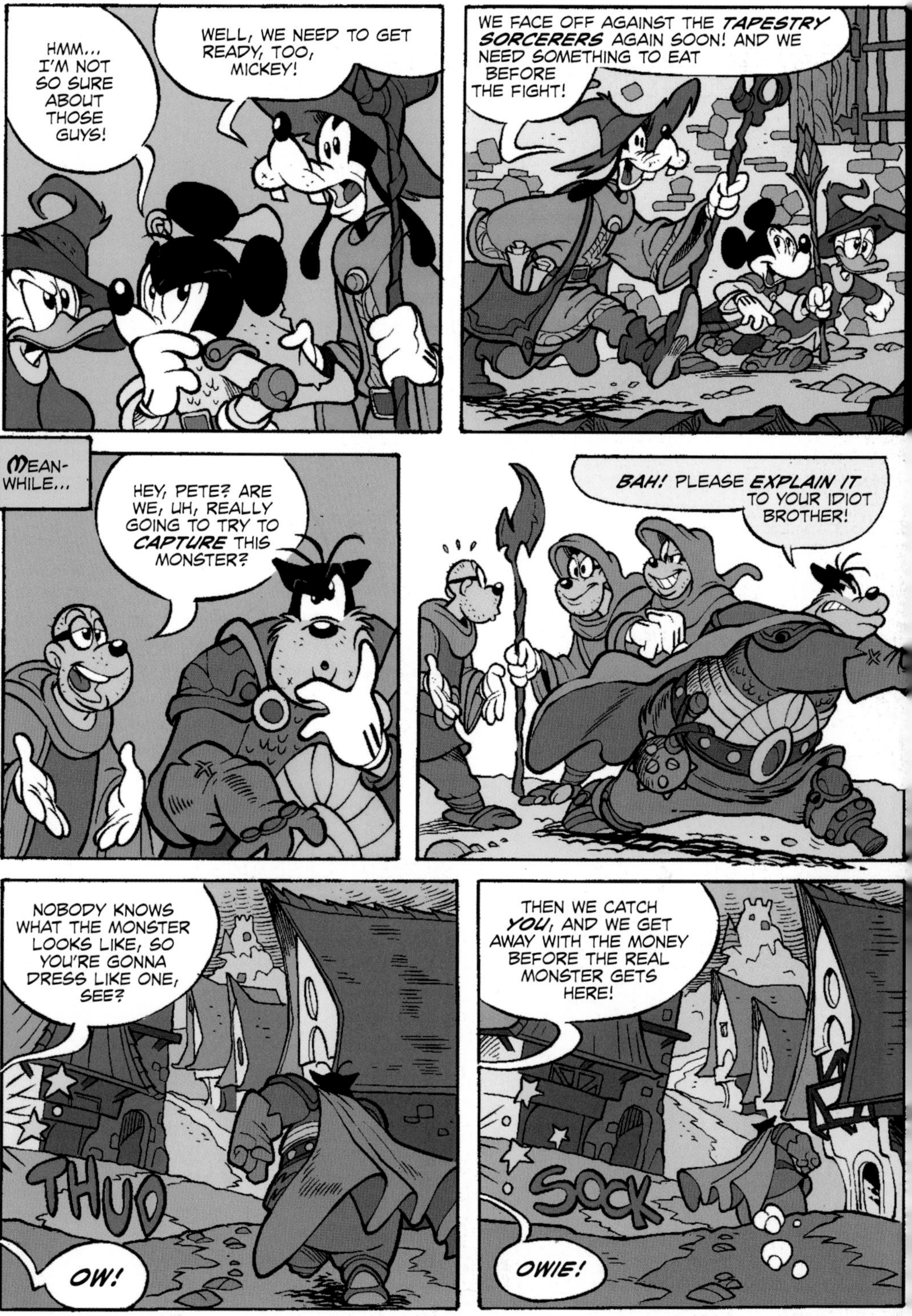
HMM... I'M NOT SO SURE ABOUT THOSE GUYS!
WELL, WE NEED TO GET READY, TOO, MICKEY!
WE FACE OFF AGAINST THE TAPESTRY SORCERERS AGAIN SOON! AND WE NEED SOMETHING TO EAT BEFORE THE FIGHT!
MEANWHILE...
HEY, PETE? ARE WE, UH, REALLY GOING TO TRY TO CAPTURE THIS MONSTER?
BAH! PLEASE EXPLAIN IT TO YOUR IDIOT BROTHER!
NOBODY KNOWS WHAT THE MONSTER LOOKS LIKE, SO YOU'RE GONNA DRESS LIKE ONE, SEE?
THUD
OW!
THEN WE CATCH YOU, AND WE GET AWAY WITH THE MONEY BEFORE THE REAL MONSTER GETS HERE!
SOCK
OWIE!

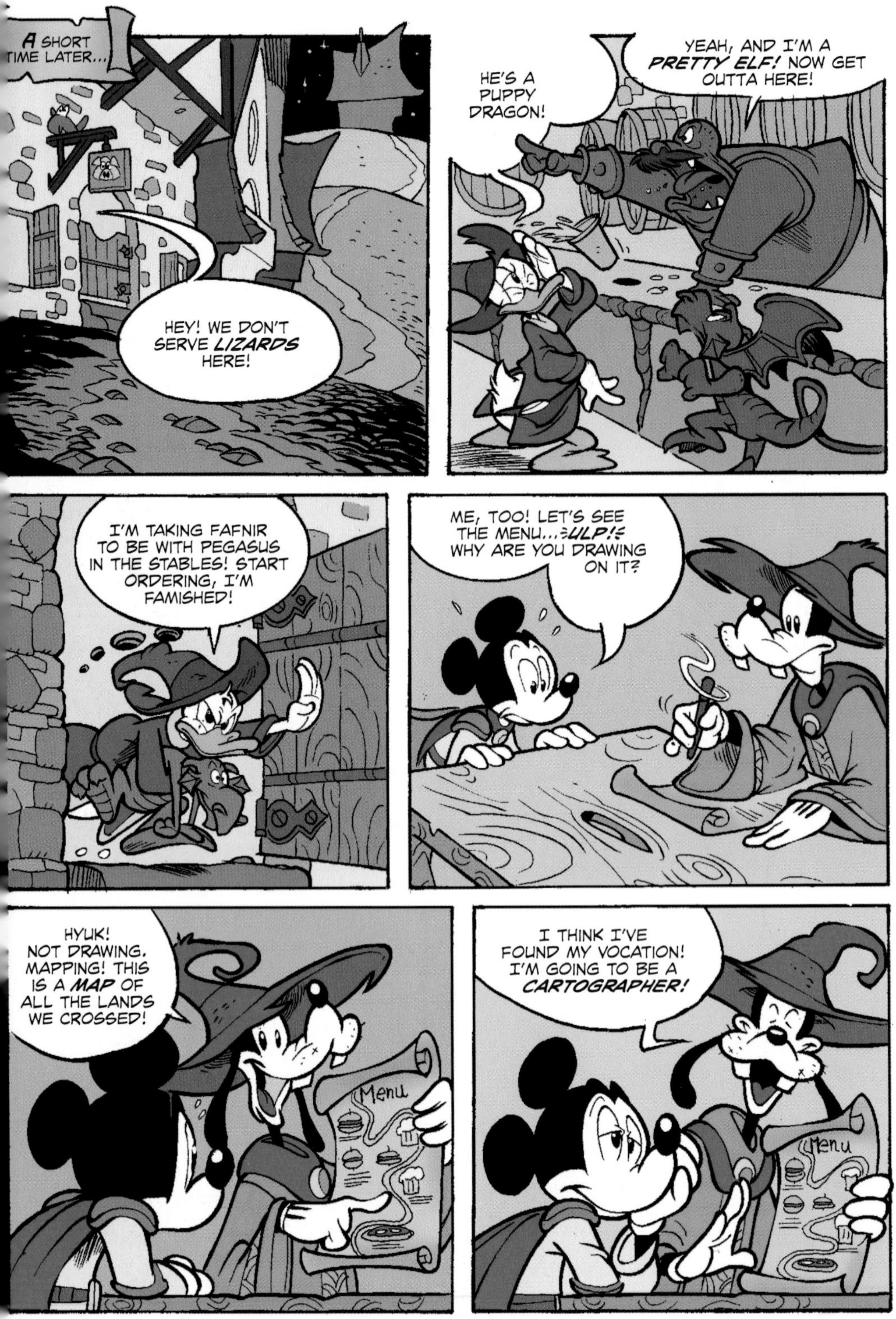
A SHORT TIME LATER...
HEY! WE DON'T SERVE LIZARDS HERE!
HE'S A PUPPY DRAGON!
YEAH, AND I'M A PRETTY ELF! NOW GET OUTTA HERE!
I'M TAKING FAFNIR TO BE WITH PEGASUS IN THE STABLES! START ORDERING, I'M FAMISHED!
ME, TOO! LET'S SEE THE MENU... ULP! WHY ARE YOU DRAWING ON IT?
HYUK! NOT DRAWING. MAPPING! THIS IS A MAP OF ALL THE LANDS WE CROSSED!
Menu
I THINK I'VE FOUND MY VOCATION! I'M GOING TO BE A CARTOGRAPHER!
Menu

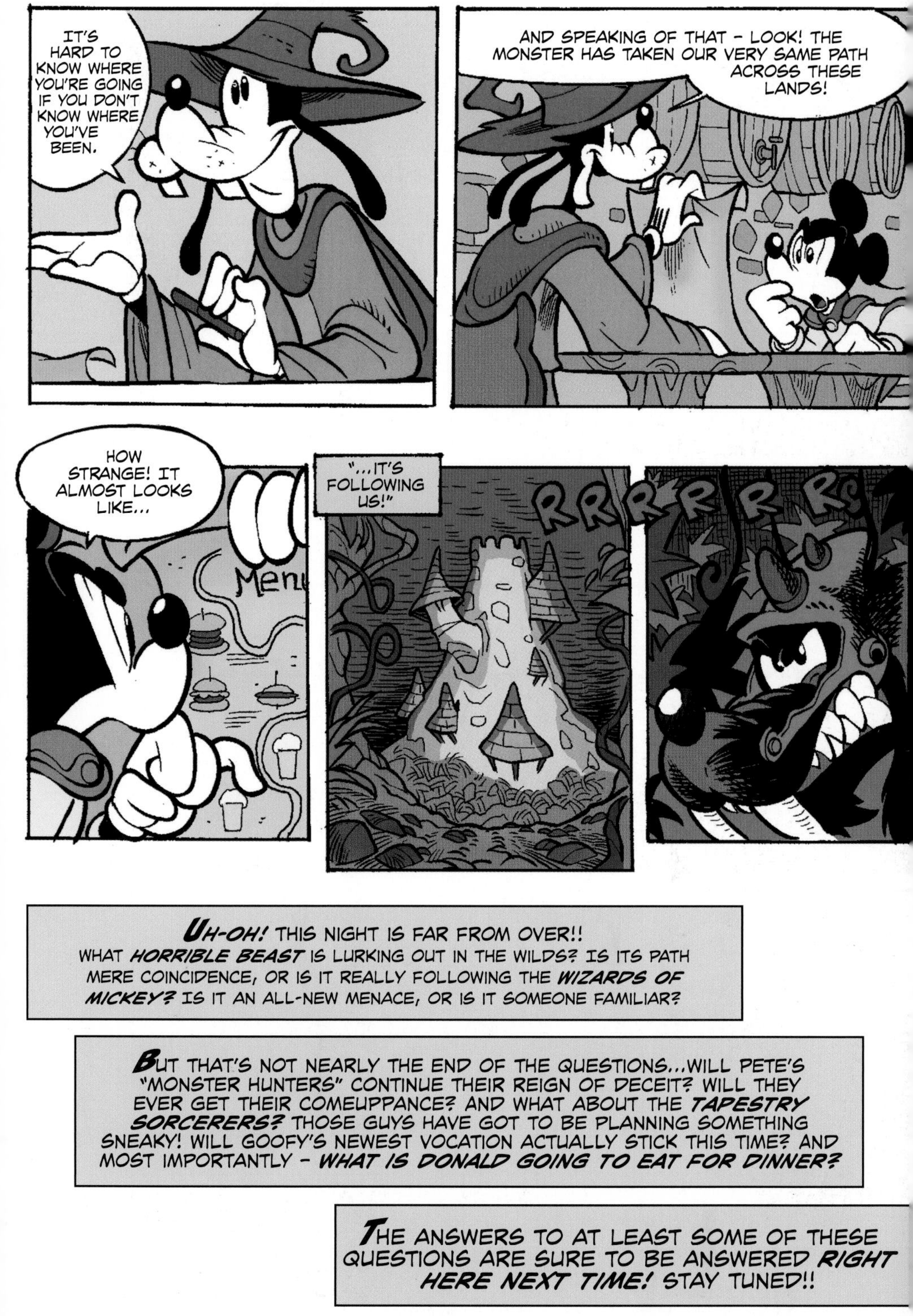
IT'S HARD TO KNOW WHERE YOU'RE GOING IF YOU DON'T KNOW WHERE YOU'VE BEEN.
AND SPEAKING OF THAT – LOOK! THE MONSTER HAS TAKEN OUR VERY SAME PATH ACROSS THESE LANDS!
HOW STRANGE! IT ALMOST LOOKS LIKE...
"...IT'S FOLLOWING US!"
RRRRRRS

UH-OH! THIS NIGHT IS FAR FROM OVER!! WHAT ***HORRIBLE BEAST*** IS LURKING OUT IN THE WILDS? IS ITS PATH MERE COINCIDENCE, OR IS IT REALLY FOLLOWING THE ***WIZARDS OF MICKEY?*** IS IT AN ALL-NEW MENACE, OR IS IT SOMEONE FAMILIAR?

BUT THAT'S NOT NEARLY THE END OF THE QUESTIONS...WILL PETE'S "MONSTER HUNTERS" CONTINUE THEIR REIGN OF DECEIT? WILL THEY EVER GET THEIR COMEUPPANCE? AND WHAT ABOUT THE ***TAPESTRY SORCERERS?*** THOSE GUYS HAVE GOT TO BE PLANNING SOMETHING SNEAKY! WILL GOOFY'S NEWEST VOCATION ACTUALLY STICK THIS TIME? AND MOST IMPORTANTLY – ***WHAT IS DONALD GOING TO EAT FOR DINNER?***

THE ANSWERS TO AT LEAST SOME OF THESE QUESTIONS ARE SURE TO BE ANSWERED ***RIGHT HERE NEXT TIME!*** STAY TUNED!!

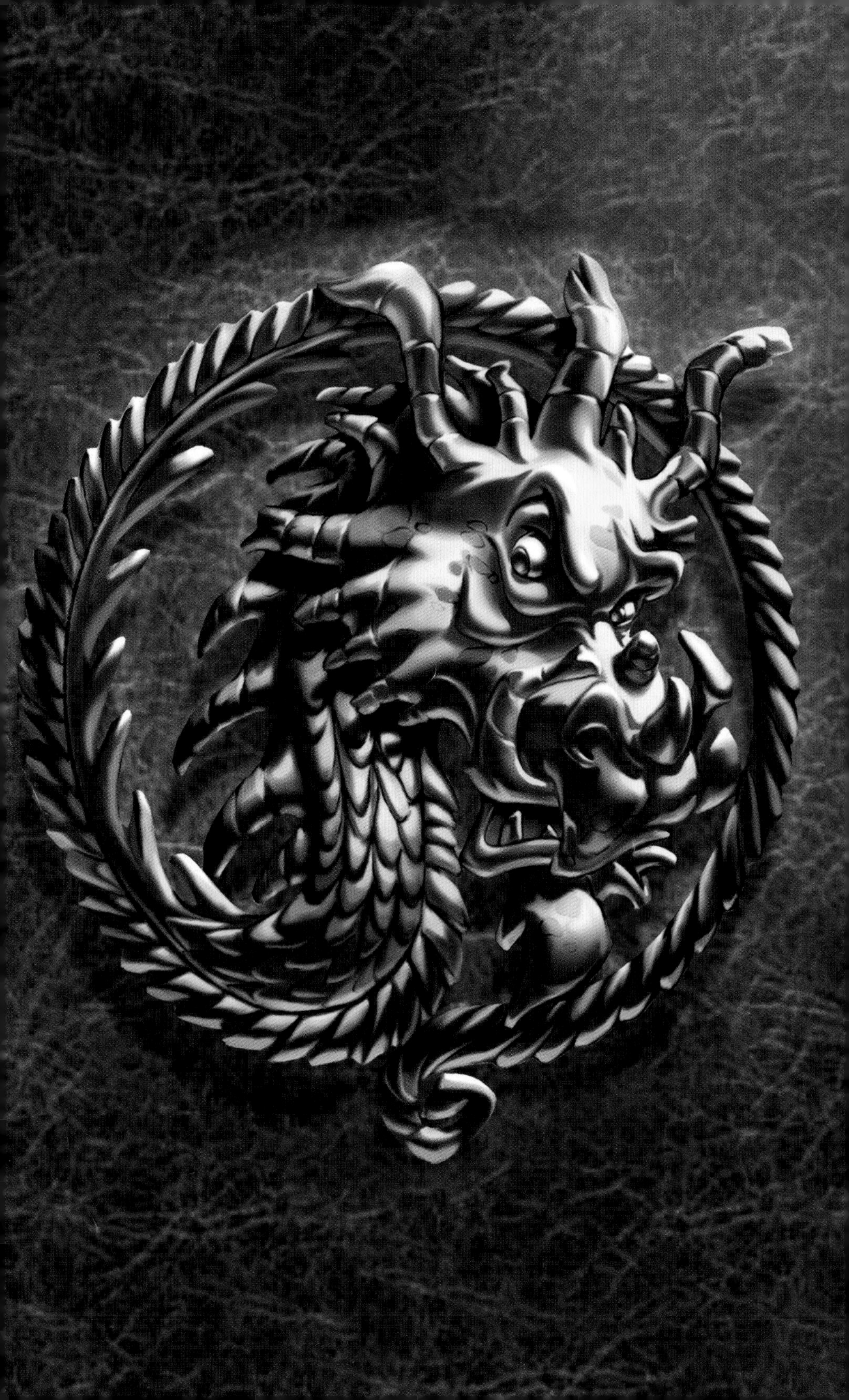

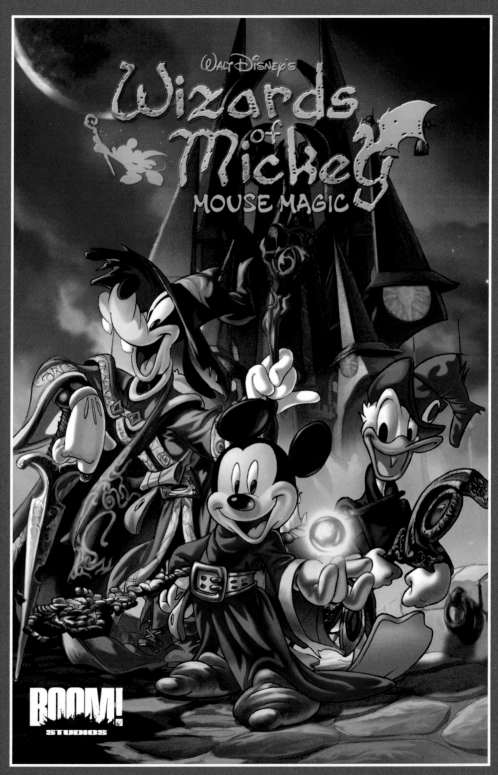

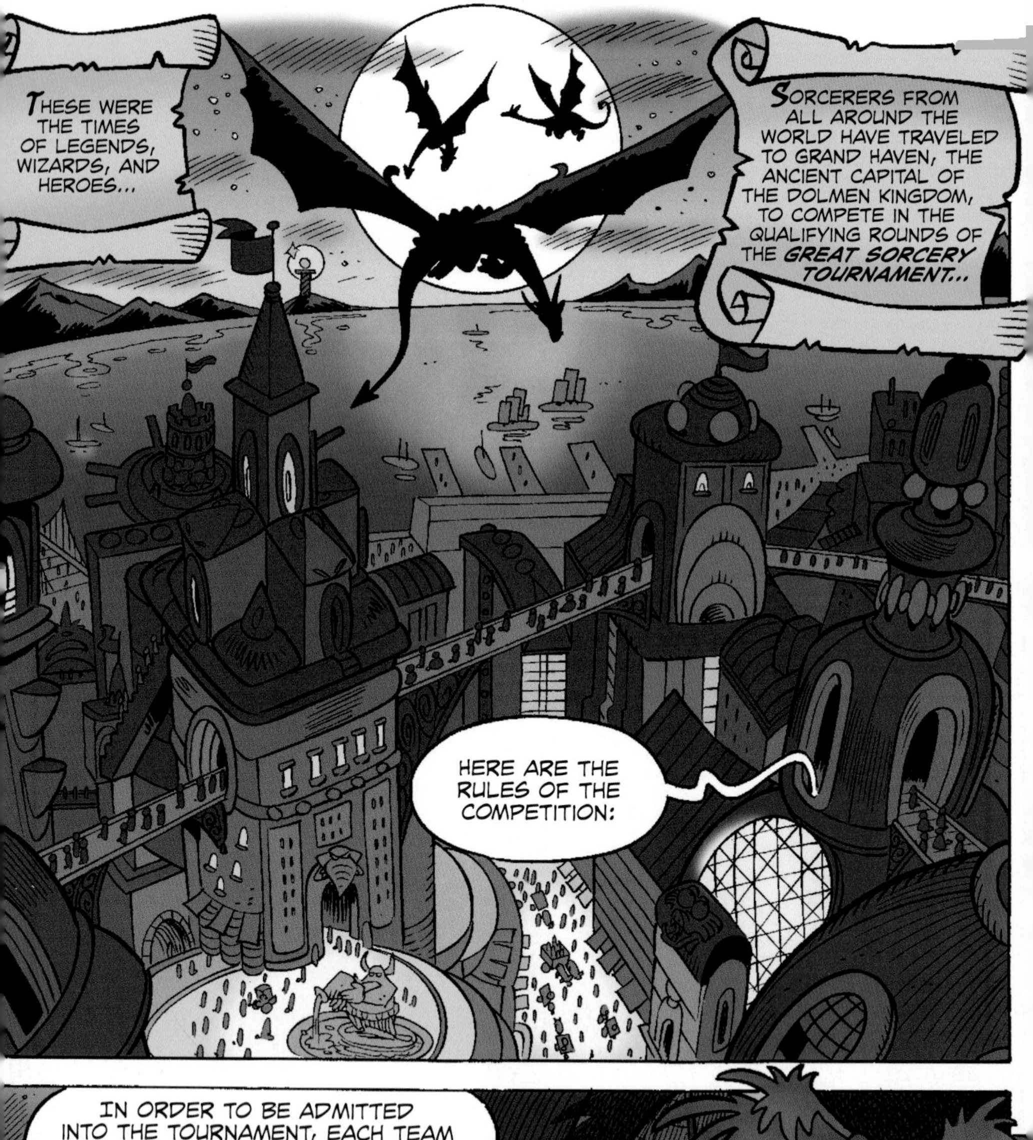
THESE WERE THE TIMES OF LEGENDS, WIZARDS, AND HEROES...
SORCERERS FROM ALL AROUND THE WORLD HAVE TRAVELED TO GRAND HAVEN, THE ANCIENT CAPITAL OF THE DOLMEN KINGDOM, TO COMPETE IN THE QUALIFYING ROUNDS OF THE GREAT SORCERY TOURNAMENT...
HERE ARE THE RULES OF THE COMPETITION:

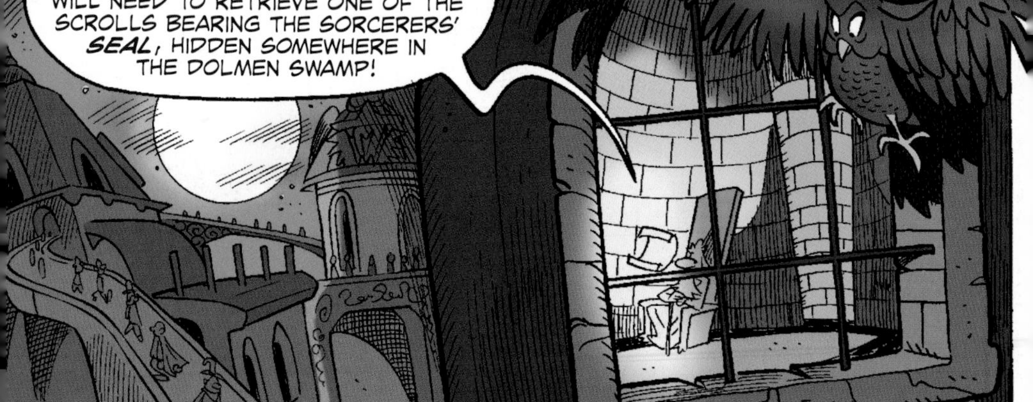
IN ORDER TO BE ADMITTED INTO THE TOURNAMENT, EACH TEAM WILL NEED TO RETRIEVE ONE OF THE SCROLLS BEARING THE SORCERERS' SEAL, HIDDEN SOMEWHERE IN THE DOLMEN SWAMP!

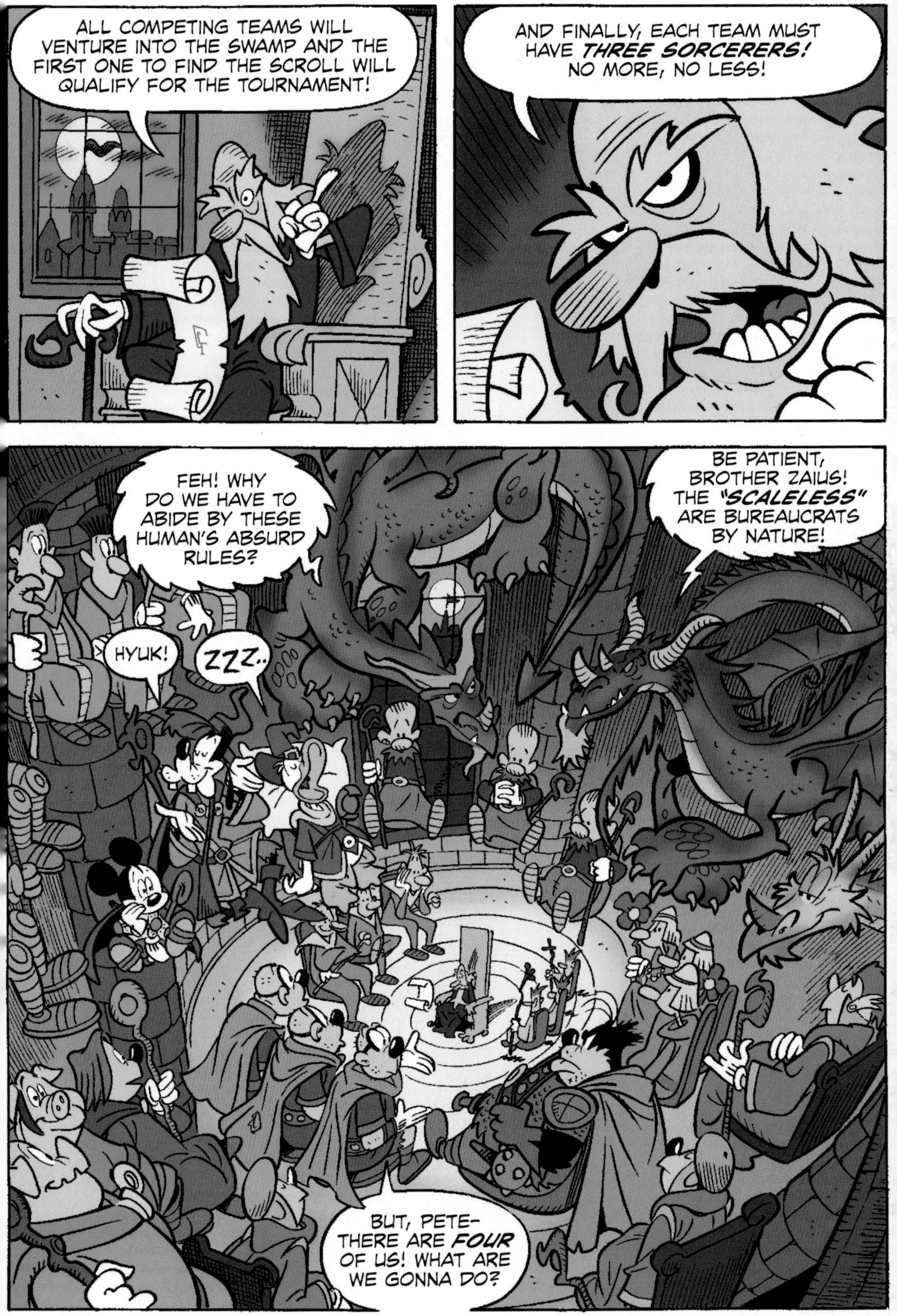
ALL COMPETING TEAMS WILL VENTURE INTO THE SWAMP AND THE FIRST ONE TO FIND THE SCROLL WILL QUALIFY FOR THE TOURNAMENT!
AND FINALLY, EACH TEAM MUST HAVE *THREE SORCERERS!* NO MORE, NO LESS!
FEH! WHY DO WE HAVE TO ABIDE BY THESE HUMAN'S ABSURD RULES?
BE PATIENT, BROTHER ZAIUS! THE *"SCALELESS"* ARE BUREAUCRATS BY NATURE!
HYUK!
ZZZ..
BUT, PETE— THERE ARE *FOUR* OF US! WHAT ARE WE GONNA DO?

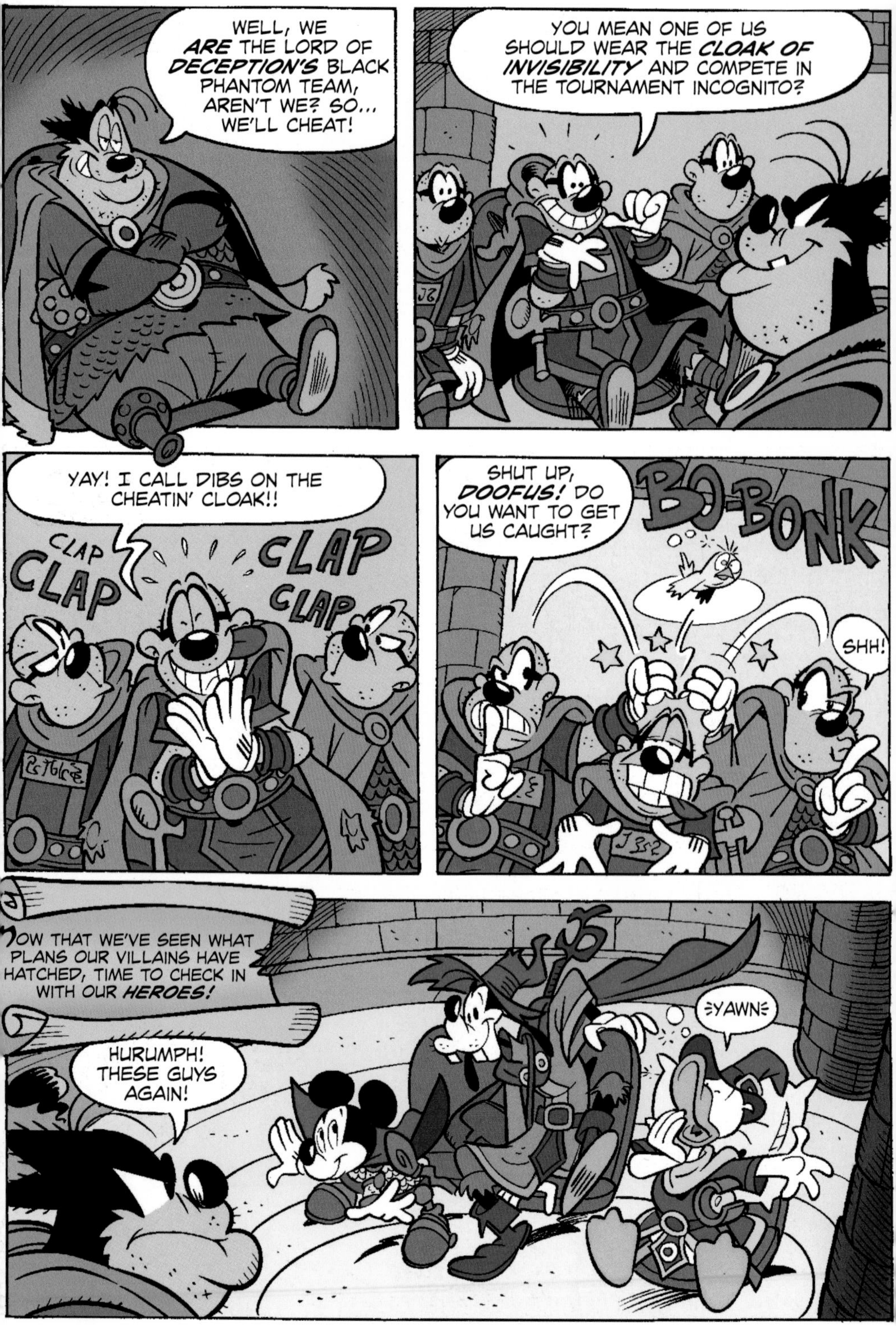

WELL, WE ARE THE LORD OF DECEPTION'S BLACK PHANTOM TEAM, AREN'T WE? SO... WE'LL CHEAT!
YOU MEAN ONE OF US SHOULD WEAR THE CLOAK OF INVISIBILITY AND COMPETE IN THE TOURNAMENT INCOGNITO?
YAY! I CALL DIBS ON THE CHEATIN' CLOAK!!
CLAP CLAP
CLAP CLAP
SHUT UP, DOOFUS! DO YOU WANT TO GET US CAUGHT?
BO-BONK
SHH!
NOW THAT WE'VE SEEN WHAT PLANS OUR VILLAINS HAVE HATCHED, TIME TO CHECK IN WITH OUR HEROES!
HURUMPH! THESE GUYS AGAIN!
YAWN

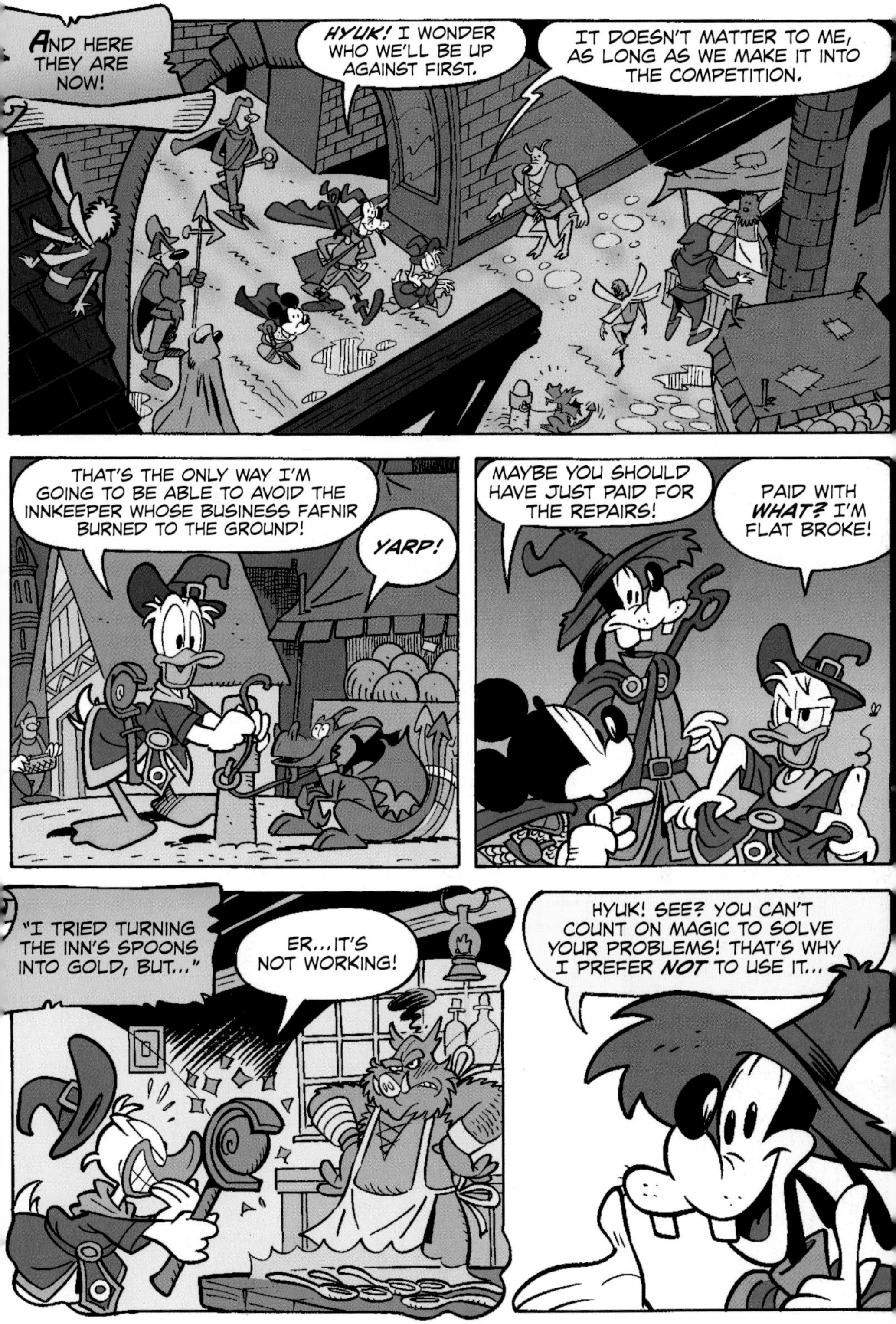
AND HERE THEY ARE NOW!
HYUK! I WONDER WHO WE'LL BE UP AGAINST FIRST.
IT DOESN'T MATTER TO ME, AS LONG AS WE MAKE IT INTO THE COMPETITION.
THAT'S THE ONLY WAY I'M GOING TO BE ABLE TO AVOID THE INNKEEPER WHOSE BUSINESS FAFNIR BURNED TO THE GROUND!
YARP!
MAYBE YOU SHOULD HAVE JUST PAID FOR THE REPAIRS!
PAID WITH WHAT? I'M FLAT BROKE!
"I TRIED TURNING THE INN'S SPOONS INTO GOLD, BUT..."
ER...IT'S NOT WORKING!
HYUK! SEE? YOU CAN'T COUNT ON MAGIC TO SOLVE YOUR PROBLEMS! THAT'S WHY I PREFER NOT TO USE IT...

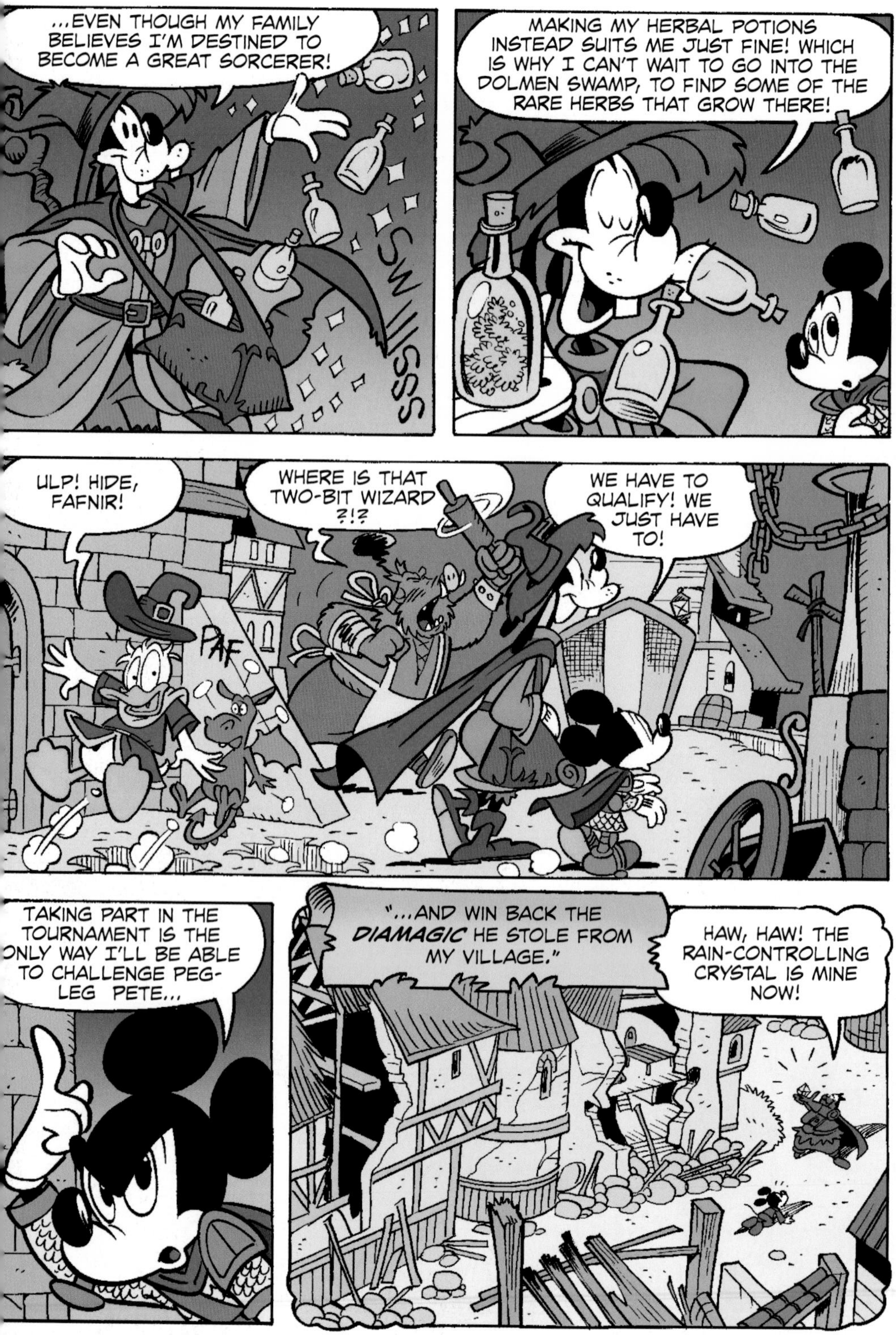
...EVEN THOUGH MY FAMILY BELIEVES I'M DESTINED TO BECOME A GREAT SORCERER!
SWIIISSS
MAKING MY HERBAL POTIONS INSTEAD SUITS ME JUST FINE! WHICH IS WHY I CAN'T WAIT TO GO INTO THE DOLMEN SWAMP, TO FIND SOME OF THE RARE HERBS THAT GROW THERE!
ULP! HIDE, FAFNIR!
WHERE IS THAT TWO-BIT WIZARD ?!?
WE HAVE TO QUALIFY! WE JUST HAVE TO!
PAF
TAKING PART IN THE TOURNAMENT IS THE ONLY WAY I'LL BE ABLE TO CHALLENGE PEG-LEG PETE...
"...AND WIN BACK THE *DIAMAGIC* HE STOLE FROM MY VILLAGE."
HAW, HAW! THE RAIN-CONTROLLING CRYSTAL IS MINE NOW!

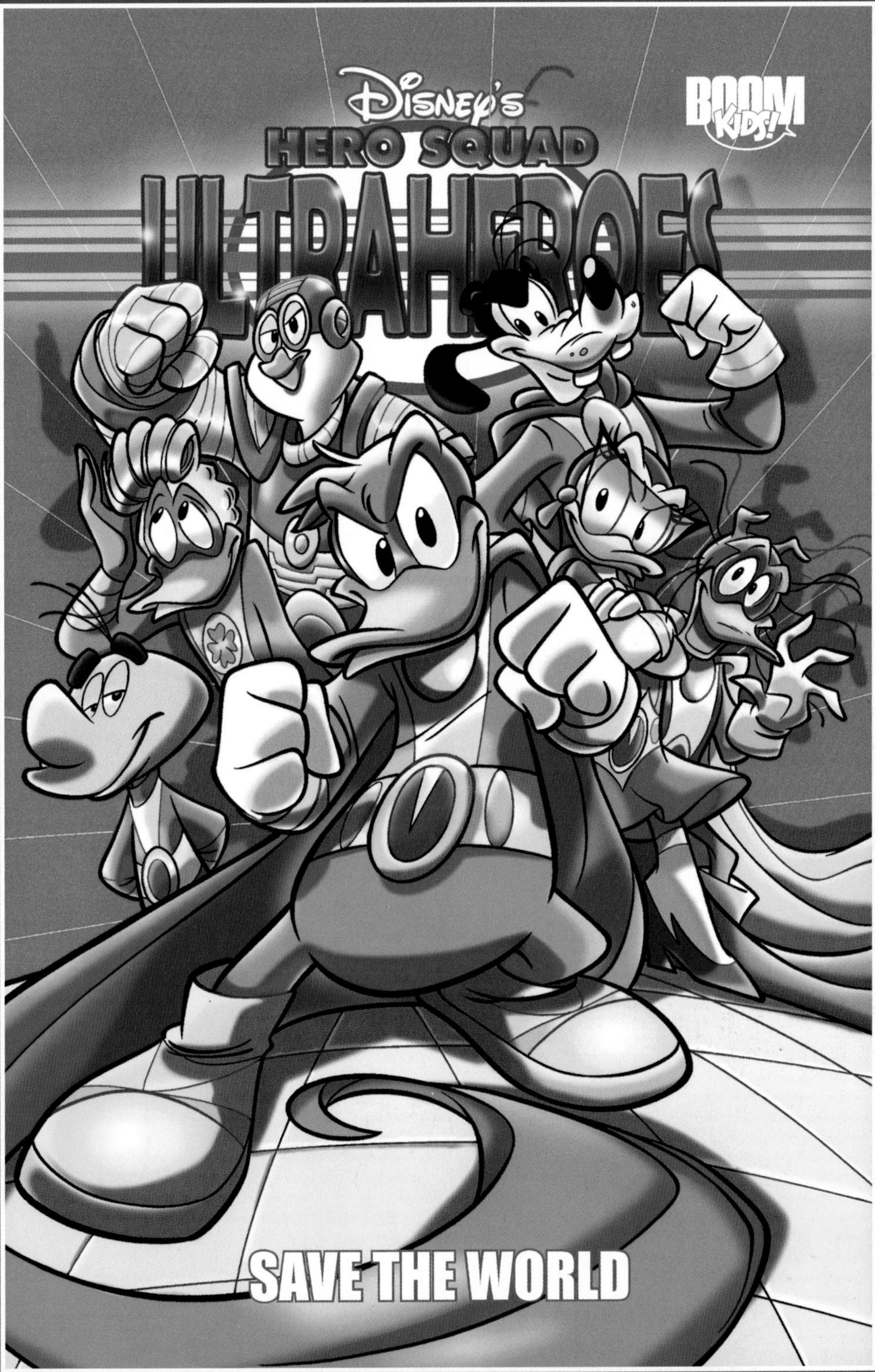
Disney's
HERO SQUAD
ULTRAHEROES
BOOM KIDS!
SAVE THE WORLD

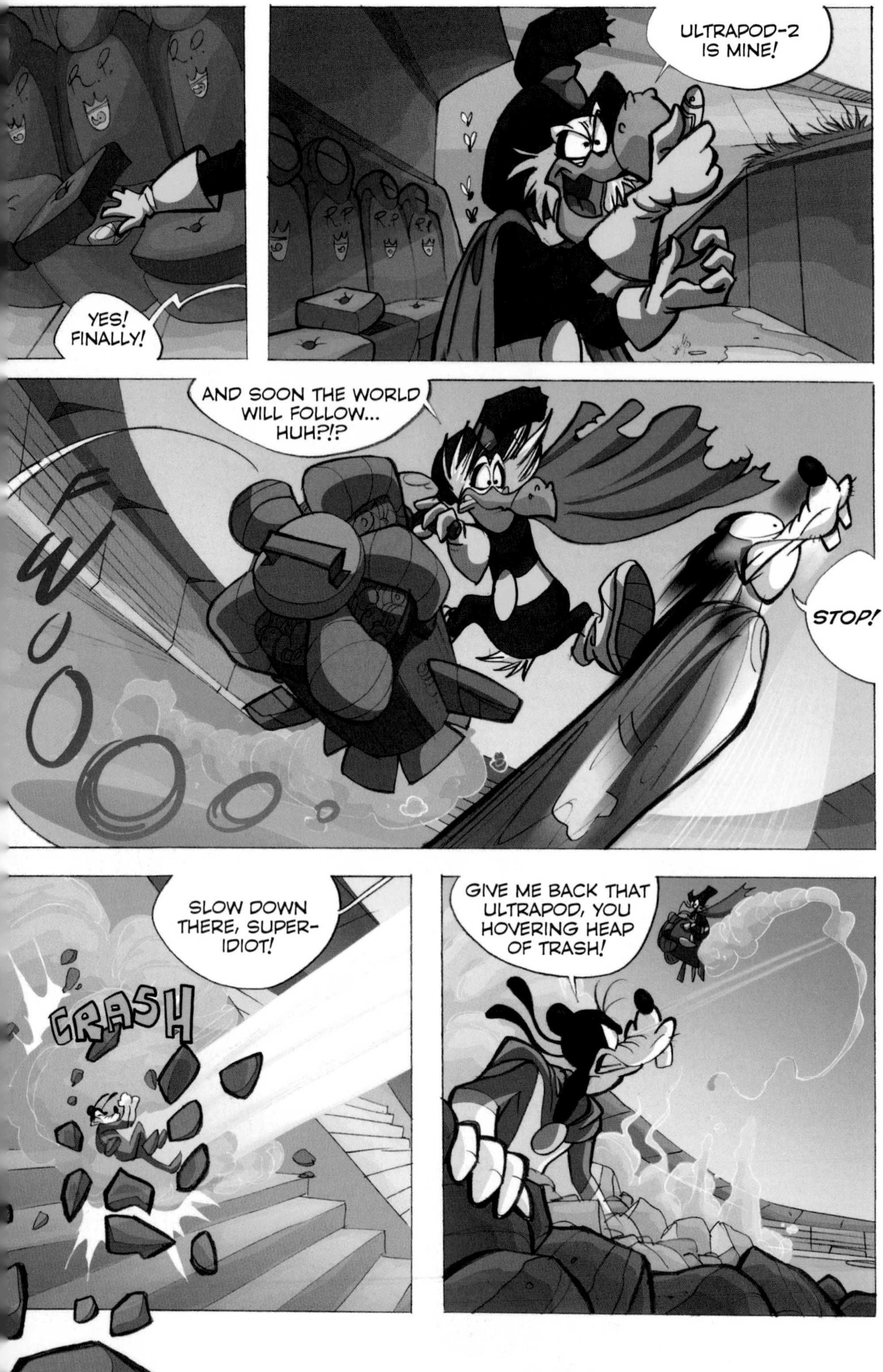
YES! FINALLY!
ULTRAPOD-2 IS MINE!
AND SOON THE WORLD WILL FOLLOW... HUH?!?
STOP!
WHOOOO
SLOW DOWN THERE, SUPER-IDIOT!
CRASH
GIVE ME BACK THAT ULTRAPOD, YOU HOVERING HEAP OF TRASH!

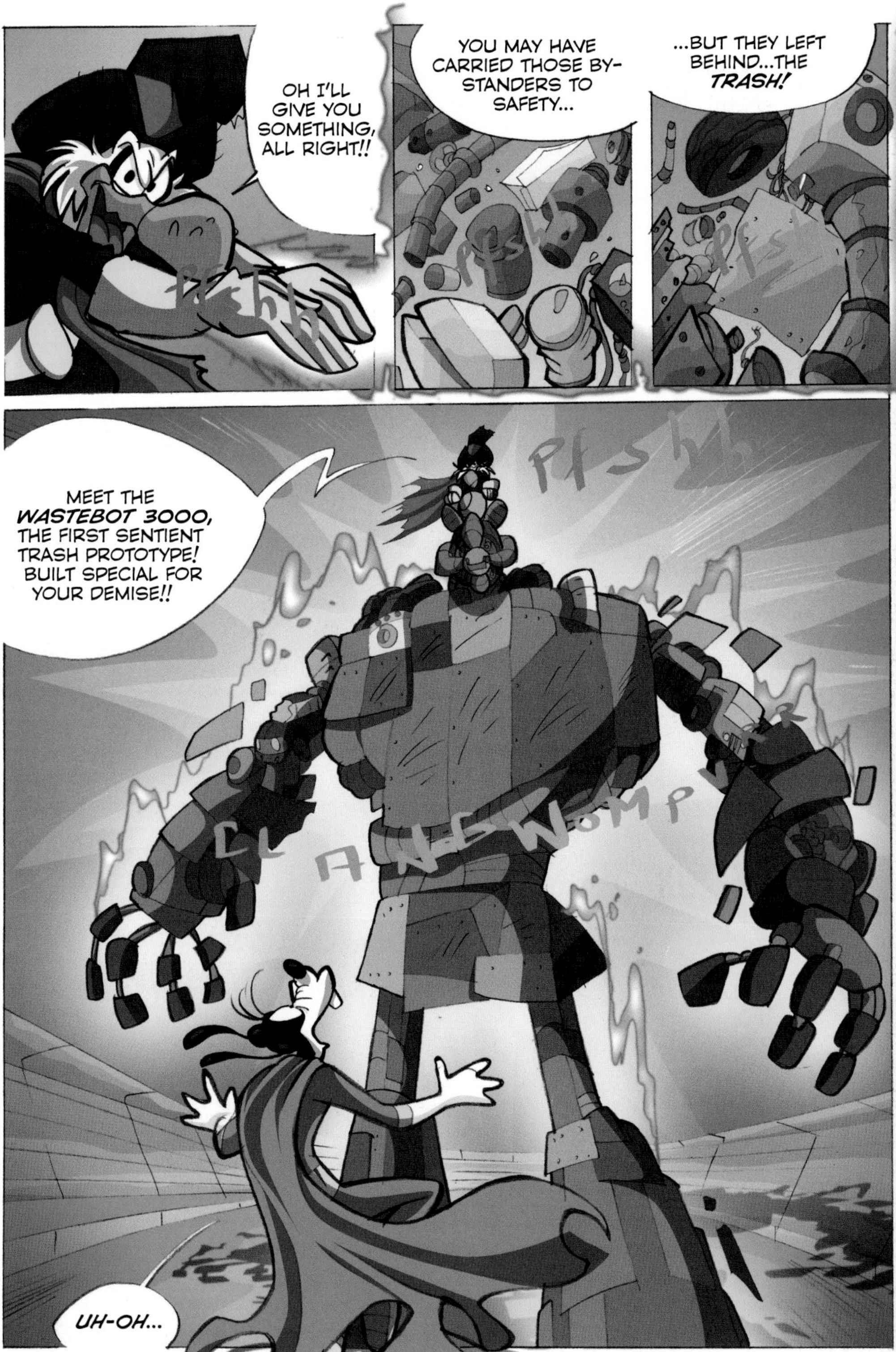
OH I'LL GIVE YOU SOMETHING, ALL RIGHT!!
YOU MAY HAVE CARRIED THOSE BY-STANDERS TO SAFETY...
...BUT THEY LEFT BEHIND...THE *TRASH!*
MEET THE *WASTEBOT 3000,* THE FIRST SENTIENT TRASH PROTOTYPE! BUILT SPECIAL FOR YOUR DEMISE!!
UH-OH...

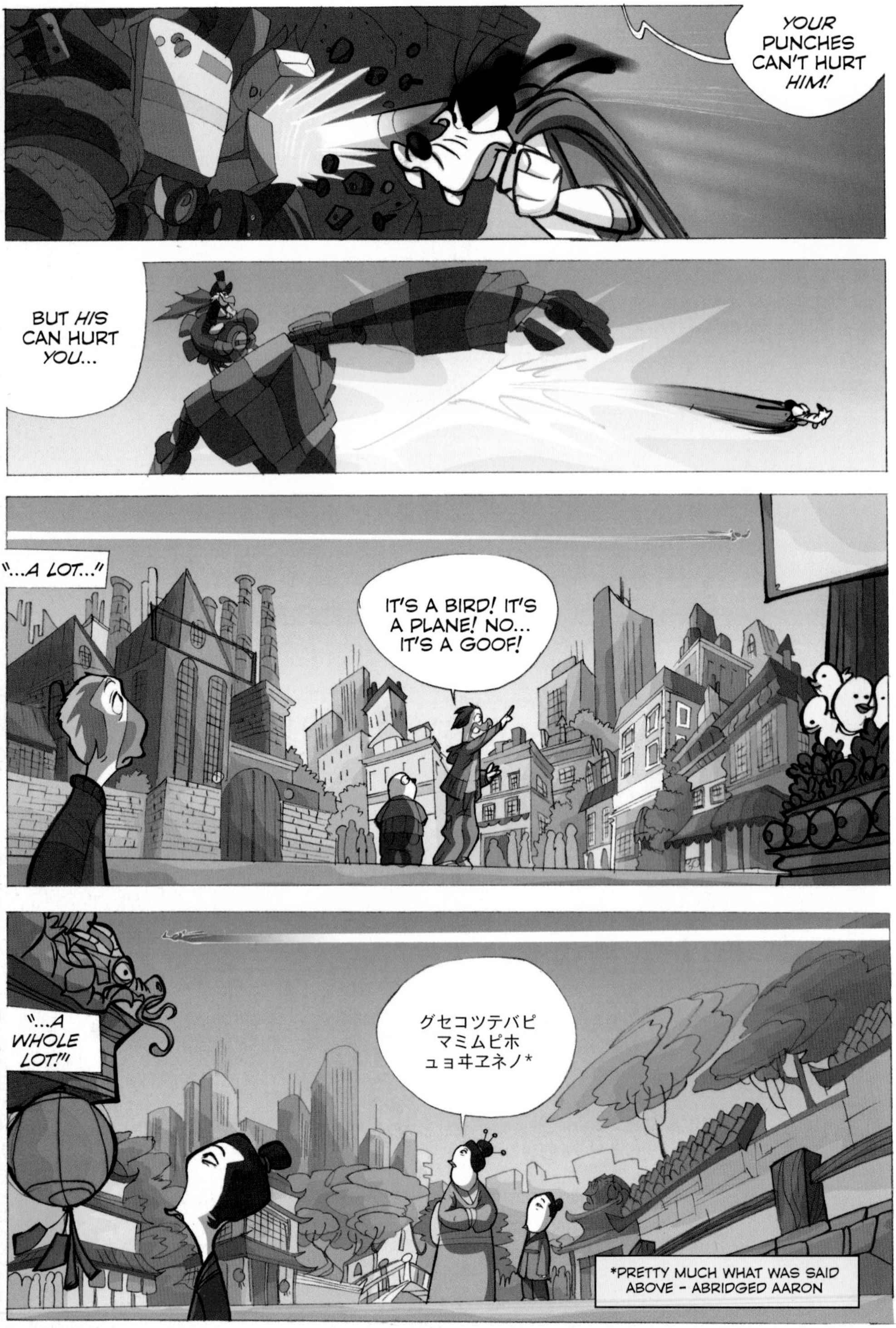
YOUR PUNCHES CAN'T HURT HIM!
BUT HIS CAN HURT YOU...
"...A LOT..."
IT'S A BIRD! IT'S A PLANE! NO... IT'S A GOOF!
"...A WHOLE LOT!"
グセコツテバピ マミムピホ ュョヰヱネノ*
*PRETTY MUCH WHAT WAS SAID ABOVE - ABRIDGED AARON

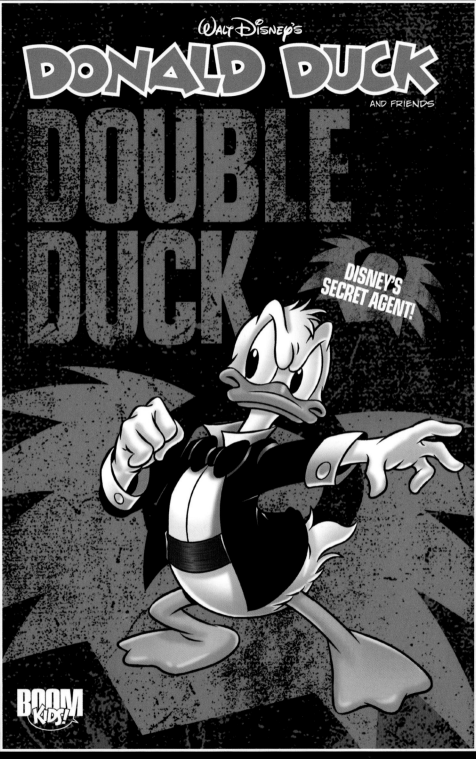

Donald Duck...as a secret agent? Villainous
fiends beware as the world of super-sleuthing
and espionage will never be the same! This is
Donald Duck like you've never seen him!

DONALD DUCK AND FRIENDS: DOUBLE DUCK
DIAMOND CODE: DEC090752
SC $9.99 ISBN 9781608865451
HC $24.99 ISBN 9781608865512

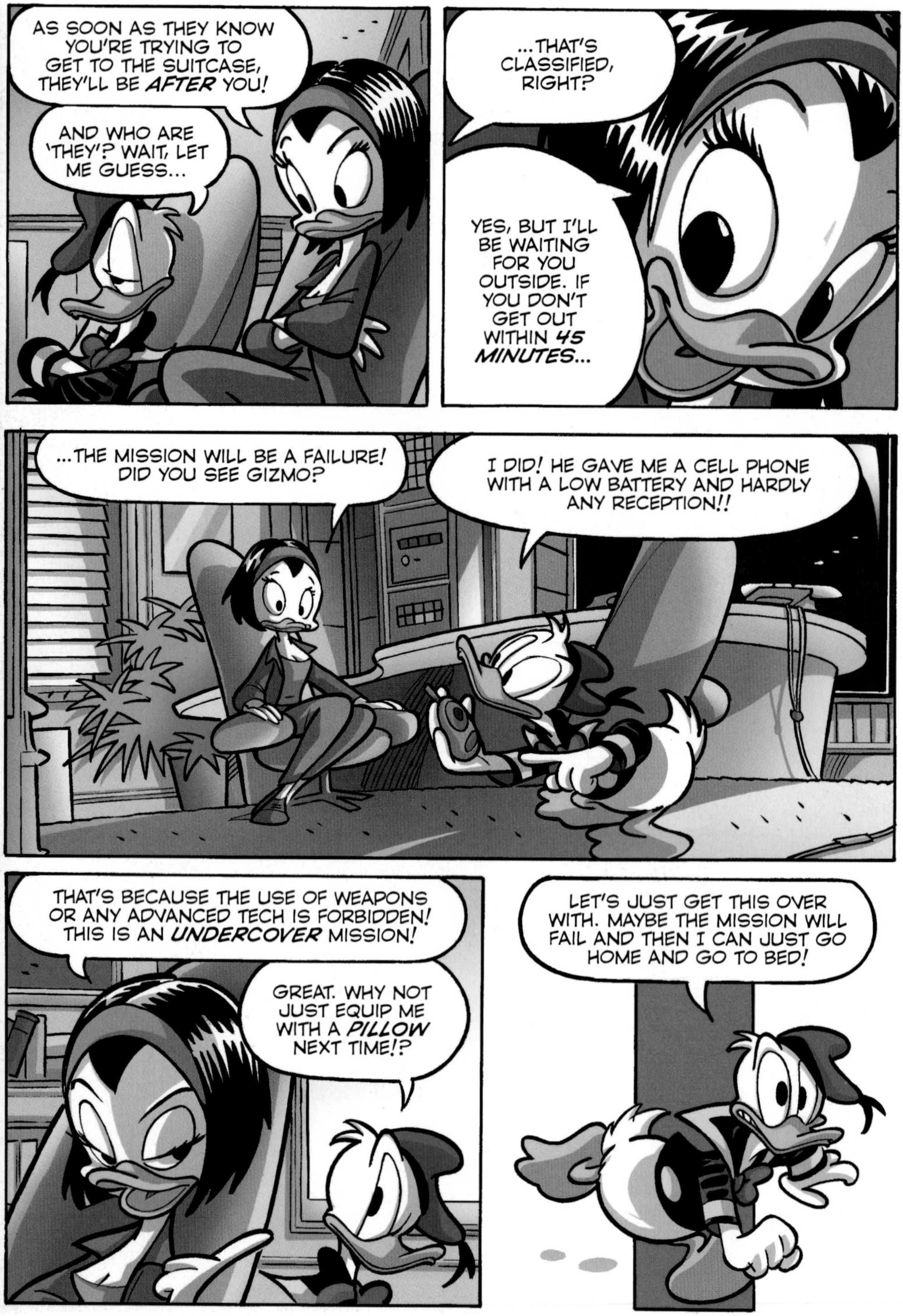
AS SOON AS THEY KNOW YOU'RE TRYING TO GET TO THE SUITCASE, THEY'LL BE *AFTER* YOU!
AND WHO ARE 'THEY'? WAIT, LET ME GUESS...
...THAT'S CLASSIFIED, RIGHT?
YES, BUT I'LL BE WAITING FOR YOU OUTSIDE. IF YOU DON'T GET OUT WITHIN *45 MINUTES*...
...THE MISSION WILL BE A FAILURE! DID YOU SEE GIZMO?
I DID! HE GAVE ME A CELL PHONE WITH A LOW BATTERY AND HARDLY ANY RECEPTION!!
THAT'S BECAUSE THE USE OF WEAPONS OR ANY ADVANCED TECH IS FORBIDDEN! THIS IS AN *UNDERCOVER* MISSION!
GREAT. WHY NOT JUST EQUIP ME WITH A *PILLOW* NEXT TIME!?
LET'S JUST GET THIS OVER WITH. MAYBE THE MISSION WILL FAIL AND THEN I CAN JUST GO HOME AND GO TO BED!

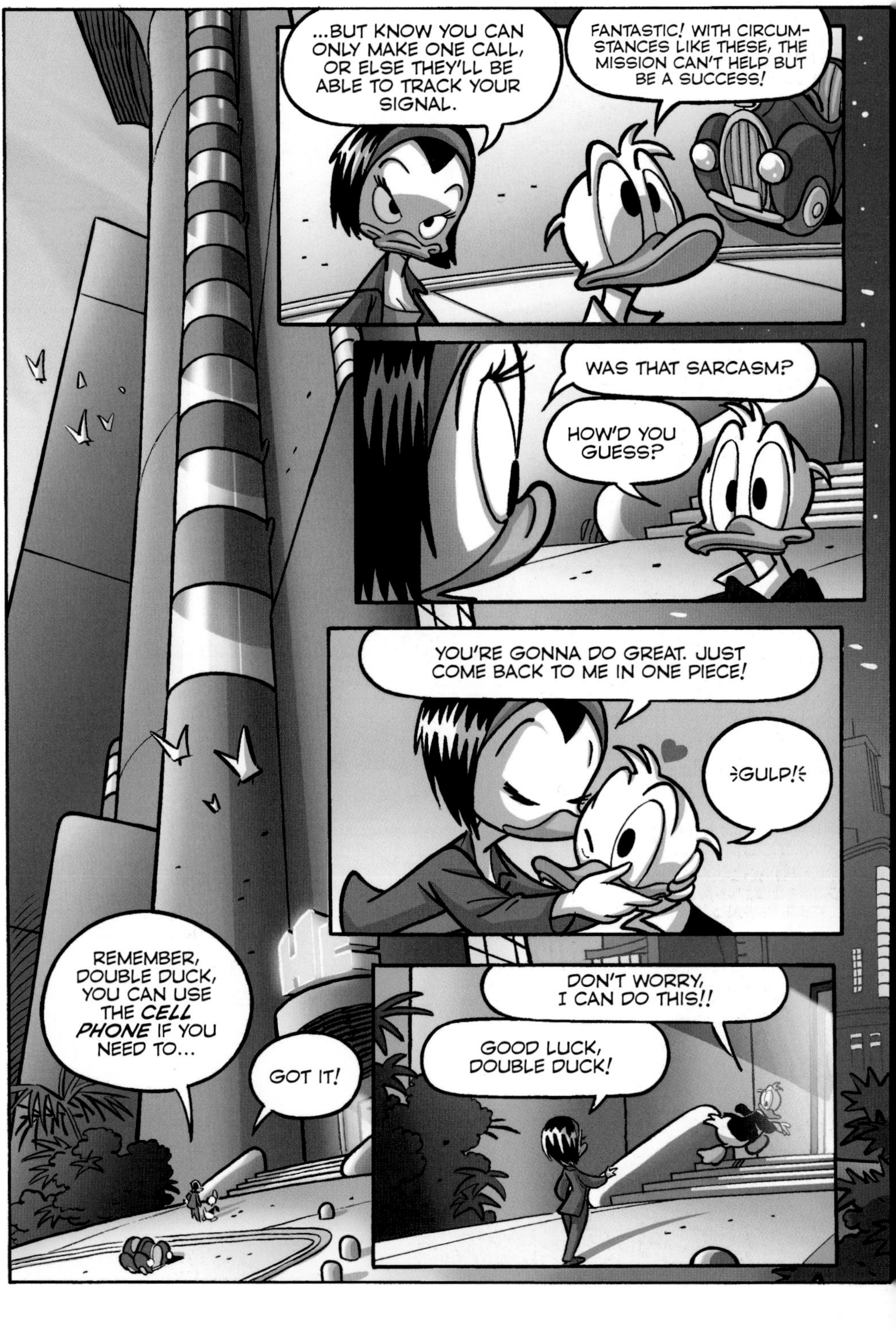
...BUT KNOW YOU CAN ONLY MAKE ONE CALL, OR ELSE THEY'LL BE ABLE TO TRACK YOUR SIGNAL.
FANTASTIC! WITH CIRCUMSTANCES LIKE THESE, THE MISSION CAN'T HELP BUT BE A SUCCESS!
WAS THAT SARCASM?
HOW'D YOU GUESS?
YOU'RE GONNA DO GREAT. JUST COME BACK TO ME IN ONE PIECE!
GULP!
REMEMBER, DOUBLE DUCK, YOU CAN USE THE CELL PHONE IF YOU NEED TO...
GOT IT!
DON'T WORRY, I CAN DO THIS!!
GOOD LUCK, DOUBLE DUCK!

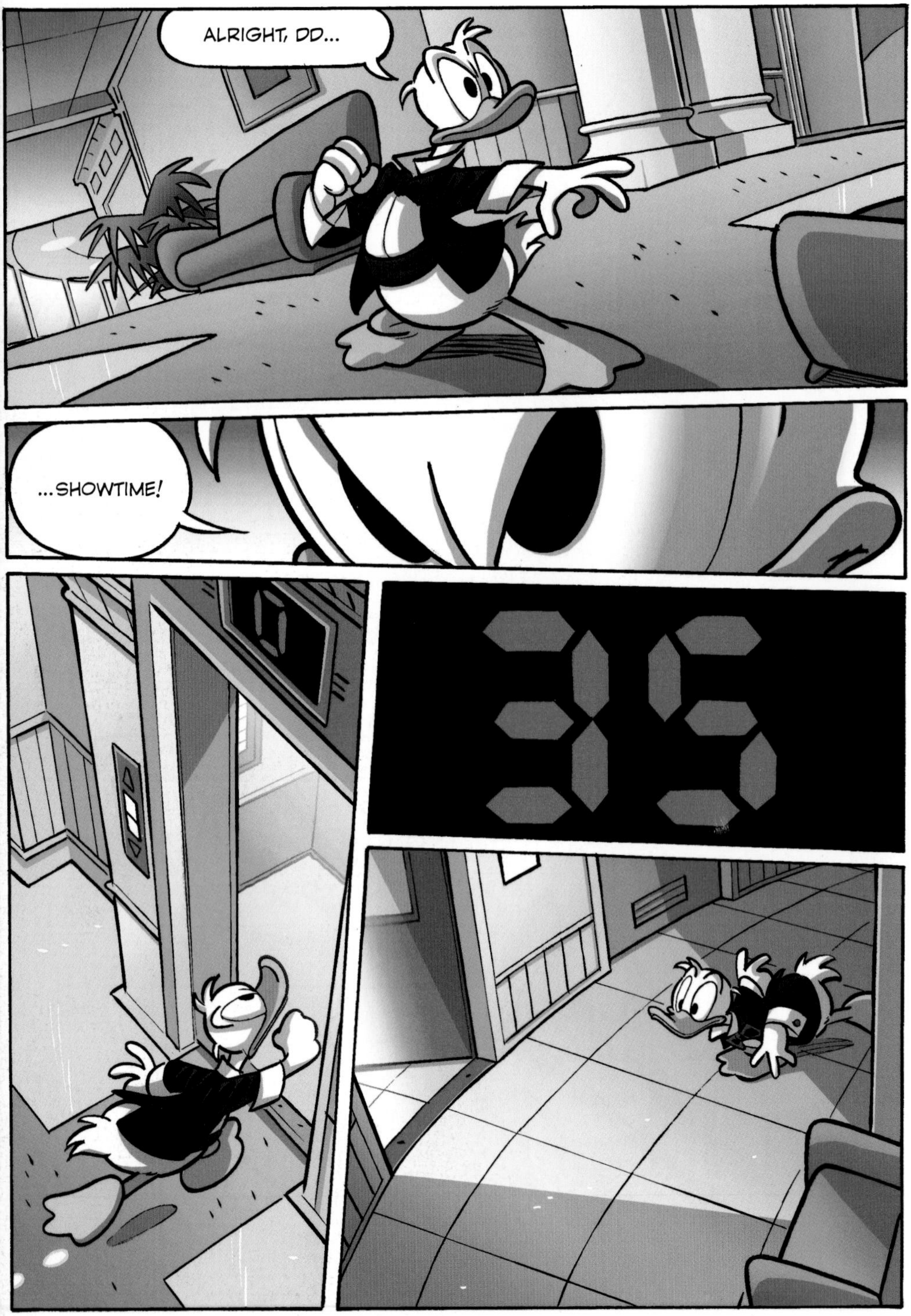
ALRIGHT, DD...
...SHOWTIME!

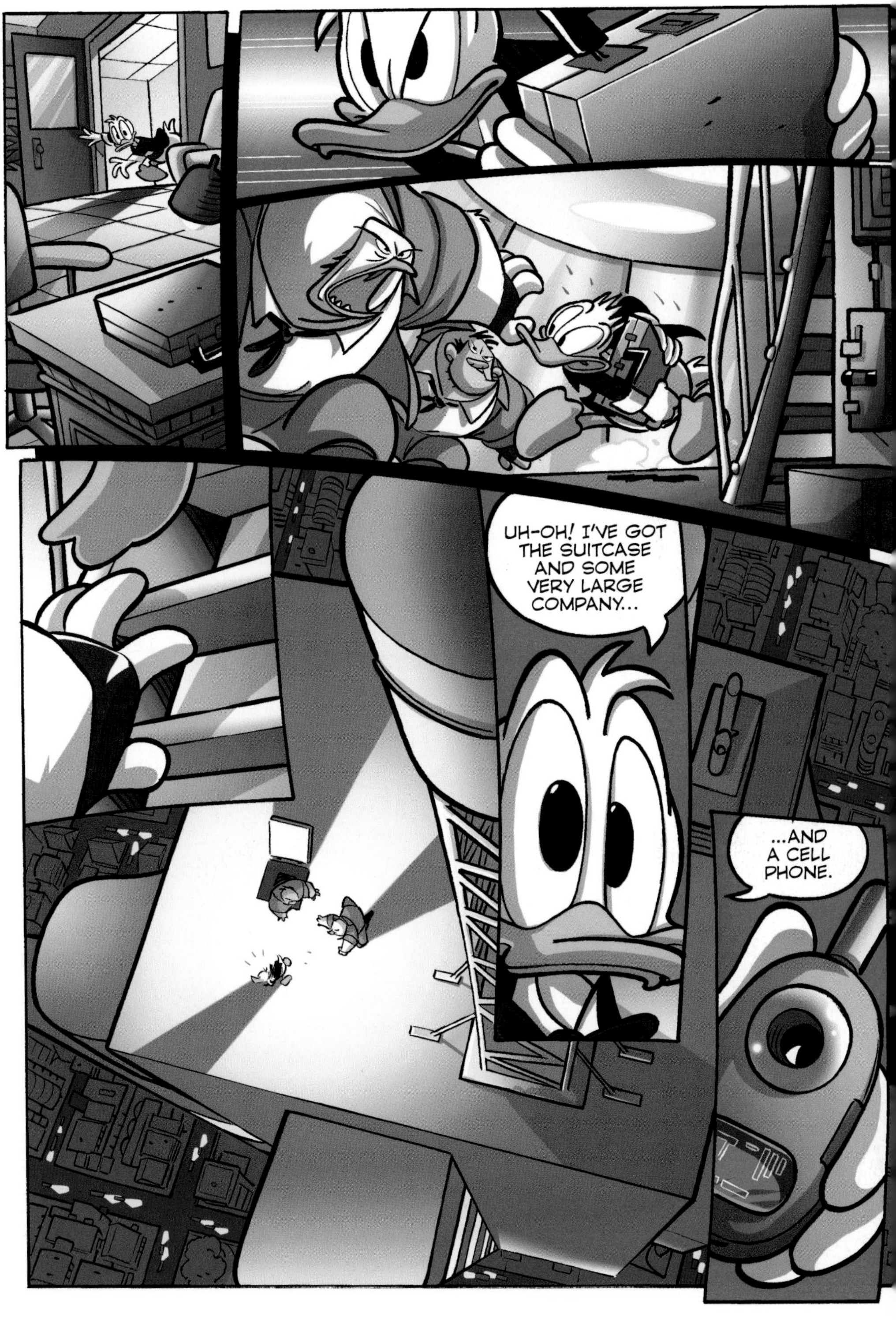
UH-OH! I'VE GOT THE SUITCASE AND SOME VERY LARGE COMPANY...
...AND A CELL PHONE.

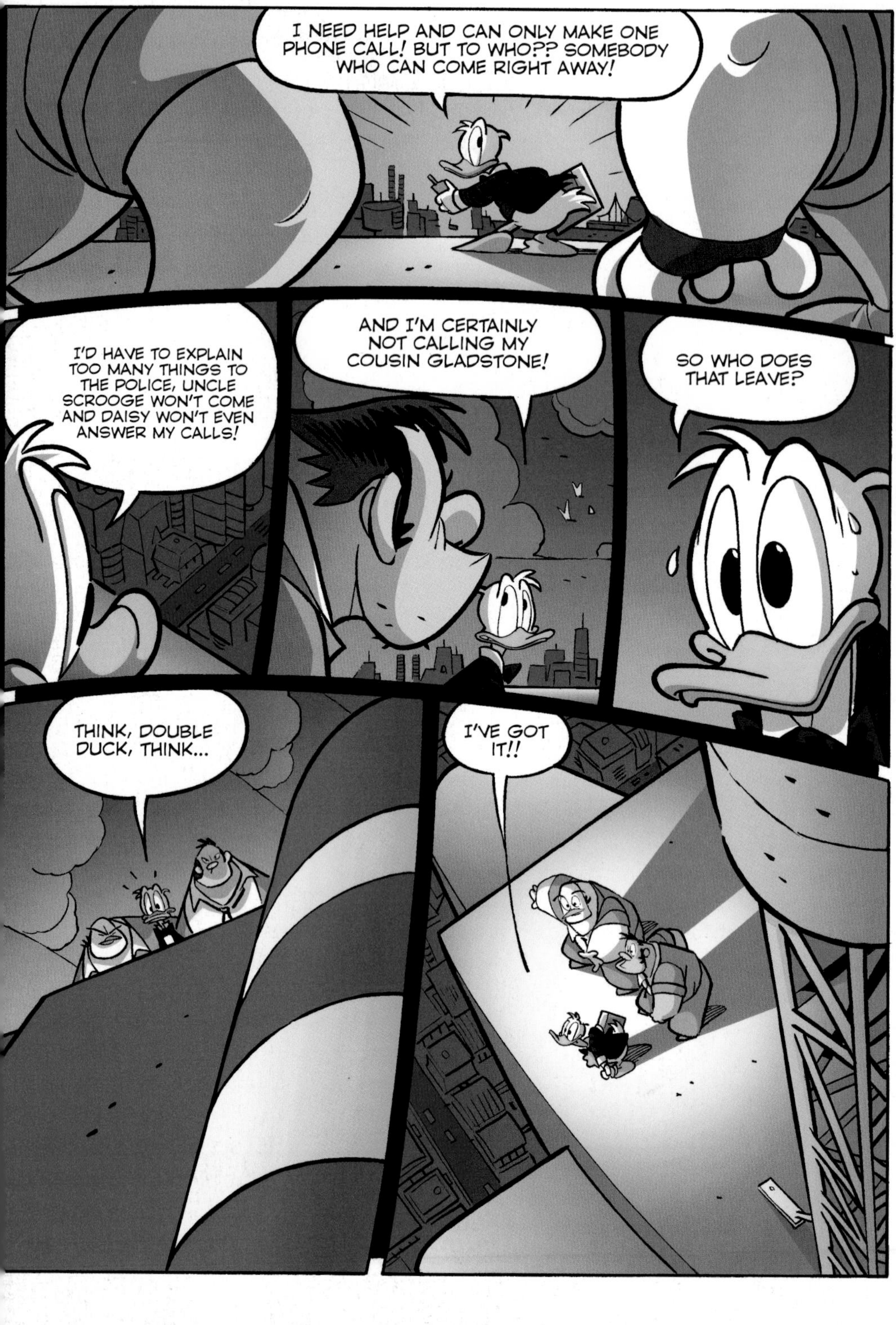
I NEED HELP AND CAN ONLY MAKE ONE PHONE CALL! BUT TO WHO?? SOMEBODY WHO CAN COME RIGHT AWAY!
I'D HAVE TO EXPLAIN TOO MANY THINGS TO THE POLICE, UNCLE SCROOGE WON'T COME AND DAISY WON'T EVEN ANSWER MY CALLS!
AND I'M CERTAINLY NOT CALLING MY COUSIN GLADSTONE!
SO WHO DOES THAT LEAVE?
THINK, DOUBLE DUCK, THINK...
I'VE GOT IT!!

Peter Pan (Kermit) whisks Wendy (Janice) and her brothers
o the magical realm of Neverswamp! Also starring Captain
Hook (Gonzo) and Piggytink (Miss Piggy), this hilarious spin
on the timeless tale is one that you'll never forget!

MUPPET PETER PAN
DIAMOND CODE: OCT090802
SC $9.99 ISBN 9781608865079

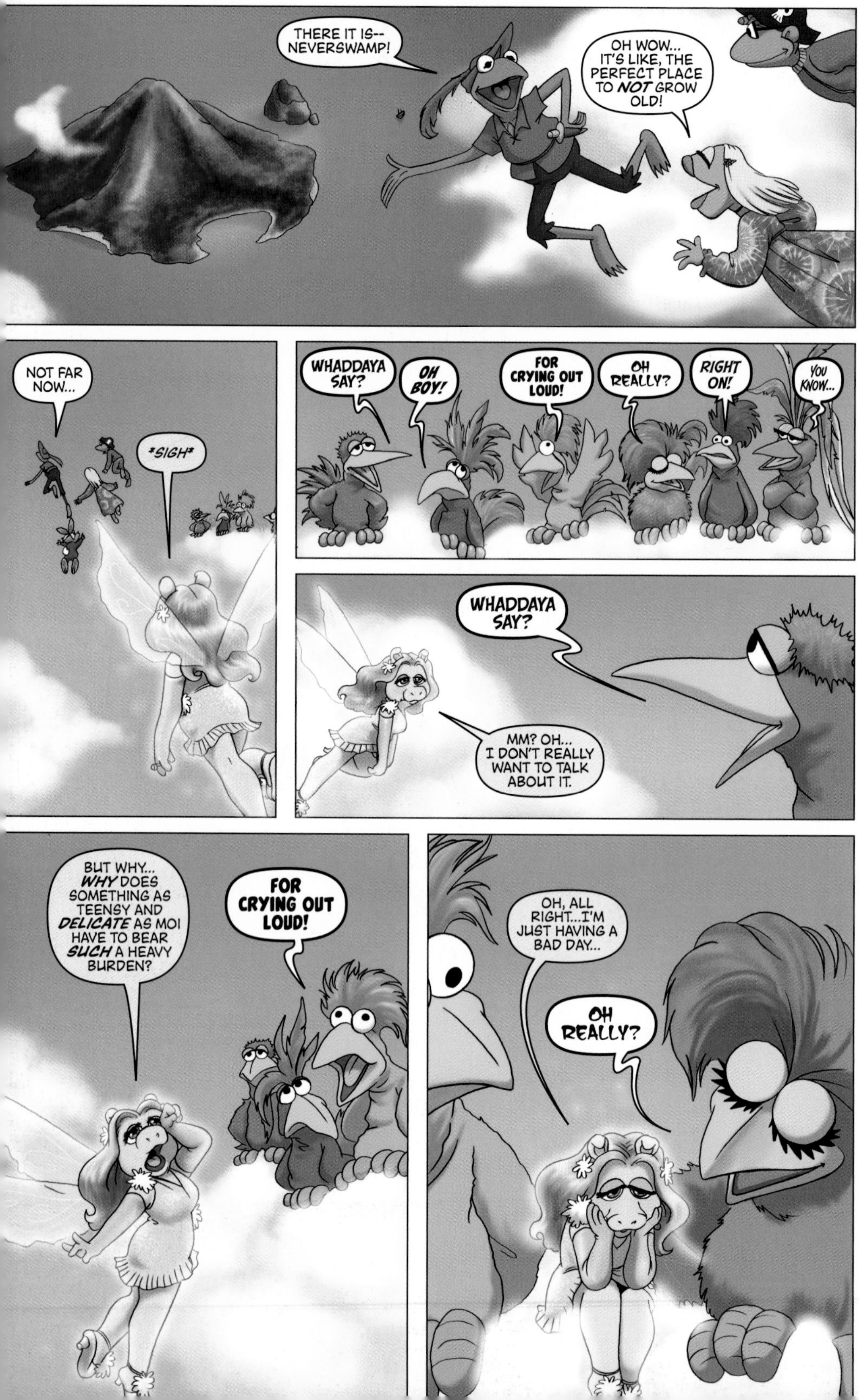
THERE IT IS-- NEVERSWAMP!
OH WOW... IT'S LIKE, THE PERFECT PLACE TO NOT GROW OLD!
NOT FAR NOW...
SIGH
WHADDAYA SAY?
OH BOY!
FOR CRYING OUT LOUD!
OH REALLY?
RIGHT ON!
YOU KNOW...
WHADDAYA SAY?
MM? OH... I DON'T REALLY WANT TO TALK ABOUT IT.
BUT WHY... WHY DOES SOMETHING AS TEENSY AND DELICATE AS MOI HAVE TO BEAR SUCH A HEAVY BURDEN?
FOR CRYING OUT LOUD!
OH, ALL RIGHT...I'M JUST HAVING A BAD DAY...
OH REALLY?

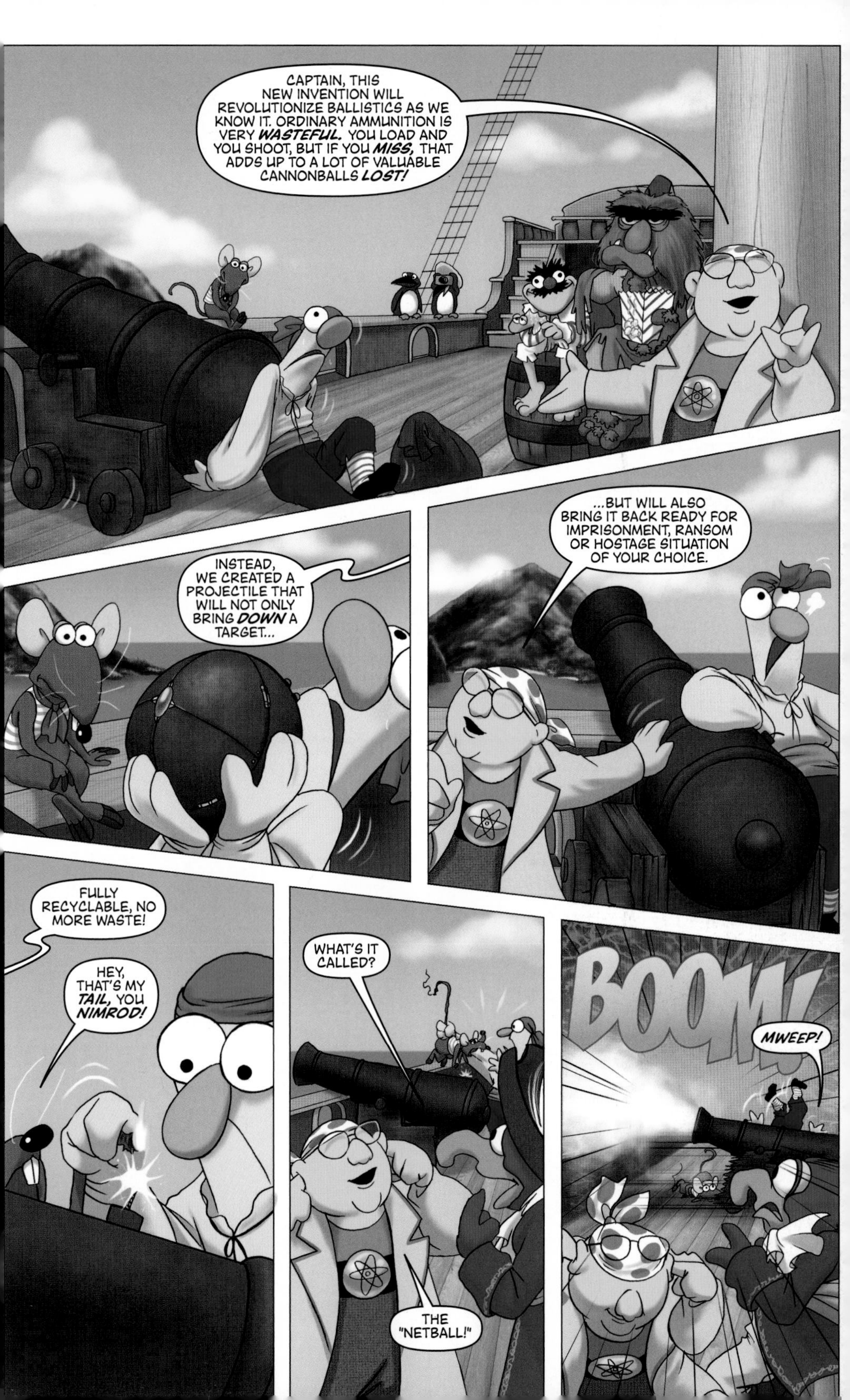
CAPTAIN, THIS NEW INVENTION WILL REVOLUTIONIZE BALLISTICS AS WE KNOW IT. ORDINARY AMMUNITION IS VERY WASTEFUL. YOU LOAD AND YOU SHOOT, BUT IF YOU MISS, THAT ADDS UP TO A LOT OF VALUABLE CANNONBALLS LOST!
INSTEAD, WE CREATED A PROJECTILE THAT WILL NOT ONLY BRING DOWN A TARGET...
...BUT WILL ALSO BRING IT BACK READY FOR IMPRISONMENT, RANSOM OR HOSTAGE SITUATION OF YOUR CHOICE.
FULLY RECYCLABLE, NO MORE WASTE!
HEY, THAT'S MY TAIL, YOU NIMROD!
WHAT'S IT CALLED?
THE "NETBALL!"
BOOM!
MWEEP!

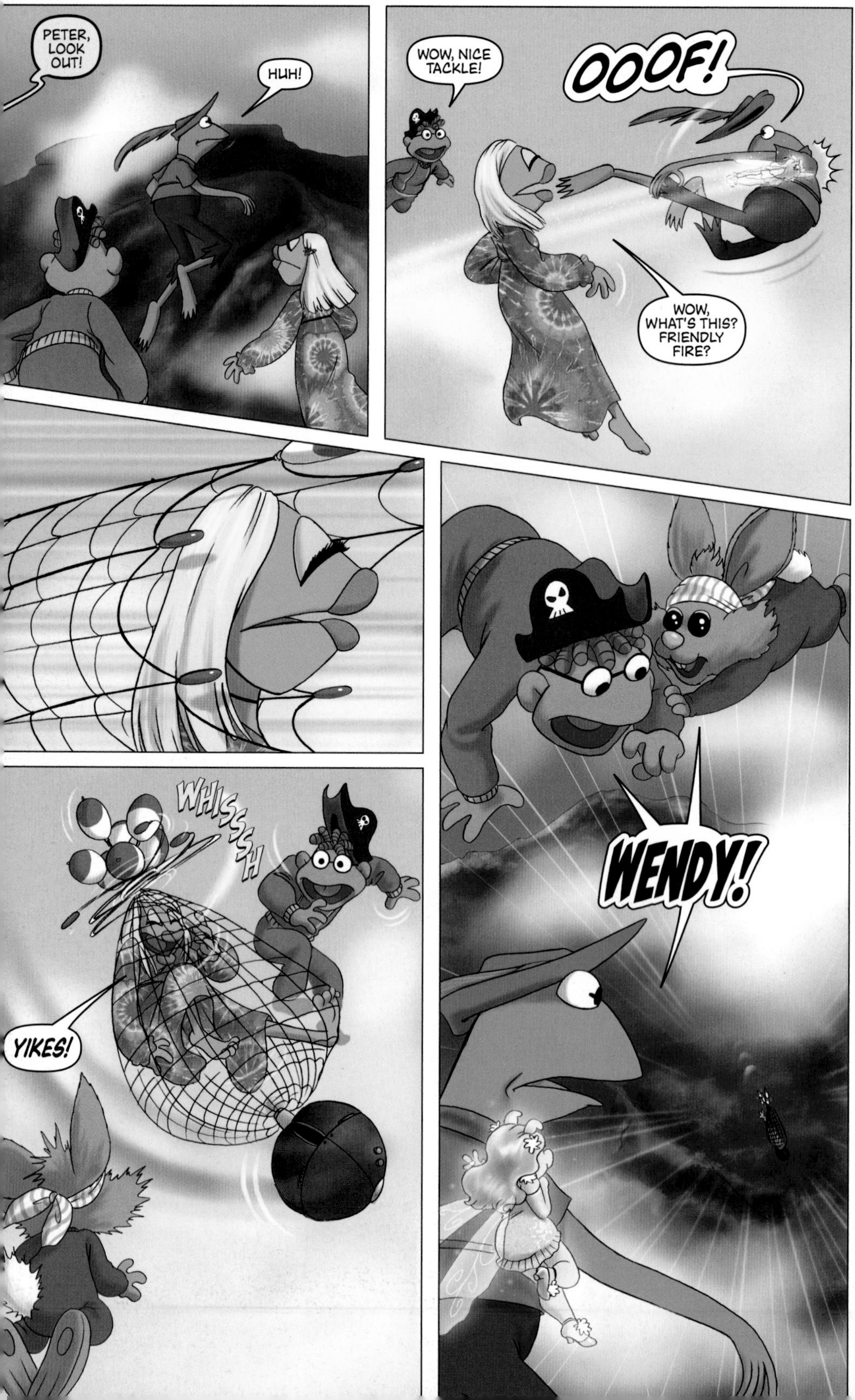
PETER, LOOK OUT!
HUH!
WOW, NICE TACKLE!
OOOF!
WOW, WHAT'S THIS? FRIENDLY FIRE?
WHISSSH
YIKES!
WENDY!

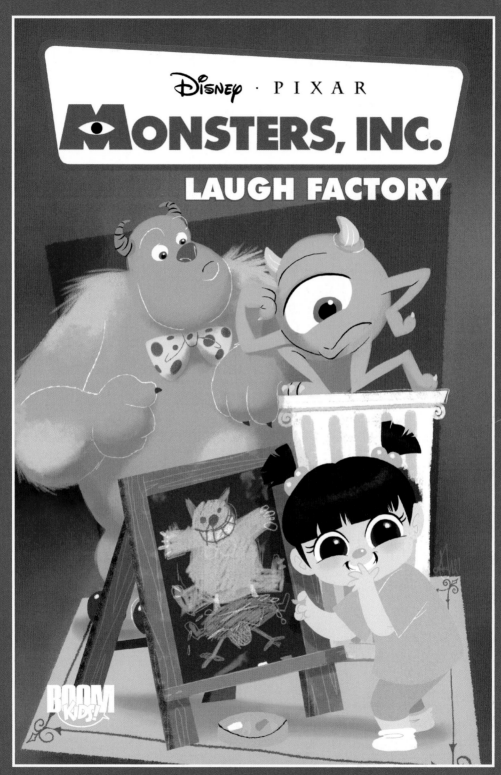

Someone is stealing comedy props from the other employees, making it hard for them to harvest the laughter they need to power Monstropolis...and all evidence points to Sulley's best friend, Mike Wazowski!

MONSTERS, INC.: LAUGH FACTORY
DIAMOND CODE: OCT090801
SC $9.99 ISBN 9781608865086
HC $24.99 ISBN 9781608865338

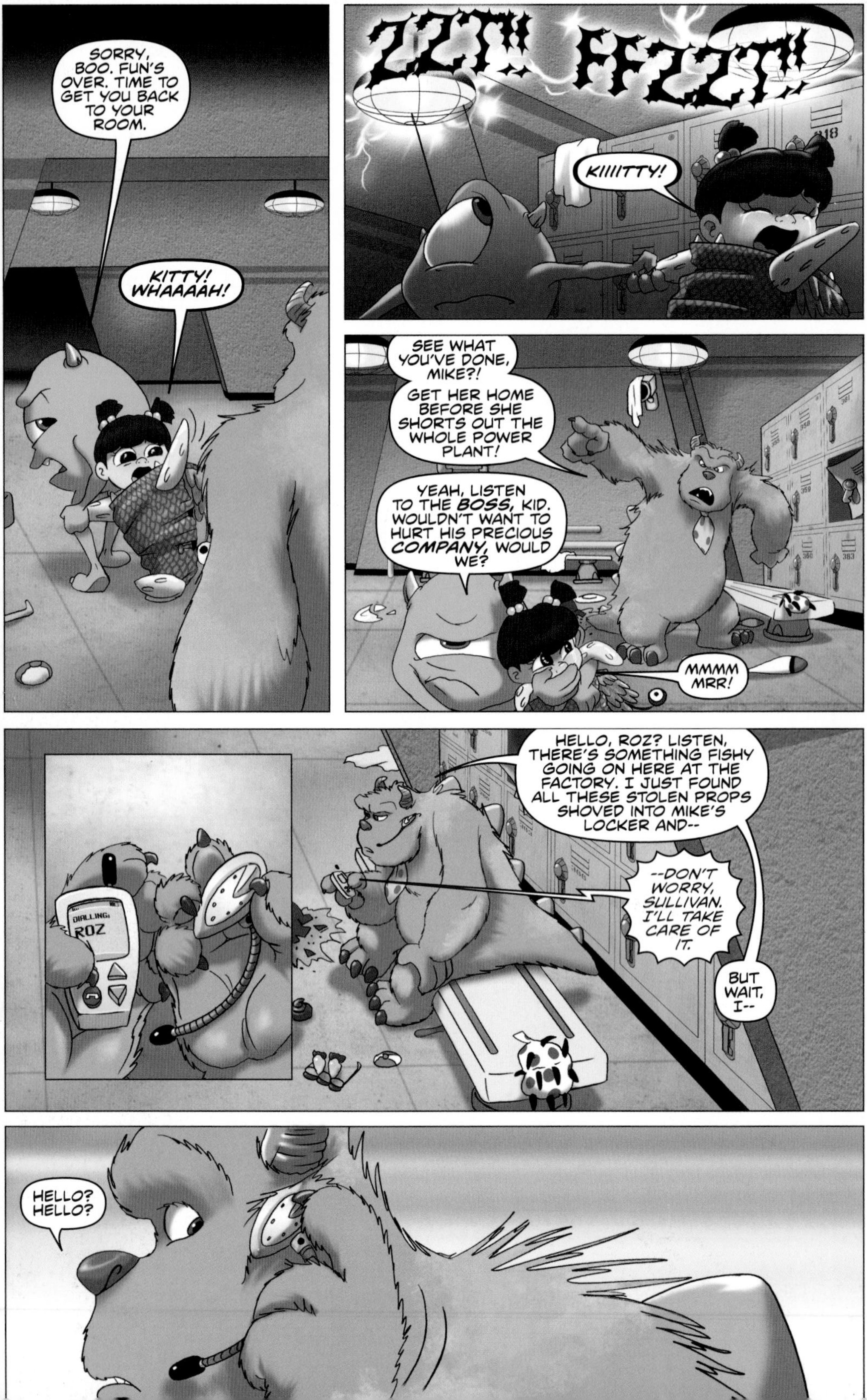
SORRY, BOO. FUN'S OVER. TIME TO GET YOU BACK TO YOUR ROOM.
KITTY! WHAAAAH!
ZZZT!! FFZZZT!!
KIIIITTY!
SEE WHAT YOU'VE DONE, MIKE?!
GET HER HOME BEFORE SHE SHORTS OUT THE WHOLE POWER PLANT!
YEAH, LISTEN TO THE BOSS, KID. WOULDN'T WANT TO HURT HIS PRECIOUS COMPANY, WOULD WE?
MMMM MRR!
HELLO, ROZ? LISTEN, THERE'S SOMETHING FISHY GOING ON HERE AT THE FACTORY. I JUST FOUND ALL THESE STOLEN PROPS SHOVED INTO MIKE'S LOCKER AND--
DIALLING: ROZ
--DON'T WORRY, SULLIVAN. I'LL TAKE CARE OF IT.
BUT WAIT, I--
HELLO? HELLO?

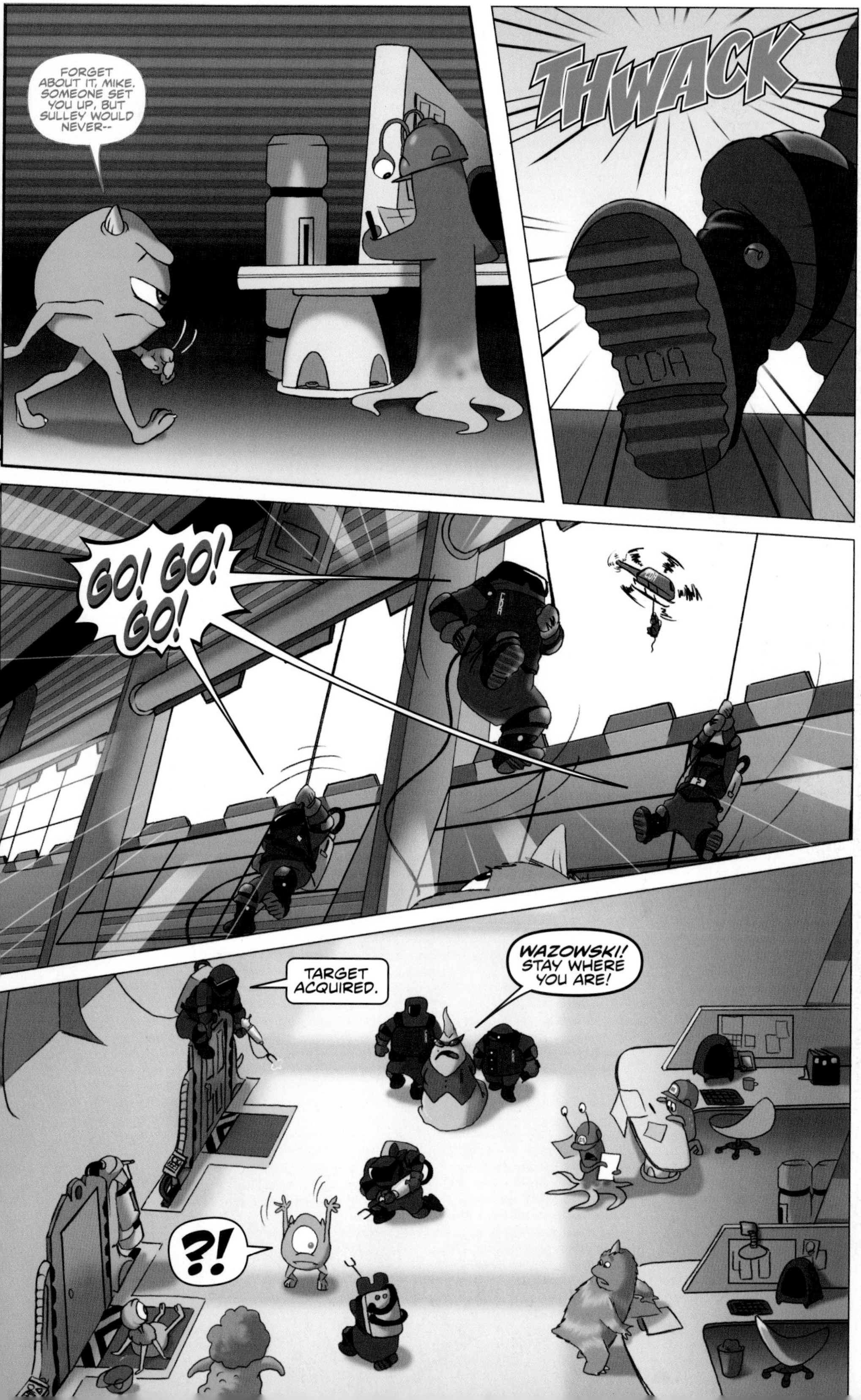
FORGET ABOUT IT, MIKE. SOMEONE SET YOU UP, BUT SULLEY WOULD NEVER--
THWACK
CDA
GO! GO! GO!
TARGET ACQUIRED.
WAZOWSKI! STAY WHERE YOU ARE!
?!

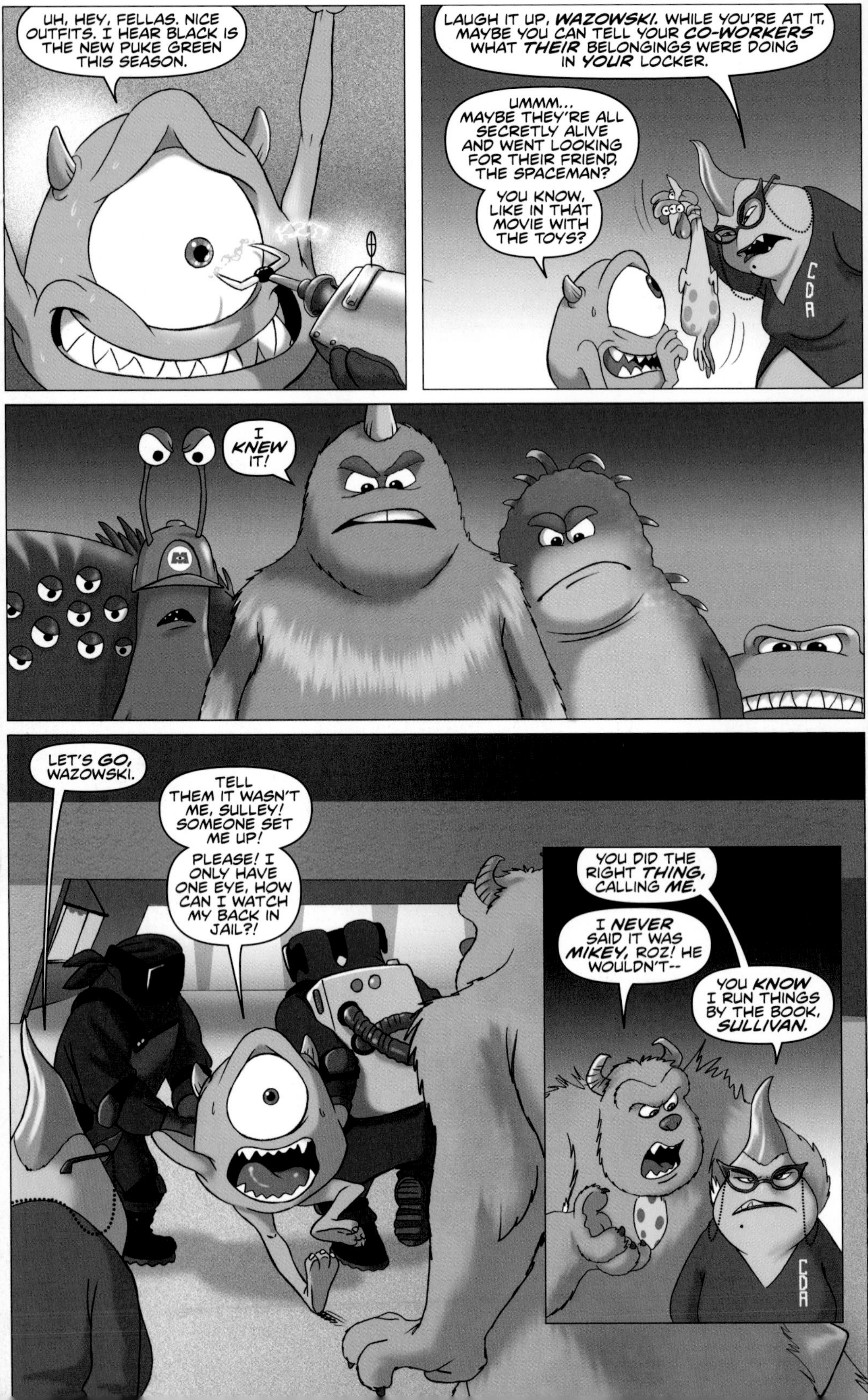
UH, HEY, FELLAS. NICE OUTFITS. I HEAR BLACK IS THE NEW PUKE GREEN THIS SEASON.
LAUGH IT UP, WAZOWSKI. WHILE YOU'RE AT IT, MAYBE YOU CAN TELL YOUR CO-WORKERS WHAT THEIR BELONGINGS WERE DOING IN YOUR LOCKER.
UMMM... MAYBE THEY'RE ALL SECRETLY ALIVE AND WENT LOOKING FOR THEIR FRIEND, THE SPACEMAN?
YOU KNOW, LIKE IN THAT MOVIE WITH THE TOYS?
CDA
I KNEW IT!
LET'S GO, WAZOWSKI.
TELL THEM IT WASN'T ME, SULLEY! SOMEONE SET ME UP!
PLEASE! I ONLY HAVE ONE EYE, HOW CAN I WATCH MY BACK IN JAIL?!
YOU DID THE RIGHT THING, CALLING ME.
I NEVER SAID IT WAS MIKEY, ROZ! HE WOULDN'T--
YOU KNOW I RUN THINGS BY THE BOOK, SULLIVAN.
CDA

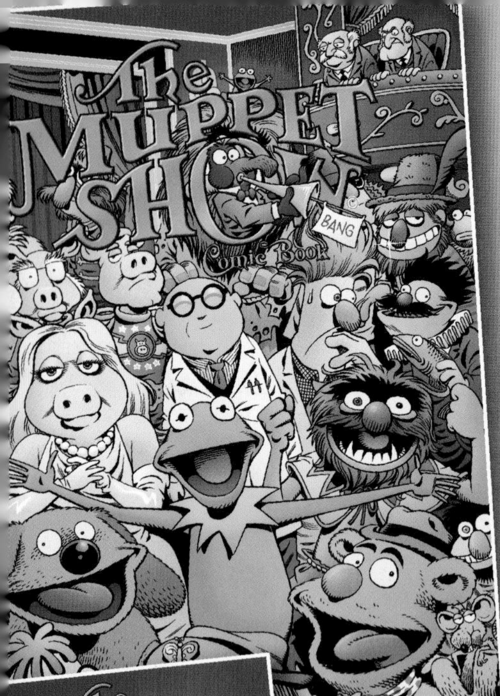
The Muppet Show
Comic Book
BANG

THE MUPPET SHOW COMIC BOOK: MEET THE MUPPETS

Collecting the first four issues of the Eisner Award-nominated THE MUPPET SHOW COMIC BOOK, written and drawn by the incomparable Roger Langridge! Packed full of madcap skits and gags, this trade is certain to please old and new fans alike!

SC $9.99 ISBN 9781934506851
HC $24.99 ISBN 9781608865277

THE MUPPET SHOW COMIC BOOK: THE TREASURE OF PEG-LEG WILSON

Scooter discovers old documents which reveal that a cache of treasure is hidden somewhere within the Muppet Theater...and when Rizzo the Rat overhears this, the news spreads like wildfire! Can Kermit keep everyone from tearing the theater apart?

SC $9.99 ISBN 9781608865048
HC $24.99 ISBN 9781608865307

THE MUPPET SHOW COMIC BOOK: ON THE ROAD

With the Muppet Theater destroyed, the Muppets take their act on the road...but with two very familiar hecklers in every town, will the show be a hit, or will our Muppet minstrels be run out of town in tar and feathers? Also: PIGS IN SPACE!

SC $9.99 ISBN 9781608865161

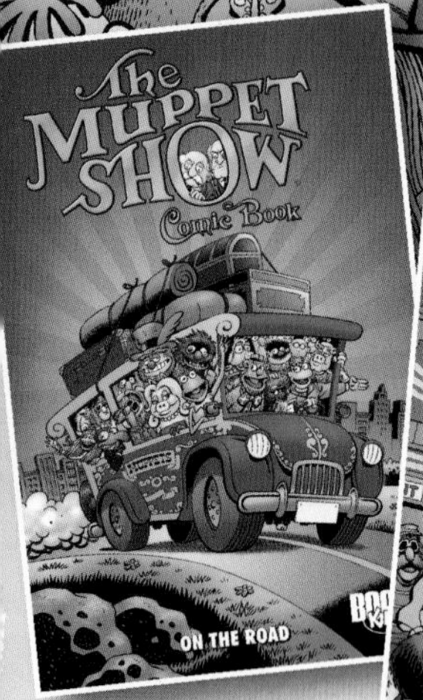
The Muppet Show
Comic Book
ON THE ROAD

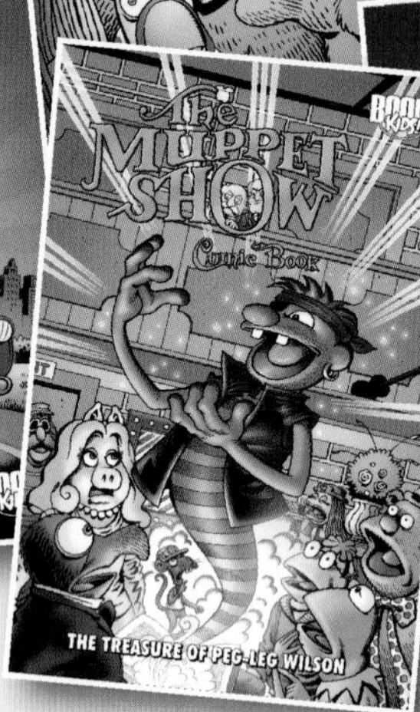
The Muppet Show
Comic Book
BOOM Kids!
THE TREASURE OF PEG-LEG WILSON

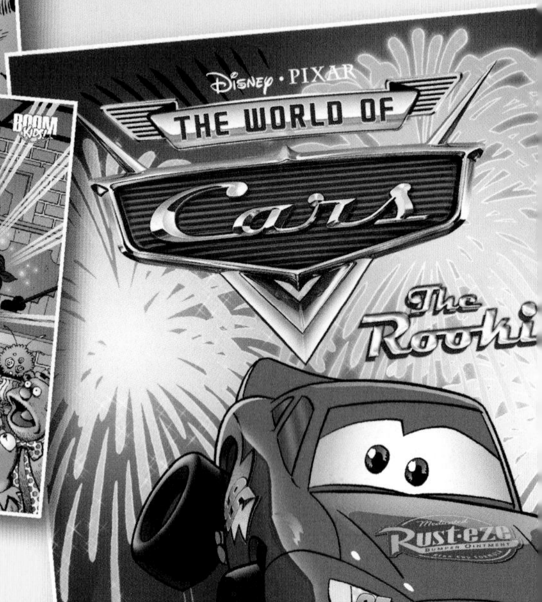
Disney • PIXAR
THE WORLD OF
Cars
The Rooki
Rust-eze
95

CARS: THE ROOKIE

See how Lightning McQueen became a Piston Cup sensation! CARS: THE ROOKIE reveals McQueen's scrappy origins as a local short track racer who dreams of the big time... and recklessly plows his way through the competition to get there!

SC $9.99 ISBN 9781934506844
HC $24.99 ISBN 9781608865222

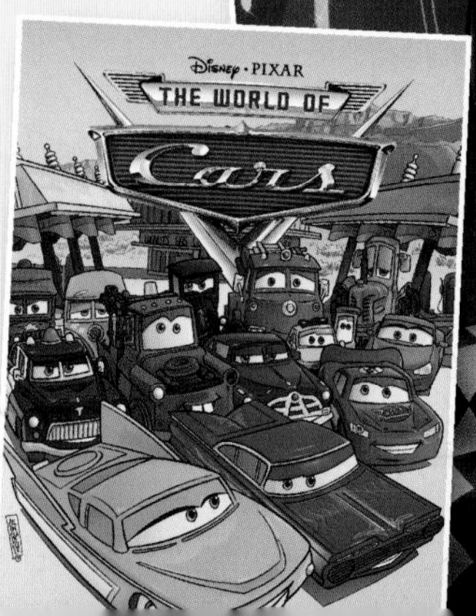
Disney • PIXAR
THE WORLD OF
Cars

CARS: RADIATOR SPRINGS

Lightning McQueen is hanging out with his friends at Flo's V8 Café when he realizes that everyone knows his story...but he doesn't know anyone else's! McQueen wants to know how his friends ended up in Radiator Springs...and more importantly, why they decided to stay!

SC $9.99 ISBN 9781608865024
HC $24.99 ISBN 9781608865284

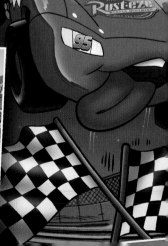

WALL•E: RECHARGE

Before WALL•E becomes the hardworking robot we know and love, he lets the few remaining robots take care of the trash compacting while he collects interesting junk. But when these robots start breaking down, WALL•E must adjust his priorities...or else Earth is doomed!

SC $9.99 ISBN 9781608865123
HC $24.99 ISBN 9781608865543

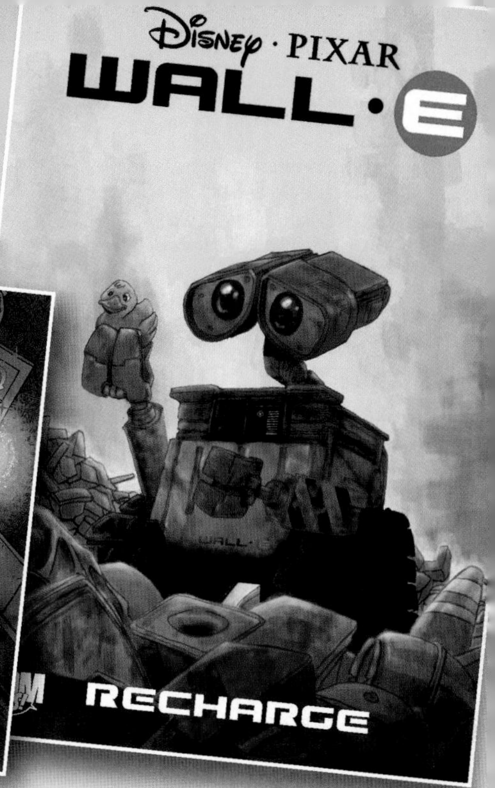
Disney · PIXAR
WALL·E
RECHARGE

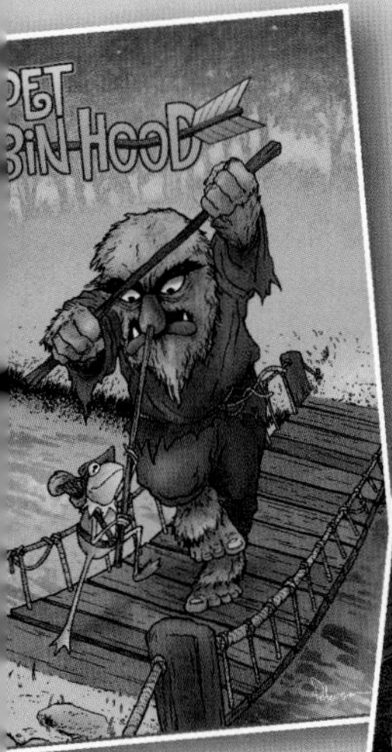

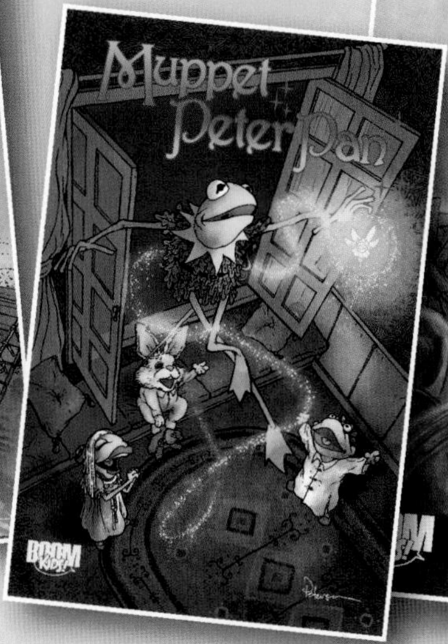
Muppet Peter Pan

MUPPET ROBIN HOOD

The Muppets tell the Robin Hood legend for laughs, and it's the reader who will be merry! Robin Hood (Kermit the Frog) joins with the Merry Men, Sherwood Forest's infamous gang of misfit outlaws, to take on the Sheriff of Nottingham (Sam the Eagle)!

SC $9.99 ISBN 9781934506790
HC $24.99 ISBN 9781608865260

MUPPET PETER PAN

When Peter Pan (Kermit) whisks Wendy (Janice) and her brothers to Neverswamp, the adventure begins! With Captain Hook (Gonzo) out for revenge for the loss of his hand, can even the magic of Piggytink (Miss Piggy) save Wendy and her brothers?

SC $9.99 ISBN 9781608865079
HC $24.99 ISBN 9781608865314

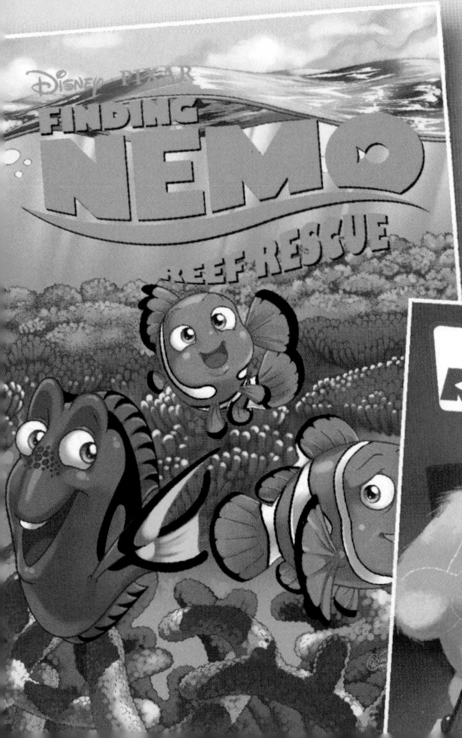
FINDING
NEMO
REEF RESCUE

FINDING NEMO: REEF RESCUE

Nemo, Dory and Marlin have become local heroes, and are recruited to embark on an all-new adventure in this exciting collection! The reef is mysteriously dying and no one knows why. So Nemo and his friends must travel the great blue sea to save their home!

SC $9.99 ISBN 9781934506882
HC $24.99 ISBN 9781608865246

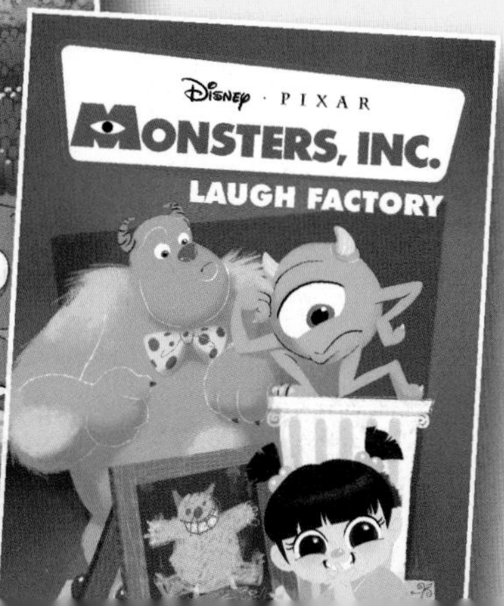
Disney · PIXAR
MONSTERS, INC.
LAUGH FACTORY

MONSTERS, INC.: LAUGH FACTORY

Someone is stealing comedy props from the other employees, making it difficult for them to harvest the laughter they need to power Monstropolis...and all evidence points to Sulley's best friend Mike Wazowski!

SC $9.99 ISBN 9781608865086
HC $24.99 ISBN 9781608865338

DISNEY'S HERO SQUAD: ULTRAHEROES VOL. 1: SAVE THE WORLD

It's an all-star cast of your favorite Disney characters, as you have never seen them before. Join Donald Duck, Goofy, Daisy, and even Mickey himself as they defend the fate of the planet as the one and only Ultraheroes!

SC $9.99 ISBN 9781608865437
HC $24.99 ISBN 9781608865529

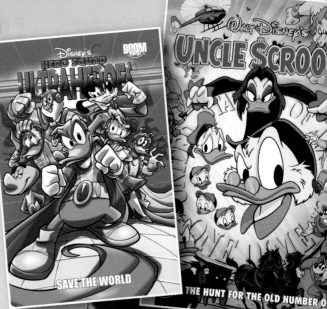

UNCLE SCROOGE: THE HUNT FOR THE OLD NUMBER ONE

Join Donald Duck's favorite penny-pinching Uncle Scrooge as he, Donald himself and Huey, Dewey, and Louie embark on a globe-spanning trek to recover treasure and save Scrooge's "number one dime" from the treacherous Magica De Spell.

SC $9.99 ISBN 9781608865475
HC $24.99 ISBN 9781608865536

WIZARDS OF MICKEY VOL. 1: MOUSE MAGIC

Your favorite Disney characters star in this magical fantasy epic! A student of the great wizard Nereus, Mickey allies himself with Donald and team mate Goofy, in a quest to find a magical crown that will give him mastery over all spells!

SC $9.99 ISBN 9781608865413
HC $24.99 ISBN 9781608865505

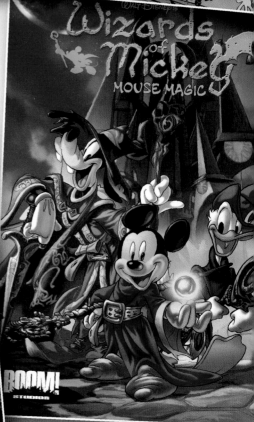

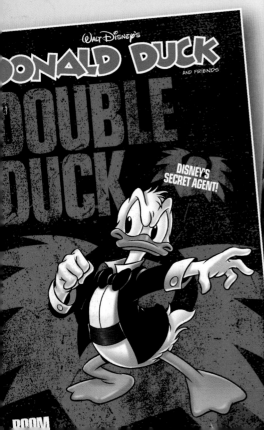

DONALD DUCK AND FRIENDS: DOUBLE DUCK VOL. 1

Donald Duck as a secret agent? Villainous fiends beware as the world of super sleuthing and espionage will never be the same! This is Donald Duck like you've never seen him!

SC $9.99 ISBN 9781608865451
HC $24.99 ISBN 9781608865512

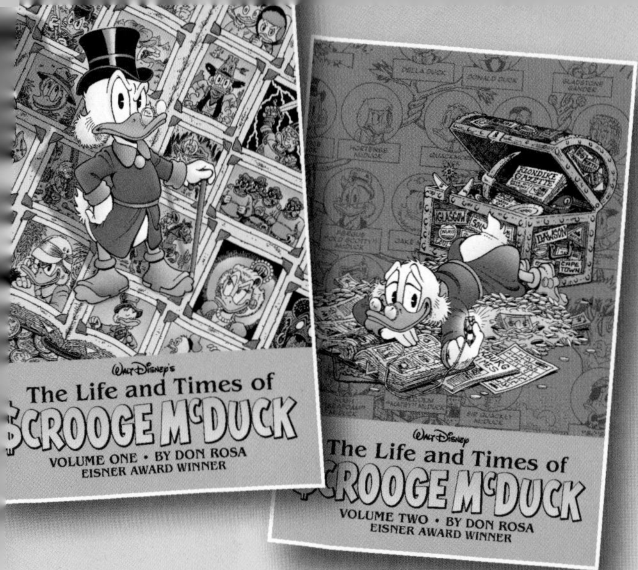
Walt Disney's
The Life and Times of
SCROOGE McDUCK
VOLUME ONE • BY DON ROSA
EISNER AWARD WINNER
Walt Disney
The Life and Times of
SCROOGE McDUCK
VOLUME TWO • BY DON ROSA
EISNER AWARD WINNER

THE LIFE AND TIMES OF SCROOGE McDUCK VOL. 1

BOOM Kids! proudly collects the first half of THE LIFE AND TIMES OF SCROOGE MCDUCK in a gorgeous hardcover collection – featuring smyth sewn binding, a gold-on-gold foil-stamped case wrap, and a bookmark ribbon! These stories, written and drawn by legendary cartoonist Don Rosa, chronicle Scrooge McDuck's fascinating life.

HC $24.99 ISBN 9781608865383

THE LIFE AND TIMES OF SCROOGE McDUCK VOL. 2

BOOM Kids! proudly presents volume two of THE LIFE AND TIMES OF SCROOGE MCDUCK in a gorgeous hardcover collection in a beautiful, deluxe package featuring smyth sewn binding and a foil-stamped case wrap! These stories, written and drawn by legendary cartoonist Don Rosa, chronicle Scrooge McDuck's fascinating life.

HC $24.99 ISBN 9781608865420

MICKEY MOUSE CLASSICS: MOUSE TAILS

See Mickey Mouse as he was meant to be seen! Solving mysteries, fighting off pirates, and generally saving the day! These classic stories comprise a "Greatest Hits" series for the mouse, including a story produced by seminal Disney creator Carl Barks!

HC $24.99 ISBN 9781608865390

DONALD DUCK CLASSICS: QUACK UP

Whether it's finding gold, journeying to the Klondike, or fighting ghosts, Donald will always have the help of his much more prepared nephews – Huey, Dewey, and Louie – by his side. Featuring some of the best Donald Duck stories Carl Barks ever produced!

HC $24.99 ISBN 9781608865406

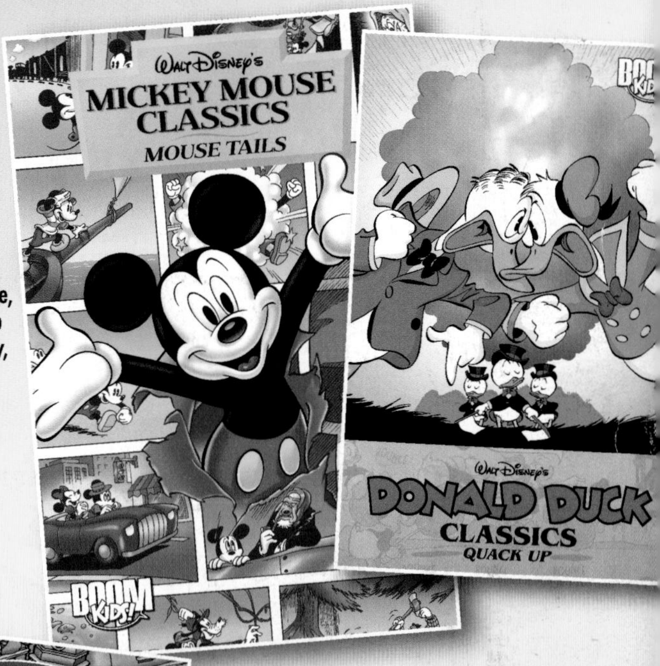
Walt Disney's
MICKEY MOUSE CLASSICS
MOUSE TAILS
BOOM KIDS!
Walt Disney's
DONALD DUCK
CLASSICS
QUACK UP

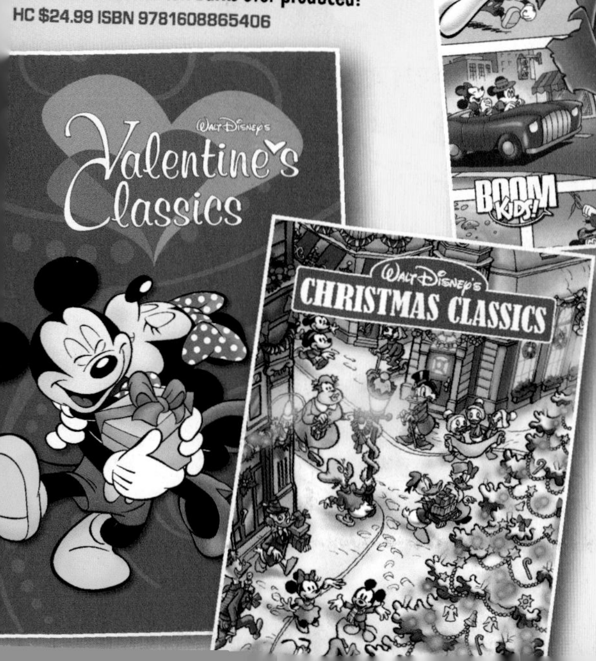
Walt Disney's
Valentine's Classics
Walt Disney's
CHRISTMAS CLASSICS

WALT DISNEY'S VALENTINE'S CLASSICS

Love is in the air for Mickey Mouse, Donald Duck and the rest of the gang. But will Cupid's arrows cause happiness or heartache? Find out in this collection of classic stories featuring work by Carl Barks, Floyd Gottfredson, Daan Jippes, Romano Scarpa and Al Taliaferro.

HC $24.99 ISBN 9781608865499

WALT DISNEY'S CHRISTMAS CLASSICS

BOOM Kids! has raided the Disney publishing archives and searched every nook and cranny to find the best and the greatest Christmas stories from Disney's vast comic book publishing history for this "best of" compilation.

HC $24.99 ISBN 9781608865482

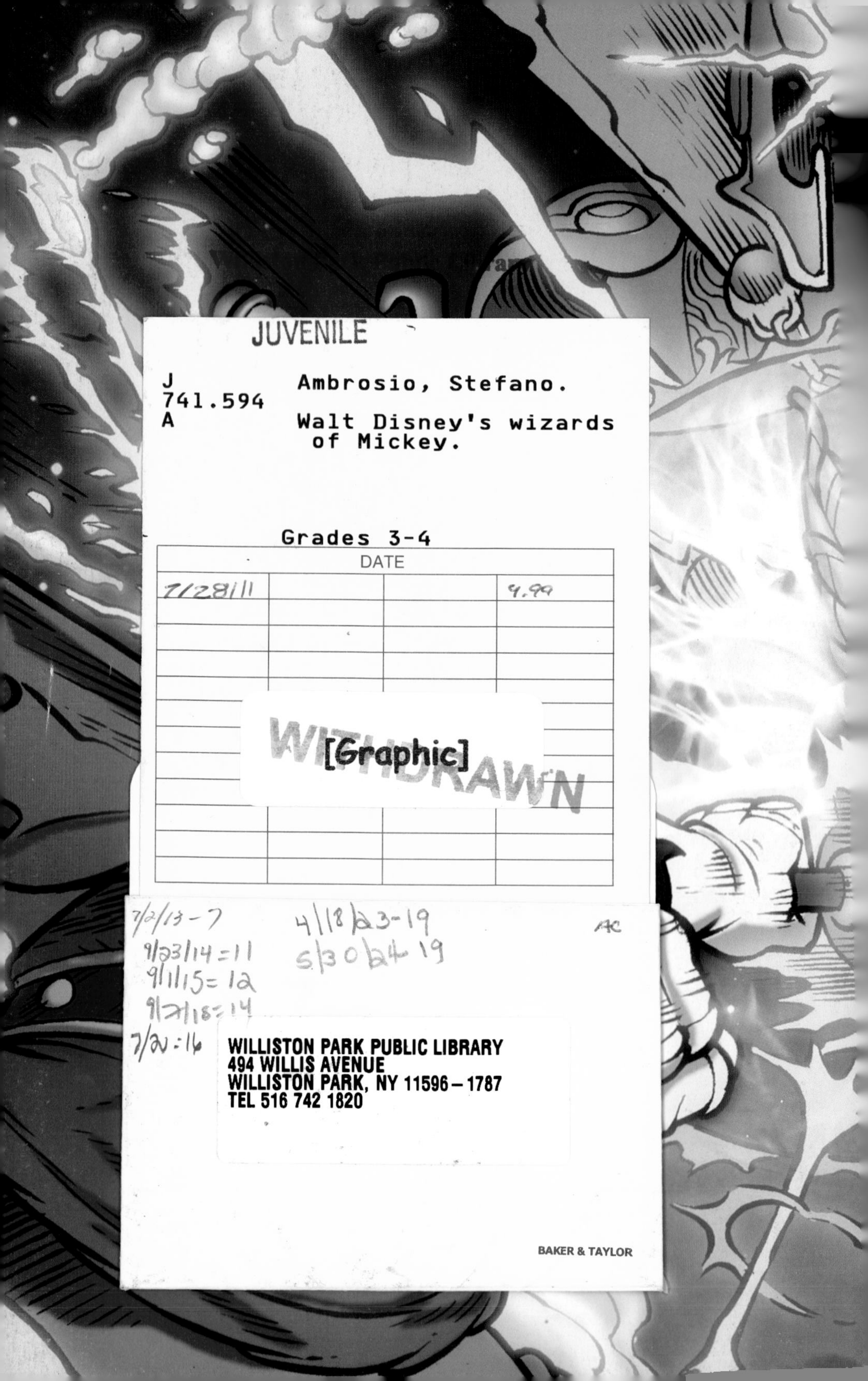